MW01127851

A *H*EARING *H*EART

Copyright © 2012 by Bonnie Dee
ISBN 978-1-47768-388-0

A Hearing Heart

Bonnie Dee

CHAPTER ONE

Broughton, Nebraska, 1901

Catherine Johnson stepped out of the general mercantile onto the wooden walkway, adjusting her mesh shopping bag on one wrist and the brown paper-wrapped parcels in her other arm. A stiff breeze cut through the fabric of her dress and twisted her long skirt around her legs. Grit scoured her cheeks and stung her eyes. At least the road wasn't muddy, but she faced a long walk back to the McPhersons' farm carrying all her purchases. She'd be glad when her stay there was over and she moved in with the Albrights in town. Shuttling from home to home was one of the more unpleasant aspects of teaching in a one-room schoolhouse.

Sometimes she wished she'd never left New York to come to Nebraska. On a Saturday afternoon in White Plains she'd be strolling along a brick path in the park with fountains and flowerbeds gracing the way. Here in Broughton she fought the ever-present wind and choking dust while her shoes tapped an uneven rhythm on the warped boards of the sidewalk.

The town was quiet for a Saturday, the street nearly empty. She was almost to the last building on Main Street, where the dusty road became prairie, when several men erupted from the saloon in front of her. The swinging doors crashed against the wall.

Catherine stumbled backward, dropping one of her packages, heart pounding

A raw-boned man with no chin and his stocky, black-bearded partner dragged a man between them. Behind them staggered a burly fellow with heavy-lidded eyes. He was shouting curses, using words Catherine had never heard. The only man in the group she recognized was the one the others gripped by the arms. He was Jim Kinney, the deaf-mute man who worked at the livery stable.

Jim glared at his captors through a fringe of dark hair. The burly man moved in front of him and plowed a fist into his stomach. The stable hand doubled over with a whoosh of air.

The skinny man hauled him upright and the bearded one punched his jaw, snapping his head to the side. Jim cried out, a hoarse, wordless sound. Bracing himself against the pair holding his arms, he kicked out with both feet at the man who'd hit him, landing a solid blow to his chest.

"Tie him up," the droopy-eyed man slurred. "Teach him some respect."

Catherine stood rooted to the spot, horrified but too shocked to react as one of the men grabbed a rope from his horse's saddle at the hitching post. When he began tying Jim's hands, she finally found her voice.

"Stop it! Stop!" She dropped her parcels and bag on the sidewalk and ran toward them. "Leave him alone!"

For a second, Jim's dark eyes met hers, and then the men dragged him out to the street, whooping in drunken glee and ignoring Catherine as if she was voiceless.

"Stop!" she yelled in frustration, her hands clenching helplessly at her sides.

The black-bearded man blocked her way, and she pushed past him, the sour stench of sweat and alcohol wrinkling her nose.

The leader mounted his horse and wrapped the end of the rope around the pommel of his saddle. Jim struggled to free his hands until the rope stretched taut and jerked him forward, forcing him to keep pace with the horse. The rider kneed his mount and it moved from a walk to a trot.

Jim ran behind, stumbling as he tried to keep on his feet.

Catherine screamed for help. A few men came from the saloon while others stepped out of stores along the street.

"Help!" she cried again, panic swelling in her chest. "Somebody help him."

Jim couldn't keep up with the speed of the horse. He tripped, fell and was dragged along the ground. Spooked by the creature on its heels, the horse whinnied and plunged ahead. A cloud of dust from its hooves concealed the body bumping over the ruts behind it.

The rider pulled the horse's head up, turned and rode back toward where his companions stood laughing and shouting encouragement.

People emerging from the barbershop, the mercantile and feed store all stood watching. No one was going to interfere, risking the drunken men's anger.

The horse cantered toward Catherine. Without a thought beyond stopping the stable hand's torture, she ran into the road, waving her arms and shouting. The animal reared on its hind legs, dumping its rider to the ground. For a moment all she could see was hooves flailing and the chestnut body rising high above her. How very tall a horse was when standing on two legs. The inane thought flashed in her mind before the animal came down on all fours.

She seized the bridle and her fingers grazed its warm jaw. The horse blew hay-scented breath into her face with a soft chuffing sound.

"Sh. Easy. Easy," she crooned, stroking its neck. She moved alongside and reached for the rope tied to the pommel. Even standing on her toes with her chest pressed against the horse's heaving flank she could barely reach it, and the knot was so tight she couldn't loosen it.

Catherine glanced at Jim's dusty body sprawled in the road, and the horse's rider staggering to his feet, cursing as he brushed off his clothes.

Now that the crisis was past, a couple of men from the feed store came out to the street and grabbed the leader of the thugs, while someone else ran to get the deputy. A few patrons of the tavern collared the other two roughnecks. Mr. Murdoch, the saloonkeeper knelt in the road beside Jim and untied his wrists.

Catherine walked over to the prone body of the stable hand and watched Murdoch feel his limbs for broken bones.

"Is he alive?" She squatted beside the dust-covered body, her skirt pooling around her. The man's eyes were closed and blood seeped from abrasions on his dirt-streaked face.

"He's unconscious, but I think he'll be all right. Damn! If only he'd kept out of their way," Murdoch said.

"He needs the doctor."

"Already sent someone to get him."

Catherine pulled her handkerchief from her sleeve and dabbed at the blood on Jim's forehead. "What happened?"

"Drunken fools called for another round. Shirley was tending another table so they shouted at Jim to get their drinks. Of course, he couldn't hear 'em. He's there to push a broom, not wait tables. They started yelling, grabbed him and dragged him outside."

Catherine bit back her question of why it had taken him so long to come to Jim's aid. Pushing back a lock of the man's dark hair, she examined the wound at his temple. "I thought Mr. Kinney worked at the livery stable."

"Works there too. Has a room back of the stables. Christ! Where's the damn doc? Pardon the language."

A young woman ran up to them, her skirts held high enough to show striped stockings all the way to her knees. Her red hair straggled from the bun in back to frame her round, red-cheeked face. The neckline of her dress revealed most of her bosom, which rose and fell as she panted. "Doc's out on a call, Mr. Murdoch. Is he okay?"

"Damn! Hope to hell there ain't anything broken. Guess all we can do is carry him back to his room."

Several men had gathered around, and three of them lifted Jim's body. He groaned, and his eyes opened, his gaze focusing on Catherine.

She smiled. "It's all right. You'll be all right."

He blinked, but she didn't know if he'd understood. She'd only seen the man once or twice since she'd moved here. People said he was slow as well as deaf and mute.

Walking beside the men carrying him, she kept her gaze locked on his in an attempt to offer encouragement. The eyes that stared back at her were focused and intelligent. She could almost see his thoughts busily flickering in them, but with no voice to give substance those thoughts remained locked inside. Catherine realized he wasn't mentally impaired at all.

The men carried him through the doors of the livery stable, and Catherine lost eye contact with Jim. Her stomach churned and her nerves jangled, unsurprising since a rearing horse had nearly trampled her. The deputy would probably have questions for her as the main witness of the altercation, but for now she was intent on seeing what she could do to help Jim Kinney. She followed the men into the livery.

* * * *

His body ached in a thousand places. Every bone hurt. Every inch of exposed skin was shredded. He felt like he'd been dragged down the street behind a horse. Jim smiled at the sarcastic thought, then groaned as one of the men carrying him jarred his right side.

Three faces hovered above him. Murdoch frowned. His mouth moved beneath his handlebar moustache as he said something to John Walker from the hardware store. Jim recognized the third man from the feed store. Their faces were strained with the effort of carrying him and their fiercely gripping hands hurt like hell. He wished they'd set him down and let him get himself back to his room. Even if he had to crawl it would be less painful.

Jim glanced past Walker, who was carrying his legs, and tried to catch another glimpse of the schoolteacher. She must've left.

He wondered if any of his bones were broken, wondered if someone was getting the doctor, and how he'd pay the man. How soon would he be able to work again? If his body failed him, he was in trouble. That's why he always took good care of himself, careful to keep healthy and steer clear of dangerous situations. From a lifetime of practice, he'd become adept at avoiding drunks or bullies who wanted to show their manliness with their fists and found him an easy target.

But today he hadn't been alert. He'd been thinking about Shirley Mae and what she'd done for him the previous night. He'd only paid for a hand job. It was all he could afford, but he was desperate for something more than his own touch. Shirley had given him a blowjob for free. She'd pointed to the rhinestone comb in her hair, the one he'd found one day while sweeping the bar and returned to her, then she'd bent her head and taken his cock in her mouth. With that memory in mind, he hadn't even been aware of the three drunken men until they grabbed him.

Now Walker and the other men were maneuvering Jim through the narrow doorway of his room. He gritted his teeth to keep from crying out as they jostled his body. When they laid him on his cot, he exhaled in relief.

His small room was crowded with bodies, but soon all of the men left except his two bosses, Murdoch and Rasmussen, the livery owner. They spoke together a moment. He couldn't see their lips and was too tired to read them anyway. His eyes drifted closed.

They opened again at the pressure of Murdoch's hand on his shoulder. He explained slowly that the doctor was out on a call, patted Jim's shoulder and left the room.

Mr. Rasmussen sat on the edge of the bed, pushed his glasses up his nose and frowned, a sure sign he didn't know what he was doing. He might be able to wrap a horse's strained leg, but what did he know about people? Jim inhaled a deep breath and pain pierced his side. Something was wrong with his ribs. He gestured to his side, letting Rasmussen know. The man nodded and began unbuttoning what was left of his shredded shirt.

A movement in the doorway caught Jim's attention. The schoolteacher stood framed there in her blue and white-flowered dress with her daffodil-colored hair. A faint scent of lily-of-the-valley perfume wafted to him. She was like a flower garden filling the dark, stuffy room.

She looked at Rasmussen before entering the room. Only a few paces brought her to the edge of Jim's bed.

He couldn't stop staring at her like the idiot everyone thought he was. The sight of her fresh, feminine form in his dingy room was unbelievable, besides which he was dizzy and near passing out from the pain throbbing in his head. His gaze fastened on her lips.

"What can I do?" she asked Rasmussen.

The stableman turned toward her so Jim couldn't see his reply. Miss Johnson nodded and left the room. He felt pain that had nothing to do with his injured body as she disappeared from view.

Rasmussen lifted Jim's torso, peeled off his long-sleeved shirt and undershirt, and lowered him back onto the bed. Colors and lights flashed in front of his eyes and the edges of his vision grew dark. Oh God, his worst nightmare was coming true. He would be blinded from the blow to his head and left totally helpless. His pulse beat wildly as panic surged through him. He gasped for breath and could see again. Rasmussen was frowning at him.

"Where does it hurt?"

Jim indicated his head.

"You'll be all right. I'll fix you up."

How the hell do you know? You can barely tend the horses! Jim nodded, his jaw clenching at the pain.

Suddenly the teacher was back. She carried a bucket of water in one hand and some clean rags from the tack room in the other. Offering them to Rasmussen, she glanced at Jim. Her eyes widened at the sight of his bare torso and she quickly looked away.

Rasmussen rose, indicating she should take his seat and wash the blood and dust from Jim's face and body. He was going to get liniment. The teacher looked after Rasmussen as he walked from the room, her mouth open as if to protest, then she closed it and turned back to Jim. Her smile was tense.

"You. Read. Lips?" She shaped each word carefully.

He nodded.

"I'm going to clean you." She sat on the cot next to him, her warm hip pressed against his. She dipped one of the rags, squeezed it out and leaned over him to sponge off the blood at his temple. The cloth was cold but it felt good.

He let his eyes drift closed and submitted to the pressure of the wet cloth dabbing his face. She held his chin in her other hand as she bathed his forehead, cheek and neck. Her skin was soft and the scent of lilies much stronger with her so close. Beneath the flowers, he could smell her body, a secret, womanly aroma.

Jim opened his eyes, watching her bend to rinse the rag in the bucket. Her sun-colored hair was pulled back into a bun at the nape of her neck. Tendrils of hair curled around her face. Two perfectly arched, light brown eyebrows were knitted in a frown of concentration over sky-blue eyes. Her tongue darted out, wetting her lips, and his heart jolted in his chest.

Turning back to him, she began patting again, this time on the bloody abrasion on his shoulder. The pink blush rising in her cheeks told him she was uncomfortable touching him. A lady didn't do such things to a strange man. He couldn't stop watching her eyes even though she refused to meet his gaze. He'd never seen eyes so blue.

All he knew about her was that she was the new teacher. He'd seen her around town a few times. Once, at the mercantile he'd watched as she laughed and talked with a little girl. Her smile and the sweet affection she'd shown the child had made him smile. He'd also seen her walking to and from the schoolhouse. But he didn't know her name. No one had said it in front of him and he couldn't ask. There was no reason for him to know it. Yet now he was desperate to have a word for her, a shape of the lips that meant *her*, even if he couldn't imagine what the word sounded like.

Jim touched her hand and she finally looked at him. He pointed at her and raised his eyebrows, requesting her name.

"Catherine Johnson." Her hand touched her chest and her lips moved slowly over each syllable.

Mimicking her, he felt her name with his thrusting tongue and moving lips. Without knowing the sound, he'd never forget the shapes. Memorization came easy to him.

Jim nodded and smiled, accepting the gift of her name.

* * * *

Jim was so much smarter than she'd been led to believe by the ladies in town, who'd claimed he was a harmless simpleton. Catherine had never given the young man who worked at the livery a moment's thought. Why would she when his world and hers never crossed? Now, she'd been forcefully catapulted into his life, sitting by his bedside performing a most intimate personal act. The day had veered from the straight path of "normal" onto a twisted trail.

Catherine hadn't seen so much male flesh in her entire life. It wasn't seemly for even laborers to toil shirtless in public, especially not somewhere a lady might see them. However, she'd been to the Metropolitan Museum in New York City with her aunt and cousins once and seen much more than a man's naked torso. The nude statues and paintings had shocked her—and if she were being truthful, had excited her, but she'd hidden her reaction from her more cosmopolitan relatives.

Jim's body wasn't like the smooth, white marble statues. His skin was warm and alive beneath her fingertips. The scrape on his shoulder was bleeding and other cuts and bruises marred his flesh. Washed clean of dust, his skin was tan and textured with small freckles and moles. His chest was mostly smooth with just a sprinkling of dark hair, and from his navel to the waist of his pants was a fine trail of hair. The sight of his dusky nipples sent a wave of fire burning in Catherine's cheeks and a prickling feeling between her legs. This very real male body was definitely nothing like the statues in the museum.

His stomach had been scraped raw on the road. Bits of grit were embedded in the flesh, and she could hardly ignore the area simply because it made her uncomfortable. Pushing aside her girlish hesitancy, she washed his abdomen clean as well.

As the rag stroked over his taut flesh, the muscles twitched and Catherine caught her breath. Her cheeks flamed even hotter and her sex tightened. She bent to dip the washrag in the bucket again. Luckily, by the time she'd wrung it out, Mr. Rasmussen was back in the room with bandages and liniment.

"If you could help me just a little longer, young lady, I want to wrap this around him in case there are any cracked ribs. I don't think anything's broken or he'd be in a lot more pain, but I'll have Doc Halloran check him over later."

Together they sat Jim upright. He groaned as they raised him. Catherine moved behind him to support his shoulders while Mr. Rasmussen wrapped the bandage around his middle. Jim's dark head rested just above her breast, its warmth burning through the fabric of her dress and into her body. Her nipples hardened and another wave of heat burned through her.

His hair was nearly black and very glossy. Strands fell across his forehead and she wanted to stroke them back. With his dark hair and eyes and tan skin he might have Indian blood or perhaps he was from Mediterranean stock. He certainly looked nothing like the fair-skinned German and Czech immigrants who'd settled much of Nebraska. How had he ended up in this town? What was his story? She was desperately curious to know everything about him.

"Finished." Mr. Rasmussen's voice startled her. He fastened the end of the binding with several pins. Jim's midsection looked like the wrap on the mummy Catherine had seen at the museum. "Could you go to the store and pick up a headache powder to ease his pain?"

"Of course." Catherine slipped out from behind Jim and lowered his body back to the bed. She rose, anxious to escape the alarming feelings growing in her.

Once more her gaze met Jim's. His eyes locked on hers with the strength of a vise, communicating something she didn't understand. She hurried from the room.

13

Outside the livery stable, she inhaled a deep breath of air, freeing her mind of the odd emotions clouding it before crossing the street toward the general store.

In front of the various businesses, clusters of people stood discussing the exciting event of the day. Where had they all been when she was screaming for help as Jim was dragged down the street? Catherine looked for her parcels and bag on the boardwalk where she'd dropped them, but they were gone.

"Miss Johnson, what happened? I heard you were nearly trampled!" Pearl Jalkanen, the barber's wife, hurried toward her. "Horrible! Tell me everything!"

Catherine gestured at the mercantile. "I have to go--"

"The deputy arrested those men. Got 'em down at the jail." Abe Jalkanen, smelling strongly of the pomade he used on his thinning hair, came up beside his wife.

"How's the boy?" Neal Hildebrandt, the feed store owner joined them. "Jed said most of his skin is scraped clean off."

"Please excuse me. Mr. Rasmussen asked me to get a headache powder from the store. Mr. Kinney is all right, although he might have broken ribs. We'll know more after the doctor has seen him." She nudged past Pearl and continued on toward the store.

Inside the mercantile were more townsfolk with questions and congratulations on what they called her heroic act. Catherine kept her answers brief as she bought the headache powder. Some kind soul had brought her purchases and handbag into the store, so she collected them then headed back to the livery.

On the way, Deputy Nathan Scott intercepted her. "Miss Johnson. Can you come to the sheriff's office? I'll need you to tell me about what happened."

"After I drop off this powder for Mr. Kinney. Have you questioned him yet?"

The deputy frowned, his fine, white-blond hair framing his pink-cheeked face and making him look like a puzzled cherub. "No. He can't talk. What could he tell me?"

Catherine shifted the bundles that were slipping from her arms.

Deputy Scott took them from her. "I'm sorry, Miss Johnson. Let me carry those for you."

"Mr. Kinney might not speak, but he can communicate. Both Mr. Rasmussen and Mr. Murdoch will tell you that. He's not stupid." She fought to keep the irritation out of her voice. She didn't know why she

14

felt so defensive on Jim's behalf. Up until today she'd assumed, like everyone else, that he was feebleminded. The deputy had no reason to think any differently, and it was true that Jim couldn't easily answer questions.

The big man escorted her to the livery where Mr. Rasmussen met them and accepted the paper packet from Catherine.

"He's asleep. I'll give him this later. Boy's going to be hurting bad by later tonight."

She felt a pang of disappointment that she had no reason to see Jim again. The strength of the feeling amazed her. What was the matter with her? Perhaps it was simply that, having saved him, she felt a responsibility for him. That must be it.

Mr. Rasmussen gave the deputy his estimation of Jim's injuries. Scott took notes and thanked him before turning to Catherine again. "Miss Johnson, if you don't mind going to the office with me, I can drive you to the McPhersons' after we've talked. Save you a long walk."

"All right." Catherine was suddenly exhausted and shaky as the shock of the experience caught up with her. Jim might be dead now instead of merely injured, or she might have been trampled by the rearing horse. Her anger swelled at the drunken, dangerous men who'd perpetrated the crime, and she wanted to make sure they stayed locked up.

With a final glance past the stalls at the closed door of the back room, Catherine followed Nathan Scott from the livery stable.

* * * *

Jim lay in the windowless darkness of his room and stared at the line of light around the door. He hadn't really been asleep when Rasmussen left, but wanted to be left alone to think about everything that had happened that day, including his sudden ridiculous attraction to Catherine Johnson.

He mouthed her name, feeling the shape of it and seeing her in his mind's eye. Of course he'd noticed the pretty woman who was new in town. Every man in Boughton probably had. She was beautiful and carried herself with an air of elegance far different from the women of the community. Jim wished he knew more about her, but until today, she'd been no more than a fleeting glimpse of passing beauty to him.

Now that he'd had her hands touching him all over and those blue eyes focused on him, his blood was fired with an impossible longing. He could've gazed into her eyes for hours. But hankering after

15

her was pointless. He might as well wish for the sun to come down to earth as to imagine ever having that woman in this room again. He still couldn't figure out why she'd come here at all.

His memory of the struggle with the men in the saloon was fragmented. One moment he was sweeping, the next rough hands grabbed him. The unexpectedness of the attack was almost worse than the pain. He hated being taken by surprise. But one image was clear in his mind. For a split second before they dragged him to the street, he'd seen a woman's face, eyes wide and horrified.

The dragging was a blur and he'd lost consciousness for a time. When he came back to himself, lying on the ground, Catherine's eyes had been something to hold on to, an anchor for his floating mind. Pity had probably inspired her to help Mr. Rasmussen nurse him, but at least it had brought her close.

Jim couldn't relax. His body throbbed with pain. His arms felt as if they'd been dislocated. He rubbed the rope burns on his wrists and stared into the darkness, afraid to close his eyes in his own room, afraid something would come for him while he slept.

Slowly, by careful inches, he sat and swung his legs off the edge of the bed. He rose and the room whirled around him. Hobbling over to the door, he slid the bolt he'd installed, locking it securely. He limped back to his cot and dropped onto it then pulled the blanket over him.

He was finally able to close his eyes, but still couldn't sleep as images of a different kind distracted him; shimmering blonde hair, a soft rosebud mouth that smiled and spoke directly to him, eyes as blue as an August sky which looked at him and really saw him. He was a fool to dream about a woman who'd done him a simple kindness and probably wouldn't acknowledge him tomorrow if he saw her on the street.

Still, he mouthed her name over and over. Catherine Johnson. And her shining form kept the darkness of his lonely room at bay.

CHAPTER TWO

"Temperance! That's the solution to so many of our nation's ills." Mrs. Albright spoke loudly enough for her voice to reach the entire congregation even though they were outside the church building after service with everyone standing in groups chatting or heading toward home. "We need to make our county alcohol-free for the safety of young ladies like Miss Johnson. When I think of how the situation might have ended! My dear, you were nothing short of heroic, saving that poor simpleton as you did, but you should never have put yourself in harm's way."

"Indeed. Such a terrible thing." Pearl Jalkanen, Alicia Van Hausen and Lily Hildebrandt all fluttered around Catherine, patting her arm and commending her for her bravery.

Catherine accepted their solicitations with a smile, wondering if even one person had gone to Jim Kinney to commiserate with the actual victim of the attack. She badly wanted to check on him, but didn't see how she could escape from her after-church dinner engagement at the Van Hausens. Her position as schoolteacher made her a sought-after guest in the community and Alicia Van Hausen would feel slighted if Catherine cancelled.

Most of her students attended the church, and they, too, began to gather around Catherine, eager to hear the story of how Miss Johnson had stopped the bad men so Deputy Scott could arrest them.

When the socializing was finally over, Catherine cast a longing look down the street toward the stable as she accompanied the Van Hausens on the short walk to their home.

"Do you know how Mr. Kinney is?" she asked Mr. Van Hausen. "Did Dr. Halloran see him yesterday?"

"I haven't heard," the banker replied. "That was quite a ruckus yesterday. The boy's lucky to be alive from what I understand."

"Thanks to you, Miss Johnson. It's most unfortunate you had to witness such a horrific scene." The Van Hausen's eldest son,

Charles, walked beside Catherine. In his derby hat and suit jacket with his neatly trimmed little moustache, the bank teller was considered a fashion plate and the best catch in town.

Catherine smiled, but turned her attention to his little sister, Melissa, walking on her other side. She wasn't eager to encourage Charles' attentions to her.

Melissa, one of her second grade pupils, clung to her hand and beamed up at her. "I can't wait until you come to live at our house. You're the nicest teacher I ever had."

Catherine smiled and swung her hand. "And you're a wonderful student."

Living with her students' families was both a blessing and a curse. Catherine would have loved to escape the children and all talk of school at the end of the day and have the privacy she'd taken for granted back home. But sharing in their lives gave her a much greater understanding of how she could best reach each child, and it was a window into the community in which she now lived.

At dinner, as she passed dishes of fried chicken, mashed potatoes, and a multitude of side dishes, Catherine tried to sidestep Charles' overtures without appearing unfriendly. It didn't help that his mother promoted the young bachelor's many good qualities and even suggested he give Catherine a buggy ride home. Catherine wished she could for once spend her Sunday afternoon on her own, doing exactly as she pleased.

After dinner, she thanked the Van Hausens for their hospitality, but insisted on walking to the McPhersons' farm. "I enjoy a Sunday afternoon constitutional. It really isn't far and I don't want Charles to go to the trouble of getting the buggy out for such a short drive."

"I could take you on a longer drive. We could go out to Asher Lake. Or if you prefer to walk, I'll accompany you. After yesterday's upset, I'm sure you'd feel safer with an escort."

Catherine swallowed her annoyance and forced a smile. "That is so kind of you, Charles, but I, uh, I promised to stop and talk to the deputy today. I don't know how long that will take."

Before Charles or his mother could press her further, she pinned on her hat, bid them good day, and walked out the door. Her abruptness was close to rude, but she couldn't stand one more moment of pleasantries and chitchat with the well-intentioned Van Hausens or their bachelor son.

She hurried down the street in the direction of the sheriff's office but passed it on her way to her real destination.

The livery stable smelled strongly of hay, horses and leather. Catherine breathed deeply. Although she'd never owned a horse and had rarely ridden one, she loved the big, quiet beasts with their soft brown eyes. As she passed each stall, she crooned quiet endearments at the animals, stopping to pet the soft, velvety nose of a tan horse with a white blaze on its forehead.

The livery owner, Mr. Rasmussen was nowhere in sight. The door of Jim's room was partially open. Catherine paused to knock on it, but no one answered. Of course not. He couldn't hear her knock. She hesitated then pushed the door open.

Jim lay in bed, his black hair stark against a white pillowcase. At her movement, he turned, and when he saw her, he smiled, eyes crinkling at the corners. She smiled back and raised a hand in greeting.

He waved her forward.

Catherine didn't stop to think of the impropriety of being in a single man's room. She went to him and stood beside his bed.

"How are you?" she asked, forcing herself not to raise her voice as if speaking louder would help.

He shrugged, and touched a hand to his ribs then to his head. His face looked much worse than yesterday, bruised purple and black, and swollen. A blanket covered him up to his bare chest so she couldn't see the rest of his body.

"Did the doctor come?"

He nodded and made a motion of snapping something in half then wiped it out with both hands.

"Nothing broken?" she guessed.

Jim pointed at her and mouthed something.

She shook her head in confusion, trying to read the words on his lips.

He repeated them carefully, and reached out to take her hand. *Thank you.*

A warm glow suffused her. Mr. Rasmussen must have told him how she'd helped out in the street yesterday.

She nodded. "You're welcome." The warm slide of his skin over hers sent a tingle through her. She let go of his hand. "I'm glad you're feeling better, and I'm sorry those men did that to you. Is there anything I can get for you? Water? Or something to eat? Probably something soft, right? I can't imagine you'd want to chew and swallow right now. Your jaw looks so swollen. It must really hurt. How is your shoulder? Did Dr. Halloran say when you might be able to get up and around again?" She couldn't stop the nervous words pouring from her mouth.

Jim held up a hand, stopping her. He shook his head. Palm down, he made a soothing gesture. *Calm down. Easy.*

"Too fast. I'm sorry." Catherine exhaled sharply, releasing her tension, her fingers unclenching at her sides.

Jim pointed toward something behind her.

There was a stool in one corner of the room. She pulled it near the bed and sat. "Sorry. I'm a little nervous." She indicated her flushed cheeks then made a talking motion with her hand. "Talking too much."

He grinned, displaying white teeth and the crease of a dimple in each cheek.

Catherine's already jumpy insides leaped again and her overheated body grew even hotter. She tried to enhance her words with her hands as best she could. "I don't know how much you understand."

Frowning, Jim shook his head, opened his mouth, and closed it again. Clearly he wanted to communicate and was frustrated at his inability to do so.

"Are you from here originally?" She pointed at the ground.

Jim shook his head, and made a sweeping gesture with his hand. *Far. Farther away.* He sat up in bed, wincing. The sheet slipped down, baring more of his torso.

Catherine glanced away, then back, focusing only on his face, ignoring his bruised, naked flesh. She couldn't very well talk to him without looking at him.

He pointed at her and raised his eyebrows.

"I'm from White Plains, New York. It's on the Hudson River."

20

Jim held his hands open—*Why?* then pointed emphatically down—*here. Why had she come here?* His movements and expressive face were more eloquent than many people's words.

Catherine smoothed her skirt over her knees. "It's a long story."

Go on, he beckoned with his fingers.

"I graduated from the Columbia University Teachers' College and taught high school in White Plains. I was engaged to a man named Howard Brown, a captain in the navy. He was stationed on a battleship. We were to be married when he came home on leave." She swallowed the rising lump in her throat. "You've heard of the *Maine*? He died in that explosion."

His eyes were trained on her mouth. A frown creased his brow.

"After Howard's death I couldn't feel anything. I could barely move through my days. I wanted to fall asleep and never wake up. I guess I wanted to die too." She exhaled a shaky breath, relieved to let go of the feelings she'd kept locked inside for so long. It was the first time she'd admitted these feelings aloud to anyone. Although her parents had done everything they could to comfort her, Catherine had never spoken about what she was going through. Knowing Jim probably didn't understand her made it easier to confide in him.

"Only teaching gave me a sense of purpose, a reason to go on living. But being in White Plains and seeing all my friends getting married or having children was too painful. I could have had a suitor, several of them, but I wanted something else—a change. I wanted to go somewhere and do something completely different. I wanted to fly away. Inside I felt the magnetic pull birds must feel when they migrate." She smiled at her fanciful notion, glad he couldn't hear how ridiculous she sounded.

"After reading about the great need for teachers in small communities out west, I took this job. My parents can't understand why I would go on such a misadventure. I think they expect me to give up and take a train home any day now."

She stopped talking at last and registered the confusion on Jim's face. She'd given him far too many words he couldn't understand. There must be a better way for them to communicate.

"Can you read and write?" She pantomimed both.

He held up his thumb and finger an inch apart.

"How about drawing? Do you have paper and a pencil? Or a slate?" She wished she had her school bag with her.

Jim nodded and moved to get up.

"No. I'll get it." She went to the chest of drawers at which he pointed. On top were a few items; a comb, soap, facecloth and towel, a penknife and several small animals whittled from wood. There was also a stub of pencil and a stack of paper--the blank backs of old bills and other used paper stacked on top of a Sears and Roebuck catalog. Numbers in neat columns marked the top sheet.

Catherine carried the papers and catalog to the bed and handed them to Jim. "I'm going to draw a picture of where I'm from. A map."

Sitting beside him on the bed, her shoulder and hip pressed against his, she was well aware of the immodesty of the situation, but ignored her apprehension.

I'm a teacher. This is merely teaching. She took the pencil and began to sketch.

* * * *

His inability to decipher her words was infuriating. She'd told him important things, he could tell from her sad expression, but her lips had been moving too fast. He caught something about her home, a man who had died, and something about teaching, but the word shapes he recognized were mixed with far too many he didn't.

And it was humiliating to have to admit he could barely read. He'd never been to school, although his mother had taught him the alphabet and a few words for objects and animals like cat and dog. Anything beyond that he'd figured out for himself with the aid of the Sears and Roebuck catalog, the only book he owned. He understood that printed words represented things, but needed help in deciphering which words meant which things. At least he had a firm grasp of numbers, thanks to Rasmussen. Jim knew to the last penny how much money he'd saved up in his tobacco can under the floorboard. He knew how much he'd need to get through the winter and how much he could use for his future plan.

Catherine's weight settled on the mattress beside him, her hip and thigh against his. She laid the catalog across their laps with a clean sheet of paper on top and leaned over to begin drawing.

Suddenly he was glad he hadn't understood her since it meant her having to sit close to explain things. Her body heat radiated through her skirt into his leg and his cock stirred in response.

He watched her profile as she gazed at her drawing, her delicately shaped nose and full pouting lips. A lock of her hair had escaped its pins and fell over one eye. His fingers itched to tuck it behind the pink shell of her ear.

She talked as she drew, forgetting he couldn't hear her. He was glad. It meant she was thinking of him as a normal person, a man like any other.

He looked at what her drawing and recognized the shape of the United States. He'd seen maps and understood they represented places. She drew a shape and labeled it with two words, one that started with an N, the other with a Y. Within the shape she made a black dot and marked it with W and P.

Catherine traced her finger around the perimeter of the map. "United States." Then she traced the smaller shape. "New York." At last she pointed to the dot. "White Plains. My home. Understand?"

He nodded, looking at the words again so he'd remember them. White Plains, New York.

She sketched the rest of her story using stick figures. A woman. She pointed to herself. And a man named "Howard." Far down the coast of the U.S. map she drew a little island and a ship with flames.

"Cuba," she said, then drew a ship in flames and on it a stick man.

Suddenly Jim made the connection. He remembered the etching in the newspaper Rasmussen had showed him of a burning ship, the *U.S.S. Maine*. His boss had said the United States was at war with a country called Spain over an island named Cuba. Sometimes Rasmussen was friendly like that and took the time to explain things. Other times he seemed to forget Jim existed.

Jim pointed to the drawing of the ship and the figure of the man, Howard. He mouthed the word "Sorry" and pressed a hand to his chest. Saying "sorry" when someone died was the correct thing to do. People had said it to him when his mother died even though they hadn't believed he could understand.

"Thank you." Catherine's smile was tinged with a sadness he longed to kiss from her lips. How wonderful it would be to have that privilege!

She drew the state of Nebraska and railroad tracks to show her journey to Broughton, ending with a little schoolhouse sketch. She handed Jim the pencil and pointed at him. "You. How did you come here?"

He wasn't too sure about the state shapes and names, but knew where the Mississippi River ran so he drew that and a dot near the gulf to represent Natchez. How could he tell her about the meandering journey that had brought him here, full of starts and stops marking the changes in his life?

In an attempt to improve a lifelong streak of bad luck, Papa had uprooted his family, taking a steamboat up the Mississippi before heading west. A sudden fever had taken him soon after they'd begun the journey, leaving Jim and his mother alone in a strange town. With no relatives in Natchez to return to, they'd continued toward the promising dreams of the west.

But their meager savings depleted quickly and they were stranded in another town. Mama took in washing, and male visitors too. At age eight, Jim started his illustrious career of sweeping floors in taverns, stores and inns.

One of Mama's men stuck around, and she told Jim he had a new Papa. They traveled again to another town farther south. There were fights. Jim couldn't hear the yelling, but he could see angry faces, punching fists and the bruises on his mother's face and arms. One night she woke him, told him to dress, and they left the new Papa to travel west once more.

In another town Jim made a friend named Bill, a fair-haired boy a little older and taller than he, but skinny as a rail. When they wrestled, Jim got the upper hand every time. They fished, climbed trees, built forts, and explored caves in the rocky hillside. One day Jim went to find his friend to play, but the family's shack was empty. The crops harvested, they'd moved on.

There were summers spent picking beans, cabbages, and corn; autumns gathering apples. They moved north, south and always further west, until by chance they reached this town in the middle of the Nebraska wheat fields. Jim's mother developed a cough that racked her body all winter and killed her by spring. He'd stayed here for lack of anyplace better to go.

Jim had spent most of his life alone. The solitary nature of his disability and the constant moving had made it difficult for him to make friends. With his mother's death, his last connection to a person was severed. He existed in Broughton like a ghost, doing his odd jobs, too silent for anyone to notice.

Catherine's hand touched his wrist, and he realized he'd been sitting with the pencil pressed against the black dot indicating Natchez for several moments. He looked into her eyes and shook his head. His story was too complex to tell with stick figures and lines on paper.

She nodded her understanding. "Jim, would you like me to teach you to read and write?"

He nodded emphatically. Of course! Anything to keep her coming back to him. Besides which not being able to read held him back as much as his lack of hearing did.

She smiled and the whole room seemed brighter. "We can start now, and I'll come back tomorrow after school with books for you. Can you show me what you know?"

Jim winced, ashamed to display how little that was. Although he could copy letters, words and whole sentences from the catalog, old newspapers or feed bag advertisements, he didn't know what the words meant. But he remembered cat, so he C-A-T--then drew a crude picture of a triangle-eared feline.

Catherine nodded. "Good. Can you write your name?"

He recalled his mother cupping his hand and helping him make the letters. He wrote J-I-M and looked at Catherine.

"Yes. Do know the entire alphabet? You know, A-B-C-D..."

He printed the alphabet. When he finished, she praised his work and showed him some of the text in the catalog, explaining the difference between capital letters and lowercase. Taking the pencil from him, she printed the lowercase counterparts next to all the capital letters he'd made.

While concentrating on the lesson, Jim was almost able to forget his attraction to her ... until Catherine began to demonstrate the sounds connected to the letters. She pointed to the capital and lowercase letter A and made the shape with her pretty lips. Taking

25

Jim's hand, she placed it on her throat, while she made the sound of "A."

Jim felt the buzzing beneath his fingertips, and the soft warmth of her skin. Inside her open mouth, her tongue dropped down and curved a little. He gazed intently at her lips and tongue while mimicking the movement.

"Good." Catherine took his other hand and put it on his throat. "Now make the sound of A."

He shaped his mouth and expelled air until he felt a vibration under his hand,. Whether the noise he made sounded the same as her, he didn't know, but Catherine seemed pleased.

She moved on to B, putting his fingers against her lips as she repeated the sound several times. Her lips were as soft as her neck, but a different texture. Hot breath escaped from between them in little puffs, warming and dampening his fingers.

His cock stirred again, an uncontrollable force of nature reacting to her closeness, her scent, and her touch. It was a good thing the blanket covered his lap and his growing erection. He shifted to relieve the pressure of his cock pressing into the Sears catalog. Covering his mouth with his hand, he tried to simulate the burst of air that accompanied "B."

Catherine brought his hand back to her throat so he could feel how B was different from A, shorter and sharper. The feel of her smooth flesh under his fingers made it hard to concentrate on the subtle differences in the letters as she continued through the alphabet. He lost track of the various sounds, he was so distracted by touching her. Besides, there were too many letters with very subtle differences in the buzzing they made in Catherine's throat.

By the letter K, she seemed to realize it and gave his hand a squeeze. "Very good. That's enough for today." She checked the watch pinned to the bodice of her dress. "It's getting late. I must go."

No, he wanted to protest. *I'll learn the rest of the alphabet and make more sounds. I'll draw maps and stick figures, anything you want, just don't leave.* But he nodded as she rose from the bed, leaving an empty spot beside him.

"Thank you," he mouthed and smiled at her.

"You're welcome. I'll come back tomorrow afternoon to see how you're doing and bring textbooks. Goodbye." She raised a hand then walked out the door.

Jim stared after her, rubbing his hand over his arm where it had pressed against the cotton sleeve of her blouse. The skin felt sensitive, the hairs prickling as they stood on end. Tomorrow he would see her again, be close to her and breathe in her sweet scent. He could hardly wait.

* * * *

Catherine thought about Jim all the way back to the McPhersons'. He was bright, eager to learn and would be very easy to teach. Only his disability created a challenge. She had read about signing, and knew there was a school for the deaf in New York. Perhaps Aunt Lydia could send informative literature or a book about signing. She'd send a telegram tomorrow asking her.

The sky had grayed to dusk by the time she reached the farm. She'd missed supper. Mrs. McPherson was cleaning up the kitchen while tending her baby and breaking up an argument between the older children. Catherine apologized for being late and allowed Mrs. McPherson to assume she'd been on a buggy ride with Charles Van Hausen. Then she pitched in, taking over the kitchen work so the woman could deal with her squabbling children.

Marlene and Caleb destroyed every false notion about twins being of one accord. The eleven-year-olds argued constantly and, in addition to being opposite genders, looked completely different from one another. Mrs. McPherson sent Marlene to help Catherine in the kitchen and Caleb to slop the hogs, while she carried the baby into the other room to change her diaper.

Mr. McPherson sat by the kerosene lamp in the living room, reading his newspaper, oblivious to the chaos around him. Catherine was definitely ready to move on to the Albrights' home in town where there was only one daughter, a polite sixteen-year-old with refined manners.

As she scoured pots and pans, Catherine relived every moment of her afternoon with Jim Kinney, not only her attempts to communicate and teach, but the unexpected feelings he roused in her.

27

She'd barely known he existed until yesterday, but now he filled her mind and her senses.

She'd tried to remain detached, convincing herself she felt no attraction, but her body had betrayed her. From the moment she entered the room, the sight of his naked shoulders above his bandage-wrapped torso had sent a tingling through her feminine parts. His inquisitive brown eyes and delighted smile on seeing her had made her stomach flip and her knees go weak.

Ignoring the symptoms of desire, she'd seated herself next to him to draw the map and write the alphabet. In the process of teaching, she'd almost forgotten her attraction, but when she faced Jim and put his hand on her throat, on her lips, the boundary between professionalism and sensual urges crumbled. It was all she could do to remember why she was having him touch her face and neck. His callused fingers scraped her skin, branding it with heat, and his eyes on her mouth were so intense they stole her breath away.

Luckily, Jim didn't seem to notice how his touch stirred her. He was concentrating completely on the lesson, innocent of her inappropriate thoughts.

Teaching him in the intimate setting of his room had been a bad idea. She'd risked innuendo and accusations of lewd behavior. Tomorrow after school, she would see him as promised, but suggest he come to the schoolhouse every day after classes for an hour or two of tutoring. That was the proper setting for teaching. Surely Mr. Rasmussen could spare him briefly each day for such an important purpose.

"Miss Johnson." Marlene's voice broke her reverie.

Catherine looked down. The girl was waiting, dishcloth in hand, for the next pan. "Sorry. I was woolgathering." She plunged her hands back into the lukewarm water. There were barely enough suds to finish the last of the dishes, but she didn't want to take the time to add more soap and hot water from the kettle on the stove. Oh, how she missed hot and cold running tap water, one of the many modern amenities she'd taken for granted in White Plains.

"Miss Johnson, do you have any brothers or sisters back home?"

"No, Marlene. I'm an only child. I had cousins though so I know how annoying boys can be." She commiserated with the girl's irritation with Caleb.

That bit of sympathy was all it took. Marlene launched into a tirade against her brother for the rest of the time it took to clean up the kitchen, then trailed after Catherine into the living room, still complaining.

"Leave Miss Johnson be, Marlene!" her mother commanded.

The family settled into an evening routine; the children working on school assignments, the baby already asleep in her cradle, and the three adults reading silently and exchanging occasional bits of town gossip.

Later, as Catherine dressed in her nightgown and slipped under the covers of the daybed in the closet-sized spare room, her thoughts turned to Jim Kinney again. Actually, they'd never left him even as she pretended to read *Jane Eyre*. Her mind raced with plans of how to approach his education, but beyond her enthusiasm for a challenging teaching project was simple, sensual attraction. She hadn't felt drawn to a man since Howard's death, and couldn't imagine why her mind had seized on Jim, the most unlikely prospect in Boughton. Nevertheless, in the privacy of her bed and the solitude of her room, she couldn't deny her fascination with him.

Images of his face haunted her; the strong cheekbones, straight nose, curved lips, and the charming creases in his cheeks when he smiled. What would his thick, dark hair feel like slipping between her fingers? Even lying in the dark with her eyes closed, his deep brown eyes wouldn't let her rest. There was so much going on behind his concentrated gaze, so many thoughts trapped inside his head, caged by silence.

She vowed she would give him the key to set them free.

CHAPTER THREE

School the next day was one little crisis after another. Nothing went smoothly and the children seemed more fractious than usual. Catherine's class was composed of twenty-two children ranging in age from seven to seventeen, each at a different level of development, each with opinions, desires and needs.

In White Plains she'd taught ninth grade and only one subject, English. From experience, she tended to have more patience dealing with older youths than with the flock of little ones. After a hectic first few weeks in the one-room schoolhouse, she'd learned to utilize the girls and boys in the upper grades. Whenever they were caught up in their work, she set them to helping the youngest or slowest members of the school. But even with the aid of her teenage pupils, Jennie Albright, Sarah Jalkanen and Ned Hildebrandt, the demands on her time were never-ending. Some child always needed attention, and today Catherine had no patience for it.

"Bernard Jalkanen, put your hands on your desk, palms down, and don't move them until I say you may. Next time you pull a girl's hair, I'll smack your hands with a ruler."

"But, Miss Johnson, she started it."

"Don't argue, just do it!" She turned to her youngest student, six-year-old Minnie Davis, who was standing by her desk. "Minnie, you know you may not get up from your seat without permission. What is it?"

The child's eyes glistened and her lower lip trembled. She leaned in close and whispered, "Miss Johnson, I had an accident."

"Oh." Catherine felt terrible for snapping at her. "All right. Come with me. Please take over the class for a few minutes, Jennie."

Leading Minnie to the coatroom, she helped her remove her soggy undergarment, after which she asked Jennie Albright to accompany the child home. Luckily Minnie lived in town rather than miles out on the prairie.

And that was just the morning.

After lunch and recess, the hours dragged until finally she could announce, "Class dismissed."

The children were out of their seats and through the door in seconds, as anxious as Catherine to escape the schoolhouse.

She gathered her papers to grade, essays to read, textbooks and a slate for Jim, and locked the door behind her. She walked to the telegraph office to send a message to her aunt. The postmaster/telegraph operator accepted Catherine's brief message, reading it over then glancing up at her with interest.

"You teaching Jim Kinney? I thought that boy was simple."

"No. He merely has trouble communicating. I hope to change that." She paid for the telegram, closed her purse, and walked from the office, frowning. No doubt the whole town would know what she was doing now. Despite the fact that a telegraph operator was supposed to be as discreet as a priest in a confessional, Herbert Nordstrum never kept a secret.

"Miss Johnson!"

Shading her eyes from the sun, Catherine saw Nathan Scott approaching her. The fair-haired deputy towered over her. He looked like an overgrown schoolboy with his round face and open smile. She supposed most women would find him handsome, but his Scandinavian fairness and bulky body didn't appeal to Catherine.

He swept off his hat and nodded. "How are you?"

"Very well, thank you." She returned his smile, hiding her annoyance at the interruption.

"Sending a letter?" He glanced at the building she'd come from.

"Mm."

"Funny, me running into you here. I was going to ride out to the McPhersons' later and tell you the latest news about the men we arrested. The circuit judge will be in town in a few days to hold a hearing. I expect the men will be fined and released."

"Released? They could have killed Mr. Kinney! Isn't the penalty for attempted manslaughter more than a fine?"

"They've only been charged with drunk and disorderly and malicious mayhem."

"That's all? Mrs. Albright is right. It's shameful the way drunken men are excused for their misbehavior while under the influence of alcohol."

Nathan frowned. "Given the circumstances and that no one was fatally injured—"

"Mr. Kinney or I might have been. It's outrageous!"

The deputy glanced at the nearly empty street where a wagon rattled past, then focused his pale blue eyes on Catherine and lowered his voice. "The truth is, Miss Johnson, those men work for Mr. Karak, the new owner of the granary and mill. He promised to pay their fine if the sheriff reduced the charges. Says he'll keep his boys in line from now on and not to worry."

"What?" She was shocked. Anger at the injustice swelled in her. "Who does this Karak think he is?"

"Rich, that's what. He came out here from the east and right away bought up the grain elevator, the mill, and banknotes on acres of farmland. Has his hand in the railroad too. The whole town pretty much belongs to him now."

"That's medieval! It's terrible!"

"Nothing anybody can do about it. The man hasn't broken any laws." The deputy shifted from one foot to the other, ran the brim of his hat between his finger and thumb, and cleared his throat. "Miss Johnson, on a more personal note, I wondered if I might call on you sometime, perhaps take you for a drive after church one Sunday."

"Oh!" She was speechless. His invitation was completely unexpected, so she wasn't prepared with a polite refusal. Perspiration trickled down her spine, making her blouse cling to her back.

She forced a smile. "That's a kind offer, Mr. Scott. I will consider it."

"Thank you." His transparent eyes reflected his disappointment with her less than enthusiastic reception of his offer. He nodded and his straight, fine hair lifted in the breeze. "Good day, Miss Johnson."

"Good day." She breathed a sigh of relief as the deputy moved aside on the boardwalk and let her pass. Poor Mr. Scott. She hated hurting any man's feelings, but after Howard's death, she'd had a lot of practice in letting suitors down gently. Several respectful months after his passing, men she knew had begun approaching her. She hadn't been nearly ready to let go of his memory and step out with anyone. In leaving White Plains, she'd hoped to escape that pressure, but it was starting up again, first with Charles Van Hausen and now Nathan Scott. What did a single woman have to do to get some peace from men's attentions?

Catherine's book-laden satchel dragged her arm down as she walked the rest of the way to the livery stable. On the way, several people stopped her to extend their sympathies on her "brush with death" and hear the story firsthand. She told it briefly, impatient to get on with her afternoon before all her free time was gone.

Finally she arrived at the stables and entered the dimness, breathing in the aroma of hay and horses.

"Miss Johnson." Mr. Rasmussen tipped his hat and rose from his seat near the front door, where he'd been smoking a cigar.

"Hello. I've come to check on Mr. Kinney's progress. Is he feeling better?"

"Much better. He's right over there, grooming Felicia." Rasmussen pointed to the third stall from the entrance. The top of Jim's dark head showed over the back of a bay horse.

"He's working already?" She frowned.

"I don't have him pitching hay or anything strenuous. Jim *wanted* to get back to work so I set him to currying."

"Mr. Rasmussen, I wondered if I might have an hour or so of his time every afternoon. I'd like to help Mr. Kinney learn to read and perhaps teach him sign language. Could you spare him a little each day … without docking his pay?" She smiled sweetly, making it impossible for him to refuse without seeming a selfish lout.

He hesitated. "Well, I suppose it'd be all right with me, if Murdoch can spare him some too. Jim's a hard worker. We both depend on him. It's only right both of us give up part of his time."

Catherine doubted either of the men paid Jim what his labor was worth, and it was petty of Rasmussen to begrudge him a few extra coins a week, but she smiled wider and thanked him before walking over to the stall.

Jim's shirtsleeves were rolled up to bare his forearms and the front of his shirt was open, revealing his bandaged torso. As he straightened from stroking the currycomb down the horse's neck, a lock of dark hair flopped over one eye. He flipped it back with a toss of his head and caught sight of Catherine. His dimples flashed.

Heat and nervous tension flared through her. She raised her hand in greeting, her heart racing as though she'd run all the way to the livery stable.

Jim raised the hand with the currycomb still strapped to it. He slipped the comb off and set it in a case beside him, then walked around the horse's head. He extended his hand to shake hers. A quick clasp and pump of the wrist was all the contact they made, but her skin tingled after she pulled away.

"Mr. Rasmussen says you can take a break for a lesson." She accompanied the words with gestures, feeling a bit foolish, but hoping her movements would make her words clearer.

He raised a finger signaling her to wait, picked up the carrier with the grooming supplies and gave the bay horse a last pat on the neck.

Catherine rubbed the mare's nose between its brown-velvet eyes. The animal whickered and blew warm, hay-scented breath into her face.

"She's a beauty. Does she belong to the stable?"

He shook his head.

"Someone boards her." Catherine looked around the stable. Some stalls were occupied, others empty. "Will you show me all the horses? I'd love to see them."

He led her through the building. At each stall, Catherine scratched a long nose or let the horse nuzzle her palm with soft, bristled lips. The horses lost interest immediately when it was clear she hadn't brought a treat. She'd remember to bring sugar lumps if she came back another time.

As they approached a large, black horse, Jim took Catherine's wrist, holding her back and shaking his head, warning her to keep her distance from this one. He didn't release her right away, but kept his fingers loosely circled around her wrist and led her past the horse. The big animal rolled its eyes and whickered, shifting nervously in its stall. When they reached the next horse, a small gray mare, Jim released her, but she still felt a bracelet of heat around her wrist.

Catherine wondered about the horses' names and it occurred to her that naming them would make a good teaching opportunity.

34

"Jim."

He was looking away and didn't respond to his name.

She touched his shoulder, and he turned toward her. For a few seconds, they stared into each other's eyes, something indefinable and almost palpable passing between them. The hushed atmosphere of the stables wrapped around them like a cocoon, holding them apart from the outside world. The soft chuff of horses' breath and the stamping of hooves were the only sounds to disturb the stillness.

Catherine blinked, breaking the spell. "Do you know their names?" She pointed at the horses. "Names? Maybe we could make a card for each stall. It would be a wonderful way to practice your lettering skills." She'd noticed the small carvings in his room and thought if he could practice the letters on paper first, he might then carve them on wood.

"I'll get Mr. Rasmussen to tell me their names." She hurried off, excited by her brilliant idea.

* * * *

Jim glared at his employer. This was not how he'd planned to spend his afternoon with Miss Johnson. He didn't want to share her attention with Mr. Rasmussen. The pair of them excluded him, talking to one another as if he didn't exist the way hearing people always did. Jim didn't want Catherine to see him as incapable of understanding or less than other men. Bad enough that she'd witnessed his humiliation on Main Street, getting dragged behind a horse.

He liked when she talked right to him, looking straight into his eyes and making those graceful gestures with her hands to enhance her words. Now her focus was on Rasmussen and writing down the horses' names as he told them to her. But there were many more words passing back and forth between them; information about who owned which horse, how long they'd been boarded at the livery, and other things that had nothing to do with horses at all. That's the way people talked, roaming all over the place, never one simple thing at a time, making it hard for Jim to keep up with them.

Inside, he was like them, with a hundred thoughts swirling around and evolving into new ideas, but there was no way for him to communicate any of it. For him to decipher the rivers of words

35

flowing from peoples' mouths was impossible. No wonder everyone thought he was stupid.

Catherine touched his arm, drawing his attention, and she handed him a notebook filled with yellow paper, a black slate, a piece of chalk and a pencil. "These are for you. I've printed each horse's name. You can practice copying them on the slate and then on paper. I'll show you which name goes with which horse." She spoke slowly, making sure he understood each thing before she continued on.

Feeling more like a project than a person, he trailed after her around the stable. At each stall, she said a name, showed him the printed version of it, and waited for him to copy it on the slate. Felicia. King. Lady. Old Tom.

He printed neatly and carefully, determined to show her he wasn't incompetent. There was no throat or lip touching this time, and Jim's annoyance with the lesson grew. This wasn't how he'd envisioned the afternoon at all. Instead of communicating *with* him as she'd done yesterday, Catherine seemed to be talking *at* him.

As he erased the slate once more and printed the last horse's name, Crusader, Jim looked at her with a raised eyebrow.

"Very good! You've done it perfectly. I want you to practice these words and try to connect them with the horses they represent. Do you understand?" She spoke as if he were one of her pupils. A child.

Jim turned to an empty, lined sheet of paper in the notebook and wrote, Lady, King, Zephyr, Felicia, Old Tom, Lucy, Crusader, without once checking the spelling against the words she'd printed for him. When he was finished, he pointed back and forth between each name and the corresponding horse, his finger emphatically stabbing the air.

He gave Catherine a hard stare.

"Oh." Her cheeks turned a bright rose as they'd done yesterday. "I'm sorry. I didn't mean to insult you. I didn't know the lesson would be so easy for you. I apologize."

Immediately, Jim felt terrible. Here she was, trying to help him and he'd been rude to her. The problem was he didn't want her to view him as a student. She was a beautiful woman and he wanted her to see him as a man.

Setting the pad of paper and slate on the floor, he moved close to Catherine and pressed his hand lightly to her throat, while pointing at the black stallion.

Catherine said the name. "Crusader." The sound buzzed in her throat.

Mimicking her mouth movements as closely as he could, Jim repeated the word shape, first silently, then aloud.

Her eyes widened and she smiled. "Yes. Like that."

He repeated it.

Pointing to the gray, she said, "Lady."

Her throat was warm and soft beneath his hand. He could feel her pulse and the flex of her muscles, but Jim forced himself not to be distracted by the intimacy of touching her and concentrated on replicating the word. He shaped it silently.

Catherine showed him how to curl his tongue toward the roof of his mouth and touch the tip to the backside of his teeth.

Jim cupped his own throat and attempted to say the word aloud by expelling air. He was making some sort of sound, but probably not the right one.

She gave a nod of approval. "You're making such progress."

Perhaps she was simply being kind, but Jim accepted her praise anyway and a warm glow kindled inside him.

They worked on several more names. Jim was almost more excited by his success in producing audible words than he was by touching Catherine's skin. Almost. But when he placed his hand on her lips to feel the puff of air in "Zephyr", he still had the impulse to pull her close and find out how those lips tasted.

He was struggling to make the buzzing sound of Z when the one of the cats that lived in the loft coiled around his legs, begging for food. Catherine squatted down to pet the black, white and orange calico. Lifting the cat in her arms, she looked up at Jim.

"I love cats! I had several back home and I really miss them."

He pointed to the hayloft ladder. Indicating the cat in her arms, he made the small sign with his thumb and forefinger.

"Little cats. Kittens. Up there? Oh, I'd love to see them!" She set the calico on the ground and rose, brushing loose fur off her blouse. She followed him to the ladder and lifted her skirts, ready to climb.

Jim smiled at her eagerness and motioned for her to go first. If she slipped on a rung, he wanted to be behind her to catch her. The fact her legs would be exposed didn't occur to him at first, but as she climbed, he couldn't take his eyes from her high-button shoes and the flash of white stockings and petticoats. The small bustle on her dress enhanced the curve of her rear. By the time they'd reached the hayloft, his breathing was labored, and not from the climb or his sore ribs. As Catherine smoothed her skirts to cover her ankles, he quickly adjusted his trousers in front.

He led her to the nest in the hay where the black cat had given birth to kittens. The little ones were no longer wobbly and helpless as they'd been only a couple of days ago, but were chasing each other and wrestling. At the sight of people, they disappeared into the hay. Jim knew they'd be back, curiosity outweighing their fear. He sat, and motioned for Catherine to do the same.

Sinking down on a pile of hay, she arranged her skirts so her legs were properly covered. Her modesty amused him. *Too late. I've already seen them.*

The kittens might be shy, but their mother wasn't. The big black cat strolled over from wherever she'd been hiding and rubbed against Catherine's arm. Smiling in delight, she pulled the heavy animal onto her lap.

"My cats were named Sunshine and Shadow," she told Jim, remembering to face him. "One was orange and the other black. Not very clever names, but I was seven when I named them. They're very old now. I doubt they'll still be alive by the time I return home."

"Home?" He mouthed the word and raised his brows.

"Yes. I'll probably be leaving after this school year. I miss White Plains too much."

He nodded, a pang of disappointment shearing through him.

The boldest of the kittens, a tabby male, suddenly sprang out from behind a drift of hay. Racing toward where they sat, he stopped abruptly and stared with round eyes, then he turned and raced back in the direction from which he'd come.

Catherine laughed. Her fingers stroked the plush fur of the mama cat. Jim imagined what it would feel like to have her hand stroking him like that, touching his hair, his face, running over his stomach, or slipping up and down his cock. He swallowed and

38

discarded the lewd thought, ashamed of himself for thinking of her like that.

Several of the kittens were now brave enough to stalk close. Catherine reached a hand out and held it there, waiting patiently. The tabby darted in, batted at her fingers and ran away again, but the runt of the litter, a little black female, came even closer and allowed her to touch its head. In a moment the kitten's real plan became clear when it climbed onto her lap to nurse from the mother cat.

Jim watched Catherine's face as she cooed and fussed over her lapful of cats. Her attention was totally focused on the animals, and it was his first chance to study her without fear of her seeing him. She was incredibly beautiful. Her heart-shaped face was wider at the forehead and pointed at the chin. Brilliant blue eyes were fringed in brown and accented by the arch of her eyebrows. Her skin was fair with a dusting of freckles across her small nose. Her mass of hair was neither pale wheat nor dirty blond, but a vibrant sunflower yellow. She wore it in the current magazine cover style, a wide roll around her face and piled loosely on her head. Her white blouse had puffy sleeves that narrowed to hug her forearms tightly. Hay and cat fur clung to the blouse and to her navy blue skirt.

Jim watched her pink lips moving as she talked to the cats, and imagined how soft they'd feel pressed against his. He swallowed and closed his eyes, trying to clear his head. Nothing was going to happen here. He wasn't actually going to lean in and kiss her. If he did, she'd slap his face and never come back again.

After a few moments, she looked up at him with a smile that wrenched his heart. "They're very sweet. Thank you for showing them to me."

He reached out to pet the old calico, which had joined them in the loft. Rubbing the animal's chest, he felt the strong tremor of its purr.

Catherine touched his knee to get his attention again. "Jim, have you always been deaf?"

He nodded. It wasn't quite true. His mother had told him an illness took his hearing when he was very young, but he couldn't recall a time when he could hear. It was easier not to explain all that.

"I asked Mr. Rasmussen about you. He told me your mother died after you moved here. Do you have any other family?"

He shook his head, intrigued that she'd been curious enough about him to ask questions.

"It must have been hard to be left alone with no one to take care of you. How old were you?"

Jim held up ten fingers then four.

"You've lived here in the livery ever since?"

He nodded. If he could have, he would've explained that he started working for Rasmussen and Murdoch long before his mother died. He'd been working one place or another since he was old enough to push a broom or pick produce. He was also very talented at lifting and carrying heavy things; boxes of liquor for Murdoch, bales of hay for Rasmussen. One summer, he'd worked at the freight depot, loading and unloading wagons, but when the owner had shorted him on his pay and he couldn't do anything about it, Jim had gone back to the two bosses he knew would at least treat him fairly.

"Is Mr. Rasmussen a good employer?"

He shrugged, tired of nodding, frustrated by not being able to tell her everything he wanted to. He pointed at her and mimed opening a book and writing. He raised his eyebrows.

"Do I read? Do I like reading and writing? Do I..." She spread her hands wide and shook her head. "Sorry. I don't understand."

Jim demonstrated the heights of different children.

"Children. Ah, my students. Do I like teaching? Yes. Although, not very much today." She proceeded to tell him about the misbehaving children, the rat that had gotten into the lunchboxes in the cloak room, and the fistfight in the schoolyard over a game of marbles.

He smiled throughout her story, entranced by her pantomime as she illustrated her words with her hands. He understood almost everything she said.

When she was finished speaking, Catherine looked at the gold watch pinned to her blouse and her eyes widened. "My goodness, it's late. I have to go." She put the cat off her lap and stood. The kittens, which had ventured boldly out of the hay, went flying off in all directions.

Jim rose too.

She stepped close and touched his arm. "Mr. Rasmussen said you may come to the schoolhouse tomorrow after school for a lesson. Would you like that?"

He nodded, breathing in her lily scent and basking in the warmth radiating from her body. She was so close, if he bent his head only a little, his mouth would touch hers.

Catherine's eyes were wide; the pupils dilated making the blue seem dark. Her lips parted slightly. She dropped her hand from his arm and stepped away.

"I'd better be going."

Jim descended the ladder first and waited at the bottom, deliberately *not* looking at her legs this time as she climbed down. However, when she was a couple of rungs from the bottom of the ladder, he put his hands on her waist to guide her last few steps. And when her feet were on the ground, he didn't take them away.

Another moment flickered like candle flame, flared, then blew out. She pulled away from him. Walking over to her satchel, she took two books from it and brought them to him.

"Here are a primer and a math book. You can study from them."

He accompanied her to the wide open double door where Mr. Rasmussen drowsed in his chair in the sunshine.

Catherine held out her hand and shook his once, firmly and politely. "Good day, Mr. Kinney. I'll see you tomorrow."

Folding his arms and leaning in the doorway, Jim watched as she walked down the street. She glanced back, and he raised a hand in farewell, continuing to gaze after her until she turned the corner.

Rasmussen's hand settled heavily on his shoulder.

Jim started. He'd been so focused on Catherine he hadn't been aware of his boss had stood up.

Rasmussen's red face was puckered in a frown. He shook his head. "She's not for you, boy. You know that."

CHAPTER FOUR

Catherine thought about Jim the rest of the evening and throughout school the following day. His amazing demonstration of memorization proved he was very intelligent. And his valiant struggle to make sounds that approximated hers demonstrated his eagerness to learn. She would be careful not to patronize him again. The problem wasn't going to be teaching him, but maintaining a respectable detachment. That suspended moment of time in the loft with the air as thick as honey, she'd been certain something was about to happen. The look in Jim's eyes as he leaned toward her was the same hungry look Howard used to have just before he kissed her.

Thinking about that look and the pressure of his hands on her waist when he helped her off the ladder made her shiver. Tender and aching, her breasts pressed against her corset. This was most definitely *not* an appropriate reaction to have when thinking about a student.

"Miss Johnson." Ned Hildebrandt's voice made her jump. From the questioning look on the boy's face, he must have tried to get her attention several times.

"Yes, Ned?"

He showed her the algebra problem he was having trouble with. She had to concentrate hard to lead him through it. Mathematics was not her forte, and she worked to keep ahead of some of her students in the textbook.

Finally the long day ended and she dismissed school. Little Minnie Davis threw her arms around Catherine's skirt and hugged her, looking up with an adoring smile. "Love you, teacher!"

"Well, I love you too, Minnie." Catherine's heart filled as she leaned over and hugged the child. "See you tomorrow."

Touching gestures like this made her appreciate her job here. Teaching had never been so personal in White Plains, and ninth graders certainly weren't as demonstrative as little ones.

Catherine explained to Marlene and Caleb McPherson that she wouldn't be walking home with them again today, but she didn't tell them why she was staying behind at the schoolhouse. The news about her teaching Jim would get around town soon enough.

Sitting at her desk to grade papers, she anxiously checked her watch to find only five minutes had passed since she'd dismissed the class. She was as impatient as a child waiting for Christmas morning. When the door of the schoolhouse opened, she tingled with excitement.

Jim stood silhouetted against the sunlight. He wore a collarless, long-sleeved shirt with a tan vest over it, and black pants. He wore no hat, and his hair was brushed haphazardly from the crown, the bangs falling across his forehead. She preferred his natural look to the current men's style, parted in the center and slicked flat with pomade. He carried the slate and books she'd given him and looked around the room, but didn't enter.

She beckoned him inside, pointing to one of the larger desks in the back of the classroom. "Come in. Sit down." She felt like a nervous hostess trying to make a good impression, as though she'd invited him for a tea party instead of a lesson.

The seating in the schoolhouse was in the old style with two pupils sharing a wooden bench and desk with cast iron legs bolted to the floor. Jim took the seat where Jennie Albright usually sat. Catherine sat beside him in Sarah Jalkanen's regular spot. Sitting so close, she could smell the scent of the stables mingled with soap and sweat. The aroma elevated her heart rate even more. What was it about the earthy smell that stirred her so much more than the sweet cologne Charles Van Hausen exuded?

After placing his books on the desk, Jim looked at her with raised eyebrows.

"Let's start with arithmetic." She opened the text. "Do you know your numbers?"

Jim smiled and flipped the pages to the back of the book where there were introductory lessons for long division. Copying down a problem with several digits on his slate, he solved it quickly and correctly.

Catherine was stunned. How could he know so little about words and be completely competent with numbers?

43

"Who taught you?" she asked, tapping the slate.

He hunched his shoulders and mimed pushing glasses up his nose.

"Mr. Rasmussen." His imitation was spot on, and she couldn't help but smile.

Erasing the division problem, he jotted down a column of numbers with dollar signs beside them, added them and wrote the total, also with a dollar sign. He drew a crude image of the livery stable beside the numbers. Looking at her, he pushed the invisible glasses up his nose again.

She frowned. "Mr. Rasmussen taught you to do his accounting?"

He nodded.

"Well, that's..." She couldn't have been more shocked if he'd sprouted wings and flown around the room. "Very impressive. Let's turn to reading, shall we?"

She'd thought hard about how to make correlations between the written word and life. With nouns she could draw the object next to the word. Verbs could be acted out. But descriptive words and esoteric concepts would be more of a challenge. It was strange to think of the written language as a series of symbols like hieroglyphs rather than depictions of phonetic sounds, but since Jim had no sounds to relate to the letter clusters he could only perceive them as code.

Catherine had him copy on his slate a number of simple nouns. She drew crude pictures to illustrate dog, cat, girl, boy, sun, moon, and other one-syllable words, and let him feel how they sounded by touching her throat and lips. As he had the previous day, Jim attempted to blurt out rough approximations, but the words were only recognizable because she knew what he was trying to say.

They were intensely concentrated on the work when suddenly a movement on the floor caught her attention. A flurry of brown made her jump from her seat shrieking. "Rat!"

Scrambling onto the bench as though the animal might suddenly attack her, she screamed again. She detested rodents and this specimen wasn't like the harmless brown field mice that occasionally got into the McPhersons' house. The rat was large and sleek, with a foot-long tail.

The animal paused in the center aisle of the schoolroom, gazing at her, nose twitching, before scurrying toward the cloakroom near the entrance. It was the culprit that had been getting into the children's lunch boxes, bold and clever enough to flip latches and lift lids.

Jim crossed to the woodstove and snatched up a poker, then chased the rat into the cloakroom.

Embarrassed by her display of squeamishness, Catherine climbed down from the bench and followed, lifting her skirts, ready to run if the rat ran toward her. She hovered in the doorway of the side room with its rows of hooks for the children's coats and watched as Jim kicked aside a pair of forgotten galoshes in an attempt to corner the elusive rodent. He jabbed the poker, and there was a loud squeal.

Catherine screamed too, covering her mouth with her hands, the visceral image of an impaled rat turning her stomach.

A second squeal came from the corner as Jim stabbed again. He leaned to examine the animal, then turned toward Catherine. Approaching her, he nodded to let her know the job was finished. The cloakroom thief had been dispatched.

As he stopped in front of her, the schoolhouse door burst open, and Charles Van Hausen raced in.

"Miss Johnson? Are you all right?"

He noted Jim's hand touching her arm, and Catherine could see in his eyes the moment he made the wrong assumption. Charles grabbed Jim's shoulder, pulling him away from Catherine and throwing him against the wall. "Get your hands off her!"

"Charles, no!" she yelled, as he grabbed Jim's throat and punched him square in the face.

Jim broke the man's grip on his throat with an upward thrust of his hands, and twisted away.

"He didn't do anything. Stop it!"

But the sedate banker was suddenly violently male and intent on protecting her honor. Too focused to listen, he charged. Jim sidestepped him and raised his fists, ready to punch back.

Catherine stepped between them. "Stop!" She held Jim back with a hand on his chest, and faced Van Hausen. "Charles, nothing happened. I screamed because there was a rat."

45

It took a second for her words to register. His small brown moustache twitched comically above his lip. "Rat?"

"Over there." She pointed to the corner.

Jim's heart pounded beneath her palm, and his chest rose and fell. An angry scowl knit his brows, and his nose gushed blood. He wiped it then pinched the bridge to stop the blood flow. His gaze never left Van Hausen as the man went to the corner and stooped to examine the dead rodent.

"I heard you scream. I thought... You're all right?"

"Yes. I was giving Jim a reading lesson. A rat ran across the room and he took care of it, as you can see."

Charles glanced from one to the other. "Learning to read? Can he?"

"Yes," she said succinctly and turned to Jim. "Are you all right, Mr. Kinney?"

He nodded and glared at Van Hausen.

"Sorry." Charles spoke too loudly. "Is it broken? I could get the doctor."

"I'll get a rag." Catherine hurried to the supply cupboard. "What brings you here, Mr. Van Hausen?"

"I came to get my sister's homework assignments. Mother wanted to make sure she doesn't fall behind." He bent to retrieve his hat, which had fallen off during the fight.

Knowing he was intent on courting her, Catherine doubted it was simply concern for his little sister's schoolwork that made him stop by. "How is Melissa?"

"It's just a sore throat and sniffles. She should be well soon."

"I'll get what you need after I've tended Mr. Kinney."

With clean rags from the closet in hand, she pointed Jim toward the water pail at the back of the room. Casting a last narrow-eyed look at Van Hausen through the dark fringe of his bangs, Jim stalked toward it wiht Catherine following. She dampened one of the rags in the water and reached toward his face, but Jim took the cloth and waved away her offer of help.

Catherine watched him staunch the blood for a moment, before turning away. She gathered the books and assignments Melissa needed and thrust the pile at Charles, anxious to have him gone.

He accepted the work, and hesitated as if about to say something. She knew the look. He wanted to ask her to go with him on some sort of outing. Evidently deciding the timing wasn't right, he said instead, "The least I could do is get rid of the rat. I'll take it outside for you."

"Thank you."

Catherine shuddered and looked the other way as he lifted the rodent by its tail and walked toward the door.

"Goodbye, Miss Johnson. I'm sorry about the violence in your presence. Please know that I acted with the best of intentions."

"I understand. Good day, Mr. Van Hausen." She dismissed him and sighed with relief when the door finally closed behind him. Her pulse still racing from the unexpected drama, she went to check on Jim.

* * * *

He felt Catherine near his side before he turned to look at her. She was saying something, forgetting she needed to have his attention first.

"Let me help you. Please, sit down." She reached for the bloodied rag in his hand. "I'm so sorry this happened."

Jim felt awful. His ribs still ached, the scrape on his shoulder had become infected and now his nose throbbed all the way into his brain. Worst of all, he'd just gotten beaten up in front of Catherine. Again. The look of pity in her eyes made him angry. He didn't want her fussing over him like he was some pathetic stray dog. Again he refused her offer of help with a warding gesture, but she ignored him and took the cloth from his hand. She led him to her chair behind the teacher's desk.

He lowered himself into it with a grunt of pain. Catherine's brows were drawn together over intent blue eyes and her lips were pressed tight. She held his chin in her hand and sponged carefully around his nose. Having her touch his face almost made it worth the pain.

Jim inhaled a clot of blood and tasted copper. He glanced down at his shirt. A great splotch of red decorated the front and spattered across his vest. His only good clothes were ruined.

Catherine pulled the shirt away from his chest and rubbed at the bloodstain, which only smeared it into the fabric. She motioned for him to take the shirt off.

Jim glanced at the door. The last thing he wanted was for another surprise visitor to walk in and make wrong assumptions. He shook his head.

Catching the movement of his eyes, she nodded and tugged on the vest instead. He slipped it off and handed it to her.

She carried it to the water bucket in the back of the room and rinsed both the vest and rag. He watched her wring them out. No one had taken care of him in a long time and her ministrations touched him.

Returning, she bent over and dabbed his upper lip again. Standing between his knees, her legs bumped his inner thighs. With a hand around her waist, he could easily pull her down onto his lap. The forbidden thought thrilled him. Even though his nose throbbed, pain spreading behind his eyes, his cock also throbbed from her nearness.

Catherine took the damp rag from his face, but remained poised over him. She brushed the hair from his forehead, smoothing it back, letting her fingers linger in it. Her gaze was fixed on his hair, not his face, as though if she looked into his eyes she'd have to acknowledge what she was doing.

Afraid to break the spell, he held his breath until he thought he'd pass out. The space between them was charged like the air before a storm, and he waited to see what would happen next. The realization that his attraction wasn't one-sided was a revelation. Catherine was clearly interested in him too. He'd thought maybe that was true when they'd shared a similar tension-filled moment yesterday, but had decided it was wishful thinking. Yet now, here she was, stroking his hair, her eyes wide and her lips slightly parted.

Jim tilted his face toward her, eyes riveted on those plump lips. His movement burst the bubble. Catherine stepped away from him so fast she almost tripped. He nearly groaned in disappointment.

"Mr. Kinney." Her eyelids lowered, remained closed a moment, and opened once more. Her sharp blue gaze pierced him. "We must be friends. Nothing more. Understand?"

Understand. What if he pretended to misunderstand? What if he simply stood and pulled her into his arms. What if he kissed her?

Would it be worth having that memory to savor later, even if she refused to ever see him again?

But of course he wouldn't do it. He'd never kissed a woman and wasn't going to have his first kiss be a stolen one. He wouldn't force himself on her. Even if she was attracted to him, she obviously didn't intend to do anything about it.

He rose to his feet. She stepped aside, and he walked past her to the desk at the back of the room where his schoolbooks lay. He gathered them and headed toward the door.

Catherine intercepted him. "I'm sorry."

He cut her off with a wave of his hand and made the "all right" sign with his circled thumb and forefinger.

"Will you come tomorrow?" Her eyebrows raised in question.

With a smile, Jim nodded and walked out the door. But his smile disappeared the moment his back was to her.

As he strode toward the livery, he cursed the stupid impulse that had made him lean in for a kiss, cursed Van Hausen for punching him in the nose, and cursed the rat for setting the whole thing in motion. Most of all, he cursed his deafness, for the first time truly hating the handicap that set him apart from other men. Even through the blinding pain in his nose, he'd been aware of the way Van Hausen looked at Catherine. The man wanted her and he was a prominent citizen, a banker, a well-employed, *hearing* suitor, whom she wouldn't automatically reject if he tried to kiss her.

Jim was so intent on his thoughts he was once again startled by a sudden hand on his shoulder. He spun around with his fists raised. What the hell was going on this week? He couldn't seem to keep out of anyone's way.

Deputy Scott raised his hands, palms open. "It's all right." He lifted his brows and pointed at the bloodstain on the front of Jim's shirt.

Jim shook his head and indicated his nose. *Just a nosebleed.*

"Do you understand me?"

He nodded.

"Those men who hurt you are free now. Their boss paid their fine." The deputy's mouth moved slowly as he mimed money exchanging hands. "I thought you'd want to know."

A fine? They'd gone free after dragging him down the street behind a horse? Jim nodded his acknowledgement. There was nothing else he could do.

"Sorry." Scott clapped a hand on his shoulder.

Jim nodded again and continued on his way.

The rest of the afternoon he mucked out stalls and in the evening, cleaned whiskey spills and tobacco spit from the floor of the Crystal Saloon. Murdoch beckoned him to the bar at the end of the night and poured them each a shot of whiskey. After the saloonkeeper had tossed his back, he counted Jim's pay from the cashbox.

Pocketing the coins, Jim sipped the searing alcohol slowly, making it last. He was tempted to buy a full glass in an attempt to blot out Catherine Johnson's face from his mind, but the money under the floorboard of his room wouldn't increase by wasting it on liquor.

Murdoch stroked the length of his handlebar moustache, and stared at Jim. "Bitch of a thing that happened to you. Sorry about that."

Jim didn't catch all the words, but understood the sympathy. He shrugged and finished the whiskey. Murdoch beckoned Shirley Mae over.

"On the house. My treat. You need a roll after what you've been through."

Shirley was a friendly, full-bodied girl with red hair and lots of freckles. Jim already knew what she could do with those hands and that grinning mouth. She winked and held out her hand to him.

He stared at her with the shot glass clenched in his fist. A virgin at twenty-two, not for lack of desire but for absolute lack of opportunity, Jim would've jumped at the chance for a free lay a few days ago. He'd never had enough cash to spare for more than an occasional hand job. Shirley's mouth on his cock the other night had been heavenly. Now he was being offered the whole package and all he could think of was that she was a poor substitute for the woman he really wanted.

Nevertheless, the whiskey had burned a path straight down his throat to his belly and his groin. His dick hardened as he gazed at Shirley Mae's ample cleavage. He imagined unveiling those generous breasts and rubbing his face between them. Setting his glass down, he rose from the bar stool and took her hand.

50

Her little room upstairs contained only an iron bedstead, a dresser and a washstand. Shirley stripped off her dress and underclothes and stood in front of him in garters, stockings, and nothing else. Jim hadn't begun to unbutton his shirt yet. He stared, gape-mouthed, at her large tits with their cherry-red nipples and the thatch of red-brown curls that hid her sex. He'd seen a French postcard once, but never a living, breathing, completely naked woman. Her skin was pink and white and mottled with freckles. Her generous weight filled rounded curves from her breasts to her waist and hips. A pale scar on her stomach caught his attention. The jagged mark hinted at pain in her past, making her seem a real person rather than just a means of satisfying an itch.

Jim had only seconds to take in the sight of her body before Shirley moved toward him. Her hands glided over his chest, taking down his suspenders, unbuttoning his shirt and pulling it off his arms. She ran her hands over the bandage binding his ribs and leaned to kiss his naked chest above the cloth. Her hands slid below his waist to unfasten his trousers.

Closing his eyes, Jim sucked in a breath and released it slowly. He savored her moist lips and tongue moving along his collarbones and chest and gasped when her hand wiggled inside his pants and grabbed his cock. His erection pulsed in her warm grasp.

Shirley rubbed the length of his shaft while unfastening his fly. Jim struggled not to explode, gritting his teeth and tamping down the heat of desire that burned through him. It would be humiliating to come before he was even inside her.

Opening his eyes, he exhaled shakily and reached for her breasts. The full mounds were warm and heavy in his hands, different somehow from what he'd expected a woman's breasts to be--not like feather pillows, but lumpy in texture, full of unseen things beneath the downy skin.

Fascinated, Jim rubbed his thumbs over her crinkled areolas and taut nipples. Shirley ran her tongue over her lips. Wrapping her hand around the back of his neck, she pulled his head down to one tit.

He sucked the nub of flesh into his mouth and breathed in her scent--whiskey, cheap perfume, sweat and sex. The heady combination increased his desire. Shirley combed her fingers through his hair and cupped the nape of his neck. He felt the throb of her voice in her chest, but didn't look up to see what she was saying. It didn't matter.

Switching his attention to her other breast, he sucked in the nipple and swirled his tongue around it. He nipped it lightly. She jerked and he felt another tremor that was her laughter. After a few moments, he reluctantly abandoned her breasts.

Shirley dropped to her knees to finish taking off his trousers, shoes and socks. He'd never been completely naked in front of anyone. Shirley's gaze traveled over his body and she smiled in approval, which made him feel better. He looked all right to her—normal. His cock, which had flagged a little under her exploring eyes, resumed thrust thick and eager, toward her.

Taking his hand, she led him to her narrow bed. The mattress sagged as he lay down on it and she climbed on top of him. Shirley lowered her body until she covered him, his erection trapped against her stomach. She slid against him, rubbing his cock with her soft belly and pubic mound.

Jim grabbed handfuls of her fleshy bottom. His eyes closed in pleasure, and he kissed her breast again as it brushed his face. Soon the friction of skin on skin wasn't enough. He needed to be inside her.

Shirley guided his cock to her entrance, then bore down on him, enveloping him in heat and wetness. As her body gripped him, Jim groaned. This felt even better than her mouth, hotter, wetter, deeper. He gripped her bottom and thrust his hips, filling her.

She nuzzled his neck, her curly, red hair tickling his face. It was a little greasy and smelled oily. Jim burrowed his face in it, as he pushed into her. His need was too intense, and too long restrained. He couldn't hold back any longer. Once, twice, three times he thrust, and then he released in strong, steady bursts. As he came, he imagined a curtain of blond hair lying across his face and the scent of lily perfume filling his senses.

After a few moments, Shirley sat up and pushed her tangled curls back from her face. She smiled at him and raised her eyebrows. "Good?"

Jim was still bringing his breath under control. His chest heaved as he nodded.

Rising from the creaky bed, she walked to the washstand, poured water from the pitcher into the bowl, dipped a cloth, and sponged between her legs. She glanced at him, and Jim understood he was dismissed. They were finished and he wasn't supposed to linger in her bed.

He stood and retrieved his clothes from the floor. The brief moment of fulfillment was an illusion. In the end, this was no different than the satisfaction he brought himself with his own hand. He might as well have spent another evening alone in his room as indulge in this pretense of real lovemaking.

After he got dressed, he nodded at Shirley Mae. In the middle of lighting her cigarette, she winked at him.

Jim walked from her room and went downstairs to the saloon. It was the tail end of the night and only a few drunks and card players still lingered. Mr. Murdoch sat at a table, talking with a man Jim recognized as the new owner of the granary and mill. Like Murdoch, the man had a full moustache that hid his mouth and made up for the lack of hair on his shining head. His eyes scanned the room, alert and restless despite the relaxed posture of his body. He looked like a wolf deciding which members of a flock of sheep were weakest. After years of reading people's characters by physical clues, Jim recognized a predator when he saw one.

The man's gaze touched Jim for a moment, then moved on, dismissing him as unimportant, leaving him feeling like a rabbit that had been passed over as too scrawny to make a meal.

Murdoch raised his glass in salute as Jim walked past.

Jim smiled, but with no joy behind it.

Exhausted, his nearly empty stomach burning from the unaccustomed whiskey, he trudged down the street toward the livery. His ribs and shoulder ached, not to mention his swollen nose, but most of all, he ached inside, lonelier than ever as he collapsed on his bed in his solitary room.

CHAPTER FIVE

Following her eventful afternoon with the rat, the fistfight and the intimate moments with Jim, Catherine spent a routine evening at the McPhersons' guiding Caleb through his homework, one of the bonuses for the family hosting the teacher. She explained the parts of a sentence while Caleb's leg jiggled beneath the table. She could feel how much he'd rather be anyplace besides studying nouns and verbs.

"But, Miss Johnson, how can 'sitting' be an action? There's nothing happening."

"Yes, but it's still something a person does, like running, eating or crying. Understand?"

On the other side of the table, Marlene snorted, saying without words, *Of course, he doesn't get it.*

"Shut up!" Caleb glared.

"Caleb, mind your tongue!" Mrs. McPherson spoke from across the living room where she sat with the baby on her lap.

There was a knock on the door and Mr. McPherson went to answer it.

Intent on finding a way to explain prepositional phrases that Caleb would understand, Catherine didn't look up until the sound of men's voices grew loud. She looked toward the front door. Mr. McPherson's back blocked the man he was speaking to. When he shifted to the side, Catherine caught her breath. The visitor was the man who'd dragged Jim behind his horse. There was a sleepy droop to his eyelids and the hunch of his shoulders gave him the looming aspect of a vulture. Beside him was the bushy-bearded man who had helped him.

What in the world were they doing here? Was it connected with her intervention on Jim's behalf the other day? She rose from her seat, heart pounding.

Mr. McPherson shouted at the men and pushed the leader toward the door. The man's scowl suggested he'd like to hit the farmer, but he and his partner left without incident. McPherson slammed the door behind him and stalked into the living room.

"What is it?" Mrs. McPherson picked up the rattle Baby Constance had dropped.

"We'll discuss it later." Her husband nodded at the twins.

Catherine's stomach clenched. Had she somehow brought trouble to the McPhersons?

The children were sent to get ready for bed, and when they were out of earshot, Mr. McPherson revealed the reason for the visit.

"Grant Karak bought the note on our property. The man owns half the town and now he's got the damn bank in his back pocket. Pardon my language, Miss Johnson."

"What does he want?" Mrs. McPherson bounced the fretful baby on her knees. "Is he taking our land?"

He shook his head. "The farmers will be little more than sharecroppers by the time he's bought us all out. He'll own us. We'll have to harvest our wheat, take it to his mill and sell through him. We'll be forced to accept whatever he says is fair whether it's the going rate or not. Karak even has a hand in the railroad. He's got us coming and going."

Not knowing what else to say, Catherine murmured that she was sorry and withdrew to her bedroom to give the McPhersons privacy. She felt like a drain on the family's already strained resources since supplying meals was part of a host family's responsibility. With this new development, she was even happier that she'd be moving to the Albrights' by the weekend.

As she lay in bed, she thought about the McPhersons' troubles for a while, but her mind inevitably returned to Jim and what had almost happened that afternoon. A kiss. She couldn't deny it had trembled in the air between them. All she'd had to do was lean down and take it.

It had been so long since she'd felt a man's lips pressed against hers. During her long engagement to Howard, they'd held hands, shared kisses, and just before he'd shipped out, she'd even allowed him to touch her breasts. They'd had so little time together, snatches of private moments in gardens during dances or afternoons walking in the park and necking on a particular bench beneath a willow tree. But oh, how she'd savored the memory of each precious moment in the many lonely hours without him.

When Howard was at sea, she'd dreamed of their future, not only sharing a house and having children, but of the intimate things they would do together as man and wife. She couldn't wait for him to return, couldn't wait to take the next step and feel his hands touching her everywhere. In the dark of night, she'd touched herself between her legs, a place a lady wasn't supposed to acknowledge, while she tried to imagine what intercourse would be like. She pictured Howard's deep blue eyes and easy smile and the way he looked at her like she was the most beautiful woman on earth. She loved him so much.

Then the news arrived about the explosion of the *Maine* in the Cuban harbor. A dreamy lethargy fell over Catherine as she waited to find out if Howard was among the dead. She was in a trance and so certain he'd somehow, miraculously, be all right that she was hardly worried. When Howard's parents came to inform her of the confirmation of his death, she wouldn't believe it at first. It was inconceivable that she would never see him again, never feel his arms around her, hear his warm laugh or his deep voice whispering secrets in her ear.

Dry-eyed days drifted past and it had taken months for his death to seep into her consciousness. At last she woke from her trance and exploded into tears and anger.

Catherine sighed, remembering that dark time, and rolled over to stare at the gray square of window above her bed. Howard was in the past now. She could cherish memories of him without crushing pain bearing down on her chest. And now, for the first time since losing him, she felt the stirring of interest in a man, the undeniable pull inside that brought her thoughts back to Jim again and again.

How could this have happened? Why couldn't she be attracted to Nathan Scott or Charles Van Hausen, or any other suitable candidate for her affections? What in the world drew her to Jim Kinney, and what had possessed her to run her fingers through his glossy, dark hair, practically encouraging him to kiss her?

There must be no more nonsense between them, no lingering looks or touches. She was teaching him to read so he could better relate to a hearing world. That was all. She would maintain distance no matter what her wayward body might feel.

****

The next day at school passed fairly quickly, despite Catherine repeatedly checking the time on her watch. The clock face was set in gold filigree and hung suspended from a chain pinned to her bodice. It was a present from her parents on her college graduation. She smiled, remembering her father's words as he presented it to her.

He'd rested his hands on her shoulders and kissed her cheek. "I know you'll be successful at teaching. You have a natural gift for it. I used to look in on you when you were a child with your dolls set up in rows and you'd teach them all the lessons you were learning at school."

Catherine hadn't corrected his impression that she was a born teacher. Actually she'd played school because she enjoyed ordering her dolls around and punishing them when they were naughty or didn't do their lessons. There were the younger brothers and sisters she'd never had.

Only an hour of school to go! She looked up from her watch to find Jennie Albright watching her. It wouldn't do to appear as if she was as anxious as the students for school to be over. Catherine rose to walk up and down the rows, helping any child having difficulties.

Three thirty finally came and the class was released. Chattering and laughing, the children left the building. For a moment, Catherine relaxed in her chair and simply breathed. She enjoyed her pupils, the funny things the little ones said and the tentative opinions the older ones expressed, but it was good to be alone at last.

After a bit, she went to the wash basin in the corner and primped in front of the little mirror hanging above it, tucking stray strands of hair into her coiffure. Today she wore her hair in the Gibson girl roll, in vogue back east, but a little too fancy for a town like Broughton. Usually, she wore a simple bun or French twist, but today she'd taken the time to pin her hair in the elaborate, loose chignon which illustrator Charles Gibson's models had made popular.

After powdering the shine from her nose and cheeks, she bit her lips to simulate the rouge she dare not wear in Broughton for fear of earning the Christian ladies' disapproval. She tugged on the wide shoulders of her sleeves, puffing them out, and smiled at her reflection.

A knock at the door set her stomach fluttering. It didn't occur to her that Jim hadn't knocked yesterday until the door opened and Mrs. Albright entered. Disappointment and irritation swelled inside her, but she covered it with a smile and went to greet her soon-to-be hostess.

"Good afternoon, Mrs. Albright. How are you?"

"Good day, Miss Johnson." The portly woman's gaze swept the room, including the small cloakroom, as though searching for something. "I'm fine, thank you. And you?"

"Very well. Can I help you? Jennie is doing well in all her subjects. I'm very pleased with her progress."

"I'm not here about my daughter. Or, to put it more precisely, I am, but not because of her schoolwork. I heard today from Mrs. Van Hausen that you've taken it upon yourself to tutor poor Jim Kinney."

Catherine's mild irritation grew to severe annoyance coupled with apprehension. "Yes, I'm helping Mr. Kinney with his reading."

Mrs. Albright raised an eyebrow. "Do you think that's wise? A single woman spending time alone with a man doesn't set a very good example for the young people in her care."

"Mrs. Albright, I'm simply teaching him. There's nothing unseemly about the situation." Her voice was tight despite her attempt to remain composed.

"Yes, of course. Your character is not in question, my dear." Mrs. Albright shifted her large handbag and reached for Catherine's hand, taking it in both of hers. "It was most admirable of you to step in and defend the man from those drunken miscreants and it's admirable that you want to help him better himself, but the *appearance* is the problem, as well as the fact that Mr. Kinney might misunderstand your intentions. Can he even learn to read? I thought he was slow-witted."

"Not at all. Merely deaf. He never attended school, but he already understands the rudiments of reading and is making quick progress. All he needs is someone to guide him. I hope to help Mr. Kinney better understand the people around him. Communication can only benefit us all. Don't you agree?" She adopted the tone she used with her students when they were argumentative, speaking briskly to show she'd tolerate no nonsense.

"Of course. I'm sure your heart is in the right place, Miss Johnson, but it's the idea of an un-chaperoned woman alone with—"

"I appreciate your concerns, but I assure you there's no reason to worry." Catherine sucked in a breath to cool the heat rushing to her cheeks. She would soon be living with the Albrights and shouldn't make an enemy of this woman. It might be prudent to ask her to stay and observe Jim's lesson as a chaperone, but her presence was the last thing Catherine wanted.

Just then the door opened and Jim walked in. He paused at the threshold, looking from Catherine to Rowena Albright. If he was surprised, he hid it, keeping his expression neutral and nodding a greeting at both of them.

Goodness, the schoolhouse has become a popular place these past few days. Nervous laughter threatened and Catherine suppressed it.

"Come in, Mr. Kinney."

Mrs. Albright looked at the book and slate Jim carried, then at Catherine. "Very well, Miss Johnson, but please consider my words. We may discuss this again." With that she swept out of the room, and the door closed behind her.

Jim raised his eyebrow at Catherine.

"Nothing." She erased Mrs. Albright's visit with a wave of her hand. There was no need to bring up the woman's talk about impropriety, especially since there was an undeniable element of truth in her words. "Let's begin."

Today there was a sense of formality between them as they both politely pretended the previous day's events hadn't happened and concentrated solely on reading and writing. Catherine refrained from meeting his eyes as much as possible, instead making herself understood on paper. He was so ready to learn that by the end of their hour together he was already able to write simple sentences with short words. It was as if he'd been waiting in a darkened room, the door cracked to let in a shaft of light, and she had thrown it the rest of the way open. His comprehension was immediate and Catherine barely needed to explain anything. He could practically lead himself through the McGuffey primer she'd given him.

As he bent over, copying words on paper, his hair falling over his forehead and curling at his shirt collar. She longed to touch it again. His lips shaped words he recognized from years of seeing other people make them, and it struck her as amazing he could do that with no sound to connect to the shape. His understanding was phenomenal.

Catherine started as she realized she'd been staring at him far too long. Checking her watch, she touched his shoulder, and when he looked up, she told him their time was over. There'd been no touching of lips or throat today and she planned to keep it that way. When the signing book from Aunt Lydia arrived, they would learn to communicate that way.

Jim collected his books, but before he left he reached into his pocket and held out his hand to her.

"What is it?"

He placed several coins on her palm, his fingers tickling as they brushed against her.

"Oh, no!" She shook her head. "You don't have to pay me. I want to teach you. It's no bother."

He frowned and closed his hand when she tried to give the money back. Perhaps it was his pride or maybe his way of demonstrating that he, too, knew their relationship must remain professional. Either way, Catherine had no choice but to accept the payment. "Thank you."

Jim stepped toward the door, hesitated and turned back. Once more he withdrew his hand from his pocket, closed in a fist around something.

"Please, you've given me enough," she protested.

He uncurled his fingers to reveal a small wooden object. It was a carved animal like the ones on his dresser, a plump, miniature cat curled in a lazy ball.

"Oh!" Catherine held out her hand, accepting his offering. "It's so sweet! Look at its tiny face!" Cradling the cat, still warm from Jim's hand, she examined the details and stroked its smooth back with a fingertip.

She smiled at Jim and he smiled too. It took all her willpower not to throw her arms around his neck and hug him. Fighting back the sudden urge, she quickly dropped her gaze from Jim's dark eyes to the cat. "Thank you so much. I'll treasure it."

He lifted a hand in farewell and left the schoolhouse.

When the door closed behind him, Catherine continued looking at the tiny cat in her hand. She held it up to her nose and inhaled the scent of wood, still fresh from the carving. This wasn't from his collection, but something made especially for her and quickly, too. She pictured him sitting up late at night, whittling by the light of an oil lamp.

His offer of money had declared their arrangement business, but his little gift put it right back in the realm of friendship and maybe something more.

CHAPTER SIX

Jim walked down the rows of field corn twisting ears from their stalks, shucking them with a husking knife and tossing them into the wagon drawn slowly alongside the workers. The sun beat on his head, making sweat drip down his face despite the cool autumn breeze. He glanced at the sun, gauging how close to noon it was. He was thirsty, hungry, and his hands hurt from the unfamiliar labor. Pitching hay, shoveling manure, sweeping or unloading bags of feed for Rasmussen or boxes of whiskey at Murdoch's place were tasks he performed every day. But he only helped in the fields threshing wheat in July and harvesting corn in fall after the first frost.

Mike Gunderson had notified him early that morning that he'd like the extra help if Rasmussen could spare him for a few days. The liveryman complained about the inconvenience as he always did but let him go. Jim would finish his field labor by mid-afternoon, and put in a few hours at both the stable and the saloon before dropping exhausted into bed after midnight. Since the extreme hours only continued for a short period, he was glad to take on the extra work and earn more money. It would swell his savings considerably.

He hoped Rasmussen would remember to tell Catherine that he wouldn't be able to come for lessons since he'd be harvesting for about a week. Perhaps it was best that he had to take a break. Being around her was increasingly difficult. He'd maintained a polite distance yesterday. Paying her for the lessons had been a smart idea, but then he'd ruined it by giving her the stupid cat like some schoolboy with a crush offering teacher an apple. The expression of delight on her face had made him happy, though.

Jim turned his attention to the endless stalks in front of him. Twist, pull, husk and throw, until his hands were raw, even the one wearing the husking glove, and his shoulder ached from hurling the ears at the bang board in the wagon.

Someone pushed him in the middle of his back. He turned to see Gunderson's son, Dean, a big, hulking man with the intelligence of a ten-year-old and a volatile temper. Dean was supposed to be working the next row over.

"Hurry up! Move it, dummy."

Jim nodded curtly and got back into rhythm, grasping the ears with hands so numb he could barely feel them anymore.

Dean disappeared between the stalks, and Jim caught flashes of his blue overalls and blond hair between the leaves. Periodically, he threw a broken bit of cornstalk over at Jim and urged him to go faster.

Jim carried on, refusing to acknowledge the simpleton's harassment. Over the years, he'd grown used to a wide range of treatment from people. There were those who ignored him because he made them uncomfortable, those who disregarded him because they simply forgot he was there, those who expressed pity and treated him like a child, and those who baited and teased. He'd come up with a policy that seemed to work with all types--shutting them out of his consciousness and minding his own business.

But some days childish behavior like Dean's was more annoying than others, and with the hot sun and his aching body, Jim's temper was short. If the man threw one more cob at his head, he might go after him with his husking knife.

Finally it was dinnertime, and the men were called from the field by the ringing of a bell. Jim wouldn't have been aware if Dean hadn't thumped him on the back again and pointed toward the farmhouse. "Come on, stupid. It's time to eat."

Jim followed him from the field. The Gundersons and several neighbors who had come to lend a hand for the day were assembling at the long table set up in the yard in the relatively cool shade under the trees. Mrs. Gunderson and several neighbor women had prepared a feast to keep the men's strength up for the long afternoon ahead.

As Jim silently ate the bread, ham, fried potatoes, greens and corn, he watched the interaction of the farm folk. They were different from the townspeople in clothing and manner, yet exactly the same in other ways. All of them talked and laughed together, a unified group to which he was forever a silent observer.

But there was another outsider present. From his family's expressions and the way they acted toward him, it was clear Dean Gunderson was considered less than a man. He was an annoyance, a mistake of nature, part of them by blood, but outside the circle. Jim recognized the frustration on Dean's face as he said something that was ignored. Jim understood his aggravation when people talked over and around but rarely *to* him. Impossibly, he felt a fleeting moment of compassion for the annoying man. Maybe he wouldn't gut him with his husking knife after all.

"What are *you* smiling about?" Dean thumped him on the back of the head and talked right into his face, a spray of spittle and cornbread crumbs flying from his mouth.

Jim clenched his jaw. Or maybe he would.

After the meal, he found a patch of shade under a tree away from the group and lay down in the grass. He closed his eyes to rest for a few minutes before facing the steaming jungle of corn again. When a shadow fell over him, he opened his eyes.

"Wanna see something?" Dean's big body blotted out the light.

Jim scrambled to his feet lest the imbecile decided to kick him in the ribs. Even standing, the big man loomed over him. His shirtsleeves were rolled up, displaying thick biceps, and his neck was as wide around as a tree trunk.

"Come on. I'll show you." He started walking toward the barn.

Jim hesitated.

Dean looked over his shoulder and frowned. "Come on!"

Most of the men and women still lingered at the lunch table so it wasn't time to go back to the field yet. Cursing himself for a trusting fool, he followed the eager, overgrown boy. *Asking for trouble. If you get your ass beaten again, don't complain.*

In the shelter of the barn, the air was cooler. Jim breathed in the familiar scent of manure and hay, similar to the livery but different since cows were also housed here.

Dean stood by a stall, resting his arms on the gate. He pointed.

Approaching cautiously, wary of any sudden moves the man might make, Jim looked at the animal that lay inside on a bed of straw. It was a brown foal with a white blaze on its forehead. The baby horse climbed awkwardly to its feet and stood on wobbly legs gazing back at them. It took a few halting steps toward them, favoring its left hind leg. Jim could see that leg was shorter than the others. The animal was permanently lame.

Dean punched Jim's arm to get his attention and jerked a thumb toward himself. "She's mine. My pa gave her to me. They were going to put her down, but I asked to keep her."

Jim didn't catch all the words, but understood the gist of it and nodded, understanding the pride of ownership. This man with the mind of a child would probably never leave his parents' house, and the foal might be the first property he'd ever been able to claim. He was anxious to show it off, especially to someone to whom he wanted to prove his superiority.

He looked to Jim for a reaction as he repeated, "She's mine."

Gesturing at the horse, Jim raised an eyebrow, asking permission to take a closer look.

Inside the stall, he ran his hands over the soft brown coat, felt the foal's withers and lifted the undeveloped leg to examine it. In his years of working at the livery, he'd become an expert on horseflesh and could see that, except for the stumpy leg, the animal was healthy. Putting his thumb and forefinger together in a circle, he gave Dean his approval then came out of the stall and closed the gate behind him.

The big man smiled. "She's mine," he repeated once more for good measure. "Her name is Star."

Jim returned the smile and pointed toward the barn door. *Time to get back to work.*

As he labored in the field that afternoon, he thought about the importance of owning something, how it made a person feel like more of a man. For the millionth time, he considered his plan for all the money he'd accumulated over the years. There was almost two hundred dollars now in the hiding place beneath the floorboards. When he had enough saved, he'd ask Rasmussen to sell him half of the business with the option to buy the whole livery some day. The man didn't have any family, no sons to leave it to. Jim believed he'd be open to the idea.

If Rasmussen refused the offer, he'd leave, travel to another town, and open a livery stable of his own. He knew everything he needed to about the care of horses and the operation of a business. He'd done most of the bookkeeping for Rasmussen for several years now. Despite his inability to read, numbers in columns were as easy as breathing to him. He appreciated their order and trustworthiness.

As he plucked another ear of corn and stripped it, a hard object hit Jim in the side of the head, knocking him out of his daydream. Another bit of stalk fell at his feet. He glanced at Dean in the next row, grinning and waving, evidently considering him a friend now.

He raised a hand in response and tossed the ear of corn into the wagon. Then he returned to his fantasy, imagining himself running the livery instead of working there, making the decisions, placing orders, selecting new horses, agreeing to board others, and hiring a boy to muck out the stalls and pitch hay.

In his daydream, he no longer lived in the back room. He came home at night to a small house he'd bought with his earnings. Inside, a woman waited for him. A wife. In his fantasy her hair was as golden as the ear of corn he tossed into the wagon and her eyes as blue as the cloudless sky overhead. Catherine smiled at him and he could *hear* as well as see her say his name.

"Jim! Welcome home."

CHAPTER SEVEN

Catherine set down her satchel and looked around her bedroom at the Albrights' house. The wallpaper was decorated with sprigs of roses and a pale rose-colored patchwork quilt lay over the bed. A carpet covered most of the floor. The window overlooked Main Street so she could watch people pass by.

As kind as the McPhersons had been to her, Catherine was glad to be out of the cramped room with the narrow cot and cold wood floor. While Mrs. Albright might be overbearing, she was a wonderful hostess. If only she wouldn't bring up the issue of tutoring Jim again.

Jim. Why couldn't she keep her mind away from him for two minutes at a time? Ever since Tuesday when Mr. Rasmussen had stopped by the schoolhouse to explain his absence, she had never completely stopped thinking about him. When she did manage to forget him, something happened to bring him insidiously back to mind: a telegram arrived from Aunt Lydia saying the requested books were on their way, a horse Catherine recognized as Zephyr from the livery passed by in the street, she found the page of sentences Jim had written in her desk drawer.

From the pocket of her dress, Catherine drew out the tiny cat he'd carved and placed it on the lace doily decorating the top of the dresser. She touched the figurine with her fingertip. Would Jim come back to her for another lesson when he was finished helping with the Gundersons' harvest or was he using the work as an excuse to end what they'd started?

It was only a few days since she'd seen him, but it seemed much longer. Although she'd known him for such a short time, she missed him with an anxious impatience that itched beneath her skin.

There was a knock on the open door and she dropped her hand guiltily from stroking the wooden cat and swung around. Jennie

Albright stood in the doorway, her round, hazel eyes looking startled as always.

"Hello, Miss Johnson. I didn't mean to disturb you. I just wanted to welcome you again." She offered a tentative smile. "I've been so looking forward to having you stay."

Catherine smiled. "I'm glad to be here. Please come in and sit down."

Jennie entered and perched on the foot of the bed. "May I help you with your unpacking?"

"No. Just talk to me." Catherine opened her satchel and pulled out several nightgowns, placing them in a dresser drawer. "How are you? You've seemed a bit quiet at school recently."

Jennie was silent.

Catherine turned to look at her, and the girl was blushing and picking at a loose thread on the quilt. It didn't take much to guess that a boy was at the center of her distraction. Besides, she'd seen Jennie stealing yearning looks at Ned Hildebrandt.

"Is there something you want to talk about? Whatever you tell me I promise to keep in the strictest confidence."

"Miss Johnson, I heard my mother say you were engaged, but your fiancé passed away."

"Yes." Catherine kept her gaze on the dress she took from the satchel. It would be easier for Jennie to say what she wanted to without meeting her eyes.

"I'm sorry." The girl's voice was soft and sympathetic. "It must have been horrible."

Catherine acknowledged her sympathy with a nod. "Thank you. It's been almost three years now. I've become ... accustomed to the loss." She was surprised to find it was true. When she'd arrived in Broughton a few months ago, it wouldn't have been the case.

"Can I ask what you ... how you got him to..."

"Notice me?" Catherine completed.

"Yes!" Jennie exhaled the word. "How did you know he was interested in you? And how long did you have to wait for him to *say* something?"

"To tell the truth, I wasn't aware of Howard at first. We went around with the same group of young people to parties, dances, buggy rides and other socials, but there was another boy I had my eye on at the time. Howard was just a tall, gangly fellow who was part of our set but someone I'd barely spoken to." She stopped folding the blouse in her hands and smiled at the memory. "But he noticed me and finally did something to get my attention."

"What?" Jennie leaned forward, breath held, as though Catherine would impart the secrets of the universe.

"He showed up at my door one afternoon with a bouquet of wildflowers he'd picked and asked me to go for a drive. Sounds like a simple plan for wooing a girl, doesn't it? But somehow Howard had gotten poison ivy in the mix of flowers. By the next day we both had a horrible rash." Catherine laughed. "I'd even gotten it on my face and my eyes swelled closed. It was just awful! Poor Howard was mortified, but he'd left a definite impression."

Jennie laughed along with her, visibly relaxing. When they stopped, she finally confided her problem. "Miss Johnson, there's someone at school I like, and I think maybe he likes me too, but weeks have passed and he doesn't say a word or do anything."

Catherine thought how tongue-tied and shy Ned Hildebrandt was with everyone. The boy made Jim appear talkative.

"I wouldn't be at all surprised if he likes you but is too nervous to say anything." She leaned toward Jennie and whispered, "Despite what society's rules say, sometimes a girl has to make the first move."

"Really? How? What should I do?"

Perhaps she'd gotten too familiar with her student. Love advice was not something a teacher should be dispensing. "I can't tell you that. It's different for every situation."

Jennie's eager smile dimmed. She'd clearly been expecting the magic key to understanding the opposite sex. "Oh."

Catherine threw caution aside. "I'm no expert, but one thing I believe is that women expect men to understand too much just from dropping hints. Sometimes the best approach is simple honesty, no matter how difficult it is to say what you're feeling."

"Tell him I like him? I couldn't do that. I just couldn't." Jennie's eyes were as round as quarters.

Catherine patted her shoulder. "Simply keep talking to Ned, even if he doesn't say much in return. At least you can continue being friends."

Jennie gasped. "How did you know it was Ned?"

"Sweetheart, there aren't that many boys in the class near your age."

"Oh." She rubbed her flushed cheek. "You won't say anything to my mother?"

"I can keep a confidence." Catherine returned to her unpacking.

After unburdening her secret, Jennie was almost impossible to get rid of. She stayed, chattering until Catherine wished she'd never invited the girl into her room. Finally she had to ask Jennie to give her a few moments alone.

As she hung the last of her dresses in the closet and sat on the bed to gaze out the window, she thought about the advice she'd given Jennie. *Be honest. Just say what you feel.* The words were so facile. It was easy to give guidance she couldn't follow herself.

When she spoke to Jim again, what if she stopped pretending she wasn't interested? What if she simply leaned in and kissed him? She was an unmarried woman and he a single man. What was the harm in having a relationship that went beyond simple friendship? Who would a few kisses hurt?

Closing her eyes, she sighed. The answers to those questions were obvious. A romantic relationship with Jim was impossible because of his station. She was no snob, but a man in his menial position was not a suitable partner for someone of her social standing. He wouldn't fit into her world. That was a simple fact, and his deafness only magnified the distance between them.

No. Better to maintain polite friendship when they resumed the lessons--*if* they resumed the lessons. Would he come back after his field work was finished? She fervently hoped so, and the intensity of her need to see him again frightened her.

* * * *

The following afternoon she sat in the parlor with the Albrights after Sunday dinner. Horace was fast asleep with his newspaper across his face while his wife and daughter worked needlepoint and Catherine darned the toe of one of her stockings. A loud knock on the front door made Mr. Albright start up, the newspaper drifting to the floor.

70

"I'll get it," Jennie said. "Sarah is coming by this afternoon for a visit." She tossed her embroidery hoop aside and hurried to the door.

In a few moments, she returned with Charles Van Hausen, hat in hand. When he saw Catherine, his teeth flashed beneath his neat, brown moustache. She shriveled inside, fed up with finding polite ways to discourage unwanted suitors.

"Mr. Van Hausen!" Mrs. Albright trilled. "What a pleasant surprise." From her smug smile, Catherine guessed it wasn't a surprise at all. Rowena Albright and Alicia Van Hausen were close friends. Mrs. Albright was helping her friend's ongoing effort to push Catherine toward her son.

"Good day." Charles addressed them all. "Lovely weather for October, isn't it? Miss Johnson, I've brought my buggy around, as promised, to take you for a ride."

She considered pleading a headache, but the deception would be obvious to all. It was easier to simply go with him. And despite her desire not to encourage his attentions, a ride outdoors on this crisp fall day did sound much nicer than an afternoon of darning stockings in the Albrights' stuffy parlor. "All right. Let me get my coat."

She smiled at Jennie as she passed her. The girl's expression was awed, as if Catherine had accomplished a great feat by snagging such an eligible suitor.

Outdoors, Charles gave her a hand up into the shining black buggy with flashy red-spoke wheels. He came around and climbed onto the seat beside her and slapped the reins on the bay's back. Catherine recognized the sleek horse as King from the livery. The animal moved forward and the buggy clattered over the pavement.

"I'm considering purchasing a motor car," Charles informed her. "Most people think they're only a fad, but I understand they're becoming quite the thing back east. Did you ever see any automobiles in White Plains?"

"Very few people had them, but my friend's father owned a Duryea motor wagon."

"Really? Were you able to ride in it? How fast did it go?" His boyish excitement was amusing and she liked him much better like this than his usual stilted manner.

71

"Just once. It was very dusty, and very loud, but not nearly as fast as a horse and carriage. Mr. Weller said it could reach a speed of ten miles an hour, but I don't think we were going that fast."

He shook his head. "Amazing! I would dearly love the opportunity to ride in one."

Personally, Catherine couldn't imagine motor vehicles ever being affordable or swift enough for common use, but Charles was enthusiastic as he talked about the invention and other advances in modern technology. She was happy to let him monopolize the conversation as he guided the horse out of town and into the countryside. She was surprised to find herself actually enjoying the drive through the waving prairie grass on such a bright, sunny day.

Charles didn't try to further his wooing by attempting to hold her hand, for which she was grateful. At the end of an hour he turned the horse's head and drove back toward town.

"Do you mind if we stop by the livery? We board our horse and store our buggy there. I thought we could walk back to the Albrights from there, it being such a pleasant day."

Catherine's stomach leaped at the word "livery," which had become synonymous with Jim in her mind. It would be strange to see him with Charles by her side. But how could she explain that she'd rather be dropped off at the Albrights' first?

"Of course, Mr. Van Hausen. Whatever's most convenient."

"I plan to buy property and build my own home soon," Charles said. "And you can be sure there will be a carriage house for my new motorcar."

"It sounds like you're doing very well for yourself."

"I expect a better position at the bank soon." He lowered his voice. "Please keep this to yourself, but now that Mr. Karak is a shareholder, things are changing. I'll probably be promoted within the next two months and not just because my father is in charge."

"Really?" Catherine raised her eyebrows. "Doesn't Mr. Karak own the mill? I had no idea he had influence in the bank as well."

"Oh yes. The bank, the railroad, the granary and mill--Mr. Karak is a real businessman, a bona fide entrepreneur." He radiated admiration. "You don't see that kind of forward thinking in Broughton. Mr. Karak is creating an industrial empire here, and I plan to be a part of it."

"I see."

Charles drove the buggy through the wide doorway of the livery stable and pulled King to a halt.

Jim appeared from the rear of the building. When he saw Catherine, he froze. An unreadable expression flickered across his eyes before he turned his attention to the horse. He took the harness, holding the animal steady while Charles jumped down from the buggy and came around to the other side to help Catherine from her seat.

"Just a minute," Charles said after he'd let go of her hand. He crossed to Jim and handed him a couple of coins then shouted in his face with plenty of accompanying gestures. "Give King an extra measure of oats."

Jim nodded and bent to the task of unhitching the horse. He didn't look at Catherine again. She wanted to say hello or ask if he planned to come for his lesson tomorrow, but she felt awkward trying to communicate with him in front of Charles.

Taking her arm, Charles escorted her from the building before she had a chance to shake off her indecision and approach Jim.

"How are the lessons going? Has the boy made any progress?" he asked.

"He's been working at the Gundersons' farm this week so we haven't been able to continue."

"Mm. Perhaps it's best if you don't." Charles shrugged. "There's hardly a need for someone like him to be able to read, is there?"

Catherine stopped and stared at him. "There's every need! It would open the world to Jim."

"I just meant that it might make him think about things he can never have. Rather like giving false hope, if you know what I mean." Charles gestured back at the livery. "He'll probably spend his entire life there. Do you think it's fair to give him dreams of a better life he can never achieve?"

Catherine was too angry to speak, and yet deep inside, his words struck a chord, echoing thoughts she may have had but not admitted to. Her face must have looked as thunderous as she felt, because Charles quickly changed the subject to the planned updates to the telegraph system.

It was a relief when they reached the Albrights' front door and he bid her good day with a tip of his derby. "It was lovely riding with you, Miss Johnson. I hope you'll allow me to take you out again soon."

Catherine smiled, but gave no answer. She retreated into the Albrights' house, determined *not* to take another ride with Charles Van Hausen. He might be a pleasant enough companion, but he possessed an arrogance and constant need to brag that she didn't like. She certainly didn't want to encourage his pursuit of her.

"Did you enjoy yourself, my dear?" Mrs. Albright greeted her practically at the door, suggesting she'd probably been watching them from the window.

"It was nice." Catherine drew the pins from her wide-brimmed hat and removed it from its jaunty perch on her French twist.

"We're having a light supper of cold meat and bread."

"Oh, thank you, but I'm really not hungry." Catherine unfastened the toggles on her coat. "In fact, I think after I've taken a short rest, I'll go for a stroll. I feel the need to stretch my legs after that long buggy ride."

Mrs. Albright's finely-arched eyebrows rose higher. "I see. Well..." She paused and Catherine knew she was debating the propriety of the young woman in her charge walking the streets of Broughton so late on a Sunday afternoon. "Well, be sure to return before dusk."

"Of course."

Catherine went to her room and poured a basin of water from the jug. She unbuttoned her blouse and slipped it down her arms. Clad in her camisole and corset, she washed her face, neck, chest and arms. She regarded the dusty linen of her blouse and opted for a clean one. After pinning up her hair again, she sprayed a mist of lilac perfume on her throat and buttoned the high collar of her crisp, white blouse.

Refreshed, she crossed her room to stare out the window, feeling as restless as a caged cat in the small room. She couldn't stay indoors another moment. A force inside her was driving her to walk and she knew exactly where her feet would lead her.

* * * *

74

King was restive, sensing Jim's tension as he stroked the currycomb over the horse's sweaty side. The animal whickered and shifted away from the rough brushing, rolling an eye as he looked back at his groomer.

Jim moved in front of him, patting King's nose and staring into his eyes, letting him know everything was all right. *Nothing's wrong. Good boy.* He mentally soothed the horse, then went to fetch him a measure of oats.

Tossing the currycomb into the tack box, he stood for a moment, staring out the stable doors, trying to get his temper back under control. He was a fool to have imagined something blossoming between Miss Johnson and him. Seeing her in Van Hausen's buggy reminded him that a beautiful woman like her could choose a suitor from among all the eligible bachelors in town. But a stab of pure rage had twisted his gut as he watched Van Hausen help her from the seat, her hand clasped in his.

Jim's jaw tightened now as he envisioned plowing a fist into the man's prissy face. His hands clenched from imagining the satisfying feel of flesh and bone under his knuckles and blood spraying from Van Hausen's split lip. Then what? Catherine would step over Van Hausen's unconscious body and walk into Jim's arms, lifting her face for a kiss? Hah!

Striding to the grain bin to get King's feed, he berated himself for his stupid fantasies. It was one thing to save money and plan for a better life, a future in which he might be part or even sole owner of a livery stable. It was another to add a wife and family into the picture. That could never happen for him. Especially not with a woman like Catherine Johnson, who was so far above him he'd need a ladder to face her eye to eye. He'd been stupid letting himself dream of it. Now he'd better corral his emotions with reason, keep them under control and locked deep inside him.

His fingers were stiff as they gripped the handle of the scoop and plunged it into the oats. Days of picking and husking corn had swollen the joints of his fingers, and his skin was cracked and sore.

A flicker of movement caught his attention and Jim looked toward the stable doors. Catherine stood silhouetted against the orange glow of the late afternoon sun. The light turned her golden hair into a halo around her head and shone through the thin fabric of her blouse so he could see her arms under the big, puffed sleeves. The sight of the actual shape of her body sent desire stabbing through him. Every bit of him yearned to touch her. For a second, Jim froze with the oat scoop halfway from the bin, then he dropped it and walked toward her.

She smiled a greeting and spoke, but he couldn't read her lips with her face in shadow against the dazzling sun. He stopped in front of her, his head full of the things he wanted to say to her, but all he could do was return her smile.

Walking out of the light and into the dimness of the stable, she stared past him at the stalls. "That's not the truth. I'm not just out for a walk. I wanted to see you to apologize."

Jim waited for her to explain.

She met his gaze again. "I should have said hello to you. I'm sorry. Mr. Van Hausen merely took me riding today, but it didn't mean anything. I'm not interested ... I don't..." Her cheeks were bright pink. She rubbed her hand over one of them and said something else he couldn't catch although his attention was riveted on her lips. She was speaking too fast and he couldn't concentrate on her words because of his fascination with her mouth.

"Anyway, I missed our lessons this week. Have you been able to study at all?"

He'd barely had time to sleep over the past week let alone open one of the textbooks. Shaking his head, he gestured at the horses, then mimed the act of corn husking.

When she saw the state of his hands, her eyes widened. She captured one of them in her own soft hands. Her mouth made a round "O" of exclamation.

Jim held perfectly still while she stroked her fingers over his callused palms and the half-healed cuts from corn leaves on his swollen fingers. She seized his other hand, holding them both. His breath stopped.

"You need ointment on these. Do you have any?"

He hesitated then nodded. The liniment he applied to the horses' sore joints would have to serve because there was no way he was going to pass up the chance to have her treat his hands.

She followed him to the tack room at the back of the building and accepted the bottle he offered. "This?" She frowned as she read the label. "You don't have any corn huskers' lotion?"

He shook his head.

Uncapping the bottle, she poured a measure of the thick liquid into her cupped palm and rubbed her hands together before reaching for his. The warm ointment soaked into his rough flesh as she rubbed it into his hands. The alcohol burned on the open wounds, but he didn't flinch, not wanting her to quit. The pads of her thumbs massaged his palm and each finger, sending lines of fire from his hand straight to his groin. His cock stiffened. His breathing was shallow and his body tense. He mustn't let her know how her touch affected him or she'd stop what she was doing. Keeping his eyes trained on her moving hands, he willed his erection to stop filling the front of his trousers with a telltale bulge.

Catherine continued to work the slick ointment into every chapped inch of skin. She reached for his other hand and did the same. After a bit, her fingers slowed and stopped until she was just holding his hand.

He accepted that for a moment, happy simply to have his hands cradled in hers, but then he dared to curl his fingers around hers. He ran his index finger up and down her thumb, a light, teasing stroke over her skin.

She didn't pull away.

Jim looked from their joined hands to her eyes. They were wide, the pupils big and black, ringed with just a hint of blue. Her lips parted and her cheeks were flushed.

Gripping her hand more tightly, he leaned toward her. Only a foot of space separated them. Heat radiated from her body and her warm breath brushed his face. He paused a few inches away, eyes trained on her lips, giving her time to reject his advance. When she didn't, he inclined his head and covered her mouth with his.

Her lips were yielding and warm, so warm he wanted to sigh in relief. This was what he'd been waiting for, the thing he'd craved for so long. Just this, a kiss, something most people took for granted, but which was a milestone in his life. Having sex with Shirley was nothing compared to his mouth moving gently against Catherine's pliant lips. His eyes were closed, but he felt her murmur against his mouth.

Afraid it was an objection and she'd pull away, he slid his hands around her back, holding her close. He angled his head to kiss her harder, dared to sweep his tongue across her lips. Catherine's mouth opened, perhaps to gasp in protest, and he took advantage of the opening to kiss her more deeply.

He slid his hands up her back, feeling the solid reality of her body. Beneath the light blouse was her warm flesh. How he wished he could feel her bare skin. When her tongue tentatively moved against his and her hands slid up his chest to grip his shirt, his heart thundered. She wasn't pulling away, but reaching out for him too.

Catherine's supple body filling his arms was the most wonderful thing he'd ever felt. With his eyes closed, he could concentrate all his senses on the smell and feel and taste of her. Jim inhaled her sweet fragrance and tasted mint on her tongue. He needed to breathe, but was afraid to stop kissing for even a second. She might come to her senses and end this.

Stroking the length of her back, he cupped her neck and fingered the curls at her nape. The strands were as silky as he'd imagined they would be, as soft and delicate as milkweed fluff. He longed to plunge his fingers into her hair and pull it from its pins. How would she look with her hair tumbled long and lustrous in a golden waterfall down her back?

Jim abandoned her mouth to kiss the curve of her cheek and her jawbone. Her high collar stopped him from nuzzling her neck or throat. He had to be content with grazing along the line of her jaw then returning to her lips.

Between their bodies, his cock strained toward her. He felt her body against his erection even through all the layers of fabric. She must feel the unyielding bulge of his cock pressing into her, but she gave no sign nor did she move away. Instead, she moved even closer, kissing and kissing him in the quiet, dimness of the tack room. The scent of leather and lilacs filled the air.

Hands touching and caressing, lips and tongues searching and exploring, hot bodies pressed close together, it was more than he'd dreamed possible ... and it wasn't nearly enough.

He wanted to be inside her so badly, he thrust against her. His body begged for hers even while his mind told him it could never happen. Catherine was not Shirley. She was a proper young woman who would never lie with some poor stable hand and destroy her virtue. He couldn't have her, but he could hold her as long as she'd let him.

A tremor ran through her body. Her hands left his back, moving to his chest and pushing. He broke off the kiss. His eyes opened and searched hers.

She gazed back at him, her mouth open, gasping for air. Her white blouse rose and fell with each breath. She shook her head. "No. We can't. I'm sorry."

His gut twisted. He wanted to shout, "Why? Why can I never have what I want--just once?" Jim stepped forward, denying her words or pretending not to understand. He pulled her against him again, wrapping her in his arms and covering her mouth. He'd kiss her until she forgot her protests.

Catherine melted against him. Her hands went around his back and she touched his neck, fingers threading into his hair and pulling him down to her. She didn't simply yield. She returned his kiss, moving her lips against his, accepting his tongue in her mouth and stroking it with her own. He felt the hum of sound transmitting from her mouth into his.

A groan of need rose in him. His eyes closed and he was aware of every place their bodies touched, the smooth texture of her skin, the wetness of her tongue, the weight, heat and mass of her body beneath his exploring hands. And the scent rising from her would linger with him forever. He could never smell lilacs again without remembering this moment.

Although he'd like nothing better than to sweep her off her feet and carry her to his bed, Jim knew that couldn't happen. This time he was the one to break off the kiss, pulling away with reluctance. He loosened his grip on her, but didn't let go completely, holding her loosely in the circle of his arms. Resting his forehead against hers with his eyes closed, he simply breathed, aching at his inability to express everything he felt.

There'd been many times in his life when his deafness was an inconvenience or even a danger, as it had been when those men attacked him, but there'd been few times when he'd actively hated his handicap. One was when his mother died and he could offer her no words of comfort, only hold her hand as she gasped for breath. Right now, he'd give up his sight if he could only hear and speak to Catherine for a few minutes, explain to her why she had to give him a chance and tell her he'd do anything to make himself worthy of her.

Her hand cradling the side of his face brought him from his reverie. He opened his eyes to gaze at her.

"Jim. This is—" He closed them again before she could tell him how wrong it was.

She brushed his hair from his face and stroked his cheek until he opened his eyes again. "I like you, Jim, but I can't be with you. Not this way. I'm a single woman with a reputation to protect, a teacher. It wouldn't do for me to become involved with any man."

He thought of her buggy ride with Van Hausen. It wasn't "any man" who was the problem—only him, but she wouldn't admit it. He dropped his arms from around her.

"I'm sorry. This was my fault. I shouldn't have encouraged you."

He took a step back, stopped trying to read her words. It didn't matter. They all said "No."

Maybe it was enough simply to know she was attracted to him, even if nothing could ever come of it. He took in her bright eyes and flushed cheeks, her swollen lips and rumpled blouse, which had come untucked from her skirt. She was soft, feminine and utterly desirable, and knowing she wanted him too should at least give him a feeling of pride. But it didn't make him feel any better at all.

Picking up the liniment bottle, he capped it and returned it to the shelf. They left the tack room, and he closed the door behind them.

She turned to him. "I don't want to stop your lessons because of this. I'm sure we can put it behind us and continue to work together. Will you come tomorrow?"

He nodded. Of course he would. Not only to learn, but to spend every minute of time he could with her, even if they never touched or kissed again.

Her smile lit her face like a sunrise turning the waving prairie grass to a sea of gold. He ached at the sight of it.

"All right. Tomorrow." She walked away.

Watching her leave, he knew it was going to be harder than ever to ignore his craving for her, but he'd do it, because the alternative, being apart from her, was even worse.

CHAPTER EIGHT

I'm a terrible person. Terrible! The refrain had repeated in Catherine's mind since the previous evening with barely a break for sleep before resuming the following morning. Dressed and ready to leave for school, she paused for a moment in her room, her face pressed to the blouse she'd worn yesterday. She breathed in the sharp scent of menthol from the liniment that permeated the fabric, and recalled the pressure of Jim's hands roaming up and down her back. Desire shivered through her and settled in a warm glow between her legs.

She was playing with fire. Yesterday in the stable, she'd been so overcome with yearning she would've let Jim touch her breasts or her sex if he'd wanted to. Her common sense had gone and her body's needs had taken over. As much as she'd enjoyed Howard's kisses, she'd never felt such overwhelming craving and tumultuous emotions as Jim aroused in her.

Hanging the blouse back in her closet, she told herself she'd wash it the moment she returned from school. There must be no reminders of yesterday's kisses, and when she tutored Jim today, she must adopt utmost decorum in her manner.

Catherine walked to school with her satchel in hand and Jennie Albright by her side. The girl was no longer withdrawn and shy, but chattered on about whatever came into her mind. Now that they'd shared their conversation about boys, Jennie wouldn't stop talking. But that was fine. Catherine didn't need to reply beyond an occasional "Mm-hm." It was amazing how many words people spoke without any real communication going on.

Once more the refrain echoed in her head. *I'm a terrible person. Terrible!* It wasn't fair to let Jim think he could kiss her one minute then pull away, telling him it was wrong the next. She'd always despised women who played with men's affections, teasing and then rebuffing them. She'd never wanted to act like that, and with

Howard she'd always been very straightforward about how she felt. He pursued her. She wasn't interested. Then suddenly one day she saw him in a new light and she'd never regretted her decision to become engaged to him. But with Jim it was much more complicated. Even as her body longed for him, logic told her nothing could come of it because of their social situation.

"Do you think that's a good idea, Miss Johnson?" Jennie demanded her attention, and for a moment Catherine felt as if the girl had read her mind. She had no idea what Jennie was talking about.

"What do *you* think?"

"I'm going to do it!" Jennie hugged her books to her chest and her eyes were bright. "Today! But what if he says 'no'?"

"At least you'll know." She wasn't surprised the topic concerned Ned. The sooner the girl made an overture and got a response, the sooner she could quit stewing over the boy. Too bad the answer to Catherine's infatuation wasn't so simple. She already knew the answer to the question, "Is he interested in me?" It didn't make things any easier.

Nerves made her heart beat too fast all day, and the children, sensing her anxious distraction, were disobedient and difficult. She rang the bell several minutes early in her eagerness to end the day.

She couldn't wait to see Jim, but the previous evening's kisses still lingered in her mind and on her lips. Could she ensure they maintained a proper distance this time?

The worry was taken from her hands when Jennie approached her desk after school was over. "Miss Johnson, Mama suggested I stay after today to work on my homework and grade papers for you while you tutor Mr. Kinney. I forgot to mention it earlier, since I was caught up in ... other things." A blush brightened her cheeks.

"Oh." Catherine was taken aback by Mrs. Albright not so subtly using Jennie as a chaperone. "Well, I do have some arithmetic tests from the younger students you can check for me."

"I think it's so noble what you're doing for that poor man." Jennie glanced at the students hurrying from the schoolhouse and waved at Ned Hildebrandt, who stood near the door. He smiled and raised a hand before he left.

The moment he was gone, Jennie turned to Catherine. "I talked to him at recess. It worked just as you said it would. He only needed encouragement. We're going to the social together!"

"Good for you, Jennie." Catherine smiled, and then a thought occurred to her. "Your mother will approve your attending with Ned?"

"I haven't asked yet, but I'm sure she will. His father owns the hardware. It's not as if he's a farm boy or something. Mama would never allow that."

Catherine bit her tongue. The merchant class in town definitely favored their own and looked down on the farmers--unless the farmer's last name was Gunderson or Hopewell, the two major landowners in the area. Their vast, prosperous acres bought them prestige and respectability. Now that Grant Karak had purchased the mortgage notes on most of the small farms, his holdings must put the Gundersons and Hopewells to shame.

Catherine had Jennie sit at the teacher's desk with a stack of papers to grade. She wanted a moment to compose herself prior to Jim's arrival, but Jennie regaled her with a detailed story of how she'd prompted Ned into asking her to the dance. Catherine was a little concerned at the girl treating her as a confidante. The respectful distance between student and teacher had disappeared and she wasn't sure how to regain it.

A few minutes later, the door opened and Jim's familiar frame filled the doorway, sending a jolt of excitement through her. She reflected that keeping her relationships with her students professional was becoming a chronic problem for her.

He entered the room, and his gaze flicked back and forth between them.

"Jim, this is Jennie Albright, one of my students. She'll be doing some work here while we have our tutoring session."

He nodded at Jennie, who stared at him curiously before giving a slight smile. Shifting his books under his arm, he raised an eyebrow and pointed to the back of the classroom.

"Yes. We'll sit there. Go ahead. I'll be right with you."

Catherine provided Jennie with her grade book so she could enter the scores on the tests, and thanked her for helping out. As she walked toward Jim, a shaft of sunlight from the window shone on his hair, illuminating strands of copper in the silky black. The memory of locks of his hair slipping through her fingers flashed in her mind. She thought of how his mouth had felt on hers, his hands pressed against her back. Swallowing, Catherine firmly suppressed the sensations as she sat down beside him.

His book was open, and he handed her the homework assignment she'd given him the previous week; simple sentences composed of the words he'd learned.

With her eyes on the work and with Jennie in the room, it was easier to free her mind of inappropriate thoughts and concentrate on teaching. "Today, let's try reading from the McGuffey primer."

If his gaze lingered a few seconds too long on her lips, Catherine ignored it as she opened the textbook to the stories intended for elementary readers. She set her finger under the line of type and moved it along slowly.

"Run, Spot, run." The book's illustrations made it easy to follow and very soon they'd worked through several pages. She asked Jim a few questions to test his comprehension of the words, and he printed his answers on the slate. On his own accord, he wrote a sentence based on his new vocabulary. "Cat eats rat."

He printed his name and indicated himself, before pointing to her with raised eyebrows.

"Miss Johnson," she said, and wrote the long name on paper.

He copied it with chalk on his slate. Dimples flashed in his cheeks as he added two more words--*like cat.*

Catherine made a correction. *Likes cats.*

Jim added another short sentence farther down the slate. *Jim likes...* Pausing, he gave her a significant look before finishing the sentence—*cats.*

Her throat was dry and her pulse racing from that brief, intense look. She must gain better control of herself and not encourage his flirting by staring moon-eyed at him. But she felt as girlishly enamored as Jennie, out of control of her emotions.

They'd only worked together for an hour, but she decided to end the lesson. "You've learned a lot, Mr. Kinney. Well done. But our time is up. I have assignments to prepare for tomorrow's class and essays to grade."

She'd almost forgotten Jennie's presence in the room, but a glance at the teacher's desk showed her the girl was so concentrated on her work she wasn't even aware of them. Catherine rose from the desk, putting some space between herself and Jim with his intoxicating aroma of hay and horses.

He rose and collected his things, displeasure at the short lesson in his tight lips, but he nodded politely and mouthed, "Thank you."

"You're welcome. We'll continue tomorrow."

He set a few coins on the desk then strode to the door.

It closed behind him and an empty feeling like dry leaves scudding down a vacant street swept through her. Silly to be so deeply affected by his arrival and his leaving. Silly and wrong. Why couldn't she control these feelings for a man she barely knew?

Catherine walked to the front of the room, where Jennie was so intent on her work she hadn't even heard Jim leave. When she saw what the girl was doing instead of grading papers, Catherine choked back a laugh. A page of "Mrs. Ned Hildebrandt" and "Jennifer A. Hildebrandt" in elegant script lay on the desk, and Jennie currently appeared to be writing a poem.

Suddenly aware of her presence, Jennie's head shot up and she shuffled her papers together. She blushed and rose, handing Catherine a stack of schoolwork. "I did grade them, but then I got distracted."

"It's all right, Jennie. Girls daydream about boys sometimes."

"He's in my mind all the time. I can't stop thinking of him," Jennie confided, as she put her books and papers in her school bag.

I know just what you mean. Feeling she should give the girl rational advice rather than encouragement of her crush, Catherine said, "Try to remember that, in the long run, romance is only a small part of your life. Don't let it become more important than your friends and family, your school work and other interests."

She picked up her satchel and led the way to the door.

It was easy to dispense wise counsel, but much harder to follow it. That evening she held her liniment-saturated blouse in her hands once more. She'd planned to rinse it out by hand in her wash basin, but hesitated before submerging it. She pressed it to her face and inhaled the scent once more, remembering every electric moment with Jim. The exact pressure of his hands on her body, the warmth of his lips and the wetness of his tongue teasing into her mouth—so shocking—were indelibly printed on her consciousness. How funny that the most unromantic, medicinal smell should bring passionate sensations and emotions blazing to life.

Catherine hung the blouse in the back of her closet, and emptied the water from the basin into the chamber pot. Perhaps she would wash the blouse another day.

CHAPTER NINE

Jim speared the pitchfork into the straw and tossed forkfuls on the floor of Crusader's stall. After spreading it around, he rested his weight against the propped pitchfork and wiped sweat from his forehead with the back of his wrist. He pulled his brand new watch from his pocket and checked the time. Up until this point in his life he'd never needed to know the exact time, leaving the livery in late afternoon after the horses were fed for the night and going to the Crystal Saloon. Murdoch released him sometime after midnight and Jim returned to his room at the stables and tumbled into bed. The cycle repeated day after day, year after year, and measuring time hadn't been important.

But now he had someplace special to be every day. He didn't want to miss a minute of his lesson and so he'd bought the used watch with some of his earnings from helping the Gundersons. Rasmussen showed him how to read its cryptic face. Now he didn't have to watch for the children to be released from school in order to know it was time to go to the schoolhouse.

The watch showed there was still about an hour before his lesson, as he'd already guessed from the angle of the sun on the street. He put the timepiece away with a sigh, and wondered if their chaperone would be there today as she had been every day this week. Probably it was just as well, since the girl's presence kept him in line when he was tempted to make advances. As it was, all he could get away with was a brush of a hand or an accidental leg bump.

Jim sat through his lessons each day, politely keeping his hands, if not his eyes, to himself. But his thoughts were all over Catherine, and his sexual dreams at night were growing more intense. He didn't like that loss of control over his emotions. It couldn't lead to anything good. Knowing Catherine was attracted to him too, only made being around her more difficult.

Gripping the pitchfork, he walked out of Crusader's stall. A movement at the door caught his attention. Dean Gunderson's hulking form was silhouetted against the light as he ran toward him. Jim instinctively tightened his hand on the pitchfork, but relaxed it when he saw the frantic expression on Dean's face.

"You have to come... I don't know... And Pa said..."

Jim struggled to focus on Dean's rapidly moving lips. He guessed whatever was wrong had to do with the foal. Leaning the pitchfork against the stall, he raised a hand to stop the flow of words and turned Dean so the outdoor light illuminated his face.

"Star is sick. Pa won't send for the vet. Says the horse wasn't meant to live." Dean pulled on his arm. "Come on. You have to..." The rest of his words were lost as he turned away, tugging Jim along with him.

Jim dug in his heels. He held up his palms and shook his head. *I can't help you.*

But Dean scowled and pulled harder. "You know about horses. Maybe you can fix her."

Arguing with the bullheaded man or fighting his iron grip was impossible. He'd go with Dean then get Mike Gunderson to explain to his son that Jim was no veterinarian. Besides, maybe there was something he could do to help the foal.

Jim ran beside Dean on the road leading out of town. His heart sank as he glanced at the distant schoolhouse. He wouldn't be able to see Catherine today and couldn't send her word.

When they reached the farm, Jim knew the moment he saw the foal that she was too far gone to save. Star lay on her side in the straw, breathing raggedly with her eyes unfocused and glassy. She was in the end stage of life.

Kneeling beside the horse, Jim stroked her heaving side. She didn't even lift her head in response to a strange presence in her stall. He glanced at Dean, who crouched beside him.

"What's wrong with her? Do something." Dean's eyes were nearly as wide and glassy as the animal's.

Jim shook his head and mouthed, *I'm sorry.* He cursed Gunderson for not getting help for his son's horse, but understood. The vet serviced all the towns in the region and lived miles away, and his service was expensive. A farmer couldn't waste good money on an animal that would never earn its keep on the farm.

Star shivered and thrashed her legs as though trying to stand and outrun her pain. Jim wished he could at least ease her suffering. Probably a bullet would be best at this point. He imagined Mike Gunderson had already suggested that, which had sent Dean running to Jim for help.

He made a gesture of drinking, and Dean scrambled to his feet to go for water. It let him feel like he was doing something useful. Jim leaned close and focused on Star's brown eyes. He sent calming thoughts at her as he rested his hand on her nose. It was all he could do, and it seemed to help a little. Star stilled. Her gaze locked with his until the moment her breath stopped.

Water sloshed onto Jim's shoulder making him glance up. Dean had returned with a full pail. His mouth moved rapidly. Jim rose and rested a hand on his shoulder. He shook his head.

"No!" Dean threw down the bucket, water spilled across the floor of the stall and washed over the still body of the foal. He dropped to his knees and his hulking shoulders shook with sobs.

Jim stood poised in indecision. Should he go to the house and get the man's mother? This wasn't his problem and he couldn't offer comfort. Dean might even turn on him in anger since he'd failed to help. At last he crouched beside Dean and patted his shoulder.

For a moment, Dean allowed his touch, then he lashed out, knocking Jim's hand away. Turning a red, tear-streaked face toward him, Dean bellowed something. He rubbed the heels of his hands into his eyes and repeated, "Don't ever tell. Don't ever tell I cried."

Jim nodded, torn between compassion and dislike of Dean's brutish temper. Just because Dean was simple didn't mean his mama couldn't teach him some manners.

As if summoned by his thought, Mrs. Gunderson appeared outside the stall. Jim rose and turned toward the farm woman with her stocky physique, red cheeks and blond hair straggling from her bun.

"Hello, Mr. Kinney." She glanced at Star's body. "The foal died? Well, it's a sad thing, but just as well. No place for an animal like that on a farm." She patted Dean's arm. "Should've let your pa put her down and spared the poor thing some hours of misery."

Jim couldn't see Dean's answer, then the man turned to him. "You help me bury her."

Jim had neither the time nor desire to help dig a hole in hard, drought-parched earth, but Dean wasn't asking. He didn't know why he let this softheaded bully order him around, but soon he had a shovel in hand, cracking through topsoil baked like a brick.

Jim took off his shirt so he wouldn't sweat it up. Dust settled on his perspiring skin. He was thirsty, but no refreshment was offered. It took hours to dig a deep enough hole, drag the body to it and cover it.

Whenever Jim glanced at Dean, the man was talking about the horse, his family and the farm. He didn't seem to care that Jim couldn't hear him. It was enough to have a captive audience. When the last of the earth was smoothed over, Dean clutched his shovel in one hand and stared at the brown patch of dirt surrounded by brown grass.

Jim recalled the freshly turned earth above his mother's grave on a cold spring morning. How adrift he'd felt without her, the only person who shared any connection with him. He glanced at Dean.

"You were a good horse. Amen." Dean clapped a heavy hand on Jim's shoulder. "Eat supper with us."

Jim didn't want to walk back to town in the dark and it was nearing sunset, but his stomach rumbled and he was dizzy from the heavy labor in such heat. He nodded.

Dean's dirty face transformed as a big grin split it from ear to ear. "You can wash up at the pump."

He led Jim across the farmyard to the red-handled pump. They took turns pumping and washing up with a yellow bar of lye soap under the cold spray of water. After drying off with a coarse towel, Jim put on his shirt and followed his strange host toward the house.

The screen door opened and Mike Gunderson came onto the front porch, followed by several men. Jim froze. They were two of the men who'd beaten and dragged him, the lazy-eyed and the bearded one. With them was the wolfish man who'd been talking to Murdoch the other night at the Crystal. Jim had learned he was the new mill owner, Karak.

Gunderson scowled and yelled, finger stabbing the air. Karak's face was as cold and predatory as it had been the other night. He extended his hand to Gunderson. The farmer gazed at it as though it was a dead animal someone had tossed at his feet, but finally took it. One brief pump and their hands parted. A deal had been made.

As Karak and his men descended the steps, the droopy-eyed man noticed Jim in the yard. He stared at him as though trying to place his face, then his expression cleared and he grinned.

Jim clenched his hands. Fury filled him. He longed to knock the smirk off the smug bastard's face. The man should be in jail, but he was under Karak's protection like a kid hiding behind its mother's skirts. There was no way to make any of them pay for what they'd done to him. All he could do was avoid future trouble by keeping out of their way—and damned if he wasn't sick of playing at being a shadow. He stared at the ground, sick with shame at having to back down from even the silent challenge of eye contact.

The men unhitched their horses from the post in front of the farmhouse, mounted and rode away. Dust rose in a choking cloud to settle over the yard.

Jim's attention was riveted on the departing riders. He jumped when Dean thumped him in the arm. Dean pointed after Karak and his crew. "Those guys?" He made a pair of fists and mock-punched at Jim.

He nodded. *Yeah. Those were the son of bitches.* Evidently everyone in town knew about his humiliation.

"They make trouble again, I'll take care of it." Dean jerked a thumb at his chest and slung an arm around Jim's shoulders, hauling him across the yard and up the steps to the porch.

Mike Gunderson still stared after Karak, a thoughtful frown on his lined face. He turned toward them. "Horse died?"

Jim nodded.

"Sorry, son." Gunderson reached out as though he might pat his son's shoulder, but he dropped his hand back to his side. "It's for the best. The animal could never have been any use."

Dean's jaw tightened. "Yes, Pa."

The farmer pushed a hand through his short, gray hair. "Well, best eat now." He led the way into the house.

Before following him inside, Jim clapped a hand on Dean's back and gave him a sympathetic smile. *We both know what it's like to be treated as if we're of no use.*

A grin spread over Dean's face like sunshine after a thunderstorm. "After we eat, I'll show you my marbles."

CHAPTER TEN

Catherine waited for another school day to end with more impatience than usual. Her edgy state of mind was beginning to be quite a habit, which she must make sure she didn't telegraph to her students. They were supposed to be her sole purpose here. Perhaps she lacked the proper dedication and focus to be a good teacher.

Opening her bottom desk drawer, she looked at the book that had arrived in yesterday's mail, *Signing for the Deaf.* Aunt Lydia must have bought and sent it almost immediately after receiving the telegram for it to have arrived so soon. A lovely note from her aunt had been tucked inside the book, reminding her that she could come and stay in New York City with them any time if she got tired of her adventure out west.

She had pored through the book the previous evening, absorbing the basic tenets. Signing was a complex system of expression. Each hand shape meant something different depending on the gesture coupled with it or the location on the body which was touched. For example, a clenched fist tapping the upper face meant "father," against the lower face "mother," and on the chest "fine."

Catherine could hardly wait to share the book with Jim. Finally they'd be on equal footing, learning something new together. But after his absence yesterday, she didn't know if he planned to return. Her impatience mounted as the minutes dripped by like water droplets from a leaky faucet.

At last it was time to dismiss school. Catherine reminded the students to begin thinking about their presentations for the fall program over the weekend. An evening in which the students exhibited what they'd been learning was a big event in the social life of a small town. Not only parents, but pretty much everyone for miles around would attend. As the children left the building, the chattering and laughter were more excited than usual.

"Miss Johnson, this is for you." Melissa Van Hausen stood beside her, holding up a picture she'd drawn.

"Why, thank you, Missy. That's lovely." She could paper a room with the drawings her little ones gave her on a daily basis.

The girl beamed, revealing the wide gap where her new front teeth were growing in. "And my brother said to give you this." Melissa offered a flat, slender box with an envelope attached to it.

Catherine's stomach gave an unpleasant lurch. A gift from Charles meant he'd taken their Sunday drive much more seriously than she had. She opened the note.

Dear Miss Johnson, I thoroughly enjoyed our drive the other day and hope you'll allow me to escort you someplace again this Sunday. With the community social dance coming soon, I'd hoped you might consider attending with me. Please consider it and enjoy this gift. Your devoted friend, Charles P. Van Hausen.

Catherine opened the box to find a pair of white kid gloves. "Oh my."

Melissa pulled the box down to her eye level and stroked the supple leather. "Pretty! Do you like them?"

"They're lovely. If you'll wait a moment, I'll write a note for you to take to your brother." Catherine set the box on her desk and snatched up a pen and paper. She wanted to write that his gift was too personal at this stage in their friendship, and that it was inappropriate to use his little sister as a courier. Instead she thanked him for the gift, but said she'd be too busy Sunday to go driving. She didn't mention the social at all. She'd refuse that invitation later, if he asked again.

Handing the sealed note to Melissa, Catherine thanked her again for her picture of a sunny sky, a field of flowers and a misshapen figure which, from the nest of hair on its head, must represent Catherine. The child skipped out the door.

Jennie approached the teacher's desk. "Do you think Mr. Kinney will come today or shall we go straight home?"

Catherine suppressed a sigh. Jennie was with her every day after school now like a sentinel. "I don't know. We'll wait a bit and see if he shows up."

"Ooh, what beautiful gloves!" The gift box still lay open on the desk. "Are they from an admirer? Mr. Van Hausen, perhaps?" Her eyes sparkled as she teased.

Catherine would never have spoken with such familiarity to her teachers when she was in school. She had to curtail this friendship Jennie was assuming. She covered the gloves with the box lid and set them aside without answering.

Opening the desk drawer, she took out the signing book. "My aunt sent me this from New York. I'm going to attempt to teach sign language to Mr. Kinney."

"How exciting! May I see?" Jennie bubbled over with comments as she flipped through the pages and mimicked some of the hand shapes. "This is fascinating! Can I learn it too?"

Catherine appreciated her enthusiasm while resenting her increasing intrusion. It appeared their chaperone would no longer be at a distance but sitting in on tutoring sessions. *And what's the problem with that? Why should it matter if Jennie is part of Jim's lesson?* If her reasons for teaching him were truly altruistic, it would be good to have a class of more than two. The more people in town who knew sign language and could communicate with Jim, the better.

But the whole experiment might be over before it began if Jim stopped coming. Why hadn't he been there yesterday? Would he show up today? Catherine barely had time to start worrying again when the schoolhouse door opened.

Jim entered with a smile that included them both. He handed Catherine a piece of paper. A note, written in Carl Rasmussen's slanted script explained Jim had missed his lesson because of helping the Gunderson's with an emergency concerning a horse.

She nodded, glad Jim had thought to have it written out so he didn't have to try to pantomime an explanation. She held up the book on signing.

"Our book arrived." She pointed at Jennie. "Jennie wants to learn too."

Jim looked from the book to Jennie. His smile was a little tight, but he nodded. His subtle signals were easy for Catherine to read. He didn't want Jennie's presence any more than she did, which was all the more reason to have the girl there.

Jim moved the teacher's chair by the desk so the three of them could all see the book. Catherine and Jim shared the desk with Jennie's chair in the aisle beside them.

Feeling as nervous as she did when helping Ned Hildebrandt with an algebra equation she didn't completely understand, Catherine opened to the first page of the book. But soon her flutter of nerves disappeared as she became immersed in the fascinating study of a new language. They practiced the hand shapes and movements for simple objects, making a game out of learning a list of ten common items then testing each other's memory of dog, cat, baby, man, woman, sun and sky.

Actions weren't too difficult to express. Eat, go, come and sit were all obvious. I'm hungry, please, and thank you were easy. Soon they could all express simple concepts. Catherine was as thrilled with their progress as she'd been when Jim assembled his first written sentences. But sometimes, even with illustrations it was hard to tell if they were doing things right.

Jennie peered at a drawing of a hand. "Does that look like the thumb is out or tucked inside the fingers?"

"It would be nice to have a teacher instead of just an instruction manual, wouldn't it?" Catherine glanced at the light from the windows stretched long across the floor. "It's getting late. We'd better be going. Your mother will be worried."

"Aw, just a little longer!" Jennie pleaded. Her eyes shone and her voice rose in excitement as she added, "Or maybe we could do it again tomorrow! Mr. Kinney, are you free on a Saturday?"

He frowned his incomprehension.

"Tomorrow." Jennie leaned across the desk, making sure Jim could see her. On the slate she drew a picture of the sun rising and tapped the book. "Meet tomorrow."

Catherine was just as eager to continue the lesson, and she hadn't had a chance to work with Jim on reading today. "It would be fine with me, if you can spare the time."

He shook his head and made the sign for work.

"Maybe on Sunday?" Taking the slate from Jennie, she sketched a second sunrise and held up two fingers.

He smiled and nodded. Taking a watch from his pocket, he held it out to her and pointed to a time.

"Two o'clock." Catherine agreed. "Here."

Jim shook his head and drew a rough sketch of the livery stable on the slate. Jennie took one of the stubs of chalk and printed "Livery" over the door of the building. "Li-ver-y, Mr. Kinney."

"Why there?" Catherine asked.

He mimed holding reins and clicked his tongue.

"A buggy ride?" Jennie clapped her hands. "That would be great. We'll pack a picnic and I'll ask Ned to join us. I'm sure he'd like to learn signing too."

"I don't know if that's a good idea." Catherine hated to put a damper on their enthusiasm, but doubted Jennie's mother would approve a Sunday outing with Jim Kinney. Besides, she didn't know if Mrs. Albright condoned Jennie's attachment to Ned. "We should probably meet here. It would be more appropriate for learning."

"Oh, please, Miss Johnson," Jennie begged. "It would be so much fun to have a day out."

Jim clasped his hands together, pleading too.

"Perhaps. We'll see what your mother says." She turned her attention to Jim. "But either way, I'll meet you at the stable for a lesson, all right?"

He dipped his head and made the sign for thank you, followed by goodbye.

* * * *

Jim couldn't believe he'd almost gotten Catherine to agree to go riding with him. Thank heavens for Jennie. He'd been annoyed by her presence at his lesson, which detracted from his time with Catherine, but now she'd become an unexpected ally.

It was late Saturday afternoon. Jim's work at the livery was finished for the day and he knelt on the floor of his room, counting out his weekly pay from Rasmussen. Keeping half of it aside to buy food for the next day's picnic, he put the rest in his tin box. Nervous excitement like fizzy soda water filled him. He'd never hosted anything in his life, but had been on the fringes of enough church picnics to know he must pack a blanket to sit on, and a hamper of food and drink. He had just enough time to go to the mercantile and buy what he needed before going to work at the Crystal. But Murdoch was pretty forgiving. If Jim was a little late, he wouldn't dock his pay.

As he tucked the money box in its cubbyhole and replaced the floorboard, he thought about his plans for the money. Six years had passed since his mother had died, leaving him on his own. Six years and he was still shoveling shit and pushing a broom, the most menial jobs in town. No wonder Catherine could never take him seriously as a prospective suitor. It was time to stop daydreaming about changing his life and actually do it.

After the picnic tomorrow he'd approach Rasmussen with his plan to buy a share of the livery. He might not have enough money yet, but he had a large enough sum that the old man would know he was serious about the idea. Tomorrow, for sure, he'd talk to him.

Shopping for food took more time than Jim had expected. He usually chose food items based on what was cheap, but now he had to imagine what Catherine would like or expect to eat on a picnic. The trouble was, at the church socials he'd attended it seemed women made all sorts of things like fried chicken, deviled eggs and pies. He couldn't make any of that. The best he could come up with was a loaf of bread, a block of cheese, apples, crackers and tins of sardines. Would she even like sardines?

At the last minute, after paying for everything, he realized he'd forgotten to purchase something to drink and went back for some bottles of sarsaparilla. He could set them in the river to cool at the place he had in mind to take her.

Carrying the groceries back to his room, he wondered if they'd make an acceptable lunch. But there was no use fretting about it since what he'd bought would have to do.

He was late to the Crystal, but no one noticed. The saloon was packed, although it was still early evening. Friday and Saturday nights were the busiest of the week as men frittered away their weekly paychecks on entertainment.

Jim emptied spittoons and rinsed them. He wiped beer-sticky tables since the girls had no time to do it between serving drinks and servicing men. Keeping tabs on the action in the room, Jim noted those who were happily drunk and those getting belligerent. He kept a sharp eye on strangers or anyone who looked as if he might cause trouble. After the last assault, he knew he was too easy a target for drunken aggression.

Shirley Mae perched on a man's lap, an arm slung around his shoulders. She grinned at Jim across the room. He smiled, wiping the stained rag across an even more stained tabletop.

A little later in the evening, as he was carrying a box of whiskey from the storeroom to restock the bar, Murdoch beckoned him to the table where he once again sat with Grant Karak.

Jim set the box behind the bar and went to find out what his boss wanted. The hair on his nape rose like a dog's hackles as he came under Karak's keen-eyed scrutiny.

Murdoch motioned him to sit, then pointed back and forth between them. "Jim, this is Mr. Grant Karak who's bought the mill. Karak, Jim Kinney."

Karak's gaze skewered him. "Mr. Kinney, do you understand me?"

Jim nodded. He sat on the edge of his chair ready to kick it back from the table and run if he had to. He didn't know what Karak wanted with him, but the man set every inner alarm bell ringing.

"I'm sorry for what my boys did. Nothing like that will happen again." Karak motioned to one of the girls to bring a round of drinks.

Jim weighed the man's words, wondering why Karak would bother to apologize to someone so unimportant.

"No hard feelings?"

He shook his head. There was nothing to be gained from crossing the most powerful man in town, and, for some reason, Murdoch seemed to want him to be friendly.

Karak leaned on his folded arms resting on the table. "Murdoch tells me you're a hard worker and you'll run errands, no questions asked." Karak smiled at the irony since Jim couldn't ask questions. "I might have some work for you sometime."

Jim raised his eyebrows.

"You can lift and carry, right? There will be some loading and unloading I need done. A strong man who doesn't gossip could be useful." He smiled, but the effect was of an angry dog baring its teeth. "I pay very well."

A job offer was the last thing he'd expected when Murdoch called him over. Jim glanced at his boss, but Murdoch's face gave nothing away.

His days were full with the two jobs he already had. He didn't want to do grunt labor for the man who'd bailed his persecutors out of jail, but, again, it wasn't smart to cross such a powerful man. Jim gave a half-nod.

The drinks arrived. He drank his quickly, the alcohol burning down his throat and settling painfully in his stomach, reminding him it was nearly empty since he'd skipped supper. Jim pointed across the room, indicating he had work to get back to.

"See? I told you he's a hard worker. Doesn't rest from the moment he gets here."

Karak stood when Jim did and offered his hand. His grip was hard and his hand dry and smooth. It was the hand of a man who did no physical labor since he had plenty of employees to do it for him. "I'll let you know when I need you."

Jim left the table. He shivered at the sensation of the man's eyes burning into his back. The wolf had noticed him, and he was no longer safe.

CHAPTER ELEVEN

Catherine walked briskly down the sidewalk, feeling like a bird freed from its cage. The situation at the Albrights today had been tense to say the least. Sweet, polite Jennie, who never crossed her mother, had exploded in youthful anger when Mrs. Albright had prohibited the proposed buggy ride.

"Mother, you're so unfair! Sarah has been riding with Mr. Walker for months now. I'm old enough to go out with a boy, and we'll be chaperoned by Miss Johnson and Mr. Kinney."

"Ned Hildebrandt is a fine young man. I encourage your friendship with him, but gallivanting around the countryside in the company of..." Rowena Albright had left the sentence unfinished. "Really, Miss Johnson, I'm surprised you would suggest such an outing. Besides, I feel my daughter's first meeting with her young man should be under my supervision."

Catherine imagined the poor kids sitting on the hard, horsehair-stuffed sofa in the parlor under Rowena's watchful eye as they made stiff, formal conversation. It sounded like a dreadful way for two young people to spend a Sunday afternoon.

"While I believe your education of Mr. Kinney is a worthwhile cause, I don't believe associating with the man in a social way is appropriate--not for Jennie or for you, Miss Johnson."

Catherine bit back a retort. "Well, this wouldn't exactly be a social situation, Mrs. Albright. Jennie is learning sign language along with Mr. Kinney and me. This would be a continuation of our regular lesson, with Ned joining in. We thought the pastoral setting would be enjoyable on one of the last fine days we can expect before winter."

Rowena shook her head. "I'm sorry, Miss Johnson. I don't want my daughter involved in your little project any longer. It's not proper for a young lady to spend so much time around a ... a stable hand."

It was at that point, the formerly quiet, obedient Jennie had broken loose, like water gushing through a ruptured dam. She'd railed at her mother about injustice and hypocrisy and claimed she was determined to drive Ned away with her controlling ways.

As Jennie's voice rose higher and her arguments ranged wildly between accusing her mother of snobbery and berating her for trying to ruin her life, Mrs. Albright cast a glance at Catherine as though laying the blame for such behavior at her door. She'd sent Jennie to her room. The girl had flounced up the stairs and slammed her bedroom door.

"I'm sorry you feel Jennie shouldn't participate in our lessons anymore, but I respect your wishes. Nevertheless, Mr. Kinney is expecting us, and I must at least give him his lesson as promised, even if we can't go riding."

Before Rowena could raise further objections, Catherine had escaped the parlor, grabbed her coat from the tree in the front hall and let herself out the door. After breathing the fresh air of freedom for a moment, she'd hurried toward the livery.

Now, as she entered the building, she saw Jim already had Lady harnessed to a buggy. The black surface of the vehicle shone, the metallic bits of the harness gleamed from polish, and Lady had been curried to a glossy sheen. She tossed her head and shifted in her traces, eager to be out on such a fine day. Jim was packing a wicker hamper into the back of the buggy. He smiled broadly at Catherine.

She returned the smile, a dull ache in her chest at the disappointment she was about to cause. As she approached Jim, his smile dimmed. He could tell from her expression that she was going to cancel.

"I'm sorry." She used the accompanying sign, then made the sign for mother. "Jennie's mother won't allow her to go so you and I can't go."

He spread his hands. *Why?*

"It wouldn't be appropriate without a chaperone." She didn't know if he understood the concepts of "proper" and "chaperone", but he definitely understood she was telling him no. His mouth compressed and his jaw tightened.

She held up the books she'd brought along. "But we could still have a lesson."

Glancing from the books to her face, he made a gesture that included the two of them and pointed to the buggy. He signed "Go" and held out his hand.

Catherine could hardly resist his yearning expression. Besides, the horse was hitched and a picnic lunch packed. Would it really harm her reputation to go riding with him? It wasn't fair that no one batted an eye at her spending a Sunday afternoon alone with Charles Van Hausen. In fact, Mrs. Albright had practically pushed her out the door, but Jim was unacceptable. Tongues would wag if someone glimpsed them heading out of town. She wavered back and forth.

"Hello?" Ned Hildebrandt's voice came from behind her. Catherine turned to see the lanky, red-haired youth hesitating in the doorway. "Um, Jennie said we were supposed to go on a buggy ride?"

"Yes, but Mrs. Albright had other plans."

"Oh." The disappointment in the one syllable was reflected in his freckled face. "All right." He turned to leave.

"Ned, you might drop by her house for a visit. I don't think her mother would object to that." No need to frighten the shy boy with the knowledge that any visiting with Jennie would be under her mama's gimlet eye.

Ned's smile lit up his face. "Thank you, Miss Johnson."

After he left, Catherine turned back to Jim waiting by the buggy. Once again he made the sign for "go" and offered his hand. Tilting his head slightly, he lifted an eyebrow. The tease of a smile curving his lips was a challenge. Against all common sense and better judgment, Catherine took his warm, rough hand and gathered her skirts. His other hand supported her waist as he helped her climb onto into the buggy.

After smoothing her skirt, she pinned her hat on more securely, wishing she hadn't worn the elaborate boater with roses and feathers. Hopefully, the strong prairie wind wouldn't carry it away. She should've worn an old-fashioned bonnet with ribbons to tie securely beneath her chin. The elaborate confections in vogue in White Plains weren't suitable here.

Jim walked around to the other side of the buggy and vaulted up beside her. He gathered the reins and flicked them on Lady's back. She stepped out briskly.

Catherine glanced at him, taking in his clean white shirt and vest, which he'd worn the first day he'd come to the school for a lesson. Although he'd buttoned the vest over the shirt, she could see a faint rusty stain on the shirtfront from the bloody nose Charles had given him that day. She imagined Jim bleaching the stain, trying to salvage the shirt to make it presentable. His only other clothing was the blue work shirts he usually wore. His attempt to dress in his best for this occasion sent a pang through her.

Riding out of town on Main Street, Catherine resisted the urge to duck her face in an effort to conceal her identity. Instead, she kept her head high and faced forward. If someone saw her riding with Jim and spread it all over town, there was nothing she could do about it now. Luckily the livery was located on the edge of town so they were soon past any buildings and out on the prairie.

As she'd expected, the stiff breeze tore at her hat and her coiffure. Rather than lose the hat to the wind, she took it off and held it on her lap. Soon her hair loosened from its pins and the elaborate curls spilled down. Strands whipped around her face, blinding her eyes. She held them back with her other hand. Struggling against the wind was like fighting a runaway team of horses.

Jim's hair, too, was ruffled and blown in all directions. She liked that it was longer and shaggier than the current men's style, and flashed back to the way it had felt slipping between her fingers—then to the kisses they'd shared and the warmth of his hands on her back.

Jim met her gaze and smiled. Catherine's cheeks burned as she looked across the waving grass, afraid he'd somehow read her thoughts.

Unlike the previous Sunday when she'd gone riding with Charles, there was a chill in the air today. It was another week closer to winter and this might well be the last of the pleasant weather. She'd been told to expect gray skies, frigid days, and snow from early November until May.

It felt strange to ride in silence yet comfortable. Without Charles' constant chatter about steam engines and industry, she could actually hear the world around her. Cicadas concealed in the grass shrieked their high, piercing song. Far overhead, a flock of Canadian geese flew in perfect formation, the leader honking and others responding as they headed south. Between the wildlife and the

104

incessant blowing wind, the prairie wasn't empty and silent, as Catherine had believed when she first arrived, but vibrant with life and sound. She watched the swallows swooping in big loops, diving for bugs that rose from the tall grass.

She peeked at Jim, his dark, solemn eyes gazing across the brown and gold land as his hands loosely held the reins. What would it be like to see the world without sound? In the privacy of her bedroom, she'd covered her ears, trying to get a feeling for his deafness, but even with them covered, sound bled through. It was almost impossible to know what utter silence was like. How unimaginable not to hear the cicadas, the geese, the blackbird song, or the wind.

Jim caught her watching him and his smile was broader, as though he knew perfectly well she was interested in him and that pleased him. He pointed toward the horizon to the east and made the sign for water.

He was taking her to the river, or what passed for a river in flat, waterless Nebraska. Back home, the thin stream would barely earn the title of creek. Still, it was a waterway and there were actual trees on its banks; trees which were also in short supply here. Catherine was excited at the prospect of seeing something besides the sea of grass for a change.

Settling back against the seat cushion, she lifted her face to the sunshine, while toying with the flowers on her hat, cradled on her lap. The buggy jounced over ruts as they turned off the main road onto a faint track that seemed to cut right through the wilderness. There was no sign of trees ahead to mark the river, but Catherine knew this land was deceptive and not really as flat as it appeared. There were subtle rises and falls. What appeared to be level land in front of them was a swell, and when they reached the top of it, a shallow valley spread below them. The buggy bounced down the slope toward the trees marking the meandering path of the river.

By the time they stopped beneath the shade of the trees, Catherine was flushed and hot. She'd pulled out the last of her hairpins rather than lose them, and her hair straggled around her face. Just the sound of splashing water coming from the stream made her feel cooler.

Jim set the brake on the buggy and jumped down. He went around to Catherine's side and helped her climb from the seat. She abandoned her useless hat and stood finger-combing her hair into a semblance of order, while he unhitched Lady and tied her to a sapling. The horse immediately began cropping grass.

Jim unloaded the picnic hamper and spread a blanket. Catherine gazed at the muddy brown river that flowed rather sluggishly until it reached a small drop-off. There the water churned around stones before continuing on its way. The opposite bank was only a few yards across--definitely a creek rather than a river by her measuring. A small cloud of gnats circled just above the water's surface, which glinted in the shafts of sunlight piercing the canopy of branches overhead.

Jim came up to stand beside her and gaze at the water.

Catherine fished a ribbon from her handbag, determined to tie back her unruly mane, but as she started to bind it into a ponytail, Jim stopped her with a hand on her arm. He reached out to run his hand over her hair. She froze, letting him stroke her, too startled at the unexpected gesture to do the right thing and push his hand away.

He stood close to her, smoothing her tangled locks, and she held her breath, staring into his eyes. He tested the texture of the strands between his thumb and forefinger, tucked a lock behind her ear, and stepped away.

Suddenly she could breathe again.

Jim pointed upstream. She lifted her skirt to keep the hem from dragging on the muddy ground and followed him.

After walking several yards, he squatted by a little eddy of the river. The surface of the shallow pool was smooth and free of ripples. In the dappled light the shadowy shapes of minnows darted beneath the surface. Jim set a pair of pop bottles at the edge of the water to cool. He pointed out a larger fish, at least a hand's length, suspended in water. Catherine dropped down beside him, but she could barely see the muddy brown shape until suddenly the fish twisted, fanning its tail left and right, stirring up silt. Its silvery-blue belly flashed before it swam out of the pool and back into the current.

Leaning close, Jim pointed to some perfectly round shapes in the bottom of the pool. He made hand motions, trying to tell her something about them, but she didn't know what he was trying to convey.

He rose and drew her to her feet, leading her back to the buggy. On his slate he sketched a school of fish, drew one of the shallow dips at the bottom of the pool and filled it with little pearls.

"Eggs and nests. It's a breeding ground."

Catherine searched for the words in the signing book. Pointing to the fish he'd drawn, she made the sign for "fish" and Jim copied it.

"Fish," she said aloud, encouraging him to shape the word with his mouth as well as sign it. Then she looked up the signs for nest and eggs.

Both of them were so pleased with their new knowledge, they grinned at one another.

Jim marked on the slate and showed it to her. He'd crossed out the eggs and nests, and he pointed up. Catherine blinked, trying to figure out what he was telling her. No fish. The sky. Suddenly the message clicked. It was fall, not the time for fish to breed. The nests were left over from the previous summer. She nodded.

Jim gestured to the hamper and made the sign for eating, which they'd learned the other day.

"Yes." Her stomach rumbled reminding her of how long ago breakfast had been. She sat on the blanket, arranging her skirts around her.

Jim laid out plates and food from the picnic basket on the blanket. While Catherine sliced bread and cheese, he went to get the pop bottles from the pool. They were dripping and a little muddy. He opened them and offered one to Catherine. She swallowed a deep draught of the sweet, fizzy root beer, lowered the bottle and belched. Her hand went to her mouth, and she flushed at the unladylike sound before remembering Jim couldn't hear it.

As she nibbled on bread and cheese, she thought how strange it was to eat in silence. It was contrary to the natural impulse to make small talk over a meal. She could hear the chewing sounds her mouth made, the slight smacking of lips. But then she started to focus on the birdsong coming from the treetops and the rush of water where it ran over stones farther along the stream. It was so very tranquil here.

Jim held up a tin of sardines.

She shook her head. "No thank you. I would like an apple, though."

He cut one into bite-sized slices for her with his penknife.

While she nibbled, Catherine gazed at a leaf riding on the surface of the slowly moving water. The tang of apple contrasted nicely with the sharp cheese, and she savored the flavors as she watched the yellow leaf drift inexorably toward the drop-off. Suddenly it was caught up in the churning water, zipped around a stone, and disappeared in white froth. If she walked downstream, would she see the leaf again, rising buoyantly to the surface after it made its way through the turbulence?

When they'd finished their meal and Jim had packed the remnants away, they washed their hands in the river.

"I suppose we'd better start your lesson." She glanced at the golden sunlight slanting through the leaves. The daylight hours were short by October, and they'd begun their ride rather late in the day. But here on the prairie, evening seemed to last a lot longer than in New York where the sun plunged behind the Catskills all at once.

They settled side by side on the blanket to study the signing book. Catherine was aware of his shoulder brushing hers, the quiet sound of his breathing and the intimate atmosphere of this pastoral spot.

After reviewing what they'd already learned, she began to add new signs. Since water was already part of their repertoire, Catherine searched for the different forms of it; river, lake, ocean, drinking water. The slate came in handy for sketching different types of water—raindrops falling from clouds, the choppy surface of the sea—and the book demonstrated the differences between their signs.

A dragonfly darted down and settled on the open book, beating its delicate wings slowly. She caught her breath, gazing at the intricate pattern of the four wings and the iridescent green and blue shimmer of its body. After a moment, it darted away.

She printed the word dragonfly, then began searching through the book for anything about insects or wildlife. "I can't seem to find a specific way to sign it. Maybe a combination of fly and—"

Glancing up, she met Jim's eyes watching her with the same fascination with which she'd studied the dragonfly. His gaze settled on her lips like the light touch of the insect alighting. Her mouth tingled at the invisible pressure. So did other parts of her she wasn't supposed to acknowledge, private parts that always simmered with life when she was around Jim.

The moment spun out like a filament of spider web shining in the air between them, connecting them loosely but tenaciously. Catherine knew she should drag her attention back to the book on her lap, but she couldn't look away. She allowed the moment to continue and become more intense. She wanted him to kiss her, craved it with every part of her. But she suddenly realized Jim wasn't going to. He wouldn't risk her rejection again. She must make the decision. If there was going to be any kissing today, she'd have to be the one to initiate it.

Her conventional inner voice bade her snap the slender filament between them. All the logical arguments against becoming involved with Jim chased through her head. But beneath the bubbles of thought was a strong, undeniable current, which had been leading them to this moment all day. Longer. Perhaps ever since the day they'd met.

She couldn't resist the pull of that current, even if it meant tumbling into rough rapids. Catherine lifted her hand and cupped Jim's jaw, her thumb tracing the corner of his mouth. His eyes nearly closed and his lips parted on a soft exhalation.

She leaned in and covered his mouth with hers, lightly, carefully testing the water. And finding it good, she plunged in.

CHAPTER TWELVE

Soft. Her hand was so soft, like cat fur, like bird feathers, like... everything soft he could think of. Her thumb caressing the corner of his mouth and her lips when they first touched his were tentative.

Jim held still, accepting her kiss without responding, not wanting to frighten her away. If she sensed the powerful need raging through him to seize and possess her, she'd run away. So he only parted his lips slightly, letting her explore his mouth, first with a soft kiss, then with an inquisitive caress of her tongue. His abdomen clenched from stomach to groin, and his cock surged to full life. His fingers clenched into fists, but he didn't put his hands around her yet. *Wait. Give her time to show you what she wants. Give her time to admit to what she wants.*

But he couldn't stop the animal groan that rose to his lips. He felt the reverberation in his throat as he surrendered to the sensation of her mouth invading his. The point of her tongue flicked against his as though asking it to play and she cupped the back of his neck. He was surprised at her willingness to take control, but then she'd had a fiancé and more experience at kissing than Jim had.

After a moment, he pressed his mouth more firmly against hers and stroked his tongue over hers, becoming an active participant in the kiss. When at last Catherine pulled away, Jim opened his eyes and he stared into hers from inches away. As blue as the wildflowers on the prairie. As blue as the sky.

His lips vibrated and he sucked the bottom one into his mouth, tasting her flavor before letting it go. Catherine continued to gaze at him. Her lips parted as though she might say something, but instead, she kissed him again.

This time Jim slid his hands around her back, pulling her close. She melted against him, her soft curves pressing into his chest, his hip. She tugged on his hair, sealing their mouths even tighter together. The force of the kiss sent heat sweeping through his body.

He twisted to face her more and he pushed the signing book off his lap and onto the ground. His hand roamed her back, feeling the bumps of her spine and the silky sweep of her hair. His fingers tangled in the thick, soft strands as if it were the gauzy threads of a coweb—one from which he was in no hurry to escape.

Catherine moved her mouth to his jaw, pressing soft little kisses. A shiver went through him at her tickling lips against his skin. He laid back on the blanket, pulling her down on him, her body half covering his. Her skirts fanned across his leg, and her hipbone pressed against his erection.

Jim relieved the painful pressure in his throbbing cock by thrusting against her just a little, not enough so she'd notice, he hoped. Her breasts were flattened against his chest and her hair swept over his face. It smelled sweet like her, the natural scent of her body mingled with a whiff of lilies. He lifted his chin so she could continue kissing the curve of his jaw and his throat. The tickling became too intense and he jerked away with a laugh.

Catherine lifted her head from his neck. She gazed into his eyes. "I haven't heard you laugh before." A smile curved her mouth. "I want to hear more." Suddenly her hand plunged for his side and began tickling.

Jim twisted away and grabbed her wrist. "No." He put air behind the word, giving it sound.

"No?" Her eyebrows arched. She pressed full length against him as she attacked his other side with her free hand. Now she was right on top of his erection, grinding against it. There was no way she couldn't feel his hardness now. Squirming to get away from her tickling only made it worse as his cock rubbed against her.

He seized her, flipping her onto her back and straddling her body. He pinned her arms to the ground, holding each wrist in a firm grip. Catherine's eyes were bright and crinkled at the corners. Her body shook with laughter he longed to hear. He planned to tickle her breathless, but instead took possession of her mouth, kissing and kissing her. He couldn't get enough of the taste and feel of her mouth under his— an impossible fantasy come true.

Her arms wrapped around his back, holding him to her and not pushing him away this time. He kissed her soft cheek, her delicate jaw, and unbuttoned her high-necked collar so he could reach her throat. The little pearl buttons clung to their loops, fighting his clumsy fingers, but at last the column of her neck was revealed.

When he reached the hollow of her throat, he didn't stop, but kept unfastening buttons all the way down her chest. He kissed each bit of skin he exposed, savoring the incredible warmth of her flesh.

Catherine shifted beneath him. He felt her chest purr beneath his mouth. It could have been a moan of delight or a protest, but he didn't wait to find out which. Pushing her blouse open, he kissed the swell of her cleavage above her corset.

Her hands were in his hair, caressing his head as she thrust her chest toward him. She wanted this, wanted his mouth pressed right here against her breast. Beneath it her pulse beat rapidly like a trapped bird in the double cage of ribs and corset. Jim wanted to set her heart free, but unlacing the corset was a step too far. He contented himself with stroking and brushing his lips over the upper swell of her breasts.

Suddenly Catherine reached to unfasten the front of the constricting undergarment. She pulled it apart and only her chemise covered her breasts. Through the nearly transparent fabric, the shadow of her nipples was visible, their points clearly outlined by the material. For a moment, Jim froze, unable to believe what she was offering.

He'd fantasized things like this, but the most he'd dared hope for was a little kissing and touching. He cupped her loosened breast, cradling the weight and warmth in his palm. He covered her other nipple with his mouth, wetting through the thin fabric and stroking the erect bud with his tongue.

Catherine shifted beneath his touch and she continued to sift his hair through her fingers. Another vibration went through her chest.

Pleased by her reaction, he took the other bud between his thumb and forefinger and rolled it. This was more than he'd ever expected, but it was no longer enough. He craved the sight and the feel of her naked breasts. He pulled down the neckline of her undergarment and the beautiful mounds bobbed free, full and round and topped by nipples like pink rosebuds.

He grazed one stiff nub with his thumb and circled around the crinkled areola, then bent his head and drew it into his mouth, swirling his tongue around before sucking hard. The effect on Catherine was dramatic. She arched her back, pushing her breast into his mouth. Her fingers gripped his shoulder. He glanced at her ecstatic face. Her lips were parted and her eyes closed.

Jim kneaded and suckled first one breast then the other for long, contented moments then pulled back to study them, the nipples red now rather than pink, glistening and standing at attention. Her breasts were beautiful, but suckling them had stoked his raging lust to outrageous proportions. His cock throbbed with the need to fill her.

He wanted to experience the moment of union he'd had with Shirley Mae, two bodies locked together as one. He knew if he shared intercourse with Catherine it would mean so much more--a melding of spirits as well as bodies. He craved her desperately. Did she feel the need for him too?

He slid his hand down her belly, reached the waistband of her skirt and kept going, feeling her body beneath skirt and petticoat. He pressed his palm against the hardness of her pubic bone. Jim glanced at Catherine's face to judge her reaction. Her hair tumbled in a golden halo, spreading over the rough, brown blanket. Her tongue swept over her lips, her cheeks were flushed and her forehead shone with perspiration. As he cupped her sex, she lifted her hips, pushing into his touch. She wanted it, wanted him, although probably not nearly as much as he desired her.

He lowered his face and resumed sucking one of her nipples, gently scraping his teeth against it and pulling it with his lips. At the same time, he began to gather the folds of her skirt. There were yards of material to pull up. Beneath it her legs were encased in stockings that covered her legs to her thighs.

Jim reached beneath the folds of skirt and petticoat, searching for bare skin. Above the tops of her stockings, he discovered several inches of smooth thigh. He groaned and suckled her tit deeper into his mouth, pressed his aching erection against her leg, and his fingers explored even higher. Flesh, heat, moisture, downy hair, and then...

She jerked beneath him and pushed against his shoulder, forcing him away. He let her nipple slide from his mouth. She struggled to sit, eyes wide open and glassy. She shook her head. "No."

He continued touching the warm skin of her thigh right at the crease. Would she continue to protest if he didn't stop, if he slipped his fingers just a bit higher into the warm, wet slit that waited for him? If he touched her sex, could he make her desire him so much she wouldn't want to quit?

But she pulled his hand away and her legs pressed together, shutting him out. She continued to shake her head, repeating, "No. We mustn't."

Jim took his hand from underneath her skirt and smoothed the material back in place, covering stocking clad legs. They were a mystery once more, hidden beneath the long skirts women wore to try to fool men into thinking of them as something other than human, as sexless angels perhaps.

Catherine slipped her breasts back into her chemise and fastened the front of her corset, cruelly confining them. She began buttoning her blouse.

"I'm sorry. No." Her mouth continued to pour a stream of explanation and apology. Jim didn't need to understand all the words. Sorry, sorry, sorry, but no, they all said.

He'd pushed too far. Now he'd be lucky if she even let him kiss her again. His erection still pressed painfully against his trousers. He shifted it as unobtrusively as he could and moved to sit beside her on the blanket.

When she'd finished straightening her clothes, Jim put his arm around her back, half expecting her to move away from him. But she sat still, staring at her hands in her lap. He kissed her temple and reached to hold her hand. He tightened his arm around her in an effort to let her know he was happy simply to hold her. Much as he'd love to have more, he would gladly take this.

Catherine relaxed and rested her head on his shoulder. Her hair brushed against his jaw, and he leaned to inhale another whiff of her. She touched his face, stroking her fingers over his cheek.

He turned his head to press his mouth into her palm and mouthed the words "I love you" against her skin. This was what his mother used to say to him before she hugged him. He understood the words meant you cared for a person. And he was certainly feeling some powerful, warm emotions for Catherine.

There was so much he wanted to share with her, his thoughts about life, his ideas and plans for the future. They both needed to learn signing faster so they could communicate about more than simple, everyday things. He leaned to pick up the discarded book from the grass and handed it to her.

Catherine opened the book and turned to face him. She made a sign they'd learned the other day. "I like..." She touched her lips.

He smiled and signed back at her. "I like kissing you too."

"I like it too much." She signed and said the words, her cheeks turning pink. "No more touching below the waist." She marked across her waist with a slicing motion.

He nodded. But she hadn't said they couldn't kiss so he leaned toward her, cupped her face and settled his mouth over hers, soft and searching.

After a moment, he sat back and resumed his lesson. He made the hand over heart sign and added the one for eyes, pointing at Catherine.

"I love your eyes. I love your mouth. Love your neck. Your hands. Your hair. Your nose." Fixing her with a simmering smile and a heavy-lidded stare, he signed all the body parts he'd learned. "I love your breasts. Your body. Your brain."

Catherine's face glowed brighter with every part he mentioned.

When he'd listed every part he knew, Jim made an all-inclusive gesture, and without a smile, so she'd understand the depth of his sincerity, he shared what was in his heart.

"I love you."

CHAPTER THIRTEEN

I love you. The words rang in her head as if he'd shouted them aloud. The message in his eyes was profound enough to make up for the lack of sound. That powerful, breath-stealing moment played over and over in Catherine's mind while Mrs. Albright continued the scolding she'd begun when Catherine returned from her afternoon ride.

"I don't know what else to say, Miss Johnson." Rowena Albright reiterated her much-repeated message. "I believe you're essentially a respectable young woman and a very good teacher and your intentions in educating Mr. Kinney are honorable, but this continued association with such a man is unsuitable. Your example means so much to impressionable young minds. The young ladies of our community look up to you and copy your behavior. Spending time alone and unchaperoned with that stable hand is simply unacceptable."

"I understand your concerns, Mrs. Albright. I'll certainly take them to heart." Catherine spoke politely, but didn't promise to change her behavior.

Mrs. Albright lowered her voice, but although she sounded calmer, her face was still a mottled pink. "I would hate to have to bring this matter up to the school board. I believe it can be handled privately, and I trust you to do the right thing."

Catherine took refuge in silence. She knew the woman wanted her to give up her lessons with Jim even though she claimed to believe it was a good cause. Having a chaperone present wouldn't be enough to appease her. The ticking of the clock filled the quiet parlor as neither woman spoke for several moments.

"I believe I've made my position clear and I'll leave it at that." Mrs. Albright straightened the doily on the back of the chair behind which she stood as if it was a lecturer's podium.

Rising from her hard seat, Catherine took her leave. "I understand your concerns are well-intentioned, Mrs. Albright. Now, if you'll excuse me, I must prepare for tomorrow." She turned and fled the stuffy parlor, escaping upstairs to her room.

Closing the door behind her, she leaned against it and touched her fingers to her lips. Only a couple of hours ago, Jim had kissed her, pressed his hard body into hers, pinning her to the ground. Oh, the feeling of his shoulders beneath her hands and the hard ridge at his groin rubbing against her sex. He'd touched a place that sent licks of fire blazing through her body, and when his mouth had descended the column of her neck to kiss the tops of her breasts, the little flames became an inferno.

Good Lord! Mrs. Albright was right to worry about her being unsupervised with Jim. She'd not only let him kiss her cleavage, but had actually loosened her corset and encouraged him to suckle her! What kind of a woman did that? But it had felt so right, so good. The memory of his hot mouth tugging on her nipple, his callused hand gently squeezing her breast, sent a fresh wave of desire coursing through her. Her breasts ached and her sex tightened. Her drawers were damp from the clench and release of her body.

Catherine walked to her window to gaze out on the darkening street. The last rays of sunlight reflected on windows, turning them bright orange. Knowing that Jim was so close, that if she went out the front door and a few blocks across town she could be with him in minutes, made her legs tremble with the desire to run. In that moment, she felt she could give up everything, her respectability, her position in society, to feel his mouth on her breasts again and his hand moving beneath her skirt. If she had let him, he would have touched her there as they lay on the bank of the river, a cool breeze blowing across the water and cicadas whirring in the treetops.

She relived those moments again with her eyes squeezed shut. Her hand slipped from her breast down her stomach to press against her skirt over her mound, igniting a warm glow. What would it have felt like to let him touch her most private place?

Pulling the curtains over the window, Catherine began to remove her clothes. A quick sponge bath at the basin and she'd pull her nightgown over her head and climb under the covers. She could grade papers for tomorrow while sitting in bed.

117

But once she'd unlaced her corset and removed her chemise, her hands slowed, fondling her breasts. Her eyes closed again and she imagined Jim's hands cupping the soft mounds, his rough fingers tugging at the nipples, twisting enough to hurt before releasing them. She slid her hands up and down her torso, tingling at the touch on her skin. She'd never allowed her hands to linger lovingly on her breasts, the bones of her rib cage, the taut drum of her stomach, the swell of her hips.

She unfastened her skirt and petticoat and let them drop to the floor. She shivered as air cooled her naked skin, and slid her hand down her stomach to cup the hairy mound of her pubis. One finger parted the lips of her sex, exploring the damp crevice.

Blood enflamed her face as she dared to look down at herself. Spreading the lips of her sex wide, she gazed at pink folds and the dark shadow of her opening. She touched the erect red bud standing sentinel over her labia and a lightning flash of excitement stabbed through her. She rubbed the hard nub, and another jolt of energy radiated from that point.

Sucking in her breath, she removed the pressure from the tiny nerve bundle and let her finger drift lower. Between her folds, her flesh was wet. She continued to examine this hidden part of her body, watching her finger disappear inside. Her sex was so hot and wet inside. There were muscles that clenched around her finger. What would it be like to have a man's penis probing her? Would it hurt as her mother had warned her to expect on her wedding night? Would it feel strange, disgusting, painful, or maybe exciting and fulfilling?

All she knew was that when a man touched or kissed her, as Howard once had, and now Jim, she felt a strong yearning between her legs, a voracious hunger. The act of intercourse couldn't be too awful or her body wouldn't crave it so.

Withdrawing her glistening finger, she moved it back to the red bud and began to circle it again. Her eyes closed and her breathing quickened as she dove deep into the sensation and imagined Jim touching her there. Oh how she wanted that.

Little beats of pleasure grew stronger, tugged deeper at her core until suddenly something exploded inside her in hard quakes. A small cry escaped her lips and she clamped her mouth shut for fear Jennie might hear her in the bedroom next door.

As soon as the trembling died away, the pleasurable sensation was replaced by shame. What kind of a young lady stood naked in her room and fingered herself? What did it say about her that she yearned for the touch of a man she wasn't even engaged to, that she'd let him suckle at her breast and wanted him to do much more?

After scrubbing her hands clean at the washbasin, she dressed in her nightgown and climbed into bed, propping the pillow against the headboard so she could sit up and do her work. With a sigh, she gazed at the stack of essays she'd taken from her satchel. The top one was a misspelled, blot-ridden offering from Caleb McPherson on "Why Baseball is Our National Pastime."

The brief paragraphs didn't really address the subject, but was a fervent discourse on why Nap Lajoie of the Philadelphia Athletics was the best player in the history of the game. The essay was a tedious compilation of Nap's batting average and other statistics. Well, at least the boy was reading something, if only sports news.

Catherine's attention drifted as she automatically marked errors in red. The words on the page grew blurry, replaced by images from earlier that afternoon; Jim turning to look at her with the sweet smile that melted her insides, his hands moving fluidly as he signed, his expression when he formed the words, "I love you."

Did he know what he was saying to her; the difference between liking and loving something? He might use the same gesture to say he appreciated cheese. Perhaps he hadn't understood the significance of those words, the emotion they conveyed.

But deep inside she knew he understood. The strength of feeling in his eyes was undeniable. She was playing with fire, allowing this relationship to continue when there could be no future in it. Jim could be badly hurt by her careless behavior in allowing him to think she might love him too.

And even if the fluttery, excited yearning inside her *was* the first stirring of love, what kind of future could they share? The thought of taking him east to introduce him to her parents was unimaginable. They were quite simply from two different worlds.

Once more Catherine resolved to steel her heart and break off their flirtation, but already she knew she'd break that promise. She wouldn't end his lessons and the first chance she got to be alone with him, she would without a doubt kiss Jim again.

* * * *

The younger children scattered across the schoolyard like a handful of marbles dropped on a wooden floor. The older ones dismissed a little slower, stopping to exchange the latest gossip then sauntering away with the ungainly grace of long-legged colts. Catherine stood on the doorstep of the school watching them, the wind whipping her skirts around her legs and blowing dust into her eyes. She glanced at the leaden gray sky and wondered if the clouds would ever produce rain.

Jennie had claimed to be running an errand for her mother today and wouldn't be able to stay for Jim's lesson, but Catherine saw her walking with Ned farther down the street and guessed the girl had an agenda of her own. When the couple entered the pharmacy where the soda fountain was, she smiled, wondering what Mrs. Albright would have to say about it. Catherine would never be the one to tell her.

She was both pleased and taken aback about the loss of Jennie as her chaperone for Jim's lesson today. Without the girl's presence to keep them on task, how much learning would be accomplished?

A figure walking up the street caught her attention. Nathan Scott was heading toward her. Oh dear. She hadn't spoken to him since his request to take her out, and she'd hoped to have discouraged his interest. She considered ducking into the building, but it wouldn't help her avoid him. Besides, he was already raising a hand in greeting.

"Good afternoon, Miss Johnson," he said when he'd crossed the schoolyard and stood at the foot of the steps. His fair complexion was pink, either from exertion or shyness. Removing his hat, he held the brim in both hands.

"Hello. Lovely weather we're having, isn't it?" She indicated the flat gray clouds that shrouded the world from horizon to horizon.

He looked up with a comical expression of bemusement. "Er... It's..."

"I'm teasing, Mr. Scott."

"Oh, yes." He flushed even brighter. "Of course. We certainly could use a good rain. Perhaps it will break soon."

"Yes." Silence fell between them, and Catherine wondered how it was she could spend hours of quiet time with Jim and not feel ill at ease. Her discomfort in Jim's presence was for an entirely different reason. "Is there something I can help you with?"

"I haven't seen you since just after the incident with the horse. I wondered how you've been doing."

"Very well, thank you. And you?"

"Fine." He cleared his throat and his hands clenched on the hat. "I was wondering if you'd considered what I said the other day about going out sometime. There's a social at the grange hall next weekend."

"I hadn't thought about—"

"Perhaps you're already going with someone?" He spoke at the same time.

"No. I'm not." She could have kicked herself the moment the words were out. They sounded like encouragement.

He smiled. "Good. Because I heard you'd been riding with Charles Van Hausen, so I thought maybe he was taking you."

"No." She searched for a gentle way to let him down. "Actually, Mr. Scott, I hadn't planned on attending the dance."

"You must! Everyone will be there."

He was right. She could hardly sit at the Albrights while the rest of the town was at the social event of the season. She'd be expected to make an appearance.

"Well, I suppose I'll go, but it will be with the Albrights. I don't intend to go with an escort."

"Oh." He looked so crestfallen she felt as if she'd kicked him.

"I could save you a dance, though." She tried to soften the refusal.

Nathan smiled. "Make that two dances?"

"All right. Two." She returned his smile.

Just then she noticed Jim approaching, his books under one arm, his gaze on them. A nervous flutter stirred inside her, as she realized how they would appear to him--flirtatious. Why couldn't he have arrived a few minutes late today?

Nathan followed her look. "So it's true, you've been tutoring him. That's what I've heard around town."

"Yes." *Leave now.*

"How's that going?"

"Very well. Mr. Kinney is a quick learner."

As Jim reached them, she nodded and gave him a reflexive smile. "Good afternoon, Mr. Kinney." *And stop looking at me like that before you give us both away.*

His gaze was riveted on her until Nathan stuck out his hand. Jim turned to him and pumped his hand a couple of times—hard.

Oblivious of the animosity blazing in those dark eyes, Nathan smiled. "Hello. How are you?"

Jim shrugged. Catherine was glad he couldn't speak, because she could imagine the sharpness in his voice if he answered the deputy.

"Well, we'd better begin our work." She interrupted the exchange. "I'll see you later, Mr. Scott."

"At the dance," he confirmed.

"Yes. Right." She turned, listening for Jim's footsteps to follow her into the schoolhouse.

He closed the door, and she turned to face him, deciding to act as if she wasn't aware of his jealousy. "Ready to start?"

He jerked his thumb behind him, eyebrows raised.

"Deputy Scott asked me to the dance. I said no." She needn't feel guilty. She hadn't done anything wrong and had merely been polite to Nathan. It wasn't her fault he liked her.

"Dance?" he mouthed the word then signed "day," a horizontal arm representing the horizon, the other hand signifying the sun moving across it.

"Next Saturday." She held up five fingers to show how many days away the social was. How odd it would be to live unaware of what was happening in the community around you. To be ignorant of general events everyone was talking about.

He pointed at her.

"Am I going? Yes. With Jennie and her family." *Please, God, don't let him ask me. He must realize we can't be seen together in public. He can't be ignorant of the problems that would cause.* The nervous flutter in her stomach increased, but Jim simply nodded.

Sucking his lower lip between his teeth, he gazed thoughtfully at her. The movement made his dimples flash, melting her heart. How could she have such conflicting emotions, wanting to distance herself one moment and ravage him with kisses the next? She was in turmoil.

Jim took a step toward her, then another, his eyes never leaving her face. They had a predatory gleam, like a cat stalking prey, and the dimples deepened as a genuine smile curved his mouth. Setting his books on a student desk, he moved closer.

Catherine caught her breath and she froze, anticipating a kiss.

Instead, he slipped one hand around her waist and clasped her hand in his. He swayed her back and forth, keeping time to an unheard beat. Together they moved in a small circle on the wooden floor, his hand on her back guiding her.

She marveled at his ability to mimic the people he lived among, who existed in a completely different world from the one he experienced. What power of attention it must take to understand the concept of music without hearing melody or rhythm.

The shuffling movement slowed then stopped until they were simply standing in a silent embrace. His hand gripped hers tighter and the one on her back drifted lower to rest just above her bustle. She could feel the pressure of his hand even through the padding.

Tilting her face, she rose on her toes and her eyes drifted closed. There was a breathless pause as he kept her waiting before his mouth covered hers. The light pressure of his lips wrung a little moan from her. Her hand slipped from his shoulder to the back of his neck, and she untangled her other hand from his to join it. How she loved the feel of his neck, so strong and warm beneath her palms, his hair tickling the backs of her hands. She relaxed into him as his arms encircled her.

His lips might be soft, but his body was hard and solid, all sinew and bone without an ounce of fat. Jim was only taller than she by about a foot, not a towering giant like Nathan or dear Howard. She liked that he was closer to her height. It was easier to look into his eyes without having to crane her neck.

Her breasts pressed against his chest and between her legs, her sex was slippery. She clenched her muscles, trying to control the pulsing, and only succeeded in stimulating herself more. Desire flooded her and she opened her mouth, encouraging Jim to kiss her deeper.

But, after one quick trace of his tongue between her lips, he pulled away and stepped back. She was leaning into him so hard he had to put his hands on her shoulders to steady her.

Catherine's eyes flew open. Releasing her shoulders, he pointed past her to the schoolbooks on the desk. As she followed Jim, she caught a glimpse of his profile when he picked up the books and slate. He was smiling smugly, enjoying teaching her that two could play at heating things up and abruptly cooling them down.

Indignation and amusement competed in her as she took her seat beside him and he handed her the paper he'd written. He'd printed a brief description of their picnic in short sentences and single words, like a poem without rhyme.

"Fish swim water. Sky. Trees. Leaves. Eat food. Drink."

She smiled at him.

He touched his lips, puckering them in a kiss, and indicated the signing book.

She looked up the sign for it.

"Fingers touching thumbs as both hands come together," the text read, "trembling slightly to indicate the degree of passion."

Catherine made the movement as she repeated the word aloud. "Kiss."

Jim copied the movement, shaping his lips like hers. He pointed to the slate and offered her the chalk so she could spell the word. He studied each letter as she wrote it, before printing them himself: K-i-s-s.

Catherine's blushed at seeing it written in glaring white against the black slate. Kiss. Somehow there seemed to be no denying or hiding it now that it was written down. She glanced at Jim's lips and her nipples hardened at the memory of his mouth sucking them. Inhaling deeply, she looked away until Jim's movement pulled her attention back to him.

Eyebrows raised, he held a hand in front of him and one lifted in the classic waltz pose.

"You want to know the word for dance?" She printed the word and looked up the sign—fingers in a down-turned "V" moving like dancers over the palm of the opposite hand. Jim copied the gesture and printed the word.

The lesson went on this way, with him leading it by asking for the words he wanted to know. He would make a sketch on the slate or act them out. Catherine would identify the word, spell it and look up the sign.

Once they had a number of nouns established, they started on the actions that modified them, or other concepts indicating distance, time, duration or strength.

As she became more focused on the work, Catherine's urgent desires faded. After a while of intent study, they'd progressed to where they could pose each other basic questions and answer them, all with signs.

She was working out a combination that would mean the livery stable, when Jim pulled out his pocket watch. He indicated that he had to leave. Disappointment out of all proportion to the announcement flooded her. She wanted more time with him, a full evening of talking and learning and laughing and sharing more kisses. The hour they were able to share each day was too brief.

Jim stood and collected his things.

Catherine reluctantly rose too, and just as she was beginning to think he would leave with only a polite nod, Jim abruptly pulled her into his arms with bone-crushing strength. There was nothing polite or gentle about this kiss. It was passionate, demanding, possessive, and she felt it all the way down to her toes.

As his tongue dominated hers, Catherine clung to him. Not until he set her back on her feet did she realize he'd lifted her off them. Her legs trembled and she thought they might collapse. Breathless, she gazed into his dark eyes. They held a promise of other things he could and would do to her given time and opportunity. The look frightened and excited her. Jim seemed suddenly dangerous and unpredictable, capable of more passion than she might be able to handle.

He cupped her cheek, tracing a thumb over her lips still buzzing from his kiss. Then he picked up his books and walked from the building.

Catherine stood shaken, aching with lust, and more torn than ever.

CHAPTER FOURTEEN

Jim rehearsed once more how he was going to present his plan to Rasmussen. With his long-held daydream moving closer to reality, he felt as twitchy as a skittish horse. It was one thing to daydream approaching his boss about a partnership. He could fantasize Rasmussen embracing the plan and telling Jim he'd like nothing better than to make a partner of such a hard worker, or that he held Jim in his heart as the son he'd never had.

It was quite another to actually face Rasmussen with his dream. But he would do it. Had to do it. After what he'd witnessed today, he knew there was no time left. With both Van Hausen and Nathan Scott moving in on Catherine, if Jim didn't do something soon to make himself more worthwhile in her eyes, he'd never have a chance. He had to prove he could be successful.

Rasmussen leaned in the doorway, staring out at the sky that still hadn't given any rain. His arms were folded and cigar smoke wreathed his head. He didn't hear Jim's quiet approach until he was beside him. Rassmussen glanced at him and pointed up at the sky. "No rain."

Jim nodded, staring at the clouds for a second before bringing his gaze back to his boss. His throat was so dry he could barely swallow yet his palms were sweating.

"What?" Rasmussen put a finger to the bridge of his glasses and pushed them up his nose. "Something wrong with one of the horses?"

Jim launched into his presentation. He handed Rasmussen a piece of paper on which he had written the number of dollars he had in his savings, as well as the payments he expected to make over the upcoming years. The final figure of his buy-in was circled at the bottom of the page.

"What's this?" Light reflected off the old man's glasses as he looked up so Jim couldn't read his eyes—not a good thing when every nuance of expression was critical.

Jim held up the box with his savings and opened it, showing the cash inside. He pointed at the top figure on the paper. Closing the box, he made the motion of handing it over to Rasmussen then indicated the building around them. After setting the box on the ground, Jim made a back and forth gesture between himself and Rasmussen and joined his hands together in a link. Then he waited.

Rasmussen looked at the numbers on the paper, the moneybox, and at Jim. The reflected light vanished and Jim could see the astonishment in his eyes.

"You want to buy my business."

Jim made a link with his hands again and once more gestured between them. He crossed two fingers to add to the point.

"A partnership?"

Jim nodded emphatically.

Rasmussen rubbed his jaw, his hand covering his mouth, but Jim caught the flash of a smile. His stomach twisted. It was an easy sign to read. The man thought his offer to buy was a joke, and that Jim was a fool.

Jim stabbed his finger at the paper showing the payment schedule he'd worked out. He wasn't so dumb as to think the funds he had were enough to buy a share in a prosperous business. Rasmussen knew he was no idiot, having entrusted him with his bookkeeping for several years now. Indicating the numbers for payments over several years, Jim pointed to the bottom line again.

Rasmussen breathed in deeply and exhaled slowly. When he looked at Jim this time there wasn't a trace of humor on his lips. He shook his head. "I can't make this deal."

Jim's chest ached so badly he could barely draw breath. His entire body was rigid as he nodded, all his hopes crashing into pieces like a broken pane of glass.

Rasmussen clapped a hand on his shoulder. "I'm sorry, but I can't."

With a curt nod, Jim backed away from the man's hand.

He pointed at the building around them. "I'm going to sell this and move away. Understand?"

Jim spread his hands. Who was Rasmussen selling to? He pointed to the money box and the paper. *I'll buy it. Just give me time.*

The man shook his head and adjusted his glasses again. "No payment plan. I need the money in a lump sum so I can move back east. I want to see my family again."

Jim made the sign for time by tapping his wrist.

"I don't have a buyer yet, but I hope by next summer."

Summer was a long way off, but not nearly long enough for Jim to earn what Rasmussen would want. To make things worse, if the livery sold to someone else he might be out of both a job and a place to live. Maybe the new owner would let him stay on, but he couldn't count on it. And the work he did at Murdoch's wasn't nearly enough to keep him fed, clothed and housed. Besides, the thought of endless years of earning pennies a day working for other men was intolerable.

He needed more money and fast.

Rasmussen waved a hand for Jim's attention. "I'm sorry. I'd ask the new owner to let you stay here as part of the deal."

Jim held up a hand, stopping his apologies and explanations. He stooped to pick up the cashbox and walked away.

In his room, he closed and locked the door behind him. He weighed the tin box in his hand then flung it across the room. It hit the wall and fell, coins scattering across the floor, bills fluttering down like falling leaves.

Hurling the box felt good so he swept his arm across the top of his dresser, knocking everything onto the floor, the ridiculous carved animals, the pitiful toiletries and useless old catalog he could never afford to order from. These paltry items were the sum of his entire dismal life.

He kicked the frame of his bed, knocking the light cot away from the wall. He cried out his rage and frustration, tore the covers off the bed and punched the pillow. Dragging the thin mattress from the metal cot, he tossed it on the floor then stopped to stare around at the destruction of his room. He had a lot more rage in him but there was nothing else to tear apart since he owned so little.

Jim sank onto the mattress on the floor, his legs drawn to his chest, forehead bowed to his knees, and hands cradling the back of his neck. He breathed in hitching bursts. He had no future, definitely no woman, and soon maybe, no home. What the hell could he do to improve his life?

He breathed slowly until he'd calmed himself and his raging thoughts had settled. All right. He wasn't completely without prospects. That man Karak had offered him odd jobs with good pay. Sure, Karak's men had beaten the crap out of Jim, but a chance for higher wages was worth working alongside the sons of bitches.

He rose to his feet, wiped his wet cheeks with his hands and regarded his wrecked room. It only took a few minutes to set his meager possessions to rights. He put on a clean shirt, combed his hair, washed his face and headed across town to to see Grant Karak.

The tall granary tower and mill were located near the railway depot. There was a side track past the granary so the grain could be loaded straight into the freight cars. It was early evening and the mill was closed when Jim arrived, but a light shone from the windows of Karak's office on the side of the building.

He glanced through the frosted glass as he walked past the window and saw the blurred shape of a person inside. After pausing on the doorstep to gather his nerve, Jim knocked on the door. He hesitated, torn between waiting for the door to open and simply entering. If Karak was yelling for him to come in and had to get up to answer the door, he'd start the interview in an irritable frame of mind. But if Jim simply strolled in uninvited, he might annoy the man too. At last, he tried the handle. The door opened and he entered Karak's lair.

The office wasn't what he'd expected for the wealthiest man in town. It was cramped and small, barely bigger than Jim's room at the stable. Crammed into the space were several filing cabinets and a massive desk that filled most of the room. The dark wood was scarred from years of use and the surface covered with files, papers and books. Karak sat behind the desk, his bald head gleaming in the light of the green-shaded desk lamp.

He gazed at Jim with a curious tilt to his eyebrows and motioned him toward the seat across the desk. "Mr. Kinney. Sit down."

Jim sat on the edge of the straight-back chair, heart thumping as he faced a man with the power to change his future for the second time that day. Before he could begin his pantomime of asking for work, Karak spoke.

"You've come for a job?"

He nodded.

"All right. I have some work you can do. Come back tomorrow at noon." He held up ten fingers then two. "Twelve o'clock, understand? My manager will tell you what to do."

Again Jim nodded, shocked at how easy this had been. But how many hours was Karak offering, enough to replace both of his other jobs? And if he quit the livery, where would he sleep at night?

"I'll pay you a dollar a day six days a week. That's six dollars a week. Got it?" Karak held up six fingers to make sure.

Jim stared at him, stunned. That was more than he made in a month at both his jobs, but what the hell was Karak going to have him do to earn that kind of money?

The man swiveled his chair to a cupboard behind the desk and took out a pair of glasses and a decanter. He poured two fingers of the amber liquid in each glass and offered one to Jim.

With a slightly shaking hand, Jim raised his glass to match Karak's salute. The whiskey slipped smoothly past his tongue and set fire to his throat. His eyes watered but he didn't cough. His new employer might take it as a weakness if he couldn't drink liquor without choking. Clenching the glass tightly in his hand, Jim waited to see what else Karak would say.

"You'll work in the mill." He pointed toward the building next door. "But, sometimes you'll do other things."

The burn in the pit of his stomach flamed hotter.

"Nothing hard. Unloading boxcars. Railroad cars. Understand?"

Again Jim nodded.

"Good! You'll do fine and make good money. More as time goes on."

When Karak had finished speaking, he wrote a note for Jim to show to Murdoch and Rasmussen explaining about his new employment then he rose and held out a hand.

They shook over the cluttered desktop. The man's grip was firm, the expression in his hooded eyes satisfied.

He'd treated Jim with respect and forthrightness, so why did Jim feel like he'd just made a deal with the devil and would come to regret this agreement? Maybe because Karak's men had dragged him down the street like a piece of trash and their boss had gotten them out of jail by paying off the sheriff. Still he'd work for the man, nonetheless, and accept his money.

As he left Karak's office, Jim encountered two of his tormentors walking across the mill yard toward the office. He cursed the bad timing that had brought them there at the exact moment of his leaving. The sleepy-eyed one who'd dragged Jim stood at the foot of the steps, his skinny friend just behind him. They blocked his way and he couldn't pass until they moved aside.

It was dark outside, only the light from the office window illuminating the men. Jim couldn't see the leader's lips to read them. His hair prickled and he wanted to open the door of Karak's office and let the man explain he was part of the team now. But that was no way to earn respect, so he forced himself to walk down the steps.

He stopped inches away from the droopy-eyed man. The sour stench of alcohol sweating from his body and on his breath wafted into Jim's face. His every heartbeat urged him to run before this man plowed a fist into his face, but he stood his ground and stared into bleary eyes.

For a long moment, they stood face to face. The man shook his head and muttered something then he moved aside, but he bumped shoulders with Jim as he went up the stairs. His partner, the skinny man poked a finger into Jim's chest and yammered something on the way past.

Jim glanced back to make sure they were really going into the office and not jumping him from behind. Only after they'd closed the door did he continue on his way to the saloon.

The Crystal was quiet, with only a few customers standing at the bar or sitting at the tables. A group of the girls clustered in a corner of the room chattering. For once Murdoch wasn't harassing them to get back to work. Jim saw Shirley Mae was the center of the women's attention. She held a blood-stained rag to the side of her face.

Shirley noticed Jim across the room and turned her face to show him her cut cheek and swollen jaw.

Jim mouthed, "Who?" but didn't recognize the name she said. He pressed his palm over his heart. "Sorry."

She nodded, accepting his thanks.

It didn't happen often, but sometimes one of the whores bore marks from a rough customer, black eyes, fat lip or bruised arm, and probably other hidden part. He hated to see Shirley hurt like that, but couldn't do anything to help her. He headed to the back room for his cleaning supplies.

At the end of the evening's work, he stopped at the bar to show Mr. Murdoch the note Karak had written about the new job. Jim hoped to keep working at the Crystal in the evenings if he could.

He waited nervously for Murdoch to finish reading. This was nothing to how he was going to feel when he gave Mr. Rasmussen notice after all these years. The question of where he'd live if not the livery flashed through his mind, followed by the realization he would no longer be able to meet Catherine in the afternoons. How could he have overlooked that fact when she was a large part of the reason he was making such a huge change in his life? If he couldn't spend time with her, he'd not only lose the chance to get closer to her, but also the opportunity to learn.

Murdoch handed the paper back to him. "Be careful. Karak is a dangerous man."

Jim nodded.

"The man who works for him, the one who dragged you, beat up Shirley earlier tonight." Murdoch pointed to his eyes and to Jim's. "Keep your eyes open and stay out of his way."

Jim pictured the droopy-eyed man using his fists on Shirley and white hot rage flashed through him. Why did scum like that get away with the things they did? The fact that Droopy-eyes and his friends were under Karak's protection said a lot about their boss too, but Jim didn't want to think about the connection. He just wanted a job that paid good money. He'd pegged Karak as a wolf among sheep the first night he'd seen him, but that didn't mean he wouldn't work for him.

Jim mouthed a silent "Thank you" to Murdoch for his advice and for the years of underpaid employment.

He headed home to bed, exhausted from the emotional ups and downs of the day. The jealousy he'd felt on seeing Catherine with the deputy, the exhilaration of kissing her, frustration at Rasmussen's rejection of his proposal, and guarded optimism at the prospect of working for Karak, not to mention the whiskey he'd drunk, all combined to give him a sour stomach and dull headache.

He dropped into bed and almost immediately fell asleep, but deep in the night, something woke him. He sat up in the pitch darkness of his room. Something had brought him out of sound sleep—a sense of something not right.

Jim lit a lantern and walked out into the stable, bits of straw and grit clinging to his bare feet as he padded across the floor. The horses were moving in their stalls, nervous. High-strung King tossed his head, eyes rolling in fear.

Something wrong. The hair on Jim's neck prickled as he scanned the dark room. So many places someone could hide. Images of the droopy-eyed man and his cronies leaping out and attacking flashed through his mind. Clutching the lantern tighter, he eyed the pitchfork leaning against Lady's stall. The mare stretched her neck over her gate and blew a warm breath against his cheek. Jim stroked her nose, still ready to dive for the pitchfork at any sign of movement in the shadows.

He took a breath and suddenly realized what was wrong. Mingled with the familiar scents of the stable was the acrid tang of smoke. He followed the faint odor out the side door.

The smell was stronger on the night breeze. Jim searched in all directions for an orange flicker that would indicate fire, but saw nothing in any of the buildings in town.

Then a glow in the western sky caught his attention. He rounded the corner of the building and gazed across the dark prairie. Several miles away the McPhersons' barn was engulfed in flames. Smoke illuminated by the fire billowed in clouds above it. A line of flames spread out from the barn. Fire was devouring the dry prairie grass.

Jim turned and ran down the sidewalk intending to wake Rasmussen at home and get him to spread the word, but already others had been roused by the smell of smoke. Neal Hildebrandt and his son, Ned emerged from their house by the dry goods store. Further down the street, Nathan Scott ran from door to door, pounding and waking residents.

Those who had horses stabled at the livery would be coming for them. Jim returned to the stable, lit a few lanterns and opened the main doors for the rush of people he expected. He led Crusader from his stall and began saddling him.

John Walker from the hardware was the first to arrive, carrying an armful of shovels and burlap sacks, which he loaded in the bed of a wagon. He harnessed Zephyr to it.

For the next twenty minutes, Jim checked out riding horses to their owners, and harnessed others to wagons of supplies for firefighting. There was no point in attempting to carry enough water in barrels to quench the flames. The best the townspeople could do was to build a firebreak, preventing the fire from spreading.

After all the horses were gone except for Old Tom, Jim mounted Crusader. He rode across the open prairie to where the men were digging ditches and setting up a controlled burn. The breeze rushing against his cheeks was also feeding the flames and driving them faster. Urgency drove Jim's heels into Crusader's sides, making the horse race faster too. He had to hurry, had to help.

Ned Hildebrandt had been put in charge of tethering and caring for everyone's horses. The boy had them pegged to the ground out of range of the workers, but it wasn't far enough from the growing fire to please the horses. They whinnied and pulled against their picket lines, anxious to escape the smell of smoke.

Jim leaped to the ground and tossed Crusader's reins to Ned. He grabbed a shovel and joined the line of men breaking sod and churning up earth. He pressed his foot against the spade head, digging into the rock-hard soil. After a rainless month, the grass was as dry as straw. Flames would easily leap the narrow trench they were digging. But on the other side of it, Nathan Scott orchestrated the setting of smaller fires that would scorch the grass between the trench and the wildfire. This burned zone should provide enough of a buffer to divert if not extinguish the fire.

Smoke filled Jim's lungs when he inhaled. He coughed as he tied a bandana around his mouth and resumed shoveling. His shoulders ached as he broke foot after foot of turf. When his digging met the tilled earth where John Walker was working, he stopped to wipe his sweating face, lean on his shovel handle and stare at the McPhersons' farm in the distance. Both the barn and house were engulfed in flames. He prayed the family had gotten out safely. His stomach lurched as he remembered they had a couple of little kids and a baby.

The line of men fanned the smaller fires they'd set, encouraging their spread. The men were silhouetted against the oranage wall of fire advancing toward the firebreak.

A hand smacked between Jim's shoulder blades, making him jump. He turned to see Dean Gunderson's round face, red and shiny in the glow of the fire. Dean held up a dripping wet burlap sack and said something. Jim had no idea what he wanted until he slapped the rough, soaking sack into his hand and beckoned him to follow.

In a moment, Jim saw what needed to be done. On the town side of the firebreak, sparks from the bigger fire were showering from the sky and igniting the grass. Some of the younger boys from both farms and town were beating out the fledgling fires before they could spread. Jim abandoned his shovel to help Dean and the others beat out flames with wet burlap.

Choking smoke rose from the ground in front of him, stinging his eyes until he could hardly see through the tears. Jim struggled to breathe through the bandana covering his mouth. He spotted a patch where flickers of flame had taken hold and were fanning in all directions. Running over to the area, he beat the ground with the sack then stamped out the embers beneath his boot heels.

On the other side of the break, the wildfire had met the scorched earth in some places. Flames raced along the sooty edge, searching for more fodder to burn. The fire died out in some places, but raged even fiercer in others as a renewed gust of wind fanned it. There were other spots where embers jumped the break, and now everyone worked at putting out the hot spots.

The fire-fighting went on and on as the sky turned gray with the approach of sunrise. But at last every sizzling blade of grass was trampled out, the final flame smothered. Soot streaked everyone's faces as they gathered in groups to discuss the fire.

Jim noticed McPherson was part of one of the groups. His wife and children weren't with him so they must have been driven or walked into town. The farmer's face was nearly black from smoke and ash. The whites of his eyes gleamed against it, and his expression was as desolate as the burned out buildings of his farm.

John Walker clapped Jim on the shoulder and said something then walked on. Wanting to get a head start back to town so he could be at the livery when the horses were returned, Jim took Crusader from the picket line. Before he rode away, he surveyed the wide band of scorched earth, tendrils of smoke still rising. A mile beyond was the charred ruins of the McPherson farm, blackened beams jutting up like clawed fingers.

No lightning strike had started the fire since the storm they all waited for still hadn't broken. A kerosene lantern knocked over into dry straw in a barn could get out of control quickly, but why would a lantern have been lit in the dead of night? Unless perhaps one of the livestock had been sick and McPherson had been tending it.

With no answers for his curiosity, Jim turned Crusader toward town and nudged his flanks. It didn't take much encouragement to set the horse cantering. Crusader was anxious to get away from the smell of smoke and have a breakfast of oats and hay.

The sky was a pearly gray and the breeze cleared the smoke from Jim's lungs and cooled his sweat-soaked body. He was exhausted and sorry for the McPhersons, but on a personal note, full of the hopefulness of a new day. Today he would quit his job at the stable, leave the familiar cocoon of the livery and enter the world a new man.

CHAPTER FIFTEEN

Adelaide McPherson's face was streaked with soot and wide-eyed with shock. She clutched Baby Constance too tightly, seemingly unaware that the little one was squirming and screaming.

"I'll take her." Catherine volunteered, easing the child from its mother's arms. She'd rarely held a baby and Constance was heavier than she'd expected--a bulky bundle that wiggled and twisted until she nearly dropped her. The baby flung out a fist and hit her in the nose hard enough to bring tears to her eyes. And the wailing went on and on.

"Let me." Mrs. Albright bustled across the room and swept the baby out of Catherine's arms, holding the child upright against her ample shoulder. Almost immediately Constance quieted.

"Why don't you take Adelaide upstairs, help her clean up, and find her something to wear?" she advised Catherine. "And Jennie, you can find something among your old clothes that might fit Marlene. When you've done that, I want you to go over to the Hildebrandts' house and see if there are any outgrown clothes from Ned they can give Caleb."

For the first time, Catherine was actually comforted by Rowena's imperious orders, as she supervised the care of the devastated McPhersons.

"Come with me, Adelaide." Catherine spoke softly, for the first time using Mrs. McPherson's Christian name, as she took her elbow and guided her upstairs. The woman was silent and clearly in shock, unable to comprehend that her family had just lost everything they owned all in one night.

In her bedroom, Catherine filled the basin with water, wishing she could offer a full bath. "Sorry the water's not warm. If you want to rinse of the worst of the soot, I'll go downstairs and bring up the kettle."

Adelaide continued to stand in the middle of the room for a moment, before finally moving over to the washstand. Catherine watched her dip the face cloth into the basin, then went downstairs to the kitchen where Mrs. Albright was cooking breakfast for everyone.

"Shall we heat water for baths?" Catherine asked.

Mrs. Albright turned from the stove where she was laying slabs of bacon on the griddle. "That's a lot of water to heat and a lot of time involved. For now, let's just get them fed and put to bed. We'll worry about bathing later."

"What about school? Will people expect it to be open? Shall I go over in case the students show up?" She felt completely indecisive and was willing to take whatever direction the older woman gave, uncertain what her job as teacher was in the middle of this tragedy.

Mrs. Albright pulled out another skillet for eggs. "Yes, perhaps you'd better be there at the regular time in case anyone comes."

Taking the steaming teakettle from the stove, Catherine started toward her bedroom, but stopped in the living room on the way. Caleb sat where Mrs. Albright had put him, on the couch with his baby sister sleeping in his arms. Constance frowned even in sleep and most of her fist was stuffed in her mouth. The boy stared across the room at the ornate mantle clock with the mechanical blacksmith hammering his anvil beneath the clock face.

Catherine touched Caleb's shoulder and leaned to look into his eyes. "Are you all right?" she whispered so as not to wake the baby.

After a moment, his eyes focused on hers. They were bright with unshed tears. "I--I didn't do it. I swear I didn't leave the lantern lit after I did my evening chores." He gulped and swallowed. "I know I didn't."

"No. I'm sure you didn't," Catherine soothed. Even if it wasn't true, there was no need to make the boy feel any worse than he already did. She patted his shoulder. "I have to get this water upstairs for your mother and sister. Your turn will come next as soon as Jennie gets you something to change into, all right?"

He nodded, and resumed staring at the inexorable rise and fall of the blacksmith's arm.

Catherine went to Jennie's room, where Jennie was searching through her closet for an outgrown dress for Marlene, and poured boiling water in the wash basin. Marlene looked as overwhelmed as her mother and brother.

Jennie whispered to Catherine, "It's terrible what happened to them. They might've been killed! How do you think the fire got started?"

"I couldn't guess." *And you shouldn't. That's how rumors get started.* Catherine changed the subject. "School's cancelled, but I'll go over there in a bit."

Jennie pulled a pink, flowered calico from the far corner of her closet. "How about this?" She held it up against her, checking the length of the sleeves.

"I'm sure it'll be fine."

Catherine continued on to her room to find Mrs. McPherson standing by the window in only her camisole and petticoat, gazing at the horizon. Perhaps she could still see a plume of smoke from her destroyed home.

Catherine poured fresh water into the basin, and went to stand beside Adelaide. "Would you like to clean up a little more? I have hot water for you now."

"It was so fast," she murmured. "If Mark hadn't woken when he did..."

Catherine rubbed her back. The woman's whole body was trembling. Catherine suddenly realized that a few weeks earlier she would've been sleeping in that house too, and forced to flee in the night. The thought sent a shiver through her. "But, you're all fine," she soothed. "You're all safe."

"With no home and our wheat burned." Adelaide looked into Catherine's eyes with a fierce gleam in her own. "It wasn't an accident. It was Karak's men. I know it. He must have found out what Mark was saying to the others."

"What others? What happened?"

"About not taking our grain to Karak's mill or using his railroad to ship it. Mark talked to some of the other farmers about banding together to take our grain to Reederville instead where we might be able to get a fair deal. He was stirring up trouble. *That's* what this fire was about. Karak burned us out."

A chill ran down Catherine's spine at the accusation. "You really believe that?"

The dark gleam in Adelaide's eyes answered her question.

"You and Mark should talk to Sheriff Tate and tell him your suspicions."

"A lot of good it would do. You know Karak has the man in his back pocket."

"Deputy Scott might be able to help." Catherine encouraged Adelaide toward the washstand, handing her a fresh bar of soap.

Plunging her hands in the water, Adelaide scrubbed her face and hands clean. She took the towel Catherine offered and dried off. "We have no proof, only a suspicion. What could he do?"

"Investigate! Maybe he'd find evidence linking the fire to Mr. Karak."

Adelaide shrugged, the expression on her face saying she'd already given up. "Even if he found something, it wouldn't help. We have no power. It's not as if it had happened to the Gundersons or Hopewells, someone with standing in this community."

Catherine was surprised by the bitterness in her voice. Although she knew there was a difference in social status between the townspeople and country folk, she hadn't thought much about the disparity between modest farmers like the McPhersons and wealthier landowners.

"What will you do?" she asked.

"Go home to my family in Virginia, if we can scrape together enough for train fare."

The injustice set Catherine's blood raging. If it was true about Karak's men starting the fire, someone must do something to punish them and him. She pulled up the covers of her unmade bed, making it ready for Adelaide, while the woman put on the dress she'd given her.

"Mrs. Albright has bacon and eggs ready for you, unless you'd rather lie down and rest for a while?"

"I couldn't possibly sleep. I need to be with my family, to know they're really safe."

"Of course."

Catherine led the way downstairs.

After the McPherson family had eaten breakfast and been tucked away to sleep, Mrs. Albright dismissed Catherine from helping with the kitchen clean up. "You go on ahead to the school. It's doubtful any child would come today, but better to be there."

Catherine was only too happy to get out of the house for a while. She'd dressed long ago, during the tense early hours of the morning. While the men fought the fire, the women had anxiously watched the orange glow from the upstairs windows of the houses in town. Putting on her jacket and picking up her satchel, she headed outside.

The air was crisp this morning, leaving no doubt it was nearly winter, and it was tinged by the sharp smell of smoke. She could only imagine the horror of waking to choking smoke and a fire advancing on one's home in the middle of the night.

As she hurried down the street, her gaze was magnetically pulled toward the stable at the far edge of town. Had Jim been involved in the fire fighting? Was he all right? When Mr. Albright had arrived home, he'd said no one was injured, but Catherine still felt a strong need to see Jim and make sure for herself.

She unlocked the schoolhouse door and went inside. Normally, on such a cool morning, Ned Hildebrandt would have come early to start a fire in the woodstove, but today there was no point in heating the building. Catherine kept her jacket on, breath puffing in a silver cloud as she shivered at her desk. She opened her grade book and began entering the scores of the last group of essays. When she checked her watch, it was nearly nine o'clock. No students would be coming. She rose, packed her satchel and left the school, locking the door on the way out.

Catherine wasn't anxious to return to the Albrights so she decided to make some stops first. She went to the bank to withdraw some cash from her account, and asked the teller if Charles Van Hausen was in his office.

A slight smirk played over the man's lips. "He is. Let me check and see if he has time in his schedule to see you."

The teller disappeared through the door leading to the offices, and moments later Charles came out. He was very dapper in a checked coat and pants, a sporty look compared to the dark suits the other men in the bank wore. With a smile, he opened the little swing gate, granting her access to the world on the other side of the counter.

"Miss Johnson! I'm pleased you stopped by. So terrible about the McPherson farm, isn't it?" He ushered her toward his office with his hand pressed against the small of her back.

"Yes. The McPhersons are staying at the Albrights. They're devastated by this disaster."

"It could've been worse. The fire might have spread to town." Charles gestured her to one of the two seats facing his desk. "Please, sit down."

Catherine perched on the edge of the chair. She doubted Charles had been one of the men fighting the fire or he wouldn't be so fresh and bright-eyed this morning. His casual tone, as if the farm was a minor loss, strengthened her intention to curtail any notion he might have of courting her.

Rather than distance himself by sitting behind his desk as he would with a loan applicant, Charles took the chair next to hers. "I hope you enjoyed my gift the other day. Perhaps it was too personal, but I couldn't resist giving the gloves to you. Have you considered my invitation to the dance this Saturday?" His gaze riveted on her, as if the power of his will alone would influence her decision.

"I've received several invitations," she said lightly. "But I've decided to go with the Albrights. I'm sorry and thank you for the invitation. As for the gloves, they're beautiful, but I can't accept them. I didn't know I was stopping by here this morning or I would have brought them. I'll return them to you shortly."

His mouth thinned in a hard line of disappointment as the light in his eyes dimmed. Charles waved a dismissive hand. "No. Please. They were a gift." His tone was curt, his posture rigid.

"I'm sorry, Mr. Van Hausen. I did enjoy our ride that day, but I don't want you to think it was more than a one-time occasion." She met his gaze as she let him know she had no intention of furthering their relationship.

He rose from his seat, seeming anxious to have her out of his office after this rejection. Two red spots marked his cheekbones. "Of course. If your affections are given elsewhere..."

"No. At this time I'm still in mourning for my fiancé back east and not ready for any new involvement." Memories of Jim's kisses, his warm hands and hard muscles invaded her mind, igniting a fire that burned low in her belly.

Gripping the handle of her satchel tightly, she rose. "I'm sorry if I've misled you in any way."

Charles led her to the door. "Perhaps after more time has passed you'll feel differently."

She smiled without answering, and didn't offer to save him a dance as she had Nathan Scott.

Back on the street, Catherine breathed deeply, relieved to have the interview over.

After stopping at the general store and purchasing some personal toiletries and a shopping bag full of items for the McPhersons, Catherine walked toward the livery. She needed to see Jim to tell him their lesson was still on for later that afternoon if he wanted to have it.

Only delivering a message, she told herself. *It's not like I'm desperate to see him, to know he's all right, and maybe steal a kiss if Mr. Rasmussen isn't around.*

The livery owner was there, but Jim wasn't. As Catherine entered the stable doors, Rasmussen was cursing loudly. He'd just sloshed water down his pants leg from the buckets he was carrying.

Catching sight of her, he set the pails on the ground, more water sluicing down their sides. "Miss Johnson. You're here to see Jim?"

"Yes. He isn't here?" She glanced around the barn as if he might appear from one of the stalls.

"No." His tone was curt and his expression stormy. "The boy's found himself a new job. Left me in the lurch after all I've done for him."

"What?"

"He's working for Grant Karak at the mill."

"Oh!" Catherine's mind flew as she tried to comprehend Jim working for the very man whose employees had beaten him. For the man who may have ordered the McPhersons' barn burned. "When did this happen?"

"This morning." Rasmussen rubbed the back of his neck. "Or maybe, yesterday. Jim came to me with a proposition to buy into the stable. Had some money saved up and plans for making payments. I felt bad telling him no, but I've been making my own plans. I want to sell the business outright and leave town. Maybe I can even sell it to Grant Karak, the man seems bent on owning all of Broughton."

He shook his head and glanced at Catherine. "I felt bad for Jim. I didn't want to have to turn down his offer. Anyway, it seems he was offered this job with Karak last night, and started today."

"He left, just like that? No notice?"

"Came back from the fire and took care of the horses, showed me some note Karak had written for him, then left." Rasmussen shrugged. "I told him he could keep his room, at least until I get someone else, and Jim agreed to continue to help out here when he can."

How convenient to continue to let Jim use a postage stamp of a room for which Rasmussen had no other use in return for free labor.

"Do you know what hours he'll be working?" she asked. "It doesn't sound like he'll have any free time to continue his lessons."

"Not likely. A shame, because he's really bright. It's been good of you to try to teach him to read and everything." Rasmussen's eyes, magnified by his glasses, focused intently on hers. "But maybe it's best. Spending time with you may have raised some false hopes in the boy."

Catherine's pulse quickened. What did Rasmussen know? What might he have seen? She covered her fear with a sharp reply.

"I'm sure there's never a time when lack of education is better than learning. Thank you, Mr. Rasmussen, and please let Jim know I stopped by. Tell him he can stop at the school whenever he has a chance and we'll arrange a time to continue our work."

She started to walk away.

"Miss Johnson. I'm not trying to be nosy, but I really am fond of Jim. He's been with me since his mother died, and I'd hate to see him get hurt. Jim's a lonely man, and liable to read something into your kindness, maybe take it for a deeper kind of caring. So be careful."

Catherine nodded curtly. "Your point is taken. I'll be considerate of his feelings."

As she walked past the shops on Main Street, her mind worried frantically at Rasmussen's words. What did he know or guess about their relationship? What might others in town be saying? If gossip was spreading, would it affect her position here?

She despised herself for worrying about her reputation and her job, but couldn't help but consider them. Then she thought of the image of a lonely, loveless man which Rasmussen had evoked. Poor Jim, with no one to talk to or to care for him, and only the company of horses all these years. No wonder he'd taken to Catherine and blossomed at her attention. Rasmussen was right. She must be very careful how she treated Jim's tender heart.

Chapter Sixteen

Jim's new work at Karak's mill was no more challenging than carrying boxes of alcohol at the saloon or shoveling manure at the livery stable. There was a lot of heavy lifting as he filled sacks of grain from the silo, tied then loaded them onto handcarts, and hauled them out to a railroad car. Dusty chaff floated in the air making him sneeze, and it tickled in his throat even when he was outdoors.

After spending a day loading fifty-pound sacks of grain, on top of a night of breaking prairie sod, his shoulders ached so badly he could barely move them. Pain radiated up the back of his neck too.

As he trudged toward home, he knew there was no way he could work at the Crystal tonight. He needed to tell Murdoch he wouldn't make it in. And he really needed to contact Catherine about the change in his situation. But instead, he stumbled through the stable, ignoring the horses' whickers of greeting, and he collapsed onto his bed to sleep like the dead until morning.

The second day of working for Karak was a repeat of the first, except without a pre-dawn fire to wake him. Jim tended the horses, feeding and watering them. He knew Rasmussen wouldn't exercise the horses and King couldn't stand being penned for too long, so Jim took King on a hard canter across the prairie. He rubbed him down and returned him to his stall before heading to the mill.

His muscles had stiffened overnight. Each movement was agony as he lifted and carried the heavy bags. After a while, the foreman gave him a break, setting him to some general cleaning, sweeping up the golden chaff from the mill floor and organizing a storage room. The mindless work gave Jim plenty of time to think about Catherine. Had she been disappointed when he didn't turn up yesterday? When he skipped the lesson again today, would she suppose he'd given up? Did she miss him at all?

He must explain to her that he wanted to continue, but it would have to be on Sunday, the only day he had a few hours to himself. He'd write a note this evening and slip it under the schoolhouse door.

As he worked, he relived the times they'd kissed and touched, particularly at the river. He was tormented by memories of her pale skin dappled by sun and shadow, her breasts rising and falling as she breathed and the taste and feel of them. He glanced around at the other workers intent on their tasks, then reached to adjust the bulge in his pants before returning to cutting the twine on a bundle of coarse linen sacks.

As he stowed the sacks in their bin, a tap on his shoulder startled him. The constant throb of the machinery that turned the mill wheel shook the floor beneath his feet, so he hadn't felt the subtle vibration of approaching footsteps.

It was the foreman, Tom Peters. "Go to Karak." Peters pointed toward the office and repeated, "Karak."

Jim nodded.

It was nice to get out into fresh air, if only for the few moments it took to walk around the side of the building to the office. He gazed into the slate-gray sky, watching a flock of geese winging south. The clouds still lingered, but there was still no rain. When would a storm finally break?

Passing the clouded windows of Karak's office, Jim saw a couple of figures moving inside. His boss had company. Should he interrupt or wait for the man to leave? Jim hesitated at the side of the building in the overgrown weeds, waiting but also enjoying a brief break in the long, back-breaking day.

The office door opened and two men emerged, Jim's droopy-eyed attacker and Karak. The hair on Jim's neck bristled as he watched Droopy-eyes descend the few steps from the office to the hard-packed dirt of the yard. He stood talking to Karak at the top of the steps. Jim could read the man's lips as he argued with his boss.

"No one got hurt. I did what you..."

Jim's gaze turned to Karak. A finger stabbed the air, punctuating his words. The brush of his moustache hid his mouth, and he was in profile so it was impossible to see what he was saying, but he was clearly angry. His flunky had done something wrong again.

Droopy-eyes shook his head and talked on. Jim couldn't catch everything, but saw the word "fire" mixed into the long explanation.

147

Fire? His pulse raced as the ramifications hit him. If Karak's men had set the fire to drive out the McPhersons, Karak was behind the action. Maybe not directly, since it seemed he was angry about it, but he'd likely sent his boys to cause some kind of trouble for the farmer. What had McPherson done to anger Karak?

Jim realized he'd potentially learned information that might be lethal to him. If the two men saw him standing here and realized how much he'd understood, he had a suspicion he'd mysteriously disappear, taken somewhere out on the prairie for the coyotes to pick clean. He held still in the shadow at the side of the office. Any movement to retreat from the spot might draw attention.

After several more seconds of arguing, Droopy-eyes stalked toward his horse, which he loosed from a hitching post. Mounting, he gave the animal a sharp kick with his heels. The horse's hooves churned up a cloud of powdery dust as it galloped away.

Jim covered his mouth and held back a cough as he waited for Karak to go inside. Then he waited a few minutes more before walking up the steps to knock on the office door. Without waiting for an answer, he turned the knob and entered.

Again, Karak sat behind his cluttered desk. He waved Jim toward the chair he'd occupied during his interview. No matter how polite Karak might act, he made Jim nervous. He hid the tension in his hands clenched in his lap as he waited to find out what Karak wanted.

"Remember I said you'd have other chores? I want you to stay after the mill closes today to unload a railroad car." Krak took a money clip from his pocket and unfolded a pair of bills from the thick stack. He held them up so Jim could see them. "Two dollars for a few hours work."

Jim stared, stunned. What the hell was going on here? He focused every bit of his attention on Karak's mouth under the shaggy moustache so he wouldn't miss a word.

"Unload boxes. Count them. Enter the numbers on a sheet, and keep quiet about the job. That's all you have to do. Understand?"

Jim's throat was dry. He swallowed hard as he nodded.

"Good. There's not many men I can trust, but I know you won't talk." He held the bills toward Jim.

As he took them, Jim felt as if he was sticking his hand into a pile of squirming maggots, the same feeling he'd had when he shook

Karak's hand. Whatever was on the boxcar must be stolen or the man wouldn't demand his silence. This, coupled with the conversation about the fire, made him wonder what the hell he was getting himself into. Was his silence worth two dollars? Was his life?

He fingered the bills as he tucked them in his pocket. But if he could make money like this, so fast, so easy, it was worth it. Not only could he continue to put money aside for the future, but he could buy a suit and new shoes, so when he went to the dance on Saturday Catherine would see he could look like any other man.

* * * *

Miss Johnson. Jim stared at the words he'd written. He'd been sitting on his bed for an hour and that was all he'd finished of the note.

How could he tell her everything he wanted to say with words like cat, sat and mat? Since he'd last seen her, only a couple of days ago, he'd fought a fire, quit his longtime job and had been hired by a man who paid him more than he'd ever dreamed of earning. At this rate, he'd soon have enough money to strike out on his own.

So what if the boxes he and the other two men had unloaded from the boxcar were stolen property, and Jim had no doubt they were. The letters U.S. and a symbol were stamped in black on each box he carried into the shed or loaded onto a waiting wagon. But it wasn't his concern. He was only doing heavy lifting as he'd always done, but getting paid a lot more for it.

The rust-colored boxcar had sat on the side track beside the mill, left behind when the train moved on. The foreman, Peters slid open the door of the compartment and climbed inside to pass boxes down to Jim and another man, whose name Jim didn't know—a big, brawny man who could carry two boxes to Jim's one.

The boxes and crates were different sizes, shapes and weights. Some were so heavy he staggered. Others were light enough to make him wonder if they were empty. But they all had that U.S. stamp in common. What did the symbol and letters mean? Something tugged at the edge of his mind, but he couldn't figure it out. Better not to. Better to concentrate on the note he was trying to write to Catherine.

There were many things he had to tell her, but what he really needed to say was simple. "I've missed you so much and ache to see

149

you again. Every moment of the day no matter what else I'm doing you're in my thoughts. I want to ... *need* to see you again. Please come to me."

Pressing pencil to paper, he wrote. "See me. 7. Jim." He thought a moment and added "Livery Stable." Folding the paper, he wrote "Miss Johnson" on the outside.

He put on his jacket, then walked across town to slip the note underneath the door of the schoolhouse. On his way home, he imagined her arriving in the morning and seeing it, reading it and understanding his message. The power of communication was an amazing thing. But would she come? What if she didn't see the note? What if it stuck to the bottom of her shoe as she walked in the door, or it got kicked across the room, or was swept up as trash?

Worse, what if she read the note and chose not to come. She might be angry with him for missing his lessons, or have decided it was best for her to stay away from him.

Jim shrugged off his fears. If she didn't come tomorrow, he'd simply find some other time, some other way to reach her—maybe at Saturday's dance. He pictured himself in his brand new suit seeing Catherine across the room and crossing the floor with confidence to offer his hand for a dance. He'd hold her close as he'd done that day in the schoolhouse, and sway her back and forth. In his imagination, he could hear the music of the fiddle and banjo. They sounded like the taste of sweet summer strawberries, or perhaps like the warmth of sun on his skin.

He smiled at the foolish fancy, but as he reached the livery and started his final chores of the evening, he couldn't suppress the buoyant hope that swelled in his chest. For the first time in a long time, he dreamed that things might get better for him. Someday he might even own a home and now he could picture more than a faceless wife waiting for him inside. Now Catherine's bright smile welcomed him home.

✳ ✳ ✳ ✳

Jim was late in getting ready for Catherine's visit the following evening. He'd spent a routine day of work at the mill with no after-hours tasks, but on his way back to the livery he'd stopped at the mercantile to buy a suit for the night of the dance. Although it was even closer. It wasn't enough. They needed to devour one another. They needed to become one.

Jim pressed his throbbing cock against her softness. Her moan buzzed against his lips as he thrust. Rubbing against her felt good on his aching cock, but only made him want more.

Catherine untangled her fingers from his hair to glide her hands down his back, slowly, as if feeling the texture of his skin and the strength of his muscles. She scratched her fingernails lightly up the length of his back, and he groaned with pleasure. Finally her hands gripped his shoulders, holding on as she pressed into him as hard as he was pushing into her. The fabric of her dress tickled his chest and stomach. He longed to feel her naked skin pressed against his, her soft breasts unbound. If they were naked, it seemed their flesh would melt together from the heat.

The yearning to merge with her became almost unbearable. Jim thrust into her skirts and the solidity of her body underneath. Cupping her rear, he settled her more firmly against his erection. He kissed her throat, sucking lightly on the hollow where her pulse beat, and buried his face into her fragrant neck. He thrust again and again, grunting a little each time and feeling the growing urgency that warned him he was on the edge of release. But he couldn't stop himself. He pushed hard once more and froze as ecstasy swept through him like a wildfire, igniting all his senses.

His fingers dug into her bottom as he shuddered from the intensity of his orgasm and from embarrassment at the come wetting his trousers. Did Catherine realize what had happened? Did she know he'd lost control from wanting her so badly?

He stayed pressed against her for several moments, loath to pull away from her. When Catherine shifted against him, he lifted his face to see her beautiful eyes shining with tears. His heart pounded and his throat constricted. What had he done? Hurt her or humiliated her with his animalistic grunting and thrusting?

She smiled and touched the side of his face, stroking it gently. "Jim." With that light shining in her eyes it was as if she'd said, "I love you."

He kissed her then set her down on her feet. He picked up the clean shirt he'd meant to put on after washing up. Slipping his arms into it, he buttoned the front quickly and reached for her again. He couldn't stop touching her, and she seemed happy to be in his embrace again. She gripped his back and her mouth yielded to his kisses once more.

When Jim finally pulled away, a movement in the corner of his eye caught his attention. Sheltered as they'd been in a back corner of the building, he hadn't stopped to think of someone discovering them. Now, over Catherine's shoulder, he saw Nathan Scott approaching.

The deputy stopped several yards away, his face slack with shock. Jim released Catherine and stepped away from her, at the same moment, she realized someone was there and turned around.

The secret between them was out now. A third person had witnessed their love which made their relationship feel more real somehow. Jim knew he should be concerned about Catherine's good name. He didn't know how much Scott had seen but surely enough to ruin Catherine's life if he spread the news around town. Yet, somehow, all Jim felt was joy. At last they could be a real couple in front of the entire community of Broughton.

His sense of hopefulness about the future swelled. He took Catherine's hand, entwining his fingers with hers as they faced the deputy together.

CHAPTER SEVENTEEN

When she was ten, Catherine had flown on her friend Janie's swing, digging her heels into the ground then sailing toward the branches overhead. With each pump of her legs she'd striven higher and higher—until the worn rope on one side of the swing broke and sent her crashing to the ground. She could still remember gasping for breath, her lungs failing her. For a moment, she'd been certain she was dying, but then she'd finally gotten air inside her. After that, the other aches and pains of her fall became apparent, but it was always that feeling of the breath driven from of her body that she remembered.

As Nathan gazed at her with shock, disappointment, disapproval, hurt and a host of other emotions darting through his eyes, Catherine felt the same horrible winded sensation. The pleasure and joy that had lifted her up only seconds before evaporated.

She let go of Jim's hand, extricating her fingers from his grip and hurried after Nathan as he walked away.

"Wait!" she called, but he only walked faster.

She followed him through the stable, past the horses shuffling in their stalls, to the dark outdoors. She grasped his arm, stopping him just outside the door. "Please wait!"

Nathan stared at the street as a wagon rattled past. "What?"

Now that she'd stopped him, she didn't know what to say. Her throat was so dry she could barely swallow.

"I know it must look bad. Very bad. Jim is my student, and it's wrong to become involved with a person I'm tutoring. But, we've become very close over the past weeks as I've gotten to know him." She drew a shaky breath. "Believe me I haven't entered this relationship lightly."

"Relationship?" He finally looked at her. "How can you possibly have a relationship with someone you can't even talk to?"

"But I can talk with him, Mr. Scott. We communicate through signing, on paper and... other ways." How could she explain the silent communion between them just through a mutual gaze? He'd think it was merely lust drawing them together, a base, animal attraction, but Catherine knew better. Jim might not be able to share his innermost thoughts and feelings yet, but as their level of communication increased, he showed more and more of himself and she liked the person she was discovering. She liked his interest in the natural world and his gentleness with his horses. She admired his work ethic and she enjoyed his teasing humor.

"It must seem impossible to you, I know. But Mr. Kinney ... Jim and I have a strong connection. I may not know him completely, but I already care for him very much."

"So I saw." Nathan's tone was as dry as dust. She hadn't thought him capable of sarcasm. She wondered exactly how much he'd witnessed, only that final embrace and kiss, or the erotic interlude prior to it?

Blood pounded in her temples and she felt faint as she imagined the deputy watching their intimate moment. It made the passion she'd felt in Jim's arms suddenly seem crude and dirty.

"Mr. Scott, may I ask that you keep silent about what you've seen here today?"

He stared at her hard, as though seeing her for the first time. "You don't have to ask that, Miss Johnson. In my line of work, a man learns the value of discretion."

She nodded, accepting his promise and wishing she hadn't asked the question. Now she'd insulted him by suggesting he might gossip.

"I only came here because I've been following up on this fire investigation," Nathan said. "You probably know the McPhersons accused Grant Karak before they left town."

She nodded. The community had rallied around the McPhersons over the past days, donating clothing and collecting enough money to buy the family railway tickets to Virginia. Meanwhile, Adelaide had spread the rumor to anyone who would listen that she laid blame for the fire at Karak's door. Mr. McPherson had remained silent on the subject. He seemed broken, defeated and anxious to leave town before something else happened to his family.

"The general opinion is that the fire was no accident," Catherine agreed.

"But suspicion isn't enough to arrest a man. Since Kinney is working for Karak now, I thought he might have heard, I mean seen something that could help with the investigation."

"You should talk to him." She was grateful for the change in subject. "He's observant, and sometimes people forget he's around. He may well be able to help you."

Nathan glanced at the door of the livery and back to her.

"I'm not much in the mood for questioning him tonight. In fact, I think it's best I put some distance between us the way I'm feeling." His blue eyes, usually so open and friendly, narrowed. "Honestly, I don't much feel like talking to you either, Miss Johnson, so if you'll excuse me..."

She nodded, aching at the loss of his good opinion. "I'm sorry, Nathan," she said softly as he turned away. It was the first time she'd used his given name.

He paused, the rigid posture of his back telegraphing his hurt and disapproval. "I'm sorry too. Guess I mistook who you were."

He strode away down the boardwalk.

Catherine released a long breath she hadn't known she was holding. What a tangled web she'd woven for herself. She'd never asked Nathan Scott to like her, so that part wasn't her fault. And she'd certainly never meant to become involved with Jim, but she'd followed her impetuous heart. She'd allowed it to run away with her common sense.

What would Howard think of her behavior? The man she'd been engaged to for almost two years, who'd only fondled her breasts a little in all that time. What would he think if he'd seen her writhing and thrusting against Jim Kinney like some sluttish saloon girl? Nathan was right: *Guess I misunderstood who you were.* She wasn't sure she knew herself anymore.

It was nearly eight and she must get home. As it was, Mrs. Albright would have something to say about her taking a walk alone after sunset, but first Catherine had to say goodbye to Jim and tell him about Nathan's reaction.

She turned to go back inside the livery. The excitement with which she'd entered it less than an hour earlier had been replaced by heavy-hearted dread. She didn't want to see Jim at the moment, or continue to dwell on the ramifications of their impossible relationship.

Jim waited only a few yards from the door, leaning against Lady's stall and scratching her forelock. He raised his eyebrows.

"Nathan won't tell." She pressed a finger to her lips. "We're safe."

Jim's expression was unreadable. He took a step toward her, pointed to her and himself and twined his fingers together with another questioning tilt of his brows.

She shook her head. "I don't know. I don't know if we're together. Please don't ask me this tonight. I need time to think."

His gaze was riveted on her lips, then her eyes. He appeared calm, but she noticed the telltale tension in his jaw. She wished she could give him a better answer and tell him everything he wanted to hear. But to wholeheartedly say "I love you and want to be with you" would be a lie right now. Her conflicting feelings were tearing her apart.

Walking over to him, she kissed his cheek. "I'm sorry," she whispered near his ear so he couldn't see her words. "I don't mean to hurt you. I want to love you, but I'm afraid."

She stepped back and gave him a small smile. "I have to go now, but I'll try to see you soon."

Jim nodded, but his earlier joyful expression had dimmed. The hopeful light was gone from his eyes.

Catherine felt his gaze on her back as she left the stable. Hurrying to the Albrights' house, she relived the evening. After arriving at the livery with every intention of talking to Jim, she'd seen his half-naked, muscular body, his dark hair sleek and wet, and she'd lost all control. Her mind fled and her body surged toward him as he reached for her.

She'd never had patience with people who made excuses for their actions, claiming they couldn't help themselves when they did wrong. It was a child's excuse. Now, for the first time, she understood, because whenever she saw Jim, she felt as if an outside force invaded her and controlled her actions. He was in her blood, in her thoughts, and rapidly working his way into her heart.

When she entered the front hall, Mrs. Albright was waiting for her, arms folded, expression stern. "I was about to send Horace looking for you. I know Broughton may seem like a nice, safe town, but a young woman out alone after dark is putting herself in harm's way. Look what happened in broad daylight with those drunkards. There are some rough characters about."

"Yes. You're right. I hadn't counted on how quickly it gets dark now and I walked too far. It won't happen again." Catherine said as she removed her coat and hung it.

"I don't mean to scold. I'm only concerned for your safety."

"Of course. Thank you."

Mrs. Albright eyed her sharply, clearly wanting to say more, and maybe suspecting that Catherine had done more than take a walk. "Well, no harm done, I suppose." She picked up a yellow telegram envelope from the hall table and held it out. "This arrived for you while you were gone."

Catherine's pulse quickened as she took the envelope. News from back east not sent through the postal service often signaled an emergency. What had happened? Were her parents all right? She ripped open the envelope and read the message inside.

Coming to visit November 14. Last chance before snow. Will celebrate Christmas early unless you're ready to come home. Miss you, darling. Mother.

Catherine relaxed as she realized there was no family crisis, but the uneasy rumbling in her stomach remained at the thought of her parents' visit.

"Everything all right, dear?" From the eagerness of Rowena's expression, Catherine guessed she'd been anxiously waiting to learn the contents of the telegram.

"My parents are coming in a couple of weeks."

Could she convince them not to? Mother hated traveling by train. A steamships to Europe was more her cup of tea. She'd despise everything about this poky little town, where the dresses in the mercantile window were fashions from several years ago and a nosy biddy like Rowena Albright was considered the epitome of society.

"How lovely! They must stay with us, of course." Rowena clapped her hands together and offered a genuine smile.

"I wouldn't want you to put yourself to any trouble. My parents will be happy to stay at the hotel." There was no polite way to explain that her mother would probably prefer it.

"Nonsense. It will be my pleasure to host them."

While Mrs. Albright started planning a welcoming tea party, Catherine made an excuse and hurried upstairs.

If her mind had been in turmoil about Jim and their discovery by Nathan Scott, it was now in a complete uproar, her jumbled thoughts clamoring like monkeys at the Bronx Zoo. Her mother in Broughton was the last complication she needed in her life.

* * * *

The evening of the harvest social, rain pelted the windowpanes as Catherine removed her evening dress from the bottom of her trunk. She laid the tissue-paper wrapped garment on the bed and unfolded the transparent paper to reveal black silk voile over blue satin. The dress was as beautiful as she'd remembered— purchased as part of her wedding trousseau for the honeymoon tour of Europe she'd never taken.

Black cord embroidery enhanced the hem, neck and sleeves, and a yoke of cream net and Valenciennes lace decorated the bodice. She fingered the beading at the sleeve edge. She should've taken the dress out much earlier and hung it in her closet, but it wasn't too badly wrinkled, and would do for this evening's festivities.

She laced her corset tight. It would take some work to compress her figure into the form-fitting bodice of the dress. Likely she'd feel faint after spending just a little time in the crowded, overheated grange hall. Well, it would be a good excuse to complain of an illness and leave early. She wouldn't have minded skipping the social entirely, but neither Jennie nor her mother would allow that.

All three men Catherine wanted to avoid would likely be present tonight. Since she'd bluntly rejected them, both Charles and Nathan would probably steer clear of her, but what about Jim? She hadn't had a chance to see him since two nights ago when she'd told him she didn't know how she felt. What if he approached her at the dance in front of everyone?

Oh, Lord, I'm as bad as mother! How could she be so bound by convention? She who'd promised herself to never be a snob? How could she be transported with joy when Jim held and kissed her, yearning for him all the time, yet be embarrassed to acknowledge him in public all because of his lowly station in life?

ready-made, it took a while to find one in his size and to choose a color—a sober, dark blue, although he'd been mighty taken with an expensive checkered one similar to Van Hausen's.

Picking a shirt, tie, new socks and shoes all took longer than expected. He would've waited to tend the horses until later in the evening, but could see Rasmussen had done a terrible job of caring for them. He hadn't mucked out stalls, curried them or treated Lady's injured leg. Jim did as much as he could, but finally had to abandon work to get ready.

He went to the pump, located inside the stable to make filling the horses' troughs easier, stripped off his shirt and worked the handle until water ran from the faucet. He plunged his head and torso underneath the stream. He shook water from his hair, blindly reached for the towel on the hook and wiped his face dry before opening his eyes.

Catherine was standing right in front of him. Early. She wore a pink dress that made her look like a rose, but her smell, when it wafted toward him, was lilacs. Her wide blue eyes skimmed his body before returning to his face.

"Hello," she signed. "How are you?"

Bone tired. Excited. Worried. Hungry for you. "Good," he signed. "You?"

"Good."

Their gazes locked together in a silent exchange that communicated more powerfully than words or hand signs. Raw desire surged in him and there was an answering hunger in her eyes.

Jim dropped his towel on the ground and moved toward her and she stepped into his open arms. He pulled her against him, hugging her tight enough to bruise her ribs. Their mouths fused in a kiss that crackled through his body like a bolt of lightning.

Mine. The thought shone like a star, clear and true. This was meant to be. He felt it deep in his bones as he lifted her off her feet and pinned her against the wall with his body. Her arms went around his neck and he pushed her skirt up to make it easier for her to wrap her thighs around his hips. His hands braced against the wall on either side of her head, and he possessed her mouth with his.

Her tongue slid over his in a sensual mating, fingers twining in his hair and tugging hard enough to hurt when she pulled his head

151

There was a soft knock at her door, and she realized she'd been staring at the dress with her corset half-laced. "Yes?"

"Miss Johnson, may I come in?"

"If you help with this dress. I believe I've gained some weight from your mother's good cooking."

Jennie entered the room, glanced at Catherine in her undergarments and looked away, blushing. "I could come back."

"Nonsense. Please help me put this gown on. I don't know if I can even lift my arms high enough to get it over my head. After that I'll dress your hair as I promised."

The girl gathered the shimmering folds of the gown while Catherine finished tying her corset. It constricted her so she could barely draw breath. She raised her arms and Jennie settled the dress over them. It fit snugly, but Jennie was able to fasten the buttons up the back. When she was finished, she stepped back and gazed at Catherine with an awed expression.

"You look beautiful!"

"As do you. That rose color is lovely with your complexion. And your hair will look perfect caught up in my coral comb. Sit down."

Catherine pulled the small chair from the corner and Jennie sat on it. As she moved around the girl, pinning her long, brown hair up in loose, artful curls, she thought that this was what having a little sister would have been like. Catherine felt an almost maternal fondness for Jennie and had to admit the girl's admiration for her was flattering.

"Miss Johnson. May I ask you something?"

"Of course. What is it?" Catherine separated a hank of hair with the comb and deftly pinned it in place.

"Did you like going to college?"

"Absolutely! I'd wanted it all my life and I really enjoyed my days at Columbia. Why? Are you considering higher education? You should. You're so bright." *Too bright to settle for marriage and family right out of high school.*

Jennie heaved a loud sigh. "It's Mother. She wants to send me to a finishing school back east. She's almost got Father ready to agree to it."

"Oh." A finishing school prepared a woman for making an advantageous match, to carry herself well in society, but had little to do with higher education as far as Catherine was concerned.

"She doesn't approve of Ned," Jennie burst out. "She won't say it, but I know she thinks I can do better than a merchant's son. It's in her tone every time she talks about him. But I love him! I don't want to leave Broughton. I want to marry Ned!" Her shoulders were heaving and her face twisted in distress when she'd finished her confession.

Marry? You're only seventeen! Catherine knew better than to say the first thought that rose to her lips. She remembered her own tendency toward stubbornness at that age and resenting adults acting as if she didn't have a mind of her own. She must let Jennie know she respected the strength of her emotions.

"I know you care for him very deeply," she offered. "And he for you. That's why there can be no harm in taking some time apart when high school is over. If your parents are willing to send you east for further education, you should take advantage of the opportunity to see new places and meet new people. You'll have the rest of your life to be with Ned after you return."

"Do you think so?" Jennie tilted her head to look up at Catherine. "I *would* like to see New York. But what if something happens and he falls in love with someone else while I'm gone? I couldn't bear it!"

"'Love that's tested and tried is true,'" she quoted. "Taking some time to pursue your own interests can only strengthen what you feel for one another."

"I suppose." Jennie fell silent. Catherine thought she'd disappointed her by not supporting her defiance of her mother's wishes.

Quickly pinning the last sections of Jennie's hair, she inserted the coral comb into her coiffure. She pulled her from her seat and guided her to the small mirror that hung over the washstand then gave her a hand mirror so she could see the arrangement from behind.

"You look like you've stepped right out of an issue of Harper's Bazaar," she said, resting a hand on Jennie's shoulder. "Enjoy yourself at the dance tonight and try not to think about the future."

CHAPTER EIGHTEEN

The grange hall was crowded, the air stifling and ripe with the smell of heated bodies doused in perfumes and pomades. At one end of the room, a band made up of a fiddle, bass and banjo played a reel. The dancers faced in rows down the middle of the hall dancing the steps of a country promenade. Couples met and twirled then moved down the line to take their place at the end. The fiddle was irresistible, and Catherine's toe tapped in time to the beat as she stood with Rowena and Horace Albright near the door. Jennie had gone to find Ned the moment they arrived.

It seemed every family in the surrounding countryside had come to the event. For one night, the social barriers were relaxed as the poorest farm families and wealthiest merchants mingled. However, the difference in attire between them was noticeable, with the town ladies' gowns being only few years outdated while their country counterparts wore styles that could have blended in at a barn dance a decade earlier. In her copy of a Parisian fashion with its layers of lace and fabric and beaded trim, Catherine felt ostentatious and out of place. She didn't want anyone to think she was trying to be a peacock, and wished she'd chosen a less showy gown.

As a waltz began, couples paired up to circle around the floor. A passing thought of Howard roused a dull ache inside her that she would always be with her now. How many dances had she gone to with him? How many times had he held her and looked into her eyes with such love and joy? It was on the night of a dance such as this that he'd pulled her outside to a garden for a breath of fresh air and went down on one knee to propose.

"Miss Johnson, your dress is simply gorgeous!" Two of her older students, Sarah Jalkanen and Mabel Driscoll, broke her from her trance.

"The style is so modern." Sarah fingered the material and examined the drape of the modest bustle and skintight bodice.

"I'd give anything to own a gown like this," Mabel sighed.

After a while, Catherine managed to extricate herself from their enthusiastic attentions. "Thank you, girls, but I believe I'm needed over at the refreshment table." She crossed the crowded room to the buffet.

Several of the ladies were setting out platters of cookies and tarts when others were emptied. Again, Catherine was surrounded by an admiring group of women, complimenting her dress and hair and asking a hundred questions about life back east. She reminded them that she was hardly a big city girl herself. White Plains wasn't New York. But they soon had her telling about social events she'd been to, her university classes, and the wonders she'd seen while visiting her relatives in the big city.

While she talked, Catherine glanced around the room. Charles Van Hausen was near the window talking to Beatrice Hildebrandt, Ned's older sister. Nathan Scott was in deep conversation with Mike Gunderson. But there was no sign of Jim. Relief and disappointment warred in her, and she cursed her fickle emotions. Why did she have to be attracted to him? Why couldn't she maintain a proper distance as she'd managed to do with every other man since Howard's death?

"May I have this dance, Miss Johnson?" Herbert Nordstrum, the telegraph operator, stood at her side, a smile lifting the corners of his pencil-thin moustache. He looked very dapper with his hair parted neatly in the center and slicked back, and wearing a pinstriped suit and string tie.

"That would be lovely, although I must confess I don't dance well."

"I don't believe that." He took her hand, and they moved onto the crowded floor. He swept her into a fast-paced two-step. They glided around the floor among the other dancers, and soon Catherine was flushed and smiling. It felt good to dance again.

When the song was over, the band took a break and the dancers left the floor, going to find friends or relatives or stepping outside for air.

"Let me bring you a glass of punch," Herbert offered.

Catherine fanned her face. "Thank you, Mr. Nordstrum." She watched as he disappeared through the milling throng in the direction of the refreshment table. For a moment, her gaze met Nathan Scott's across the room. His expression was blank, and then he turned away. Her nerves prickled as she imagined the damage he could do her if he chose to share what he'd seen in the livery. But Nathan was an honest fellow. If he said he'd keep her secret, he'd do it—unlike what she imagined Charles Van Hausen might have done with such information.

The thought of how much Nathan may have seen invoked memories of that night, the magnetic pull that had taken her straight into Jim's arms the moment she saw him, the passionate kisses and frantic groping, the feeling of his body thrusting against hers until he suddenly froze. She'd realized with a shock that he'd done what men do during intercourse right then, in his trousers, all because of his desperate need for her. That knowledge sent a thrill through her and the heat between her legs hovered on the edge of igniting. Given a few strokes more she would explode too. But Jim had eased her down to her feet, kissing her softly, before turning away to put on his shirt.

Memories of his naked skin gleaming golden in the glow of the lantern awakened need once more. Her sex throbbed with her heartbeats, and her breasts, beneath the skintight bodice, felt as if they were bruised. Her body yearned for the touch of his hand or mouth.

As though summoned by her thoughts, Jim suddenly appeared across the room. At the sight of him entering the door, Catherine's breath caught and her desire burned hotter. Dressed in a navy suit with a crisp white shirt and dark blue tie beneath it, Jim looked as if he'd stepped from the pages of a magazine. The material of the suit was understated, unlike the current rage among young men for houndstooth, wide stripes and other flashy fabrics. The soberness of his attire, coupled with his erect posture, gave him an austere, elegant appearance. His black hair was newly trimmed quite short, but thank heavens the barber hadn't lacquered it flat with pomade. Shiny as a crow's wing, it was brushed in natural waves. An errant lock fell over his forehead, making her fingers itch to delve her hands into that lustrous hair.

As Catherine took in Jim's stylish new appearance, she realized others were doing the same. The people near him turned to look, particularly the women. People leaned together to whisper, as if he could hear their words. Many pairs of eyes focused on Jim at the same moment that he caught sight of Catherine. His eyes shone as he smiled at her. Everyone who'd been staring at Jim immediately looked to her.

No, Jim. Don't look at me that way as if you could devour me with your eyes. Everyone will know. They couldn't help but know what you feel.

Catherine schooled her expression to neutrality and nodded at him then turned toward the refreshment table. Her heart pounded and her body was as rigid as a flagpole. She prayed no one would notice the fiery red of her cheeks.

Over by the punch bowl, Herbert caught her eye and held up two filled glasses. He made his way back to her through the crowd.

Her stomach hurt and she felt lightheaded from the too-tight corset and the crowded room. She wished she was brave enough to flaunt convention, walk across the room and take Jim's hand. But she was a coward and so she ignored him and smiled at Herbert as she accepted the glass.

She sipped punch while staring off to the left, examining Maizie Banks' gown, anything other than look back toward the door and catch Jim's eye again. The fruit punch was overly sweet, but cooled her parched throat. She drank the small cupful down in two gulps. Pressing a hand to Herbert's arm, she leaned in to be heard above the noise.

"Excuse me, Mr. Nordstrum. I must talk to Mrs. Albright about something."

"Save another dance for me later?"

"Perhaps."

She quickly walked away before he could try to extract a promise from her. Over near the door, people had resumed their conversations and Jim was no longer in sight. She frantically scanned the room, praying he wouldn't approach her. She remembered how he'd danced with her in the schoolhouse. Would he want to do that here? Dance to music he couldn't hear? What would people say about the schoolmistress dancing with the stable hand?

Then Catherine saw Jim again, leaning against the wall, arms folded. People passed back and forth between them, but she caught glimpses of his face. His expression was tense and unhappy and his eyes still focused on her.

She ducked behind a large man to hide and chatted with various people to keep the distance of a room between them. Knowing Jim might be here tonight, she'd planned to greet him politely as a teacher would treat a student since everyone knew she was tutoring him. But that smoldering look he'd given her had changed everything. Surely if they got within a foot of each other the entire town would see the combustible attraction between them as if they'd shouted it aloud.

Better to accept a dance with some white-bearded farmer who swung her around hard enough to rip her bodice seam beneath one arm. Better to help Mrs. Hildebrandt cut cake at the refreshment table, or gush over Polly Flint's new baby, or spend a moment in the coatroom fixing Jennie's straggling curls. Better to chat or dance with every member of the Broughton community than admit to the fact that Jim was standing solitary and friendless in his brand new suit, waiting for her to acknowledge him.

At one point, it seemed he might come to her as he moved through the crowd in her direction. But when Catherine flitted away, putting more distance between them, he stationed himself by the wall once more, leaving it up to her to come to him.

To her infinite shame, she didn't, not even to say a quick hello, and when she next stole a glance toward him, he was gone. She looked everywhere, but it seemed he'd left the building. She had no idea how long he'd been gone.

The anxiety she'd felt with him in the room was replaced by heartsickness from knowing she'd cold-heartedly snubbed him. What kind of person had she become to let a man believe she cared for him, let him kiss and hold her, then hurt him so?

The tight feeling in her chest built until she knew she would either burst into tears or faint right there in the middle of the room.

"Excuse me," she interrupted Sonia Parkins, who was explaining how her family had moved to Broughton back in 1872. "I'm sorry. I need some air immediately."

With a growing ringing in her ears, she slipped past the jostling bodies and out the door of the hall to gasp in great draughts of the cold night air. She pressed the heels of her palms against her eyes, as if she could force back her tears. She'd brought these horrible feelings on herself and deserved them. How could she remedy the pain she'd given Jim? Maybe it was better for her to, at long last, leave him alone. Let this slap in the face end their relationship once and for all before she caused him any more grief.

She picked her way across the yard, avoiding the puddles from the rain earlier in the day, seeking drier spots where her heels wouldn't sink in. Without conscious thought, she headed toward the boardwalk. From there she knew her feet would take her to the livery stable. She was weak and drawn to Jim like a compass needle to north. If she explained her behavior, perhaps he could find it in his heart to forgive her.

Lifting her skirts high, Catherine was so concentrated on avoiding the mud that she didn't see the man standing in front of her until she almost ran into him. A cry of surprise startled from her, and she looked up at the tall figure looming in the dark—the horrible man who'd dragged Jim behind his horse.

"Hello there. Where you headed?" The words slurred and he swayed on his feet.

"Pardon me." Catherine attempted to step around him and continue on her way, but his two companions, the black-bearded man and the chinless one, flanked him on either side, blocking her path.

Catherine attempted to turn back toward the lights and noise of the grange hall.

"Wait a minute!" The leader grabbed her arm and peered into her face. "I know you." His breath was sour and hot. She didn't have to see his expression in the dark to know his eyes were bloodshot and his mouth slack. The man was as drunk as he'd been the day he'd assaulted Jim.

She attempted to wrench her arm free from his hard grip. "Let me go right now or there will be repercussions." She glared at him. Inside she was screaming, but she mustn't show fear or weakness.

"Hey, Sanborn, best let her be," one of his cronies warned. "We don't need any more trouble with Karak than we already got."

"Shut up." Her assailant gripped her harder and began to drag her with him away from the grange hall.

The bearded man protested again. "I'm not gonna be part of another one of your messes."

"Let me go!" Catherine fought to maintain an authoritative tone, but she could hear how pleading she sounded. She realized she was in serious trouble and just as she decided it was time to scream for help, Sanborn pulled her close and covered her mouth with his big hand. One of the slender heels of her shoes broke off in a crack in the boardwalk as he dragged her toward the dark mouth of an alley.

CHAPTER NINETEEN

Jim's heart felt as if Catherine had taken and squeezed it in her fist, compressing it into a hard little ball. Every time her gaze swept past him, looked right through him, was like another contraction—tighter, tighter until there was only a solid stone left in his chest. That was when he'd gone outside.

Cold air filled his aching lungs. It tasted fresh and sweet after the closeness of the crowded room. Too many people all pressed together always made him uncomfortable, as if something might attack him from an unexpected quarter.

Despite the chill, he took off the jacket of the ridiculous suit, barely resisting the temptation to fling it on the ground and trample it into the mud. How could he have thought a new job and new clothes would be enough to bridge the social chasm that separated him from Catherine? He tossed the jacket over his shoulder and stalked across the yard toward the road.

It was not as if he'd believed she would suddenly throw her arms around him in front of all those people, or dance with him. But he'd imagined she'd at least spend some time communicating with him in their new language. Deep inside he'd fashioned a fantasy in which their hands flew as they signed back and forth while everyone looked on in amazement. Many people would realize for the first time that he wasn't feebleminded and could share his thoughts as well as any of them given a chance. Stupid daydream.

A hand fell on his shoulder and he spun around, throwing up his arm to knock the hand away.

Dean Gunderson lumbered back a step, raising his palms. "It's me."

Jim lowered his fists, but his pulse still raced.

"Come on." Dean gestured toward the back of the building.

What the hell? He had nothing better to do besides sulk in his room. He followed Dean around the corner. In the back of the grange hall in the glow from the windows, clusters of men stood passing jugs or bottles around. No fruit punch here. A party wasn't complete without some local moonshine.

Jim could tell from the broad gestures and slack mouths as they laughed that many of the men were well on their way to drunk. How many were back here drinking because they'd been rejected by a woman? For a moment, he felt a flash of kinship with them. They were not too different from him.

Dean grabbed his arm and dragged him toward a group that included several farmers and John Walker from the hardware store. One of the men shook his head and waved Dean off, pointing toward the building. "No. Go back inside."

Dean argued and reached for the bottle. The man refused to pass it to him. Jim couldn't see the words, but understood Dean was being denied his right as a grown man to drink with the others. Probably they were afraid of what Mike Gunderson would do to them if they let his dim-witted son get liquored up.

If Dean could work as hard in the fields as any man, he had a right to get stinking drunk with them if he chose to! Jim stepped forward and held out his hand for the bottle. He stared hard at the farmer, and after a long moment the man shrugged and tossed him the half-empty bottle. Jim took a swig, the grain alcohol searing his throat worse than the whiskey at the Crystal. He blinked tears from his eyes and passed the hooch to Dean.

Dean gulped a mouthful and choked as it went down, coughing and spraying liquor from his mouth. The farmer said something. Everyone laughed except John Walker. John gave a reply that shut the man down and made the others laugh even harder. Jim wished it wasn't so dark out here. He'd have liked to have seen the comment that put the man in his place.

After that, Dean and Jim were a part of the circle. As the bottle came around several times, the hard knot in Jim's chest dissolved and his head floated in an unfocused haze. He felt a lot better.

By the time they cracked open a new jug, the men were singing. Walker's arm was slung around Jim's shoulders. Dean's head tilted back, his eyes closed as he howled the words to the song.

Jim needed to piss, and pulled away from Walker's drunken embrace, staggering slightly until he got his balance. He wandered across the yard to the tall grass where the prairie began. He unbuttoned his fly, pulled out his cock and let a long, steady stream arch over the grass while he gazed at the glittering stars scattered across the sky.

When he was finished buttoning his trousers, he glanced at the yellow windows of the grange hall, imaging Catherine dancing with someone else. He looked at the shadowy shapes of the men gathered out back and considered rejoining the group. He should probably drag Dean away before he made himself sick, but Jim decided he'd rather just go home. The temporary euphoria of the alcohol was already wearing off and his stomach was churning.

He was almost to the boardwalk when he saw several figures a dozen yards ahead. A woman was struggling with a man who was pulling her along. Two other men followed. Jim saw the flash of a blue dress. The woman was Catherine. The fog in his brain evaporated as he raced toward them.

Recognizing Karak's men, blind rage ripped through him. He threw himself at the man holding Catherine tight against him with a hand clamped over her mouth. Jim barreled into the man's side and grabbed his arm, trying to break his grip. The sudden attack surprised the man enough that he loosened his hold. Catherine wrenched free and stumbled away from him.

The droopy-eyed man lost his balance under Jim's assault. He staggered backward and fell with Jim landing on top of him. Bracing a hand against his opponent's chest, Jim pushed himself up and straddled him. He punched a fist into his face, snapping his head to the side. Pain reverberated from his knuckles all the way up his arm. Jim got in a couple more good blows before one of the other men grabbed the back of his shirt and hauled him away.

A fist like a sledgehammer drove into his gut, knocking the breath out of him. He wheezed for air as the pain in his belly doubled him over. He glanced up to see Catherine caught by the black-bearded man. She was struggling against him, her eyes and mouth open wide. *Screaming*, Jim thought.

The skinny man, who'd punched his stomach, took another swing. Jim twisted aside and the blow clipped his shoulder. Since he was already bent over, Jim rammed his shoulder into the skinny man's stomach, knocking him back.

Droopy-eyes had climbed to his feet and now he grabbed Jim. Both men were attacking him at once. Jim twisted and lashed out with fists and feet, dodging blows and trying to hit back, but these were men whose business was using their fists. He kept swinging until he was knocked to the ground. A hard kick to his still-tender ribs sent pain shearing through him. His vision went dark. As he tried to crawl away, a boot heel came down on his hand. He yelled and tried to pull away, but the heel ground his hand into the mud. Only the fact that he was lying on the soft ground saved his bones from being crushed.

Then, all of a sudden, the boot and the man attached to it were gone. Jim rolled to his side and looked up. Dean Gunderson had grabbed Droopy-eyes and his skinny partner. His big hands were wrapped around the backs of their necks and he thumped their heads together.

Climbing to his feet and cradling his injured hand to his chest, Jim searched for Catherine, and saw her running toward the grange hall. People were spilling out of the building. The black-bearded man had disappeared from the scene.

Jim turned back to the fighters in time to see Dean slam his fist into the leader's face. The skinny one was about to hit Dean from behind with a big rock. Jim knocked him away from Dean. He slammed his uninjured fist into the side of the man's head. But his opponent was as slippery as the snake he resembled. He kicked out a leg, taking both Jim's legs out from under him. Once more, he toppled to the muddy ground. The man leaped on top of him and began hitting.

But Jim managed to flip him so he was on top. He punched the skinny guy's nose, and then suddenly hands were hauling Jim off of his opponent. He fought against them until he realized it was men from town breaking up the fight. A couple of them grabbed Karak's men and Dean, who was still throwing punches.

Abe Jalkanen kept holding Jim's arms even after Jim stopped struggling. He looked from one face to another, trying to figure out what was happening. Dean fought against the men holding him back and shouted at the man he'd been beating on. The droopy-eyed man was talking. Everyone was talking. Catherine's hands gestured as she explained what had happened. Deputy Scott moved in front of Jim, his back blocking Jim's view of her.

Then Abe released Jim's arms and patted him on the back. The barber leaned so Jim could see his face. "Okay." He made a circle of his thumb and forefinger. "Good."

Nodding, Jim curled his injured hand to his chest and held his arm across his aching ribs and sore gut. His brand new clothes were torn and covered in mud.

Dr. Halloran appeared in front of him, reaching for his hand. Jim let him examine it. Sheriff Tate joined the group. He and Scott were taking Karak's men away with them, presumably to jail. Maybe they'd stay locked up a while this time. Even Karak couldn't save them after they'd assaulted a woman.

Mike Gunderson was frowning and talking to Dean. Since the man always frowned, it was hard to tell if he was praising his son or yelling at him for drinking and fighting. Mrs. Gunderson was there too, her arm around a red-faced and upset Dean.

Jim gasped as Dr. Halloran pressed his fingers. He looked at the doctor's mouth and he was saying something about bandages. Jim searched for Catherine and found her in the midst of a cluster of women like a colorful group of hens. He wanted her to see him, desperately needed to have just a moment of eye contact with her, but Mrs. Albright moved between them and her huge head of hair blocked Catherine from his view.

At least, she was all right. The men hadn't done anything to her. But if he'd arrived any later... Jim shuddered at the images flashing in his mind. He pictured Shirley Mae's battered face. Murdoch should've done something about Droopy-eyes right then to prevent him from attacking other women. But a whore getting beaten by a customer wasn't uncommon and, like everyone else in town, Murdoch was afraid to cross Karak.

Jim felt disoriented and confused, which might have something to do with that last punch in the head he'd received. Events continued to move in disjointed flashes. The sheriff, deputy and prisoners left. So did some of the men. Others stayed behind and talked. Some people went back inside the grange hall. Others came out to see what had happened.

Dr. Halloran waved a hand in front of Jim's face to get his attention. "I need to wrap your hand." He held up a finger, telling Jim to wait, and walked over to Dean Gunderson to examine his injuries.

Jim waited, as he was told, shivering from shock and cold. In the midst of all the activity, he stood alone, as always. He longed to curl up on the ground and pass out, sleep until the throbbing pain in his hand and ribs and head went away. But even more, he longed to see Catherine just for a moment, to touch her and know for certain that she was all right.

Suddenly, there she was, walking toward him. With her golden hair and pale skin, she practically glowed in the darkness. Her eyes never left his face as she held out her hands to him. He glanced at the people around them. Surely she didn't mean to take his hand in front of everyone. Uncertain, he extended his left hand, the other still curled against his body.

"Thank you," Catherine signed before taking his hand between both of hers and clasping it. Her hands were so soft. Fury surged through him that the droopy-eyed bastard had dared to touch her. He'd like to go after the man and kill him. He fought an equally strong urge to pull Catherine into his arms.

"I'm sorry." She squeezed his hand. "Sorry I didn't come over to you tonight."

He nodded, accepting her apology but also offering his understanding of why she'd ignored him. Maybe she understood everything his nod conveyed. Maybe she didn't.

Mrs. Albright swept up beside them, glanced at Jim and began talking to Catherine. She tugged on Catherine's arm. With a smile for Jim, Catherine allowed herself to be pulled away from him. He watched her go until John Walker stepped into his line of sight.

"Good work." Walker grabbed his injured hand and shook it, making him wince and yelp.

Jim pulled his hand away. Others came up to him then, clapping him on the back or shoulder and congratulating him, smiles on their faces, respect in their eyes. It was a new feeling to be looked *at* instead of *through*, but having so many people focus on him at once was a little alarming after being ignored every day for most of his life. He wished they'd leave him alone.

Then Dr. Halloran was beside him again, beckoning. "Come with me."

Dean threw an arm around Jim's shoulders, practically knocking him off his feet, and gestured wildly with his other hand.

His mouth was moving, but Jim was too exhausted to try to read his lips so he simply nodded. He allowed himself to be dragged along with Dean and his parents toward the doctor's office.

* * * *

Jim bent low over Crusader's neck, the wind scouring his face as he rode hard across the open land. He closed his eyes and imagined himself as a hawk soaring high above the earth, wild, free, boundless. Riding always made him feel as if he could accomplish anything, handle whatever the world threw at him. His body and hand still ached from last night's fight and jolting along on horseback didn't help, but it was worth a little pain to have a moment of freedom for himself and the horse.

Poor Crusader had been cooped up indoors or in the paddock all week, and was happy to run as far as Jim would let him. Rasmussen never exercised any of the horses, and with Jim's new job he hadn't had time to take them out. He wondered why someone who didn't seem to care much for horses would choose to own a livery stable.

Finally deciding he'd gone far enough, Jim reined in Crusader and headed him back toward town. Broughton looked small on the horizon, like a child's blocks tumbled across the grass. Jim remembered the wooden squares and rectangles he'd played with as a boy; hours spent building houses, bridges, barns and forts with them. Seeing Broughton from a distance, it was hard to imagine all the people who lived there going about their daily business, each with plans, hopes and emotions they kept hidden inside.

As he cantered closer, the town loomed larger. The charred ruins of the McPhersons' place lay on his left. He thought of the conversation he'd witnessed between Karak and the droopy-eyed man, who was now sitting in a jail cell as far as he knew. There was no way either of those men would be released after what they'd attempted with Catherine. If Karak somehow convinced the sheriff to accept another payoff, Jim would find some way to keep the men from hurting anyone again even if he had to kill them.

Could he actually do that? He was no killer. But didn't working for a man like Grant Karak make him just as bad as those men? Jim guessed Karak's crew were guilty of causing the

McPhersons' fire and yet he told no one. He was sure the goods he'd unloaded from the train were stolen, but he accepted payment for his labor and kept the knowledge to himself. How was he any better than any of Karak's other henchmen?

The invigorating feeling riding had given him began to evaporate as worries gathered in his mind. Should he try to explain to the deputy what he thought or keep silent and accept bribe money? Would Scott even listen if Jim drew him a picture or offered to lead him to the storage shed? Better to keep quiet a little longer. Next time Karak asked him to do after-hours work, he'd check inside one or two of the boxes and find out exactly what they contained.

The town was quiet as Jim rode toward the livery stable. It was Sunday morning and every good Christian person was at church. The rest were sleeping in after a late night of drinking at the Crystal. Not everyone had attended the harvest social and Murdoch's place had probably been almost as busy last night as it was any other Saturday.

Inside the stable, Jim dismounted and bent to unfasten the saddle and lift it off the horse's back. After setting it aside, he grabbed Crusader's bridle to lead him to his stall. He looked up and froze at the vision in front of him.

Catherine stood in the dim interior of the stable looking as fresh as spring in a pale lilac dress. She smiled at him, and his heart swelled, filling his chest almost painfully, as if it would actually burst through. He felt as free and invincible as he had felt racing across the prairie.

Jim reached out his hand and she walked toward him and took it.

CHAPTER TWENTY

One benefit of being accosted by drunken men and nearly dragged into a dark alley was that it was easy to convince Mrs. Albright she needed to stay home from church and rest. There was no need to fake a cough or lie about a headache. From her window, she could see the church and the stream of people entering it. She quickly hurried downstairs and out the front door.

Last night Catherine had learned several things about herself. She was a despicable coward when it came to standing against society, and she loved Jim Kinney—not only because he'd swooped in like some dark avenging angel to protect her from those men, although that had certainly helped solidify the realization. When he'd stood in front of her, battered and muddy, the emotion she could no longer deny surged through her.

Everything had happened so quickly last night it had hardly seemed real. One moment she'd been wondering how to apologize for snubbing Jim, the next she was being attacked, then Jim was pulling her free. She'd watched him fight like a wildcat, twisting, kicking, punching and crying out—a wordless, eerie yell. She was terrified the men would finish what they'd started when they'd dragged him down the street. They might kill Jim this time. Then Dean Gunderson came roaring in like a steam engine. In what seemed like seconds, the fight was over. Nathan took her statement and the sheriff apprehended the men.

Pushing her way through the crowd of fluttering, concerned women, Catherine had walked toward Jim. That was the moment when the proverbial light had gone on inside her. Seeing him standing alone, tattered and blood-streaked, his eyes shining with love for her, the endless doubts of the past month vanished. A single truth shone clearly: *I love* this *man. Right or wrong, obstacles be damned, I love him.*

She might have embraced him right then in front of half the town, but there was still enough of her mother's chiding voice inside to restrain her. Social conventions bound her like a corset she didn't dare take off in public. She couldn't bring herself to do more than hold Jim's hand and offer her apology, then Mrs. Albright pulled her away. When she'd glanced back, men surrounded Jim, but she'd planned to go to him at the first opportunity. Hopefully he'd forgive her callous treatment of him when she did.

On her walk to the stable that morning she saw not a soul on the street. Unfortunately, the livery was equally vacant. Neither Rasmussen nor Jim was there. When she saw Crusader's empty stall, she decided Jim must be out on a ride. She patted a few of the horses, and sat on a straw bale to await Jim's return.

She heard the rhythmic thud of hooves before Jim and Crusader entered the open doors. Jim sat astride the huge horse with a grace and ease in the saddle that was thrilling to see. He didn't see her waiting, so she enjoyed watching unobserved as he dismounted and removed the saddle. His bandaged hand and swollen left cheek, injuries received on her account, made her want to hold him and kiss away all his aches and pains.

The moment he saw her, she knew she was forgiven. His expression contained such pure joy and pleasure that her throat thickened and her eyes blurred with tears. His lips parted and for a moment, it seemed as though he might say something—perhaps her name. She almost forgot that he couldn't, he communicated so much through his glorious smile and his beautiful eyes.

Walking toward him, she reached for his bandaged hand. He gave it to her, smiling as she pressed it to her lips.

"I'm sorry," she said, looking into his eyes, then she let go of his hand to say the same thing in sign. "Sorry for how I ignored you last night. I worry too much about what people think." She signed the words they both knew as she spoke. In summary, she pointed at herself and made the sign for bad.

"No. Not bad. I understand." With a series of gestures he illustrated that she had everything to lose and he had nothing. When he was finished, his hands dropped to his sides.

We just had a conversation about important things and said it all more or less silently. Imagine how well we could communicate after years of practice.

Jim gestured toward Crusader, and Catherine nodded. She watched as he efficiently removed the horse's tack, rubbed him down, and returned him to his stall. He put away the saddle, washed up and returned to her.

There wasn't much time. Although there was a social hour after service, the Albrights would return home in a little over an hour, and she must be back in her room. She didn't want to waste these precious minutes with Jim. She walked into his embrace, nuzzled her face into his shoulder and inhaled the scent of horse, imagining she could even smell the sunshine and wind from his ride across the prairie.

After a few moments of clinging to him, she pulled back and tipped her face up. His eyes zeroed in on her lips and he slowly leaned to kiss them. She felt the gauze bandage tickle her skin where he cradled her neck. His other hand pressed the small of her back, urging her hips closer to his. His hardness rubbed against her tender parts and her sex clenched. Memories of his eager thrusting the other night heightened her excitement. She wanted more of that, more of him. *All* of him.

Her breathing quickened as she closed her eyes and indulged in the sensation of his lips moving against hers. He sucked her lower lip into his mouth, tugging gently before letting go. His tongue slipped between her lips and brushed hers. A quiet moan rose in her throat at the delicious warmth and wetness. She clung to him, wanting more of him than she could have standing in the middle of the stable.

Catherine pulled away from his seducing mouth and pointed toward his bedroom. "Bed?" she signed.

He stared at her as if making sure he'd understood correctly. He looked toward his room and back to her. "Bed?"

She nodded emphatically, making a commitment at last.

Jim swallowed hard. "Bed. Small. Very small." His finger and thumb illustrated a tiny increment. He pointed up to the loft above them.

Catherine nodded.

Once again, she climbed the ladder and inhaled the yeasty scent of fresh hay, sneezing at the dust that floated in the air as her feet stirred up chaff. The creak of the board floor announced Jim's presence behind her. He'd brought blankets from his room, and he pointed at a spot near the small window where a stream of light poured in.

Walking across the loft, Catherine's senses were magnified in the hushed stillness. She heard Jim's quiet breathing, the movements of the horses below, the coo of mourning doves in the rafters. The hairs rose on her skin as though electrified as nervous excitement filled her. Jim's touch on her elbow made a connection between them like a telegraph wire, a silent transmitter of messages. Her chest hitched as she drew in a lungful of the dusty air and sneezed. Jim's soft chuckle bathed her in warmth and set her flesh tingling. It was like having a fever but much more pleasurable.

He spread the brown blankets over a drift of hay and held out his hand to her.

Her stomach lurched as the reality of the moment hit her. They weren't going to just lie together and kiss. She knew that. But was she really ready for the act men and women did together that blessed their union as husband and wife?

She looked into Jim's solemn eyes as he offered his hand. Yes. She was ready. This *was* what she wanted.

She took his hand, and he pulled her down with him onto the nest of blankets. The hay compressed beneath the weight of their bodies, and Catherine felt the hard wood floor underneath.

Jim's gaze never left her face, as if he could read her every thought by her slightest reaction. He seemed to sense her nervousness so didn't assail her with hungry kisses. Instead, he put an arm around her, pulled her close and simply held her. The fingers of his other hand laced with hers, thumb tracing slow circles on her palm. Pleasure radiated through her from where his thumb stroked. How did he do that with such a delicate touch?

His hand was tan and rough, the knuckles swollen and scraped from last night's fight. It made her own slender fingers look small and delicate, incapable of hard labor. There'd been servants in her parents' home. She was educated but probably couldn't cook a simple meal, although she had learned to help out with household chores at the McPhersons'. What kind of a partner could she be for a workingman, who'd expect a wife to know how to keep house?

Jim brought her hand to his mouth and pressed his lips to her palm, and she stopped worrying about the future. She immersed herself in the sensation of his nuzzling mouth, his breath tickling her hand. Dark hair tumbled over Jim's forehead and black lashes fanned against his cheeks. He appeared enraptured at the touch of her hand against his face, his expression like a painting of a saint meditating on God. Then his eyes opened. Half-lidded and dreamy, they focused on hers with naked hunger. Fresh desire roared through her at his starving look.

Jim reached to touch her face with his bandaged hand. She sucked in a breath at the sight of his swollen, bruised fingers against the white bandage. She seized his hand and kissed each fingertip.

He made a quiet whimpering sound and pulled his hand away—only to grab hold of her and pull her on top of him. Catherine felt hard muscle and bone beneath her and his strong arms around her back. She hadn't worn her corset so only a thin lawn dress and camisole separated her breasts from his solid chest. Having her breasts unbound felt decadent, and she realized deep down she'd known they would be together like this when she dressed to come here today.

She leaned to kiss his lips, marveling at their softness, but how hard and challenging they became when he kissed her back. Jim groaned into her mouth and slid his hands up her back and into her hair, pulling it loose of its pins, getting it snarled around his fingers before tugging them free. His passionate kisses fed the heat wakening her body like the spring sun after a long, cold winter. All her doubts and hesitation were crushed under a crashing wave of pure lust.

Rolling Catherine onto her back, he worked the buttons at the front of her dress, his swollen fingers fumbling. She gently moved his hand away and unbuttoned her bodice all the way down to her waist, her own fingers trembling. His eyes glittered as they beheld the shape of her breasts beneath the thin camisole. Slipping his hand inside the open bodice, he cupped one and squeezed lightly.

Catherine moaned as he fondled one mound, then the other, bringing her nipples to hard peaks with tugs of his fingers. Jim lowered his head and sucked one into his mouth, wetting the fabric so it molded to her body. The warmth of his mouth sent electric shocks from her breast down to her sex. She squeezed her thighs together against a gush of moisture.

Slipping his hands beneath her camisole, he pushed it up to reveal her breasts. Her nipples tightened even harder at his intent examination. He brushed his fingertips all over her breasts, making her tremble in anticipation, then bent his head to nuzzle her breasts and kiss them all over.

Catherine cupped the back of his head, fingering the softness of his hair and arching her back to offer more of herself to his seeking mouth. At last he sucked her nipple back into his mouth, and the insistent tug nearly put her over the edge. The tension and slippery wetness between her legs increased.

Jim slid his hand down her stomach and beneath the waistband of her petticoat. Through the fabric of her underwear he touched the juncture of her thighs in the place where her need was strongest. He rubbed her there and she thrust into his hand.

He licked the undersides of her breasts and kissed his way down her rib cage to her stomach; soft little kisses that made her flesh twitch. Her breathing grew shallower when he laid his head on her belly, loosened the drawstring on her underwear and slipped his hand inside.

She gave a startled cry and clutched a fistful of his hair when he touched her sex. His finger grazed the hard bud at the apex, making her jerk at the electric current that shot through her. He slipped his finger lower, delving between her folds, and made a soft, yearning sound in his throat that melted her insides. Her body was on fire by the time he slid his fingers inside her.

Catherine held very still, the lips of her entrance tensing around his fingers. She wasn't sure how she felt about the intrusion. Sensing her discomfort, he withdrew his fingers and moved them back to the sensitive nub. She relaxed under his circling finger. She could grow to like this part very much.

Jim knelt above her to strip off his shirt and undershirt. Her gaze traveled over his sinewy arms, the muscles of his chest and the flatness of his stomach. She longed to trace a finger down the soft trail of hair from his navel to the waistband of his pants to see what it led her to.

Catherine sat so he could pull her bodice down her arms and remove her camisole. With both of their upper bodies bared, he gathered her close to him again. Her breasts pressed against his hard chest and the glide of their skin together was like being stroked with silk. Cool air tickled her bare back, and Jim's hands roamed her flesh, leaving trails of heat in their wake. She wanted to feel his hands everywhere and was ready to finish shedding her dress to let him see and touch her wherever he willed.

Her face buried against his shoulder, she breathed in his male scent and listened to the soft contented sounds he made as he cuddled her close. His lips pressed against the side of her head, her neck, the top of her shoulder. She felt so warm and cherished in the protective circle of his arms.

At last, he pulled away to cup her face in his hands and kiss her again. The scratch of his bandage against her cheek, his fingers warm against her skin, the taste of his mouth, the stroke of his tongue, the dusty air and the distant whicker of horses—all these details held a deep significance. *I will never forget this moment. No matter what may happen later, I will always remember this.*

Jim rose and pulled her to her feet. He helped her out of her dress and petticoat, unbuttoned her shoes and unfastened her stocking garters. She sat as he tugged off her shoes and stockings. When he cradled her naked foot in his hands and kissed the top of it, she whimpered at the unexpected sensation. He caressed her foot, massaging the bottom with hard presses of his thumbs. It was heavenly. He glanced at her face and smiled at her reaction. She must be wearing an expression of bliss.

After rubbing both her feet, he set them down and turned his attention to removing the rest of his clothes. Catherine crossed her arms over her breasts, suddenly self-conscious. It was unbelievable that she sat clad in only her drawers, watching a man undress himself. She was about to see what that bulge in his trousers looked like uncovered.

Jim finished undoing the row of buttons and hesitated, tongue flicking over his lips betraying his nervousness. He took his trousers off, revealing a pair of drawers that fit tight to his form, ending just above his knees. She could clearly see the shape of his erection straining against the fabric, and she swallowed. It looked huge, not at all like the little members which could easily be concealed by a fig leaf on the Grecian statues she'd seen at the museum.

Catherine remembered her mother's clipped tone as she delivered a brief, clinical explanation of sexual intercourse in preparation for Catherine's approaching wedding. She understood the male member engorged and entered the woman's body to accomplish the act of procreation, but she hadn't counted on it engorging to *that* size.

Jim joined her on the blanket again. They lay facing each other. The coarse blanket and shreds of hay scratched her bare skin. She turned her head to sneeze as dust tickled her nose, and when she turned back, he watched her with his head propped on his hand. Lord, she could sink deep into those fathomless eyes and never resurface.

He touched her wrist, slid his palm all the way up to her shoulder, turned his hand and trailed the back of it slowly down to her hand again. She shivered. Even the body parts he wasn't touching were tingling. Her sex throbbed and she wanted him to touch her between her legs again.

But he didn't, nor did he kiss her. Instead, he traced his fingertips over every inch of her face as if he were blind rather than deaf and it was his only way of seeing her. His fingers paused at the hollow of her throat as he felt her heartbeat. He traced the lines of her collarbones and the swell of each breast, his eyes feasting on her body. Memorizing all of her. The gentle stroking of his fingers made every part of her come alive, and his entranced gaze made her feel like the most desirable woman on earth.

She quivered with exquisite tension. Her sex opened, yearning to be filled. Jim had made her utterly ready for him with his slow, sensual exploration. At the edge of her consciousness, moral edicts against what they were about to do nibbled, but she refused to let them in. Here in this loft they existed in a space apart from society's rules. She would let nature take control.

Jim wrapped an arm around her and drew her closer. He kissed her, softly then more deeply, his tongue probing her mouth symbolic of his erection nudging her crotch. She felt every inch of his length rubbing against her, and when his hardness slid over the nub at the apex of her sex, waves of pleasure radiated from the point of contact.

Releasing her lips, he kissed his way down her body again. After loving her breasts for a few moments, he licked and kissed her rib cage and her belly, while she squirmed with pleasure at the tickling sensation. Then he pulled her underwear over her hips and down her legs, exposing her sex to his view.

Her impulse was to cover herself, but Jim moved her hands away, shaking his head. He held her wrists as he gazed at the triangle of hair and folds of flesh beneath. Catherine's flesh burned from the heat in his eyes.

At last he let go of her hands and nudged her legs apart, exposing all of her to his sight. Again he ran his fingers down her seam, delving inside her entrance, letting her acclimate to his touch. He stroked in and out until she relaxed. Then he did something so shocking it made her gasp. Lifting his fingers to his nose, he smelled them. Touching them to his tongue, he tasted her essence. His eyes closed and he smiled as though he'd enjoyed the most exquisite delicacy.

Then Jim did something even more shocking. With a hand on each of her thighs, he bent down to her sex and simply breathed. Then he kissed her there. Her heart thundered and her head swam dizzily as though she might swoon. Did people do such things? It seemed so primitive, like something an animal might do, but felt amazing, especially when his tongue flicked over the little bud at the apex of her sex.

Catherine closed her eyes and arched her hips, lifting herself to his wonderful, caressing mouth. She didn't care whether this act was wrong. It felt too good to regret. With the persistent stroking of his tongue, her deep pulses of desire grew stronger, sharper, brighter. She breathed in shallow bursts and her moan became a high-pitched whine as her excitement grew until the exquisite tension exploded. She cried out as shimmers of delight shattered and sparkled like shards of broken glass. Her entire body arched, her bottom lifting off the ground.

She felt outside of herself yet completely aware of the ripples of ecstasy coursing through her, and her heart beat, and the blood rushing in her veins. One of the horses below whinnied, perhaps in response to her cry. A bluebottle fly droned monotonously. The sunshine and breeze from the window poured over her body. Jim's tongue ceased lapping her sex and his breath puffed warmly against her. Catherine experienced every tiny detail, but as if she was miles above her body.

Slowly, her breathing slowed and she came back to herself. She opened her eyes and looked down. Jim was gazing at her avidly. He pressed a quick kiss to her stomach before crawling up to lie on top of her. She wrapped her arms around him, feeling the powerful muscles ripple beneath his warm skin. She slid her hands down to grip his rear. Beneath the material of his drawers she felt the tense muscles of his buttocks and in front, the heat of his manhood pressing into her. His body was trembling with need.

Catherine looked into his questioning eyes and nodded. She was ready.

Jim knelt to untie the drawstring of his underwear and slide them down his hips. His penis bobbed free, jutting out from a thatch of dark hair. She had only a glimpse of the long, thick shaft, the flushed head and the heavy sac beneath, as Jim pulled off his undergarment and tossed it aside. Then he lowered his body over her and guided himself to her opening.

Jim's shoulders and arms were tensed from holding his weight off her. His face was tense too. He was holding back. His concern touched her. She encouraged him with a smile and a tug on his buttocks.

He exhaled and pushed inside.

Her sex stretched around the girth of his shaft. Catherine had been warned to expect some pain. But the sensation wasn't really painful, merely tight. Then his penis hit a barrier inside her and pushed insistently through it. There was a burning sensation. Her body tensed, her inner muscles trying to stop his inexorable thrust. She shifted beneath him, her fingers digging into his back.

Jim opened his eyes. It took him a moment to focus on her, as though he was coming back from far away. He stopped pushing and held perfectly still, waiting for her to give him a signal to continue or withdraw.

She nodded. "Go on," she whispered.

He pushed farther. She willed herself to relax and accept the little bit of pain that accompanied the pleasure. Because it *was* pleasurable. The feeling of being filled, of surrounding and holding him inside her, a living piece of his body inside hers, was amazing. The sense of union was so satisfying it was worth a bit of discomfort.

Her legs were spread wide and flat. Jim reached down to grab hold of her thigh and pull her leg up. Catherine followed his example on the other side. With her knees bent and her feet braced against the slippery hay, her body made a cradle around his hips. And his penis hit a new spot inside her. This angle was much better.

"Oh," she gasped and closed her eyes as she immersed herself in the primitive sensations of coupling. His muscles tensed and flexed beneath her hands. She relished the harsh gasp of his breathing, his quiet grunts, the sound of their bellies slapping together as he drove in and out. Deep in her core, where the head of his member struck, the formless vapor of pleasure coalesced and grew stronger.

Jim thrust faster, harder, less gently. His increasingly desperate groans excited her greatly and abruptly the growing tension inside her unfurled. Pleasure shuddered through her, not the same intense ecstasy she'd experienced from Jim's tongue on her sex, but something deeper and more subtle.

Then Jim cried out hoarsely and withdrew from inside her. Catherine felt almost bereft at the loss of his cock inside her. His shaft slapped her belly as he pushed into her groin. Warm liquid jetted across her flesh. Jim dropped his face to her shoulder as he bucked against her. At last his thrusting slowed, stopped, and he lay on her, breathing raggedly.

Catherine stroked his heaving back, moved by the way he lost control in those moments of release, and touched by his consideration in pulling out. The risk of pregnancy, which should be uppermost in her mind, she'd foolishly barely considered. Her common sense had been swept away by a tide of passion.

She combed her fingers through the fine strands of his newly cut hair. She'd liked it better longer. There was more to play with.

All of a sudden, something sharp jabbed her hand. She shrieked and bolted upright, practically throwing Jim off her body. He moved to a crouch, instantly alert.

Catherine looked for the source of the stabbing in time to see a kitten's rear end disappear into the hay, tail raised straight as a flagpole. Thin red stripes marked her hand where she'd been scratched. The idle movement of her hand must have drawn the attack.

Grinning, she turned to Jim and found him smiling back. He lifted a corner of the blanket to wipe a smear of white fluid from her stomach. With a glance at her, he shrugged and flushed a little. She was glad she wasn't the only one who felt a bit awkward now that their interlude was finished.

His half flaccid penis was much less imposing than it had been while erect. She wished she'd had a chance to examine it more closely, but Jim was already reaching for his drawers and putting them on.

Catherine did the same, picking bits of hay out of the garment before tugging it up her legs. She searched for her camisole, but Jim laid a hand on her arm, stopping her. He pulled her with him onto the blanket again.

"Good?" he signed.

She repeated and enhanced the sign. "*Very* good."

His smile was satisfied as he stroked his hand up her arm and over her shoulder. Settling on her nape, he drew her to him for a kiss so soft and sweet it made her ache.

"Mm. I should go," she murmured against his lips.

He stopped her words by kissing her again. And again. Then he lay back and pulled her head down on his chest. His heart thundered beneath her ear.

"I can't stay," she protested, but made no effort to move.

She examined the nipple in her view with interest, the dusky disc of his areola with the tiny bud in the center, similar yet so very different from hers. Small, tight, masculine. She reached out to touch it, to trace a circle around it. Her movement spurred another kitten attack. A little triangular face suddenly appeared over the top of Jim's arm, wide green eyes stared into hers, and a white-tipped paw darted out to bat at her hand.

Catherine tapped her fingers against Jim's chest and the kitten pawed her again before disappearing below Jim's biceps. She drummed a tattoo, provoking more play. Unfortunately, the kitten attacked with claws unsheathed this time, digging them into Jim's chest.

Jim yelped and jerked. The kitten scurried away.

Catherine pushed up onto her elbow and leaned to kiss the little scratches just above his nipple. She dared to flick out her tongue and lick his skin. Underneath the salty taste of sweat was the essence of his flesh. Did he like the feeling of her mouth on his nipple as much as she had enjoyed his? He gave a contented murmur and shifted beneath her.

She smiled smugly and looked up into his half-lidded eyes. He pushed his hand into her hair, weight the mass of it.

Catherine kissed his chest once more then sat up. As much as she'd love to lie here longer, she didn't want to have to explain to Rowena Albright where she'd been so early on a Sunday morning when she was supposed to be lying in bed, overcome by the previous night's attack.

"I have to go," she said and signed.

Jim grabbed her arm and pulled her back on top of him. "No." He said it aloud, an atonal burst that sounded like, "oh."

"I would love to stay, but I can't."

She started to pull away from him, and he rolled on top of her, pinning her to the hay. He kissed her seductively, teasing at her mouth with little nibbles and strokes of his tongue, making her lose her train of thought. For several more minutes, she relaxed into the delicious pressure of his mouth and his body holding her down. His hands held hers on either side of her head, and she liked the sense of helpless vulnerability it gave her.

When he broke off the kiss and moved his lips to her breast again, sucking her nipples back to hard peaks, Catherine broke from her trance.

"No. I really must go." She pushed against his restraining hands and wiggled beneath his body. "Let me up now."

He looked up, his eyes as poignant as a spoken plea.

Catherine's heart wrenched. She wished she could spend the rest of the day with him, making love in their secret nest in the loft.

"Don't give me puppy dog eyes. I don't *want* to go. I've got to."

Nodding, he released her hands, but trailed his fingers along her inner arms, leaving sparks behind them. He rose and helped her into her clothes, fastening hooks and buttons. As Catherine worked on the row a the front of her bodice, he knelt at her feet and worked her shoe buttons into their loops. She began pinning up her hair, while he brushed away bits of hay clinging to her dress.

Checking her watch, Catherine saw there were only minutes to spare until the Albrights could be expected home from church. If they'd decided not to stay after service for the social hour, it might already be too late to beat them home.

"When will I see you?" Jim signed.

She shook her head and shrugged. He worked during the block of time after school which she could devote to him. There was no way she could sneak out to see him late in the evening. "I don't know."

His lips tightened as if she'd told him "Never."

She put a hand on his arm and gazed into his eyes. "I want to. Somehow we'll find the time."

He led the way to the ladder, climbing down and waiting at the bottom to take her hand and help her off the bottom rung. Pulling her into his arms once more, he held her tightly for a few moments before releasing her.

"I love you," he signed, his eyes conveying it more clearly than any sign or words.

She hesitated only a moment before responding with the same sign. "I love you."

It was true. But love didn't clear up all the many issues that still stood between them. She had doubts about what kind of future they could possibly have together. As she fell deeper and harder for Jim, her troubled heart continued to waver between pure emotion and the cool logic of real life—a world in which a stable hand and a young lady of good breeding could never be accepted as a couple.

CHAPTER TWENTY-ONE

Catherine's hands and lips said "I love you," but her eyes withheld what he'd hoped to see. Jim no longer doubted she cared for him, but she didn't love him in the same way he loved her—unconditionally. If she did, he'd have seen it in her eyes.

But that wasn't surprising, Jim told himself as he turned the horses out into the paddock. She had everything to lose by loving him while he could only gain by it.

All the more reason he must keep working for Karak no matter what he suspected about the man. It was the quickest way he could earn a lot of money. And money meant power. Money made people respectable. Even a man who apparently had nothing to offer, might be considered acceptable if he had decent financial prospects.

Resting his folded arms on the top bar of the corral fence, he watched Lady frisk around like she was a colt again. Her sore leg seemed completely healed.

Jim closed his eyes and relived every second of this earth-shaking morning. It seemed like a dream that would drift away when he awoke completely. If he didn't commit each detail to memory, the experience might be lost forever.

Catherine had come to him willingly, fully intending to have sex with him. Rather than Jim cajoling her to go beyond a few kisses, it had been a choice on her part, which made their union all the sweeter. How wonderful it had felt, kissing her, holding her, tasting her very essence. He had Shirley Mae to thank for the tip about using his mouth on a woman's pussy.

One evening, after the picnic with Catherine, he'd been working at the Crystal and had pulled Shirley aside to ask her what women liked during sex. Of course, the questioning hadn't been that easy. He'd had to use plenty of pantomime to get the point across. But after understanding dawned in Shirley's eyes, she'd pointed to her pussy, made a slit of two fingers and wiggled her tongue between them.

At the time, Jim hadn't been able to imagine putting his mouth down there, but when he'd been with Catherine this morning it had seemed the most natural thing in the world. When she reached her peak, fingers clutching the blanket, body arching, he knew Shirley had given him sound advice.

And then there was the wonderful moment when he was inside her at last. It was the best thing he'd ever felt. Her channel was so tight and hot, it felt as if it would melt his cock. Just remembering the feeling brought on another erection. Jim rested his forehead on his arms and reveled in images; of Catherine's face twisted in ecstasy, the glistening folds of her sex, her wide eyes gazing into his, her laughing mouth when the kitten had attacked. The smell of her sex mingled with a trace of lilacs was a perfume he'd never forget. And the taste of her...

Jim felt a tremor underfoot that brought him from his erotic reverie. Someone was approaching. He felt their slight vibration of their footsteps.

He turned to see one of Karak's millworkers walking toward him. He pointed at Jim then beckoned with a wave of his hand. "You. Come. Karak has a job for you."

Jim made sure the paddock gate was fastened before following the man from the yard. His thoughts raced as he walked across town toward the mill. He glanced at his companion, a stocky man with biceps like hams and a blue shadow of stubble on his jaw. The man's attitude wasn't threatening, but what was he leading Jim to?

Did Karak really have a job for him or did he blame Jim for the previous night's fight and his men being thrown in jail again? If Karak decided to get rid of Jim, it might not be a simple matter of being fired. Knowing about Karak's special shipments put Jim in a dangerous position.

The burly man didn't take him toward Karak's office, but around the back of the buildings to the same stretch of track where another rust-red boxcar sat. The door was open and the men he'd worked with last time were already unloading crates and boxes onto the platform.

Jim's stocky partner pointed at a four-wheel cart. Jim pushed it over to one of the piles of crates marked with the same U.S. symbol as last time. He lifted the heavy cartons onto the cart until sweat poured from his body and his back ached. When the cart was full, he pushed it toward the open door of the storage shed, struggling to move it over the bumpy ground.

Even with sunlight coming through the doors the interior of the shed was dim. Almost all the containers which Jim had moved there the other day were gone now, making plenty of floor space for the new shipment.

Jim unloaded the cart and steered it back out to the dock. His co-workers had loaded another cart. Again he wrestled it across the uneven ground to the shed and unloaded crate after crate, some heavy, others lighter. His curiosity about their contents grew stronger. The lids were nailed closed. There was no way to pry them open and hammer them shut again given his limited time alone in the shed.

After heaving the last box off the cart, he headed back outdoors again.

Mr. Peters, the mill foreman was there now, directing the loading of a couple of horse-drawn wagons. Jim piled oilskin-wrapped bundles in the bed of one of the wagons, and cartons that felt as if they were full of sand or grain in the other. Once the wagons were full, a couple of the other men tied down tarps over the contents. Jim wondered where the goods were headed, and if the real owners complained when packages never arrived at their destination.

One last small load awaited transportation to the shed. Peters set Jim to do it while the others took a break. This might be his only chance to examine the contents of one of the boxes. He didn't really want to know what stolen goods Karak was dealing in. Knowing could only cause him trouble and make him feel worse than he already did for taking this job. But curiosity won out.

As he entered the shed, Jim glanced back at his co-workers. All of them, even Peters were standing around smoking and talking. He pushed his cart to the pile of goods, and walked around back where he'd set some cardboard cartons that would be easier to open than a wooden crate. With the penknife from his pocket he carefully slit the tape sealing the box, pushed open the flaps and peered inside.

The carton was filled with tins of dry goods. He snaked his hand in and lifted a can. It had words written on it he couldn't read and was marked with the U.S. stamp. Putting it back, he closed the cardboard flap and put another box on top of the one he'd opened.

Moving farther to the back of the pile, Jim pried open the lid of another carton. This one was filled with sacks of flour. No wonder it had been so heavy. He tamped the lid down as tight as he could and glanced toward the open shed door. If anyone came, he was simply taking his time stacking boxes. But he had to see what was in the long crates that had taken two men to carry. Most of those had been loaded onto the wagons, but a couple had been brought to the shed.

Jim found a piece of iron he could use to lever the lid open. He slipped it under the edge and put his muscle into it until the nails pried loose from the wood. He checked the door. There was only empty land and sky visible through it. Crouching down, he pulled up the corner of the crate as best he could with the rest of the lid still nailed shut. A sliver stabbed his hand through the bandage. Inside the box he saw the glint of metal and he smelled grease and gunpowder. Rifles. It was what he'd guessed, but knowing for sure sent fear stabbing through him. Stolen weapons were a lot more serious than some dry goods.

After another glance at the door, Jim tapped the nails back in place with the iron bar. When he rounded the side of the pile and saw Karak silhouetted in the doorway of the shed, his heart nearly burst through his chest. Jim gulped and continued toward the cart, as though he'd been interrupted in the middle of moving the next box. He acknowledged his boss's presence with an unconcerned nod.

As Karak entered the building, Jim squinted, trying to see his face, but he was just a silhouette against the light. Once more Jim got the impression of a stalking predator. He wanted to bolt like a terrified rabbit, but remained standing in as casual a pose as he could muster.

Then Karak turned so the light struck his face revealing his thick eyebrows, hawk nose, shaggy moustache and keen silver eyes which looked through Jim as though he could read his very thoughts. "How are you?"

Jim shrugged.

The man reached into his coat pocket and Jim's heart raced even faster. For a second, he was certain his boss would draw a gun and shoot him, but Karak pulled out his money clip. Peeling off a couple of bills, he offered them.

"For your work today and for last night's trouble." It was hard to read his lips with the moustache shielding his mouth, but Karak always remembered to speak slowly to Jim. More than he could say for Rasmussen after all these years. Too bad Karak was an evil man.

He took a step closer and tapped a finger on Jim's chest. "They won't bother you again."

Jim felt each poke and wanted to rub his chest after Karak had drawn his hand away. Two of the men were in jail and evidently Karak was going to let them stay there this time. He didn't know what had happened to their black-bearded pal who'd disappeared last night.

Karak offered the money again. Jim accepted the dollars with a nod. Wanting to get away from the man's relentless gaze, Jim pointed at the boxes he still had to unload from the cart.

Karak clapped him on the shoulder. "Good man. You're a hard worker. And I know you'll keep quiet about your work here." He winked and pressed a finger to his lips.

Jim didn't breathe until after Karak had walked away. He quickly unloaded the last of the boxes, wheeled the empty cart to the corner, and left the shed. The boxcar door was closed. The other men had gone. Peters and Karak stood beside it, talking together and smoking cigars.

As Jim approached, Peters waved him off. "You can go."

With a last look at Karak, staring down the empty tracks, Jim walked away, praying no one could tell he'd tampered with the boxes. His back itched between the shoulder blades and he glanced over his shoulder to see Karak watching him. Despite the heat, Jim shivered as if touched by a cold wind.

It was already late afternoon as he walked toward the livery. He was nearly there when Deputy Scott intercepted him. Jim felt the thud of boots on the boardwalk behind him. He spun around, half expecting it to be Karak or one of his men.

The deputy pointed at him. "You. Come with me." Before Jim could respond, Scott grabbed his arm and dragged him down the street. He hurried to keep up with the taller man's longer paces. His stomach lurched. *What now?*

The deputy led him into the sheriff's office, past the desks and to the holding area in back. A stench hit Jim like a punch to the face, then he saw the cause of the metallic tang of blood and the sharp ammonia odor of piss.

Still gripping Jim's arm, Scott roughly pushed him toward the cells.

Inside two bodies lay sprawled like piles of discarded rags. One man lay half on, half off his cot. Blood dripped from his fingers to the floor. It was Droopy-eyes. In the other cell, his skinny partner was huddled in the farthest corner, his body curled in a ball as if he'd tried to make himself as small a target as possible.

Jim stared at the bodies and the puddles of red spreading out from them. Other than his parents, he'd never seen a dead person before. His mother had simply stopped struggling for breath one day. There'd been no blood or violence.

His gaze darted back and forth between the two men he'd fantasized killing. The one lying on his back had his eyes wide open, for once without the characteristic droop. His partner's face was turned toward the wall. There was a big hole in the back of his head.

Bile rose in Jim's throat and he clapped a hand over his mouth. He closed his eyes and forced it down, then exhaled a long breath before facing Scott again.

"What do you know?" the deputy asked.

Karak or one of his men did it to keep them quiet about his business. His roiling stomach gave another leap as he realized Scott suspected him in some way. Jim shook his head, keeping his face as calm as he could.

Scott stepped close, towering over him and glaring into his face. "You hated them. They hurt you, and Catherine. You wanted to make them pay."

Jim shook his head harder. *I don't own a gun!* He made a shooting gesture with his thumb and finger then wiped it out with both hands.

"Who then?" Scott demanded.

Karak couldn't bail the men out a second time, not after they assaulted Catherine. He feared they'd give information about him in exchange for their freedom. He shrugged, not knowing how to explain all that and not sure he wanted to. To betray Karak was to risk the same fate. His eyes flicked back to the dead men, away from Scott's suspicious gaze.

The deputy took hold of his chin and pulled his focus back. "You *know* something." A glare twisted his usually placid features until he looked like a baby-faced demon. "Nothing? Then you're under arrest." He grabbed Jim's arm, unlocked one of the cells and pushed him inside.

Jim stared at the balled-up dead man in the corner, at the gore oozing from his head. He looked at Scott, unable to read his fast-moving mouth as he backed out the cell and slammed the door shut. "—think about it."

The deputy stalked from the room, closing the door behind him.

Jim stood with his arms hugging his body, pressed against the bars of the cell as far away from his cellmate as he could get.

That dead man could just as easily be him.

CHAPTER TWENTY-TWO

Catherine should have known something was wrong when Jennie was so quiet on the way to school Monday morning, and later when said she didn't feel well and asked to go home. After taking attendance and noticing Ned absent, she might have been suspicious. But the fact they were both gone didn't register until halfway through the day. Suddenly, like a gaslight sputtering to life, something clicked inside her head. Catherine looked at Jennie's empty seat beside Sarah Jalkanen, Ned's next to Ronald Wilcox, and she knew.

Maybe if she hadn't spent the entire day replaying her encounter with Jim over and over in her mind, she would've noticed sooner. As a teacher, it was her job to be aware of her students, not only their academic lives, but other problems they might have. Knowing Jennie fancied herself in love with Ned and wanted to thwart her mother's plan to send her away to school, Catherine should have guided the girl instead of being so wrapped up in her own romance.

She prayed she was wrong in guessing they'd eloped, but anxiously counted the seconds to the end of the school day. After releasing the children almost ten minutes early, she hurried to the Albrights. Jennie was not sick in bed or in the house at all. Luckily, her mother wasn't either. Perhaps it wasn't too late for Catherine to find the young couple and talk some sense into them.

When she tried to imagine where they might be or what they might be doing, all she could think of was she and Jim rolling in the hay like a pair of animals. What kind of role model had she been for a young girl? Even if she'd never showed her lust for Jim in front of Jennie, the girl might have caught some sense of it in her demeanor. Or maybe Jennie and Ned would've run off together no matter what.

Whether they'd eloped or merely gone some place to spend the day together, they would probably have rented a buggy. Catherine took a last look at Jennie's smoothly made bed and hurried downstairs to head toward the livery.

Walking into the dusky interior of the stable, a perverse onslaught of arousal hit her. The scent of hay and horses immediately brought back every moment of yesterday morning. She shivered and hugged her arms across her tingling breasts. Jim must be working at the mill today, but she hoped he'd appear from the tack room at any moment.

Instead, Mr. Rasmussen came in from the side door leading to the paddock. His glasses glinted in the dim light as he came toward her. "Miss Johnson. How can I help you?"

"Jim's not here?"

"No. Not today."

It was what she'd expected, but disappointment shot through her. "I wondered if Ned Hildebrandt might have been here earlier."

He pushed his glasses up his nose as if to see her more clearly. "As a matter of fact, he came by early this morning for King and rented a buggy too."

"Was ... anyone with him?"

"No." The old man frowned. "But it did seem odd to me, him taking a buggy out on a Monday morning. I asked where he was going and he said he had to run an errand to Hastings. Now, why take a buggy, I thought. If he was picking up supplies for the hardware, why wouldn't he have used a wagon?"

Catherine's lips tightened as she nodded. "Thank you, Mr. Rasmussen."

"Is something wrong?"

"No. Probably not. Ned wasn't at school today, and I wondered where he might be."

"Seems Ned isn't the only one playing hooky. I haven't seen Jim since early Sunday morning. I don't think he slept here last night. Guess now he's working full time for Karak, he's found someplace else to stay. Except, all his things are here." He stared hard at Catherine as though she might have an explanation.

"Oh?" On top of her anxiety over Jennie and Ned this new information added to her sense of apprehension. What did Jim's absence mean? It wasn't like him to neglect the horses or move without telling Mr. Rasmussen. Something was wrong.

"Guess he'll come back for his stuff when he gets a chance."

Before Catherine could reply, Nathan Scott's voice came from behind her. "Miss Johnson."

She turned toward him. "Deputy Scott."

His usually open expression was unreadable, his face an expressionless mask. "I saw you walking and wondered if I might talk to you about the attack the other night. Can you come with me to the sheriff's office?"

"Yes, of course." She thanked Rasmussen for the information about Ned, before following Nathan from the livery.

As she walked beside him, she wondered if she should tell him about the missing children, or keep this family business confidential and go to the Albrights right now. Hastings was the nearest large town and the place Ned would have taken Jennie if they planned to elope. If that was the case, she hoped they could be stopped in time.

"I have nothing to add to what I told you on Saturday," she said, as she quick-stepped alongside the deputy. "I went outdoors for a breath of air and ran into that Sanborn fellow and his friends."

Nathan shook his head and stopped walking. "It's not that. Something's happened, and I need your help."

"What?" The panicky feeling grew worse when she realized Nathan actually seemed frightened. Her worries about Jennie and Ned were consumed by a greater fear. "What happened?"

"Those men we arrested were shot yesterday—in their cells. I wasn't on duty yet, and Tate had gone out, leaving the office empty. Someone came in and killed them both. No one knows about this yet. I moved the bodies to the icehouse. I want to figure this thing out before rumors spread. Sheriff Tate agrees. And I picked up Jim Kinney for questioning."

Catherine felt as is all the air had been sucked out of her lungs. "You don't suspect Jim!"

"No. Not really. But he was the man with the strongest motive so I brought him to the jail to show him the bodies and see how he'd react."

"Jim would never do something like that. Never!"

"A man will do most anything to protect the woman he loves." Nathan's level gaze said more than words. "But you're right, I don't see Jim shooting anyone in cold blood. Doubt he even owns a

200

gun." Removing his hat, he pushed a hand through his hair. "Still, he knows something. I can see it in his eyes."

"You believe he knows who did it?"

"I think *I* know, but I need more proof. Think about it. Who else, other than Jim, would want those men dead? Whose business might they know too much about?" He raised his eyebrows.

Her heart slipped. She put a hand to her chest as if to hold it steady. "Grant Karak."

"He couldn't bail them out again after they assaulted you. The community would be in an uproar." Nathan paused as Polly Flint passed by on the sidewalk, casting a curious glance at them. When she was gone, he continued. "I believe he'd kill them rather than take a chance on them talking. So the question is—what does Karak have to hide?"

Catherine recalled Mrs. McPherson's accusations. "The fire?"

"That and maybe a lot more. I need you to find out what Jim knows." Nathan resumed walking, and Catherine trotted alongside him.

"If he knew something about the fire, he would've told someone by now."

"You're the only one he communicates with, and maybe he only suspects something and isn't sure enough to share it. Or maybe he's just plain scared of Karak. All I know was that he looked shocked to see those men dead, but not too surprised, if you know what I mean."

They were nearing the sheriff's office. Catherine was out of breath from nervousness and from walking so fast.

"So you've had him locked up since yesterday?" She imagined Jim spending the night where men had just been murdered. How frightened he must have been, not knowing if he was accused of the killings and might stay locked up forever. "You knew he wasn't guilty. How could you do that to him?"

Nathan paused with his hand on the doorknob of the office. "A suspect can be held for twenty-four hours before being charged with a crime. I wanted to put a little fear into Jim, give him the opportunity to realize it's better for him to tell the truth."

"You should have gotten me right away." Her jaw tightened as Natahn held the door open for her to enter. She sensed smugness in

201

his attitude. Perhaps what he said was true, but he'd also enjoyed making Jim suffer. She hadn't imagined jealousy would make Nathan so mean-spirited.

The sheriff wasn't in the office as they walked through it. "I waited until I knew Tate would be gone for a few hours to bring you here," Nathan explained as he unlocked the back room. "Karak's got him pretty well in his pocket. Jim's only safe so long as Karak doesn't know I've been questioning him."

The stench of bleach in the holding cell area stung Catherine's nose as she entered the room. There were two cells, barred on three sides, a brick wall at the back, and a cot and a bucket in each. Jim rose from one of the cots and walked toward the bars, grasping them and gazing at her as if he couldn't believe she was real.

Pain lanced through her at the expression in his sad eyes. She felt his fear as if it was her own. She wrapped her fingers around his, clutching the bars. His knuckles were hard and his skin cold. The white bandage was now a dirty gray and frayed at the edges.

She looked into his eyes, offering all her love and support to strengthen him. "It's all right. You're all right." She glanced at the deputy. "Let him out! I can't talk to him like this."

He unlocked the cell and beckoned Jim forward. Catherine noted the bleached patch in the corner and the rusty shadow which still stained the floor.

"Give us a few private moments, if you want me to convince him it's safe to trust you." She stared at Nathan. "You can keep watch for gunmen and your corrupt sheriff while you're waiting."

"All right, but I need to be a part of the questioning." Nathan left the room, not quite closing the door behind him.

Jim stared after him for a second, then at Catherine. She put her arms around him and buried her face against his shoulder. His arms slid around her back and held her close. A quiet groan of satisfaction rumbled in his chest, sending a rush of desire through her. How could that soft, little sound stir her so?

At last she pulled away to sign, "How are you?"

"Bad."

"Nathan told me what happened to those men." Gazing straight into Jim's eyes, she said, "Did Karak kill them?"

Jim shrugged.

She cupped his cheek, forcing his attention back on her. "You know something. Please, tell me." His gaze flicked from her mouth to her eyes and she could see him considering. "Trust me. You're safer if the truth is out."

He paused another moment, then nodded once.

Before she could call for Nathan, the deputy returned to the room so she knew he'd been listening in. Catherine fixed him with a hard look. "You have to promise to keep Jim safe. Don't involve him in this any more than you must."

"I'll do everything I can," Nathan promised, and she believed him.

The deputy led them into the office. He'd locked the door and drawn the blinds on both windows. Jim sat at the desk. Catherine stood beside him, and Nathan gave her the paper and pencil she'd requested.

Arms folded, Nathan leaned against the wall and watched.

"Fire." Catherine scribbled a picture of a burning barn. "Karak?"

Jim's hand wavered back and forth. "Yes and no." He pointed toward the cells and held up two fingers.

"Those men did it?"

He nodded.

"But Karak ordered it."

Jim shook his head. "Angry," he signed.

"Karak was angry at them for starting the fire." She guessed Jim must have seen them arguing.

"He probably told them to scare McPherson, but didn't intend it to go so far," Nathan said. "Then he was afraid his men would implicate him so he had them killed. But we've got no evidence and only a deaf man to testify."

Jim picked up a pencil and drew on the paper a railroad track, a boxcar and a shed beside the tracks. He drew a box marked U.S. with a governmental chevron below, and connected the box to the train car and the shed with arrows. Lastly, he sketched a horse and a wagon with more U.S. marked boxes inside.

"Government supplies," Catherine said.

"Stolen supplies," Nathan added. "Where is this?" He tapped the paper, then shook Jim's shoulder and when he looked up, asked, "Where?"

Jim sketched a cluster of buildings. A tall silo identified it as the mill.

"The tracks run right past so it'd be easy to uncouple a boxcar and leave it behind. All it takes is paying off the right people," Nathan thought aloud.

Jim's hand moved swiftly over the paper, drawing a rectangular box, marking it U.S. and sketching a rifle inside it.

"Damn!" Nathan's florid face paled as the ramifications of the theft became clear.

Catherine's anxiety ramped up to fear. It seemed Karak was more powerful than the law in Boughton. A man who stole government rifles and ordered men killed wouldn't think twice about eliminating anyone who threatened him or stood in his way.

"This is bad." Nathan stared at the drawing and shook his head. "Karak has more money, more power than any man in the county, maybe even the entire state of Nebraska. Unless I have ironclad proof, I don't dare arrest him. I'm going to have to check out this warehouse and make sure this shipment exists before I wire the marshal." He paced across the office to peer out the window through the slats of the blinds. "It still might not be enough to take Karak down. A man like that can bribe his way out of anything."

Jim looked to Catherine to explain what the deputy had said. She shuddered with fear for him. He'd been carrying around this information like a loaded gun. If Karak even suspected him of betrayal, he'd be dead.

She signed the gist of Nathan's words, that he planned to check out Jim's story.

Jim rose from his chair, tapped a finger on his chest and pointed to the shed on the paper.

"It's too dangerous," Catherine protested. "You don't need to go with him. Drawing a map is good enough." She turned to Nathan. "Why don't you send for outside help before you do this? Even Karak's men wouldn't dare fire on U.S. Marshals."

"I'm not going to look like a fool calling them in only to find an empty shed. I won't seek a warrant until I'm sure there's something to this story."

"You think Jim is lying?" Her frustration flared to anger. Why did Nathan have to be pigheaded and put both himself and Jim at risk?

"What if they're not government goods? What if it's a legitimate business venture? Or what if he's already emptied the warehouse. I'm not wiring the marshal until I know exactly what kind of evidence I have." Nathan crossed his arms signaling an end to the discussion. "Why don't you hide Jim somewhere safe until this is over? The livery is the first place Karak would look for him."

The deputy laid out a fresh piece of paper and handed the pencil to Jim. Looking into his eyes, he said, "Show me exactly where the shed is at."

CHAPTER TWENTY-THREE

Jim didn't like being left behind, but Scott refused to let him lead the way to the storage shed. The man was suddenly protective now. What a difference a few hours could make.

Yesterday Jim had remained locked in the cell with a corpse until Scott came back to drag both bodies away. Together they'd cleaned up the mess in the two cells. Jim had spent the night terrified and feeling completely defenseless. If someone decided to shoot him too, there wasn't a thing he could do about it. It had been the bleakest night of his life. Wrapped in the thin blanket on the narrow cot, he'd tried to focus on memories of making love to Catherine rather than picturing dead men or gunmen in the dark. But still he'd felt utterly frightened and alone and feared he'd be locked up for life.

In the morning, Scott had brought him a bowl of oatmeal. A little later, Sheriff Tate came back to stare at him like he was a caged animal, said something to the deputy and left. Another long spell passed. Jim couldn't hold his piss anymore and used the bucket in the corner while staring at the spot where the skinny man's body had lain. He guessed what might happen next. Imprisonment or hanging for a crime he hadn't committed, or getting shot by one of Karak's men to ensure his silence. The best scenario he could imagine was being released for lack of proof and continuing to work for Karak since he feared him too much to quit. How had he allowed himself to get involved with a cold-blooded killer? He should have heeded Murdoch's advice to steer clear of him.

Then, as Jim counted the bars of the cell and the spider webs in the corners, Catherine had suddenly appeared in the doorway like a shining angel in the dingy room. She'd walked straight to him, covering his hands with hers on the bars even though Scott watched from the doorway. Her eyes glittered with tears, telling him how much she cared for him.

Shockingly, Scott released him and left them alone together. Holding Catherine in his embrace was the best thing he'd ever felt. Her lily perfume smelled like heaven after the stench in his cell.

When she'd questioned him about Karak, Jim could almost feel fate seesawing back and forth. There were moments in a man's life when his future could go in several different directions depending on his choice. He'd experienced such a moment a few weeks after his mother died when he'd decided to stay in Broughton rather than taking a job shoveling coal on a locomotive. Working for the railroad would've taken him all over the country, maybe opened new and better opportunities, but he'd chosen familiarity and safety.

Deciding to approach Rasmussen with his proposal to buy into the livery had been another pivotal moment. Daring to kiss Catherine had set a new course for his life, and taking the job with Karak had sent it careening in another direction. Now he must decide if he was brave enough to betray the most powerful man in town. By remaining loyal and pretending to know nothing, he might gain Karak's confidence and even his protection. He might be rewarded with more money than he'd ever dreamed of having. To cross the dangerous man could end in death or being forced to flee town.

Catherine looked at him expectantly with her guileless blue eyes and he knew he really had no choice. He would tell her the truth and take whatever that road led to. Karak couldn't be allowed to get away with stealing, burning out farmers, or killing people, even if they were scum.

After Jim shared everything he knew, Catherine and Scott began arguing about what should be done, forgetting his presence and treating him as if his opinion didn't matter. The deputy going off on his own with no backup was likely to get Scott shot. But Scott refused Jim's offer to help and now he was being left behind as if he couldn't possibly be of any use.

"Come with me," Catherine said. "I'm taking you to the Albrights' until this is over."

Feeling frustrated and weak, Jim went with her. As they walked through town, he searched the street for anyone who might be following them. Maybe Karak didn't know he'd been jailed, but if he did, he might be keeping watch on his newest employee. Jim was ready to push Catherine to the ground if he caught sight of anyone aiming a gun. His body vibrated with energy, blood rushing through his veins and his heart racing.

They made it to the Albrights' home without incident, although a few people on the street stared as they passed. When the door closed behind them and they were safely inside, Jim breathed a sigh of relief. He gazed around the front hall. He'd never been in such a fine house in his life. He wasn't a person whom people invited into their homes.

In the hallway was an oval looking glass in an ornate frame with an intricately carved stand beneath it. Portraits hung against green and white striped wallpaper. A flowered carpet covered most of the wood floor, and overhead was a chandelier with sparkling pendants. The living and dining rooms also had colorful carpets and fancy furniture from what he glimpsed of them through the archways on either side.

Jim absorbed all of this in a quick scan before Mrs. Albright steamed down the hallway toward them. Her lips moved too fast to read, but her body told him she was frantic with fear about something. She barely glanced at Jim before yammering at Catherine, illustrating her words with big gestures.

Catherine put a calming hand on her arm and said something. Meanwhile, Mr. Albright joined them. He looked worried too, but not nearly as overcome with emotion as his wife.

Jim focused on the lips and pieced together that they were talking about Jennie. It seemed she was in some type of trouble. She was a nice girl and he hoped she was all right.

His attention wandered from the conversation he couldn't quite follow. He looked out the window beside the front door to see if anyone was lurking nearby, but the street was clear.

Catherine took his arm, pulled him forward and explained his presence to the Albrights. He smiled stiffly, knowing that if Mrs. Albright weren't so distraught about her daughter she'd probably be staring at him like he was dog vomit. As it was, she nodded distractedly. Catherine tugged his arm, leading him into the living room.

He sat on a sofa, which was hard and covered with shiny, flowery material. He perched on the edge and stroked the smooth upholstery, tracing one of the flowers. Catherine walked to the fireplace and back, arms folded, nervous. He wished she'd sit too. He wondered what she'd told the Albrights about him, and how she felt about him withholding the truth about the fire for so long. If he'd told someone sooner those men might have been in jail and Catherine never would have been assaulted.

Jim pointed toward the front hall where Mr. Albright was putting on his coat while his wife stood and talked at him. "What happened?" he signed.

"Jennie and Ned ran away together. They took a horse and buggy from the livery and went to Hastings. Maybe to get married."

"Love?"

Catherine smiled, but shook her head as she signed back. "Yes. Love. But Jennie is too young."

"Why?" Sometimes he didn't understand the way people thought. If the girl and boy loved each other, what was the problem?

"Her parents want her home." She waved a hand as if it was too difficult to explain and changed the subject. "You must be hungry. Stay here. I'll bring you something to eat."

She started to walk away, and Jim jumped up to follow. He didn't want to be left alone here in the Albrights' fancy house.

The kitchen was clean and orderly, nothing like the chaotic kitchen at the Crystal. Jim leaned against the counter, staying out of Catherine's way as she moved around the room, pulling cold meat and cheese from the icebox and lighting one of the gas rings on the stove to heat the kettle. As he watched her, he imagined what it would be like to share a home and have her prepare meals for him every day like wives did for husbands. He banished the foolish thought from his head. Just because they'd made love once didn't mean she'd ever consider sharing her entire life with him. Still, it must have meant something to her. *He* must mean something to her.

She stopped in the middle of the room, a plate in one hand, a dish of coleslaw in the other, and looked at him. "Are you all right?"

"Yes. Good. You?"

"Afraid. Worried." She set the dishes on the counter and walked over to him.

He wasn't sure if she wanted him to hug her in Mrs. Albright's kitchen where they might be interrupted at any moment, but he did it anyway. He pulled her close and rested his cheek against her hair. She always smelled so good, like flowers, but also the scent of her own body all feminine and warm. The memory of her musky taste and the feel of her pussy under his tongue made his cock harden. How he wanted to taste her again.

Jim released her reluctantly, taking her by the shoulders and pushing her gently away. This wasn't the time or place for being close as much as he might long for it. He gazed into her eyes for a moment then she returned to fixing him a plate.

Suddenly Mrs. Albright plowed through the kitchen door like a steam locomotive. She glanced at him, then turned her back on him and spoke to Catherine.

Catherine nodded and answered while continuing to prepare the food. She set the plate on the small kitchen table and ushered Jim into the chair.

He sat, feeling self-conscious about being the only one eating, especially since the Albright woman would clearly rather have him out of her house. But his stomach didn't have such qualms. One bite of the cold turkey and it clamored for more. He concentrated on eating the meat, coleslaw, fruit and bread, all so fresh and delicious compared to the tinned foods he usually ate.

Catherine set a mug of steaming coffee in front of him, and he smiled up at her. He wished their hostess would leave so he could have Catherine to himself, but Catherine poured cups of coffee for herself and Mrs. Albright and the two women stood at the counter talking.

Jim had just finished scraping the last bite from his plate when both women looked toward the door. Mrs. Albright set down her cup and rushed from the room.

Catherine turned to Jim. "It sounds like Mr. Albright is back."

She motioned him to stay, and left the kitchen. He rinsed off his empty plate, utensils and mug under the hand pump in the sink, and stood feeling out of place and wondering how Nathan Scott was doing. The man was a fool to take such a risk. He should have accepted Jim's description of the contents of the shed and gone in with a posse.

Jim folded his stiff fingers to his palm and opened them again, clenching and unclenching for a few moments. He began unwinding the filthy bandage.

The kitchen door opened and Catherine entered, her expression considerably more relaxed. "Jennie's here. Her father met her and Ned on the road coming back from Hastings. No minister would marry them without their parents' consent."

She took hold of his hand and finished removing the bandage then gently touched the bruised flesh. "This looks painful."

She motioned him to the sink and pumped water over his hands.

As he washed with the bar of soap, he thought about the young couple in love but not allowed to be together. Ned seemed nice enough when Jim went to the hardware store. He wondered why the Albrights didn't want him for their daughter. Maybe his house wasn't as nice as this one or his family as rich.

Catherine handed him a towel to dry off with and glanced at the window. It was full dark out. "Nathan should be back by now. I hope he's all right."

Jim held up one finger and shook his head. He held up both hands, ten fingers and nodded. "More," he signed. "More men."

"You're right. We should get help. Nathan might be in trouble. I could wire the marshal in Hastings myself."

Too late. It will take too long. His gut instinct told him waiting for reinforcements from the city was a mistake.

She leaned to kiss his cheek, a feathery brush of her lips. "You stay here. I'll go get Herbert Nordstrum to send a telegram."

He caught her arm as she moved away, wanting to protest her running around in the dark by herself. But he realized letting her go on this errand was the only way he would be free to do what he needed to. Cupping her face in both hands, he kissed her. Her lips left a burning impression on his even after he pulled away. For one more moment, he held onto her, drinking in every detail of her face and form in case this was the last time he saw her.

"It's all right." Catherine smiled and touched his cheek with her fingertips. "I'll be back soon." She glanced past him at the kitchen door. "The Albrights are upset and arguing so you should probably wait here in the kitchen."

Taking a shawl from a hook in the entry, she left through the back door off the kitchen. Jim counted slowly to twenty and followed her into the night.

* * * *

Monday was one of the quietest nights at the Crystal, which was a problem. Jim would have preferred the staff be too busy to notice him. His first plan had been to ride to the Gundersons and ask Mike and Dean to help, but their farm was too far away. Besides, he had a prickling feeling inside him that Scott needed help soon. Rousing a posse of men in town would also take time and complicated explanations. So Jim decided to go alone to check on the deputy. But first, he needed a gun.

Murdoch kept a pistol behind the bar. It would be easy to grab, as long as no one noticed him. Since he didn't work there anymore he had no good reason for being at the Crystal. But Jim was like a shadow to most people, who generally didn't register his presence.

He entered the saloon through the back exit and lingered in the hallway, looking to see who was tending bar. It was Ted. Murdoch wasn't anywhere in sight. Good. Jim scanned the room. Only a few customers were seated at tables. The rest filled most of the bar stools. Not so good.

He watched Ted pour drinks, take money, and finally, leave the bar unattended while he went into the kitchen. Jim was about to walk toward the bar when a light hand touched his back. He spun around.

Shirley Mae was right behind him, a smile curving her red-painted lips. The bruises from her beating had faded to smudges of yellow and lilac, not quite hidden by face powder.

"Hello! We've missed you. How've you been?"

He nodded and turned away, anxious to be rid of her, but Shirley wasn't in a hurry to get back to work. She tugged on his arm until he looked at her.

"How's your new job?"

He shrugged.

"Your creepy boss is here." She pointed across the room.

Jim's heart flew into his mouth. Grant Karak sat with his back to them, half hidden by one of the support posts in the center of the large room.

Jim withdrew deeper into the shadows of the hallway. Shirley's insistent tugging forced his attention back to her. She was frowning.

"What's the matter? Are you in trouble? Can I help?"

He started to shake his head when a thought struck him. Jim nodded, looking directly into Shirley's eyes. He made the shape of a gun with his thumb and index finger and pointed at the bar.

"You want me to get Murdoch's pistol for you? Steal it?" Her throat worked as she swallowed. "Why?"

Clasping his hands together, he mouthed, "Please."

Shirley looked at the bar, at Karak, and back at Jim. Her eyes were wide. "No. I couldn't do that."

"Please," he asked again.

She hesitated another moment before a sudden hardness tensed her usually placid features. Her broad, freckled face was set in a scowl as she nodded.

"All right. I will."

Without waiting for Jim's response, she walked across the room and went behind the bar. She bent beneath the level of the counter and stayed there for several seconds. When she rose again, she had a bottle in her hand. After pouring a shot of whiskey, she picked it up and started back toward Jim.

Ted returned through the swinging door to the kitchen and said something to Shirley. She laughed. Sweat trickled down Jim's spine as he watched the exchange, but a moment later, Shirley sauntered past Ted and wove between tables until she reached the hallway where Jim waited. Her face was flushed and perspiring. She lifted her scanty camisole, pulled the big Colt from the waistband of her skirt and passed it to Jim.

The gun was heavy in his hand, the metal cold and hard. He grasped Shirley's warm hand and looked into her eyes again. "Thank you," he mouthed.

"Be careful," she said. "Don't get killed."

Not planning on it, but don't be surprised if I do.

* * * *

Fifteen minutes later, Jim lay belly-flat in the weeds on the far side of the train tracks, shivering with cold, staring into the darkness, and trying to decide if the blacker shape within the shadow of a building was moving or not. He'd approached the mill from cross-country rather than from town, tramping through tall prairie grass and dropping to an awkward crouching run as he neared the group of buildings. When he reached the edge of the wild land, he'd dove for the ground, positive he'd seen a patrolling guard near the storage shed.

Too paralyzed to move, he continued to search the shadows with the gun pressed painfully into his gut. Since he was lying right on top of it, he couldn't draw it to shoot at anyone even if he wanted to. He'd be lucky if he didn't shoot his own dick off.

Stupid! What good did I think I could do?

The black shape by the side of the shed hadn't moved and apparently wasn't a living thing. It was safe to go forward, but still he stayed frozen to the ground. What the hell was he going to do? Scott was probably back at the Albrights by now, while Jim cowered in the weeds like a fool.

Just as he rose to his hands and knees and started crawling backward through the grass in retreat, a bobbing lantern moving from the shed toward the mill caught his attention. He identified the tall man carrying the lantern as mill foreman, Tom Peters. Following him were the men Jim had unloaded train cars with, dragging Nathan Scott between them. The deputy was barely stumbling along, apparently almost unconscious.

Jim's already terror ratcheted up another notch. He must act before they decided to kill the deputy. Probably the men were waiting for Karak to return from the Crystal and make a decision.

He felt as if he were outside of himself, a stranger watching his actions as he reached to the waistband of his trousers and pulled out the pistol. The length of the barrel slid coolly against his belly making it prickle with heat. He'd never fired a gun before, but had seen men do it a few times. Sight down the barrel, cock it and pull the trigger, smooth and easy. Still, his hand was trembling so badly he was more likely to shoot Nathan than save him.

Thirty yards was too far to aim accurately, but if he moved closer he'd have to leave the shelter of the weeds and cross the tracks. In the moments he hesitated in indecision, the men moved farther away. They were almost to the door of the mill. Once they disappeared inside, whatever chance he had to rescue Scott might be gone.

From around the corner of the building, two more men appeared, Karak and the burly man who'd fetched Jim to work on Sunday. Everyone who dealt with the special shipments was there. Five of them, all armed, against Jim, who didn't even know how to shoot.

The group in the yard paused while Karak and Peters talked. Arms bound behind his back, Deputy Scott sagged between his captors. Jim imagined Karak giving the order to kill him. They'd probably take him far out on the prairie where a shot wouldn't be heard, or use a knife to slit his throat. Maybe Karak would question Scott before killing him. That would buy some time, but Jim couldn't count on it. If he guessed wrong, Scott would be dead.

As Karak walked away, the two men holding the deputy got him walking again. Still lying on his belly, Jim raised the pistol and supported his wrist to hold it steady. He aimed at Peters and squeezed the trigger. The gun's recoil made him jerk. Jim saw glittering shards of glass flying from the lantern before it went black. The men scattered in all directions, diving for cover.

Jim squirmed through the brush, crawling away from the spot where he'd fired. They'd come looking for him and now was his chance to move closer to the buildings.

He rose and darted across the open ground toward the mill. Reaching the building, he flattened himself against the side, breath rasping in his lungs. Jim squatted and peered around the edge of the building at the open area dimly lit by moonlight.

The men had abandoned their prisoner when they dove for shelter from Jim's gunfire. Scott had apparently been faking being incapacitated at least to an extent, because now he was running in a zigzag pattern across the yard. Bullets tore up the ground behind him, before he disappeared behind the grain silo.

Jim fumbled with the pistol, trying to figure out how to move it to the next chamber. He raised and pointed again, sighting on a man-shaped shadow crouching beside a wagon. Prepared for the recoil this time, he didn't jerk, but kept his arm loose, allowing it to absorb the impact. The man by the wagon fell backward, out of the shadows onto the moonlit ground. Jim had hit the burly man. He wasn't moving and his gun lay inches from his hand.

Jim withdrew into the shadow of the shed, flattening himself against the wall and gasping for breath. His skin was clammy and his stomach churning. He'd actually killed somebody. Suddenly the wood splintered near his head, slivers peppering his cheek. A bullet had drilled into the corner of the building. He scrambled to his feet and ran along the wall in the opposite direction. He rounded the far corner before pausing to breathe.

With no sound to guide him, it was impossible to tell where his enemies were. Out of his sight, they could be anywhere. This was his worst nightmare, the helpless feeling of being in danger because of his handicap. His gaze darted back and forth in the darkness, searching for attackers. He had to resist the urge to shoot at anything that moved. Coming to help Nathan Scott was one of the worst ideas he'd ever had. If either of them made it out of here alive, it would be a miracle.

CHAPTER TWENTY-FOUR

It took Catherine far too long to convince Herbert Nordstrum to go with her to reopen the telegraph office and send a wire. Her emergency entailed some explanation, and he didn't want to send for the marshal without Nathan's approval.

"Mr. Nordstrum, please trust me. Deputy Scott has taken on more than he can handle. Sheriff Tate is of no use. We need more lawmen and from outside Broughton to deal with this matter."

She waited impatiently for the marshal's answer and then had to send a second message to convince him this was no flight of fancy. Her description of the crates with government-issue rifles finally seemed to convince him. And perhaps the U.S. Marshalls' office had caught wind of rumors about Grant Karak already. At last, he wired back to say help was on the way.

"If Deputy Scott's in as much danger as you suggest, perhaps we should alert some men in town," Nordstrum said as he walked her back to the Albrights. Apparently he finally believed her too.

Catherine was about to protest—the authorities would handle it, no need to alert Karak that anyone was on to him until the marshal arrived—when the report of gunfire cracked through the air from the direction of the mill. Her nerves had been singing like tightly strung wires all evening, and now they snapped.

Catherine remained rooted to the spot for a moment. Who could she run to for help? Sheriff Tate was corrupt and Deputy Scott was fighting for his life. A second shot snapped her from her panic. She clutched Nordstrum's arm.

"We need to get some men to help the deputy. Who do you suggest?"

"John Walker's a pretty good shot. Murdoch and his crew can all fire a gun."

"Round up whoever you can while I go to the Crystal!" She raced in the direction of the saloon.

People were already spilling from the tavern onto the street to find out what the shots were about. Men in various states of inebriation and women wearing too few clothes talked excitedly. A few of the brave or curious started down the street toward the mill. Other doors opened on Main Street as those who lived above their stores came out.

"Mr. Murdoch!" Catherine pushed through the crowd to reach the man, who stood, arms folded, in front of the Crystal. "Please help. Deputy Scott is at the mill. He found out something about Karak and now it sounds as if he's in a gun fight!"

Murdoch looked at her then gazed down the street, stroking a hand over his chin. He stood so long it seemed as if he wasn't going to answer her.

She wanted to shake him. *Hurry! There's no time!*

He turned to the man beside him. "Ted. Get my pistol." He raised his voice. "Any man who knows how to shoot, better get a weapon and come with me."

Catherine's sense of panic eased as Murdoch took control of the situation, shouting orders and getting the crowd focused and organized. She might not be able to physically do anything to help Nathan, but at least she'd stirred someone to action.

A minute later, Ted returned from the saloon. "Gun's not behind the bar."

"What?" Murdoch snapped.

"Gone," the man repeated.

"Mr. Murdoch." The red-haired girl, who'd been there the day Jim was attacked, approached. Her hands twisted together and her face was drawn into a worried frown. "Mr. Murdoch, I—I have to tell you something, please don't fire me." The two sentences ran together.

"What did you do?" Murdoch glared at the girl, whose round cheeks were beet-red.

"Jim was by here a while ago. He wanted... He needed the gun, so I got it for him. I think it was something to do with that Grant Karak. I know I shouldn't have done it, but I wanted to help."

"You did what?" Murdoch thundered, glaring at her as though he might strike her.

Catherine would have felt defensive on the girl's behalf, but she wanted to do the same thing, slap her silly face. She pointed down

218

the street. "Jim's a part of that?" *Impossible! I left him at the Albrights. He's safe.*

"I'm sorry. It was stupid, but Jim seemed so sure, and I hate that Karak. The things he does to me..."

Catherine suddenly understood. The woman didn't only serve liquor in the saloon, her other job was something Catherine wasn't even supposed to know about. She tried to imagine what kind of cruelties Karak might commit.

With a scowl, Murdoch brushed past the girl and strode over to a man Catherine didn't know. "Give me your piece, Dodd. You're too drunk to fire it."

He took the man's gun and spoke to the group of armed men who'd assembled. "All right, let's go see what the hell's happening at the mill."

* * * *

Jim climbed a pile of pallets and crawled into the building through a window. Since he didn't know what direction the men were coming from, inside seemed safer than outside, with more places to hide. He could take stock of the situation, try to find Scott, and hopefully slip away when the search had died down.

Crouching behind a pile of filled sacks of grain, he scanned the dark interior of the large room. Only the faint light coming through the windows illuminated the machinery and bins.

Jim didn't see anyone, but that didn't mean they weren't there. He checked the pistol to see how many bullets were left in the chambers. Flipping open the magazine, he peered into the six holes. Four of them showed silver. Two were empty—a smashed lantern and a dead man. Again his stomach lurched. He'd neither liked nor disliked the burly man, but sure as hell hadn't wanted to kill him.

Just as he snapped the chamber back into place, Jim felt the brush of air on his face and the vibration of a footstep on the floorboards. Someone was approaching from his left side. He whirled, pointing the gun. But he forgot to cock it as he pulled the trigger so it didn't fire.

Nathan Scott dropped to his knees beside Jim. His round face glowed as pale as the moon in the darkness. His mouth moved, but it was impossible for Jim to read his lips. He turned his back so Jim could untie his hands. Setting the gun down, Jim picked at the tight knots, but was unable to loosen them. At last, he took the penknife from his pocket and sawed through the twine.

When his hands were free, Nathan reached for the pistol and Jim gladly surrendered it. The deputy motioned him up. Together they crept around the perimeter of the room, heading toward the door. Jim grabbed up a two-foot length of board, used for knocking the last of the flour from the grinder, to use as a club if need be.

Scott put a hand on his chest, stopping him, and gestured him to stay put. Jim kept his back to the wall and scanned the machinery, conveyors, bales, and bundles, and all the shadows they cast. Constantly in motion during the day, the mill was as still as a cemetery at night, the great wind-driven turbine shut down and the grinding stone motionless. Jim glanced toward the deputy. He'd disappeared through the doorway. Was Jim supposed to follow or remain behind?

He went to the door and peered through the crack at the yard where wagons and old pieces of machinery offered a multitude of hiding places. A bright flash, scarcely larger than a firefly, came from near the corner of the granary silo. Across the yard, another flash, then a dark figure raced across the open yard. Shooting.

With no pistol, Jim couldn't be of any help to Scott, so he returned to the spot where the deputy had told him to wait. He felt worthless, cowering in the mill until Scott came back for him. He'd come here to help. But what could he do without a weapon?

As Jim crouched in the dark, his body crackling with energy and his mind racing, it suddenly occurred to him there was an important piece of evidence needed if Karak ever went to trial. Somewhere in the man's office must be a record of his activities— both normal business transactions and illegal ones. While Nathan kept the men occupied in the main yard, Jim could sneak into the office and find information to use against Karak.

He stole along the wall toward the rear of the building where he'd entered. He didn't really expect to encounter anyone inside the mill, so when he saw a puff of steam in the darkness it took him a second to realize it was someone's breath. A man stood near the massive grinding stone and the chute which came down from the hopper.

220

Jim froze. Had he been spotted? The man wasn't shooting at him so he doubted it, but any further movement might draw attention. He clutched his piece of board, afraid to go forward.

The man left the deep shadow by the grinder and headed across the open floor toward the front of the building. Jim recognized him as Peters from the stoop of his shoulders. He would wait until Peters was well past him before continuing on his way. But then he realized Peters would get the jump on Scott, sneaking up on him from behind. Jim had to stop him.

The board in his hands would hardly be useful against a gun. Jim studied the network of conveyors and pulleys above from which large hooks were suspended. Sacks of flour or cornmeal were filled at the reservoir near the grinder, tied, hung on the hooks and moved across the length of the building. They were unhooked at the loading dock and piled on wagons or in boxcars. The conveyors should be empty of anything except hooks at the end of the workday, but someone had left several heavy, grain-filled bags suspended.

Jim grabbed hold of a bag, pulled back and let go, sending it swinging down the length of the conveyor. He was afraid it wouldn't have enough momentum to go far, but the conveyor wheels were newly oiled and the fifty-pound sack careened across the room. Peters turned toward the sound and the sack hit him square in the face, knocking him backward. The gun fell from his hand and landed on the floor several yards away.

Jim raced across the room. He smashed his board across Peters' shoulders, driving the man to the floor, then lifted the board again and brought it down on the foreman's head.

Breathing hard and lightheaded from the rush of blood, Jim stared at the man sprawled at his feet. Peters didn't move.

Jim dropped to his knees. Pressing his fingers against the man's neck beneath his shirt collar, he located a steady beat. He was glad he hadn't killed the man, but now he must tie him up.

Jim retrieved the man's gun and tucked it in his own belt. He cut several lengths of baling twine from the huge spool near the mountain of cloth sacks and bound Peters' hands and his feet securely, then he gagged him with a bandana from the man's pocket, and tied him to one of the hooks.

Jim mopped the sweat from his brow and darted a glance around the dark building, checking for more attackers. His body prickled all over like a cats' fur filled with static electricity. His nerves were on fire as he resumed his journey to Karak's office, letting himself out of the building and darting from shadow to shadow.

CHAPTER TWENTY-FIVE

Catherine stood on the street as the posse of men disappeared around the corner. She felt weak and utterly useless standing there waiting, unable to do anything to help. She shivered against the cold and wrapped her shawl more tightly around her.

"Miss Johnson?" The redheaded girl from the Crystal offered a tentative smile and a steaming mug of coffee. "My name's Shirley. I'd invite you inside to warm up, but..."

Of course, Catherine could never set foot in the saloon. According to society's rules, she shouldn't even talk to this woman. But then, Catherine had done a lot of rule-breaking lately.

"Thank you." She gratefully accepted the hot coffee and blew across it.

Shirley hovered beside her.

"I appreciate this," Catherine said to fill the silence.

"Well, we always have a pot on. Sometimes you have to sober a man up before you can let him ride home."

Catherine smiled at the saloon girl trying so hard to be friendly, and wondered what had brought her to the kind of work she did. Images of flesh on flesh flickered through her mind. Now that she truly knew what sex was, her cheeks burned at the thought of sharing such intimacies with many strange men.

Shirley played with a coral ring on her finger, twisting it around and around. "I know it ain't my place, but can I ask you something?"

Catherine nodded, swallowing the burning coffee.

"Jim's a real nice guy. He's been working at the Crystal ever since I got there. I know you've been teaching him to read and do some kind of hand talking. I think that's real nice of you." Shirley paused. "Anyway, I think he likes you a lot. A whole lot. Just now when you were asking Mr. Murdoch for help, I got the impression maybe you care about Jim too. Do you?"

"I..." How could she answer that, and why should she share her feelings with this girl? It was an odd conversation with a most unlikely person. "I do care. Very much," she admitted.

A sunny smile stretched across Shirley's broad face. "That's good."

"I'm very worried about him," Catherine added. "If something has happened to him..."

She couldn't finish as she suddenly felt the full force of what it would mean to her if Jim were hurt ... or worse. When she'd received the news of Howard's death, it was as if she'd been blown apart on that battleship with him. To learn Jim had been killed would be like dying all over again. She couldn't bear another devastating grief like that.

"I shouldn't have gave him that pistol. It was stupid," Shirley said. "But he'll be all right. He has to be." She gripped Catherine's arm, fiercely. "Someone sweet like him, who's had such a hard time all his life, deserves better. Do you think God would finally give him love then not let him keep it for a while? It ain't right!"

Catherine shook her head, her throat too tight to speak and her vision blurring. Her fears for Jim mingled with anger at herself for having held part of herself back from him all because of her fears.

"He's smart. He'll be careful. Don't you worry! And when this is over, you can both live happily ever after like in the fairytales." Shirley's outpouring of emotion moved her. Tears spilled down Catherine's cheeks as she nodded.

"Sorry. Didn't mean to make you bawl." Shirley wiped her own eyes. Her shoulders heaved as she sighed. "Women have it hard, don't we? Can't do nothing but wait when trouble happens, and we have to keep our mouths shut while men make all the decisions."

Catherine drew a shaky breath and brushed the tears from her cheeks. She noticed the fading bruises on Shirley's face. Reaching out, she took the girl's hand and squeezed it.

"But there are some things we convince ourselves we have no control over when the truth is the power was in our hands all along. There are some things we *can* change."

* * * *

In Grant Karak's office, Jim stared into cool gray eyes that betrayed no emotion. His hands were slippery with sweat against the grip of the pistol he held on his employer. Karak had been in the office when Jim entered.

"You going to shoot me?"

Jim motioned with the gun for him to come around from behind the desk and kneel on the floor, hands behind his head.

Karak stared up at Jim. "You could have made good money. Should have kept your mouth shut."

Jim wanted to laughed at the irony of his words and at the fact that Karak was one of the few people who addressed him as if he weren't an idiot.

He pushed Karak face down on the floor and planted a knee in his back. He set aside his weapon long enough to loop baling twine around Karak's wrists, tight enough that the jute cut into his flesh. For good measure, in case the twine wasn't strong enough to hold Karak, Jim rapped him in the temple with the butt of the gun—hard enough to leave a mark, but not hard enough to render him unconscious.

Jim stripped off Karak's fine silk tie and gagged him with it to keep him from yelling for help, then walked over to the desk. Behind it was an open safe from which Karak had been removing a ledger and small leather case when Jim walked in.

Flipping the latches on the case, Jim opened it. He sucked in a breath. Stacks and stacks of bills filled it, bound piles of tens and twenties. The amount was mind-boggling. The urge to grab a few packets and put them in his pockets was almost irresistible. No one would know, and Jim could turn the rest in to the authorities. No one except Karak knew how much money he had in his safe.

Jim imagined leaving town and starting over, his life paved smooth by cash. He could finally own his own business. When he was established, a real man at last, he could find Catherine again and convince her to marry him.

Jim slammed the case closed and latched it before temptation overcame him. He barely understood why it was wrong to take it. People gained money in all sorts of ways, as he'd learned from watching the world around him. Morals were for people who could afford to have them. He couldn't.

Yet something deep inside wouldn't allow him to simply take what he desired. He set the case aside and leafed through the ledger. It contained columns of numbers labeled with a lot of words that must signify the stolen shipments. He put it beside the case in the kneehole of the desk then checked on his prisoner.

Karak still lay face down on the floor. All Jim needed to do was wait for help to arrive—or for one of Karak's men to burst through the door. He cocked the pistol in his hand and aimed it for practice.

The door burst open. His finger automatically squeezed the trigger and he fired off a shot. Luckily his aim was poor and it only splintered the frame, because the man was Nathan Scott. It was the second time that evening Jim had pulled a gun on him.

Scott was followed by a couple of other men from town. One of them was Murdoch. Soon the tiny office was so full of bodies there wasn't room to move. Jim lowered the pistol and offered it to the deputy then showed him Karak's ledger and money.

A rush of activity followed as Scott hauled Karak to his feet and handcuffed him. Scott picked several men to help escort Karak and his men to jail, while others carried off the men who'd been shot. The deputy also took charge of the evidence and Jim couldn't help but wonder if some of it might end up in his pockets.

Jim leaned against the outside wall of Karak's office and watched the other men milling around. His legs trembled almost too much to hold him upright. He felt he could stay propped against the wall until he simply melted into it. Sometimes it was good to be overlooked and left alone. But after a bit Murdoch came over to him.

Murdoch looked him in the eyes. "Good job." He shook Jim's hand before pulling him away from the wall. With a guiding hand on his back, he escorted him across the mill yard. Several other men nodded at Jim or shook his hand. Soon he was part of the group walking back toward the center of town. Jim felt as if he was walking in one of those daydreams he used to have in which he did something heroic and the town acknowledged him. But he was dead tired and ready to sink into blackness and not wake up for about twelve hours.

Up ahead, clusters of people drawn by the gunfire waited to find out what was going on. Murdoch slapped Jim between his shoulder blades to get his attention and pointed at the group ahead. He said something, but it was too dark and Jim was too tired to read his lips. Would this night ever be over? He still had to go back to the Albrights and explain to Catherine everything that had happened.

All of a sudden, she was there, breaking away from a group of women and running toward him. She raced across the space between them and threw her arms around him. The force of her body knocked him back a few steps as she wrapped around him like a trumpet vine on a cornstalk.

He regained his footing and hugged her right back. His exhaustion disappeared in a second, erased by the incredible fact that Catherine was embracing him right there on the street in front of half the town. She lifted her face to kiss him. The warmth and pressure of her mouth melted away the anxiety and tensionstill floating in him and filled him with wild elation instead.

After several moments of feasting on her mouth like a starving man, he pulled away and his eyes opened. Her tear-streaked face filled his vision. His stomach dropped. Why was she crying? What had happened to her?

Suddenly he was aware of the crowd of people gathering around them. Glancing up, he saw many eyes focused on him and Catherine, mouths talking, expressions of surprise and shock. He let go of her and stepped back, although it was far too late to protect her reputation.

Catherine cupped his face, drawing his attention back to her, and her lips were moving. "...don't you? Never again!" She frowned and signed as she spoke. "Never! Understand? I love you." Her graceful hands made the love sign, which looked as if she was offering her heart to him.

At last Jim realized the reason she was upset was because he'd been in danger. If he'd doubted that she cared, those doubts evaporated under the force of her fury. He nodded and promised. He had absolutely no intention of ever using a gun again the rest of his life. The memory of the lifeless body of the man he'd shot, the wide staring eyes, haunted him.

"Good!" she finished and added, "Are you all right?"

Smiling, he joined his thumb and index finger in a circle. He pointed at her. "You?"

"Much better now." She grabbed hold of both his hands and held them tight.

* * * *

Holding Jim's hand in a firm grip to ensure that he was truly safe beside her, Catherine turned to Murdoch.

"What happened, Mr. Murdoch? Is Deputy Scott all right? Was anyone hurt?"

"Two of Karak's men were shot and died. Trace Hazen was shot, but it looks like just a graze. Karak and the rest of his boys were arrested."

"The marshal should be on his way," she told him. "He can take them to the county jail in Hastings. Stolen government goods make it a federal matter."

"Scott says it looks like supplies headed for a reservation out west, and the rifles were army issue," Murdoch said.

"An Indian reservation?" Catherine glanced at Jim to include him in the conversation. His eyes were glazed over and she could see he was too tired to care. She gave his hand a gentle squeeze.

"Blankets, food, dry goods and medicine. Karak's mill operation made a good cover and gave easy access to the rails."

"Wouldn't someone notice when the inventory was off?"

Murdoch laughed. "I was in the army for a while just after the war. The U.S. government's the biggest boondoggle you ever heard of, especially the military. There's *always* somebody skimming, making a little nest egg for after he's discharged. Army pay doesn't amount to much." His glance at the Crystal suggested he'd made such a nest egg for himself, allowing him to open his own business.

"Do you think there's enough evidence to make a good case against Mr. Karak?"

He shrugged. "There's enough evidence, but whether it will be allowed in court is another question. Karak is very wealthy and powerful. He might be in jail tonight, but men like him rarely go to prison."

Catherine thought about the injustice of Karak spending a few nights in jail the same as Jim who'd done nothing wrong. Buying and controlling an entire town hadn't been enough for Grant Karak. His greed extended to robbing Indians of the basic necessities of life so he

228

could make even more money. A man like that seemed more interested in the process of gaining power than in actually spending his accumulated fortune.

Catherine thanked Murdoch for coming to Nathan and Jim's aid and bid him goodnight.

"Come back to work for me if you want." Murdoch patted Jim on the shoulder, and walked away.

Slipping an arm around Jim's back Catherine urged him forward. "Come on. You need to rest."

Together they walked up the street, past the clusters of people who still stood discussing the evening's excitement. Faces turned as they walked by, some smiling, some frowning, but Catherine kept her arm around Jim and held her head high. She no longer feared gossip or disapproval. She knew what she'd nearly lost and was determined never to risk losing love again.

CHAPTER TWENTY-SIX

The schoolhouse was crowded with adults wedged into desks intended for children. More parents sat in chairs at the back of the room. The teachers' desk had been moved aside to make room for a temporary stage at the front. The students sat in a row of chairs along one wall, youngest to oldest, each awaiting his or her turn to display knowledge.

Melissa Van Hausen perched on the edge of her seat, her face shining with excitement. She appeared ready to jump on the stage and launch into her poem at any second, while Minnie Davis, pressed to the back of her chair, legs dangling, seemed frozen. Her face was so pale Catherine feared she might faint if she tried to walk to the platform to recite her piece. She hurried over to give words of encouragement to the stage-struck child.

"Are you going to be all right, Minnie?" she asked, squatting in front of her.

The little girl stared with dazed eyes at the people filling the room and shook her head.

Catherine had never believed in forcing a child to speak or read in front of the class when they were nearly incapacitated with fear. Some children weren't natural speakers and she'd rather ease them into losing their shyness than force them into it.

"Would you like it if Melissa stood with you while you recite your poem?" A frantic nod answered her question. "Would you do that, Melissa? Go up with Minnie?"

"Oh, yes!" The girl's already bright eyes went starry and she wiggled in her seat, clicking her polished shoes together. "Don't be afraid, Minnie. I'll be with you," she said with the aplomb of one who was a whole nine months older.

Catherine was glad Melissa's cheerful energy hadn't been dimmed by the pall over the Van Hausen family. Since Charles had been charged with illegal banking practices in connection with the

Karak case and was facing jail time or at the very least heavy fines, his parents could barely hold up their heads in the community. Luckily, the situation didn't seem to affect the youngest Van Hausen.

Catherine moved down the line, checking on each of her students one last time. In the last two seats sat Jennie and Ned. Their elopement might have been aborted but they were inseparable and said they were "engaged" although Jennie's parents hadn't approved it. She was still leaving for finishing school right after the Christmas holiday, Mrs. Albright evidently hoping to cool the romance before the long winter months locked Ned and Jennie even closer together. It would be interesting to see if Jennie's experience broadened her horizons or if she came back to Broughton to settle down with her intended.

Catherine scanned the room full of proud relatives and parents—including her own. She flashed a smile at her father and mother, who looked as out of place as peacocks in a flock of chickens. Father was dressed in a business suit that blended well enough with the other men's clothing, but Mother's brocade gown was too elegant, her hairstyle sophisticated and the very tilt of her chin rather arrogant. This was simply the way she carried herself, but her demeanor certainly made her appear snobbish.

Jim hadn't arrived yet. He was back to work at both the livery and the Crystal Saloon, so Catherine hadn't expected him to be here in time for the children's presentation. It was just as well. She would rather get through that portion of the evening before the real event of her night began—introducing Jim to her parents.

Over the past few weeks, the people of Broughton had come to accept they were a couple. No doubt there was still plenty of talk behind her back, but they'd been careful to keep their relationship out in the open, barely stealing an occasional kiss let alone sneaking off to the hayloft to indulge in earthier pursuits. Her behavior had been irreproachable.

Of course, Mrs. Albright had offered advice. "I'm speaking for your mother, dear, since she's not here to counsel you. You must realize what an inappropriate choice that man is for you. He has a severe handicap and no prospects. What could an educated young woman like you possibly find appealing in him? You must consider your future and unsuitable nature of this attachment before things go too far."

Catherine hadn't tried to explain herself, knowing Rowena wouldn't really hear what she had to say and would never understand even if she listened. Instead, Catherine had promised to consider the advice, but continued tutoring Jim and spending as much time with him as possible. To her surprise, the school board hadn't threatened to fire her, proving her fears unfounded.

But now her mother was here and would, no doubt, give the same lecture as Mrs. Albright and more. After meeting her parents at the train station, Catherine had intended to tell them everything about her months in Broughton, including her relationship with Jim, but the words had stuck in her throat. She'd talked about her students, the people in the community and mentioned that she was tutoring after school. Before she could rouse the courage to explain that Jim was much more to her than a student, Mother had launched into one anecdote after another about people in White Plains. Catherine had allowed her to prattle on, glad to put off the revelation.

As they'd walked from the train station to the Albrights, Mother had made snide comments about backwater towns, but Father had hugged Catherine with one arm and spoken about their journey and what a marvel modern transportation was. After arriving at the Albrights, Rowena Albright had monopolized the conversation, clearly trying to impress them with the fact that she was the hub of the social wheel in Broughton.

As they freshened up and ate dinner with the Albrights, Catherine had no opportunity to tell her parents about Jim. And then it was time for her to go to the schoolhouse to set up. But in the back of her mind, she knew she was putting off what she feared. Presenting Jim to her parents as the man she loved was not going to be easy. She should've warned them ahead of time and now it was too late.

She pushed her worries out of her mind and concentrated on the school program. Stepping up on the low platform John Walker had erected for the event, she raised her hand for silence. Voices lowered to a murmur, then stopped. Only an occasional cough disturbed the quiet.

"Good evening." She smiled, making eye contact with several people around the room. "Welcome to our school open house. Your children have been studying diligently and learning so much. They're very eager to display some of their newfound knowledge tonight, so without further ado, let us all rise for the Pledge of Allegiance."

She turned to face the flag and there was a rustle of clothing as everyone did the same. When the pledge was finished, Catherine stepped down from the stage and sat in the empty seat by her parents. Her father's twinkling eyes and the warm smile lifting the edges of his moustache gave a lift to her heart. He grasped her hand and continued to hold it as Minnie gave her recitation.

Catherine nearly forgot her own fears she was so caught up in Minnie's. The girl's eyes were huge and her soft voice didn't carry beyond the first row. After a few lines of *The Old Cherry Tree*, Minnie fell silent, fumbling for words. Catherine's heart beat faster, willing her to get through the piece.

Luckily, Melissa, who stood beside her frightened friend, had the good sense to whisper the next line loudly. "The blossoms fall. A drift of white..."

Minnie sucked in a breath and repeated the line. She finished the rest of the poem in one breath, her face a fiery red. Both the little girl and Catherine heaved a sigh of relief when it was over, and the audience politely applauded.

Minnie had barely returned to her seat before Melissa launched into her poem, *The Old Blacksmith*. Line after line with increasing speed and fervor, she nearly shouted the words, bringing the poem to a resounding conclusion.

The rest of the performers recited pieces, solved math problems on the blackboard or gave short geography lessons using the map at the front of the room, according to their preference. Dale Timmerman, who wasn't too creative, listed the presidents in order from George Washington all the way up to Theodore Roosevelt. Sarah Jalkanen gave a wonderful description of the daily lives of the Sioux, who had peopled the prairies prior to the settlement by pioneers.

Jennie Albright took her place on stage to recite the Declaration of Independence. When she reached the words "...that they are endowed by their Creator with the right to life, liberty and the pursuit of happiness..." she gazed pointedly at her mother.

Hostility simmered in the Albrights' house these days as formerly sweet, pliant Jennie demonstrated her rebellion in not so subtle ways every day. Her parents might have control over her life, but she wasn't going to surrender easily. Catherine tried to counsel her to look on the East Coast experience as a great opportunity to see another part of the country, but all Jennie could see was that she was being torn away from Ned.

She finished her recitation and spoke about what the words meant to her, something she hadn't pre-approved with Catherine. "I'm sure you all agree with President Lincoln that God wants us to be happy and free to live as we choose. No one should have the right to dictate other peoples' lives. This extends to the poor and the rich, men and women, young people as well as old. Thank you."

Another glare at her mother and Jennie took her seat.

Ned was the last to recite. He launched into an enthusiastic dissection of the workings of the new electric light bulb, which he believed would one day replace gas for home illumination. During his speech, which devolved into far too much detail, Catherine heard the door open. Her gaze darted to Jim entering the building and moving to stand along the wall with other latecomers. His eyes found hers and a smile curved his lips and lit his eyes.

Her heart thumped wildly. It always sped when she saw him, but tonight anxiety was mingled with love. Oh how she wished she'd taken time to properly prepare her parents for this news. She didn't want the shock on her mother's face to hurt Jim, and knew he couldn't help but read any disapproval in her expression.

At last Ned finished talking about electricity and his speech ended with the idealistic conclusion. "Electricity will revolutionize our world and the steam engine will someday be a footnote in history. Thank you."

Catherine's father leaned to whisper, "Quite the young radicals you're educating."

"I taught them critical thinking as you did for me, Daddy. What they do with it is beyond my control, although I must say I think Ned's electric-powered future seems unlikely. It could never be as cost effective as gas and it's dangerous."

Catherine went to the stage one last time, leading her little school and the audience in singing *America, the Beautiful* before calling for one last round of applause for all the pupils. She hadn't counted on being surrounded by congratulatory parents and over-excited children after the presentation. The room was packed and she was stopped every few feet by someone wanting to tell her what a wonderful school year it had been so far for little Johnny or Susie, and how much her teaching was appreciated. Although nice to hear, it didn't allow her to move toward Jim or her parents very quickly.

Suddenly, her mother was in front of her, smoothing down her skirt and looking askance at the jostling bodies around her. She smiled at Catherine and took her hands, kissing her on each cheek and speaking near her ear to be heard above the noise.

"A bit crowded, isn't it? I just wanted to tell you how proud I am of you. You've done these people a great service coming here to teach." She made the compliment sound as if her daughter was a missionary among heathens. "I'm sure this is a time you'll always remember when you've returned home. Howard would be proud of you too, but I know he'd want you to move on with your life and find someone you can make a family with." It was her typical manner of wrapping a hard nugget of meaning in a sweet candy coating.

Funny you should mention that, Mother. I have someone I want you to meet. Catherine searched for Jim in the crowd. He stood near the door, holding back and waiting for her to beckon him over when she was ready.

"Mother, Daddy. There's someone I want to introduce to you. Remember I told you I was tutoring after school hours? Well, the student is a deaf man who lives here in Broughton. I've been teaching him to read and we've both been learning sign language." She nodded at Jim to come over.

As he made his way through the room, her stomach tied in knots. Should she tell her parents that Jim was more than a student, more than a friend? Or should she save that part for later? This was only their first meeting after all.

Her gaze met her father's and his brow creased. "What is it?"

"Daddy..." She paused too long, trying to find the right words. *I'm in love with this man. He's the one I think I'm going to spend the rest of my life with.*

Then Jim arrived at her side and the moment to speak was past.

Catherine turned to him. "Jim, these are my parents, Aletha and Donald." She finger-spelled their names even though Jim knew very well what their names were, since they'd discussed the upcoming visit. She turned to her parents. "This is Jim Kinney."

Jim held out his hand and her father shook it firmly. "Pleased to meet you."

Mother hesitated a second before taking Jim's hand. "Lovely to meet you." Her questioning eyes met Catherine's.

"How was your journey?" Jim signed.

"He asks how your trip went," Catherine translated.

"Very well, thank you." Mother maintained her weak smile. "Have you always lived in Broughton?"

Jim made the "more or less" gesture.

"He moved here with his mother when he was young. After she died, he stayed. Jim works at the livery stable and does odd jobs too." No need to mention him working in a saloon.

"I see."

Catherine could either chatter on about how she'd begun tutoring Jim and how he was progressing in his studies, thus relegating him to the role of student. Or she could acknowledge their true relationship, which had deepened even further over the last few weeks. Taking a deep breath, she slipped her hand into the crook of Jim's arm, gripping his forearm quite hard for support.

"The truth is Jim is more than my student. We have a special friendship."

Mother's gaze shifted back and forth between them before settling on Catherine's hand gripping Jim's arm. "What does that mean, exactly?" Her face was composed, but the smile had completely faded.

"I believe Catherine is telling us this is her sweetheart, Aletha."

God bless you, Daddy! Catherine felt a surge of warmth toward her father. She'd expected he'd be easier to win over since he was more open minded, but hadn't imagined he'd take her announcement so casually. His face was calm and genial despite the permanent frown lines etched between his brows. He smiled. "I'm glad to see you happy again, sweetheart."

Mother swallowed. She glanced at Jim, then away, unable to manage even a small smile this time. "Well. This is unexpected, I must say."

She left it at that, too well bred to air her concerns in public, but Catherine knew she'd get an earful later.

"I know it must seem sudden, but we've been growing closer for a while now." She took her hand from Jim's arm to sign what she was saying for his benefit.

His tan complexion was a bit ruddier than usual—a blush. He was well aware her mother was appalled by this development. His hands flew as he delivered a heartfelt message to her parents. Working together over the past few weeks had greatly increased their sign vocabulary, but this was the longest sequence Jim had ever put together. Catherine interpreted his thoughts aloud for her parents.

"I know I'm not the man you want for your daughter. But I promise you, I love her and I'll do everything I can to be worthy of her."

As she spoke his words for him, Catherine's throat tightened. She stumbled over "I love her" and finished up in a choked voice.

Her father reached out to stroke her cheek. "As I said, I'm just glad my girl's happy again."

"Thank you, Daddy." She bit her trembling lower lip and blinked away tears.

"Well," was all Mother could manage.

A few moments of silence was abruptly broken by Dean Gunderson's booming voice as he bounded up beside them like an overgrown three-year-old. "Hey. Did you get cookies? There's sixteen different kinds over there. I counted them." He gestured with one hand, sloshing his drink over the rim of his cup.

Catherine introduced him to her parents. "Dean is the son of one of the local landowners. He helps out at school, cleaning up after the children, making repairs and tending the woodstove for us. We couldn't get along without him to wipe down the chalkboard and keep the rats at bay."

"Rats?" Her mother's gaze darted around the room as though expecting an attack at any moment.

"Just joking, Mother. We don't have rats ... at least not at the moment." She smiled at Jim recalling his brave defense of her against the lunch-stealing rat in the cloakroom. "Shall we follow Dean's example and see what culinary delights the ladies have at the refreshment table?"

She hooked her arm even more firmly around Jim's, and they led the way through the crowded room. Catherine held her head high and nodded at people they passed. Jim was hers now. No more hiding their relationship from anyone. She glanced at him and his beaming expression reflected her own happiness.

CHAPTER TWENTY-SEVEN

Jim stood in front of the small, wavy mirror in his room where he was getting dressed for the biggest event of his life. He adjusted his tie, but still wasn't satisfied with the results. It was the first time he'd ever worn one and he'd had to figure out for himself how to tie it.

He ran the brush through his hair once more, pleased that at least it was lying smooth on his head. Setting the brush down, he stared at the empty dresser top. No more carved wooden animals, toiletries or catalog. Just the brush, and soon it would be packed in his suitcase along with everything else he owned.

He gazed around the empty room, stripped of all that had made it his. These were the last moments he'd ever spend here. Tomorrow at this time, he'd be on a train heading across the country toward New York. He didn't feel the slightest pang of sadness at leaving this place. What was there to miss here? The future lay open in front of him. He was going to attend the School for the Deaf in New York City, and Catherine's father had offered him a job in the accounting department of his business when he finished his education. Maybe he'd do that, or maybe he'd start a business of his own. Anything was possible.

And today... His stomach fluttered like a flock of butterflies. Today he would live out his dream, walking down the aisle of the church and claiming Catherine as his bride. It seemed both impossible and inevitable. They were meant to be together. He'd sensed it from the first moment he locked gazes with her. It had just taken her a little longer to know it too.

As he buttoned his vest and took a last look at his reflection, he thought of his proposal and Catherine's acceptance of it. Several months after her parents' visit and her announcement that she and Jim were a couple, he'd begun to wonder if he really must wait until he was financially better off before asking her to marry him. Earning enough to be "worthy" of her no longer seemed so desperately important. Life was too short to waste on living apart.

Since they'd becom an official couple, Catherine had become careful to show restraint, making sure no one had any cause to judge them for inappropriate behavior. Stolen kisses and fondling were all very well, but they were no longer enough. He wanted her body, heart and soul, every hour of the day.

Jim had approached John Walker at the hardware store and took on hours there, stocking shelves and doing some bookkeeping. Even with the extra money, he could barely afford the cheapest wedding band the general mercantile carried.

Nervous about asking Catherine, even though he was pretty sure she'd accept, Jim had come up with a unique way of presenting his proposal. He'd tied a ribbon with the ring on it around one of the cat's necks. But when Catherine arrived at the livery that evening and he offered the little cat for her to stroke, the blasted thing had jumped from his arms and disappeared into the back of the stable. Nothing was harder to catch than a cat on a mission to stay out of reach. Jim spent the next half hour tracking the thing down with Catherine trying to get him to explain why it was so important to him.

Jim was red-faced and furious by the time he thrust the squirming little beast toward her. Catherine burst out laughing as she saw the ribbon and the ring around its neck. Her mouth was wide open and her eyes squinted. He wished he could hear what her laughter sounded like. Instead, as she held the young cat against her chest, Jim set his hand there too, so he could feel the vibration of her joy.

"Yes," she told him when she'd caught her breath and wiped the tears from her eyes. She put the cat on the ground and it scampered away. "Yes," she signed. "I'll marry you."

She'd said she didn't want to wait long. "I don't want to go home to New York and have my mother plan some big affair. We can marry here in Broughton, and soon."

Soon had sounded good to Jim, and so they'd planned their wedding for the end of the spring term.

Now Jim checked his watch, which hung on a new chain Catherine had bought for him, before tucking it back in his vest pocket. It was time to walk to the church. He placed his new bowler hat on his head and closed the door to his room without looking back.

Rasmussen waited in the stable. He was dressed in a suit too, a rare sight. He shook Jim's hand. "I'll miss you. You've been a good worker all these years. I have a little wedding present for you." He handed Jim a thick envelope.

Without opening it, Jim could tell it was filled with money. He smiled and dipped his head in acknowledgement, placed the envelope in the inside pocket of his suit jacket and signed, "Thank you."

"You're welcome." Rasmussen used the sign Catherine had taught him. "Well, it's about time. We'd better go."

They locked the stable door and walked to the church together.

Jim's nervousness increased the closer they got to the building. His palms sweated and his throat was dry. He was in no doubt about wanting to marry Catherine, but the thought of all those watching eyes made his skin crawl. He and Catherine had intended to keep the ceremony small, but somehow everyone in town had assumed they were invited. The church would be packed with those who cared and those who were merely curious.

Inside the building Mr. Rasmussen bid him good luck and went to find a seat in the crowded pews. Jim glanced once at the spectators, but after that the church might as well have been empty because he caught sight of Catherine. His breath was knocked out of him at the sight of her waiting for him in the back of the church.

She wore a new but simple dress of some shiny blue material. Her hair was piled loosely on her head and flowers were woven into it. She smiled at him, and he went to take her arm. They'd agreed to walk up the aisle together since her father wasn't here to give away the bride, and also to symbolize that they were entering into this marriage as partners.

Catherine looped her arm through his, and when she gave his arm a gentle squeeze, he knew the music had begun and it was time. Looking straight up the aisle where the minister waited, Jim marched forward. His chest ached with happiness and pride at having Catherine by his side.

When they stopped in front of the clergyman, Jim focused on his lips, moving too fast to read all the words. But he knew what the man was saying. Catherine's hands wove images in the air. Man and woman joined together forever. That was all he needed to know.

The moment came for him to say "I do" and he spoke the words aloud, and signed them, and meant them with all his heart.

* * * *

Jim's body swayed with the rocking of the railroad car. The motion had made him a little queasy the first few hours, but he'd adjusted to it. Now he found it soothing ... and a little arousing. Or maybe that was because Catherine stood sponge bathing at the washstand in their sleeper compartment. The sight of her wearing only her camisole and drawers made his cock stiffen.

Unrestrained by a corset, her breasts swayed beneath the light material. He longed to cup them and feel their warm weight in his hands, but he remained on the narrow cot with his hands behind his head, watching her wash her upper body with a wet cloth. Her golden hair tumbled in luxurious waves down her back and around her face. Such a lovely, smooth face, like the brightly colored picture of an angel his mother used to tack on the wall of whatever shack or rooming house they lived in. It had been one of her few prized possessions. As a child, Jim used to stare at that angel's sweet, slightly mysterious smile and imagine she talked to him in words only he could hear. Now he had his own real life angel who talked to him with her hands.

Catherine caught his gaze in the small mirror over the stand and her plump, kissable lips curved in a smile that made his heart leap. She raised her arm to run the damp cloth down the inside of it. Her breast thrust against the thin camisole, her nipple clearly outlined by the fabric.

Jim swallowed hard. His fingers drummed lightly on his naked stomach, and his cock tented the front of his drawers. He ached to jump up, grab her and haul her into the narrow berth, but he waited ... impatiently. Last night in the hotel room they'd reserved for after the wedding, they'd made love again and again, but he couldn't get enough of her. His eagerness was boundless.

In the mirror, Catherine's smile widened. Her tongue swept over her lips as she tossed the washcloth into the basin.

Jim wanted to hold out his arms. "Come to me!" but he kept them tucked behind his head, casual and relaxed. *Who, me impatient? Hardly.*

Catherine padded barefoot across the floor. There was little room on the bunk for her to sit beside him, but she wedged her hip against his and looked down at him. "Happy?" her hands asked.

He shook his head.

Her eyebrows shot up. "No?"

Finally taking his arms from behind his head, he signed, "No. I need..." He smoothed his hand up the inside of her thigh, feeling the warmth of her skin through her underwear. His palm settled on her pussy. He gazed into her eyes, his own heavy-lidded with lust.

"You need? I think you *want*." She held her hands open then closed in a grasping motion.

"Want *and* need." He made the subtly different signs before hooking his hand around her waist to pull her on top of him. Slipping his hand up her back into the mass of silken hair, he lifted his head from the pillow and angled his mouth to cover hers. She tasted of the tooth powder she'd just brushed with, and the soapy scent of her skin drove him crazy.

"Mm." His pleasure rumbled in the back of his throat.

Catherine must have liked the sound because she kissed him harder and her lips parted.

His tongue slipped between them to stroke hers before teasingly pulling away. He let his head fall back on the pillow while he gazed into her face, so close that her two eyes became one.

She drew back. "What?"

He shook his head. It was too hard to explain that he simply wanted to look at her for a moment. Pushing back the damp tendrils of hair from her clean face, he gazed at her lips, wet with his kisses. He studied the shape of her nose, the soft roundness of her cheeks and chin, and stared into those amazing sky-blue eyes.

"You look like you're eating me up." Her hands were easy to read now after months of practice.

He nodded. *I am, and soon I'll taste you down there, lap your juices until you writhe.* He loved feeling her body go stiff and shudder beneath him when she reached her peak, and he loved watching her

243

face drawn into an expression of near pain at the intensity of it. So beautiful!

Of course, he also loved filling her until he was completely enveloped in heat and wetness, thrusting until he couldn't control the tension any longer and he exploded inside her. And he loved cuddling together afterward. That part might be his very favorite. Holding her soft, warm body in his arms and knowing he'd wake up with her in the morning because he belonged there now—in her bed, in her embrace, in her life.

Aware he'd been staring too long, he cupped her face and traced his thumb over her lips. He pulled her down for another kiss, fiercer and deeper than ever. His plunging tongue possessed her mouth, claiming her as his.

After a while, Catherine moved to kiss his jaw, his neck and chest. She kissed around his nipple then licked and nipped it until he gasped. Then she did the same to the other. Her nibbles sent heat racing to his cock. He thrust against her belly.

Catherine looked at him, eyelids lowering, lips curving in a seductive smile that set his heart racing in anticipation. She reached to untie the waistband of his drawers while she licked a trail down his twitching belly. She tugged his underwear off his legs, and his cock sprang out to greet her, eager as a dog welcoming its master home.

She took his shaft in her hand and stroked it. Her gaze focused on his erection was nearly as exciting as the touch of her hand. Again she looked to Jim's face, connecting with him as she bent and licked the tip protruding from his foreskin. The sight and feel of her pink tongue licking the swollen purple head made his balls draw tight. She hadn't done this before. He hadn't known if she would and wondered how she knew what to do. Then he stopped thinking as she sucked him into her mouth. It was a wonder he didn't incinerate or melt away in that luxurious heat. Her hand glided up and down his shaft while she sucked, her cheeks hollowed with the effort.

Jim closed his eyes and indulged in darkness and silence which enhanced all the sensations coursing through him. He was aware not only of her mouth and stroking hand, but details like her hair tickling his thighs, the pressure of her arm against his leg, and the soft humming in her throat that vibrated his cockhead.

His cock swelled even more and he lifted his hips to thrust into her mouth. The tension in his groin grew tighter, like reins restraining a horse when it wanted to run. Her hand and mouth urged him onward until he had to break free, bucking and plunging. Waves of ecstasy burst through him and into her mouth. She swallowed every bit before pulling away.

His eyes opened to watch Catherine sedately wiping her mouth with the side of her hand, her expression smug. It was the same little smile she wore when he got a lesson right or pleased her by giving her a flower. She was so easy to make happy, and he vowed he'd spend the rest of his life doing it. Whatever happened after they reached New York, he'd do everything in his power to make her happy she'd chosen him.

He held out his hand to her and she moved back on top of him, her warm flesh sticking to his. Her hair spread over his chest and shoulder and against his mouth. He kissed it. His heart was so full of love for her that it wasn't enough to express it physically. Jim wanted to tell her what he felt out loud. He still wasn't comfortable speaking, having no idea whether he made the sounds right or not, but he'd practiced one phrase in particular with Rasmussen.

"I love you." He felt the vibration in his chest, throat and mouth and hoped he'd placed his tongue correctly, applied the right amount of air.

Raising up on her arms, Catherine looked into his eyes. Hers were shining as blue as a lake. "I love you too."

Jim smiled, satisfied.

She laid her head back on his chest, and he held her close, the pair of them rocking with the motion of the train like infants in a cradle. It occurred to him he'd finally taken the train he'd refused a job on before. Riding in a sleeping compartment with Catherine beat the hell out of shoveling coal.

He'd been certain he was shackled to Broughton for the rest of his life, but here he was heading out into the world to begin a brand new life. It proved anything might happen to even the most unlikely of people.

CHAPTER TWENTY-EIGHT

Catherine had given up worrying about social conventions and no longer felt guilt or shame about anything she and Jim did together in the name of love. She would never have imagined she would suck on a man's member and enjoy it, but she adored how it had made him thrust and groan with pleasure—just as Shirley Mae had said it would. Those low, desperate sounds built her arousal to a dizzying pitch. Loving a man who didn't speak made each grunt, groan or sigh all the more precious.

And the words Jim had just spoken, as unformed as they might sound, were music to her ears.

I love you too. More than I ever thought possible. My man. My husband.

Their wedding had taken place quickly and probably raised questions in the minds of everyone in Broughton, but Catherine couldn't wait to be with him any longer. She hadn't wanted to return to New York and have her mother take over the wedding plans, or try to convince her not to marry Jim. Now it was done and Mother would have to accept it.

Over the past months, as they'd grown to understand one another better, Catherine had found more and more to like about Jim. He was thoughtful, tender, hard-working, enthusiastic, even-tempered, creative, gentle, loving. She even found his flaws endearing, for he certainly could be stubborn, possessive, proud and inclined to sulk when displeased. All of those aspects were part of the sum total of Jim, and she loved all of him.

During their last month in Broughton, he'd had to give testimony at Grant Karak's trial with Catherine's aid in translating. Although Karak's money and connections ensured his prison time was brief, he'd been nearly bankrupted by the court case and fines and had sold out all of his interests in Broughton. That went a long way toward making Jim suddenly acceptable in the community. Even Mrs.

Albright learned to keep her opinion about their relationship to herself. The woman was subdued with Jennie gone away to school and Catherine thought maybe she wished she'd never sent her. Perhaps Ned Hildebrandt wasn't looking like such a bad choice for a son-in-law after all.

Now, lying in Jim's arms as the train rattled over the tracks carrying them miles away from Broughton, Catherine thought she would miss the town and people she'd come to know so well. She'd especially miss her students, who had all presented her with hand-made cards and gifts at the end of the school year.

She was excited though nervous about the future. While Jim attended the School for the Deaf, Catherine would teach at a nearby school. They'd rent a home using the small trust fund left to her by Great Aunt Mildred. Between Catherine's teaching salary and whatever job Jim could find, they would pay their household expenses. Living in busy New York City would be far different than quiet White Plains or somnolent Broughton. Catherine was glad Aunt Lydia and the cousins would be nearby to ease their transition into city life.

She sighed and put niggling concerns about the future to rest. This train trip was their honeymoon. She needn't worry about anything except enjoying her new husband, satisfying him and letting him please her, which he did so well.

She moved to lie with her back to Jim and his body spooned behind her. His arms wrapped around her and his breath tickled the back of her neck. Occasionally he pressed a kiss to her shoulder. Then he began to communicate, using her body in place of his own to make signs as his hands silently spoke to her. "Worried?"

Catherine nodded and held her finger and thumb an inch apart. "A little."

"About parents." He made the signs for mother and father.

"No."

"You sorry?"

"No!" She added emphasis with the force of her motion. "Never." She rolled to face him. "Are *you* worried?"

"What if school doesn't take me?"

"It will. If not, we'll keep working together."

As they lay face-to-face on the pillow, his dark eyes gazed at her from so close she could see the dark outer rim of his irises and the slight greenish cast in the brown.

Jim traced the edge of her ear with his finger and tugged on the lobe. "Wish I could hear your voice," he signed.

He'd never before complained about his lack of hearing. His admission was as painful as a knife to her heart as she thought of all the things Jim missed in life: music, bird song, running water, laughter, whispers, joyous shouts. There was no response she could give except to lean in and kiss him as she combed her fingers through the silky strands of his hair. His lips were firm yet yielding at the same time. Catherine imagined one day their kisses wouldn't leave her yearning and melting, but right now the mere brush of his mouth against hers awoke raging desire.

She rose to strip off her underwear, then pressed her nude body against his warm, naked torso. In the tight confines of the berth, she wrapped her leg around his hip and felt his cock swell against her.

Jim reached down to finger her sex, smearing her juices over her pulsing clitoris, and moving in tight circles until she moaned. She grasped his erection and guided it to her entrance. The head of his cock nudged inside and with a pleasured groan Jim thrust deeply, filling her. The relieved exhalation of his breath warmed her neck.

She gasped at the suddenness of his entry, but her muscles clamped around him, pulling him deeper. She loved the feeling of his hard member driving into her. The flutters of delight inside her grew stronger like caged wings trying to burst free. That's what she'd been before she'd met Jim—caged. She'd considered herself a modern woman, choosing a teaching career rather than remaining idle, but she'd still been bound by convention, indoctrinated into caring about society's—and her mother's—opinion. It had taken the love of a special man to awaken her to a new life.

Jim's soft grunts, her whimpers, the wet slapping of their bodies joining rose above the rumbling wheels of the train. Her pleasure grew sweeter and more intense with every stroke of his cock which hit someplace deep within her over and over until suddenly the caged bird burst free, soaring across limitless space. She cried out and arched against him as tremors of joy swept through her.

Jim clutched her hip and he pumped harder and faster. After a few more strokes, he froze, groaning long and low as he released in steady pulses. When the last spasm died away, Catherine relaxed against him and opened her eyes.

Jim was back with her again. His eyes focused on hers with that quiet intensity that made her stomach tighten. She reached out her hand to touch his face.

He kissed her palm and murmured into her skin, "Love you."

"I love you, and I need you," she signed. "Not *want*. Need! It took me some time, but I know the difference now."

Jim looked into her eyes and smiled. "I'm right here."

He pulled her close once more and held her until they were both rocked to sleep by the motion of the train as it steamed through the night and into their future.

The End

ABOUT THE AUTHOR:

Whether you're a fan of contemporary, paranormal, or historical romance, you'll find something to enjoy. My style is very personal and my characters will feel like well-known friends by the time you've finished reading. I'm interested in flawed, often damaged, people who find the fulfillment they seek in one another. Stop by my web site, http://bonniedee.com or for future updates on my books, join my Yahoo group, http://groups.yahoo.com/group/bonniedee/

If you enjoyed A Hearing Heart, continue reading for an excerpt of Bone Deep, another historical with an unusual hero:

Love plumbs deep below the surface.

In 1946, Sarah, a grieving war widow goes to the carnival with friends and is riveted by the tattooed man in the freak show, adorned in head to toe body art. Later she discovers the man hiding in her hayloft, escaped from imprisonment by the evil owner. She shelters Tom on her farm, fighting a powerful attraction while learning about his mysterious past and gentle nature.

When a child goes missing, Tom uses his psychic gift to find her but his assistance doesn't relieve the locals' mistrust of such an exotic stranger. Small-town prejudice tears the lovers apart and a very real threat from the carnival owner endangers them. Can the lovers rise above obstacles of fear and hatred to create the family both have always craved?

BONE DEEP

Discordant carnival music and the smell of burnt sugar, popcorn and axle grease drifted through the crisp fall air. In the dusk, the colored lights of the rusty rides shone in broken lines where bulbs were missing. Faded canvas tents housed games of chance, a fortune-teller, a fun house and freaks. Sarah walked the trash-strewn paths between booths and rides and wondered why she'd come. She hated carnivals.

"Sarah, you made it!" Grace May called across the loud music and barker's cries. She caught up with Sarah and linked arms. "I'm so glad. You spend far too much time alone on the farm. You need to get out more."

Sarah smiled without comment. It was easy to read Grace's message between the lines. 'Stop grieving. John was killed over a year and a half ago. It's time to start living again.' But Grace couldn't possibly know what Sarah felt like inside, hard as drought-baked earth longing for rain but more likely to shed water than soak it in and grow soft again. John's body had been shipped home from the front just before V.E. day ended the war. She could pinpoint April 29, 1945 as the day her heart froze. The moment she'd seen John in the coffin and realized his death was real, Sarah had stopped feeling much of anything.

She drew her light blue cardigan more tightly around her. There was a chill in the air at the end of a hot September day.

Grace squeezed her arm. "Look, I know you're going to be mad at me but—"

"Grace, what'd you do?"

"I told Mike to bring a friend along. You know Andrew Harper, who works at the hardware store? He's new in town, single, almost forty but a real sweet guy and he's looking for someone."

"Well, I'm not." Sarah pulled her arm away from Grace, annoyed at her friend's meddling. "And I don't appreciate your match-making without consulting me first."

"Come on. Don't be upset. It's only for this one evening. If you don't like the guy, you don't have to see him again. Oh look, there they are." Grace grabbed Sarah's arm again and tugged her toward two men standing near the entrance to one of the tents.

Grace's husband, Mike, was talking to a red-haired guy with a pleasant smile on his freckled face. He wore a short-sleeved shirt and a navy blue sweater-vest, and she vaguely remembered seeing the man when she had her screen door repaired at McNulty's Hardware. She might even have talked to him, but if she had, it hadn't left an impression.

Harper's grip was warm and his smile shy as he shook her hand. "Hi. I'm Andrew Harper. I work at—"

"McNulty's. I know. I've seen you there. I'm Sarah Cassidy." She pulled her hand away from his and adjusted her sweater around her shoulders, aware of Grace and Mike exchanging glances. "So, how do you like living in Fairfield?"

Harper shifted on his feet and a flush crept up from his neck, covering his freckles. "I like it just fine." He cleared his throat and looked across the fairgrounds.

"That's nice." Sarah couldn't think of a single thing to add. She didn't want to make small talk. She wished she was at home reading a book or listening to the radio.

Mike stepped forward interrupting, the awkward moment. "How about a ride on the Ferris wheel, ladies?"

"Not for me," Grace replied. "I hate heights and even if I didn't I wouldn't trust that thing." She indicated the ancient metal wheel arching against the night sky. The cars swayed as it jerked to a stop.

"How about in here?" Andrew pointed to the tent near them.

The painting on the side of the canvas showed obese, bearded, dwarfed, misshapen, tattooed, hermaphrodite freaks. You could gawk at them for only a quarter. She thought those who were willing to pay to view handicapped people were more pathetic than the unfortunates themselves. But Grace and Mike agreed so Sarah paid her money and followed the others inside.

In the hushed darkness beneath the canvas, each display was illuminated by a single bare bulb. The dim light cast odd shadows, adding to the gloomy atmosphere of the stifling tent. Heat from earlier in the day was trapped in the airless enclosure. The smell of unwashed bodies and cow manure was rank.

Sarah removed her cardigan and tied it around her hips. Only a few other people wandered from one attraction to the next. There was a placard set up in front of each 'display'. There was a calf with a fifth leg lying on a bed of straw. A two-foot-tall dwarf sat on a stool, smoking a cigarette and gazing impassively at the fair-goers. Sarah felt as if she'd stepped back into medieval times as she trailed her friends from one mistake of nature to the next. What next? Bear baiting and a public execution?

She watched the bearded woman open her robe to reveal a breast then tug on her facial hair to prove its validity. Feeling like a voyeur, Sarah dropped her gaze. She moved on to observe another woman who had some kind of growth on the side of her neck, which on closer examination proved to have stunted facial features--nature's aborted attempt at a twin.

The others lingered, studying the woman with the tumor, but Sarah moved quickly ahead, anxious to be out of the hot, oppressive tent. It felt wrong to be gaping at these peoples' anomalies.

The next station appeared to be empty. The wooden chair beneath the yellow glow of the light bulb was empty. Sarah peered into the shadows behind the spotlighted chair and saw something moving. Then the dark figure stepped into the circle of light.

Sarah drew in her breath.

The man was a walking tapestry of color. Every bit of his skin was covered in tattoos. Angels, devils, dragons, flames, flowers and skulls were tossed on blue waves. There was no common theme to the tattoos and only the decorative blue swirls connected them. It gave the impression of flotsam floating in the wake of a shipwreck.

In the center of the man's chest was a red heart, not a Valentine confection but a knobby fist-shaped lump with stubs of aortas sticking out. Wrapped around the heart were links of black chain, binding it tight. The movements of his muscles as he took his seat caused the images to expand and contract, as if they pulsed with life.

With all the ink covering his body, it took Sarah a moment to notice how very nearly naked he was. A loincloth hung from his hips. As he sat, propping one knee up on a rung of the chair, the cloth opened to reveal that his thigh was covered with images right up to his groin.

A flush of heat lanced through her, settling warmly in between her legs. She brushed her hair back from her burning cheeks and tucked it behind her ear. She knew she should move on, but couldn't stop staring at the tattooed man.

He gazed past her, across the tent, focusing on something. Sarah fought the urge to look over her shoulder at whatever he was seeing.

His body was as concealed as if he were clothed. The designs covered every limb and muscle, distracting the eye from his nudity. Even his face and shaven head were tattooed. More tentacles of the swirling blue design marked his cheeks and framed his eyes making their vivid blue seem to glow like a gas flame. When he turned his head to the side, images bloomed up the back of his neck and fanned over his scalp in a fountain of colors. The shreds of pale skin between the tattoos served as contrast to red, purple, ochre, green and inky black.

Sarah suddenly realized that her friends had already looked at the tattooed man and gone on ahead while she still stood and stared. Unwillingly, she started to walk away. Just then he turned his head and his eyes caught and held Sarah's.

Her breath stopped and her heart pounded. He was gazing at her as intently as she had been looking at him, peering deep inside her.

She felt naked in front of him and longed to run away from his searing gaze, but found it impossible to move her feet. It was as if he saw and marked her pain, still percolating underneath the veneer of dull ennui. His scalpel gaze hurt as it cut through her scars. Tears stung her eyes and she blinked to clear them.

Then the man looked away, once again staring sightlessly at that invisible mark on the opposite side of the tent.

Sarah moved on, feeling shaken and anxious, wondering what had just happened. That moment of connection had been as sharp and real as anything she'd ever experienced. She longed to go home, bury herself under her bedcovers, and forget what she'd seen tonight.

She hurried past the rest of the exhibits, but before she followed her friends out of the sideshow Sarah took a last glance at the tattooed man. A cluster of people blocked her view. She had to leave without seeing him again.

The rest of the evening passed in a blur of carnival lights and music and too much noise. She made pointless small talk with Grace, Mike, and Andrew but nothing registered. She felt as if she was walking in a dream. Her mind kept returning to the arresting vision of the tattooed man, to his intense eyes even more than the art decorating his muscular body. If only she could steal away from her friends, pay her quarter and see him one last time. Instead, she bid them all goodnight, rejected Andrew's offer to see her home, and walked over the hill, through the pasture to her house.

Look for these titles from Bonnie Dee

Contemporaries:
Four Kisses
Serious Play (w/Summer Devon)
Hired for Her Pleasure
Finding Home (w/Lauren Baker)
Opposites Attract
Butterfly Unpinned (w/Laura Bacchi)
The Final Act
The Valentine Effect
Awakening

Historicals:
Captive Bride
Blackberry Pie
Perfecting Amanda
The Countess Takes a Lover
The Countess Lends a Hand
The Gypsy's Vow
Bone Deep
A Hearing Heart
Liberating Lucius

Paranormal and Fantasy:
After the End
Dead Country
Magical Menages: Shifters' Captive
Magical Menages: Vampires' Consort
Fairytale Fantasies: Cinderella Unmasked (w/Marie Treanor)
Fairytale Fantasies: Demon Lover (w/Marie Treanor)
Fairytale Fantasies: Awakening Beauty (w/Marie Treanor)
The Warrior's Gift
Shifter, P.I.
Like Clockwork
Evolving Man
The Thief and the Desert Flower

Empath
Dream Across Time
Rock Hard
Mirror Image (w/Mima)
The Straw Man
Terran Realm: Measure of a Man
Terran Realm: Fruits of Betrayal

M/m all genres:
Undeniable Magnetism
Cage Match
Star Flyer
Jungle Heat
Ignite!
Seducing Stephen
The Gentleman and the Rogue (w/Summer Devon)
The Nobleman and the Spy (w/Summer Devon)
House of Mirrors (w/Summer Devon)
The Psychic and the Sleuth (w/Summer Devon)

Anthologies:
Seasons of Love
Hot Summer Nights
Heat Wave: print anthology
Strangers in the Night: print anthology
Gifted: print anthology
Red Velvet & Absinthe
The Handsome Prince
Beyond Desire
Secrets, Volume 23
Lust: Erotic Fantasies for Women
Best Women's Erotica
Got a Minute?: Sixty Second Erotica

Made in the USA
Lexington, KY
11 February 2016